THE FIRE
IN EMBER

Also by DiAnn Mills

A Woman Called Sage

THE FIRE IN EMBER

A NOVEL

DIANN MILLS

ZONDERVAN®

ZONDERVAN.com/
AUTHORTRACKER
follow your favorite authors

ZONDERVAN

The Fire in Ember
Copyright © 2011 by DiAnn Mills

This title is also available as a Zondervan ebook. Visit www.zondervan.com/ebooks.

This title is also available in a Zondervan audio edition. Visit www.zondervan.fm.

Requests for information should be addressed to:

Zondervan, *Grand Rapids, Michigan 49530*

Library of Congress Cataloging-in-Publication Data

Mills, DiAnn.
 The fire in ember / DiAnn Mills.
  p. cm.
 ISBN 978-0-310-29330-9 (pbk.)
  1. Frontier and pioneer life—Colorado—Fiction. 2. Ranchers—Colorado—Fiction. I. Title.
 PS3613.I567F57 2010
 813'.6—dc22
                       2010028324

All Scripture quotations are taken from the King James Version of the Bible.

Any Internet addresses (websites, blogs, etc.) and telephone numbers printed in this book are offered as a resource. They are not intended in any way to be or imply an endorsement by Zondervan, nor does Zondervan vouch for the content of these sites and numbers for the life of this book.

Published in association with the Books & Such Literary Agency, 52 Mission Circle, Suite 122, PMB 170, Santa Rosa, California 95407-5370. www.booksandsuch.biz

Cover design: Aleta Rafton
Cover illustration: Aleta Rafton

Printed in the United States of America

10 11 12 13 14 /DCI/ 23 22 21 20 19 18 17 16 15 14 13 12 11 10 9 8 7 6 5 4 3 2 1

To the Birthday Club Girls

And they that know thy name will put their trust in thee: for thou, Lord, hast not forsaken them that seek thee.

Psalm 9:10

CHAPTER I

1888 COLORADO
JUNE

A hanging is no place for a woman.

Bert cast a wary glance at the man who lifted a rope from his saddle horn and stomped her way. With her hands tied behind her back and a second man holding her shoulders, she had no hope of freeing herself.

"Horse thieves are hanged." The man they called Leon gazed up into the branches of a cottonwood and pointed. "That limb looks sturdy enough to carry the likes of you. If it breaks, we'll find another one." He tied the noose around her neck.

"But he's just a boy," an old man said. "I'm not up to hangin' a kid."

"Billy the Kid started his murderin' ways at fourteen." Leon walked toward Bert. His breath reeked of liquid courage, and the swagger in his step meant she couldn't reason with him. "He won't even tell us his name. That means this ain't the first time he's broke the law." He sneered, revealing a mouthful of black and broken teeth. "But it'll be the last time."

"Maybe he's too scared to talk. You hit him hard," the old man said.

Bert touched her tongue to the stinging side of her mouth where blood dripped down her chin. That had been Leon's first punch. She glanced his way again through one eye. The other one had already swollen shut, and it throbbed in time to her pounding heart.

"In case you've forgotten, the boss's been lookin' for that horse nigh onto six months." Leon tossed the rope over a branch. "This here's his prize mare all right, and she's wearing the Wide O brand."

"All I'm sayin' is you've taught the boy a good lesson. One he ain't likely to forget. Let's send him on his way and take the boss his horse." The man held the bridle of the sleek mare she'd been riding.

Bert stared into the face of the haggard man who was attempting to reason with her executor. His lined face and bush-like silver beard showed his age. He couldn't help her with three men determined to hang her. But maybe the others would listen to his reasoning.

Leon strode to Bert and grabbed her by the neck and out of the clutches of the man who'd held her shoulders. "Why'd you steal this horse?"

"I didn't." Bert could barely speak for Leon's hand cutting off her air supply.

"Then where'd you get it?"

She couldn't answer that.

"What do you men think?" Leon released his hold and shoved her backward onto the hard ground.

Bert knew what a beatin' felt like, and she'd lived through enough to know she'd survive. But not a rope swung from a tree branch. A crow flew overhead. The bird opened its mouth and cawed as if it were voting on tying the rope around her neck. She pulled her attention from the crow to the other men for maybe a sign that one of them might agree with the older man.

The greasy-looking man who had held her for Leon glanced at a fourth man and nodded. "We agree with you. If'n this kid has already stole a horse, what else is he gonna do? Murder a man?"

"Let's get 'er done then." Leon grinned. "How about a little whiskey to sweeten up this party?"

"This is wrong," the older man said. "The boss won't like it one bit. And you already know how he feels about drinkin' when we're supposed to be workin'."

"Who's gonna tell him, Ted?" Leon jutted out his chin. A breeze swept through the cottonwood's treetops and picked up his tattered, flat-brimmed hat. Amidst the snickers, he chased after it, cussing like her brothers. He snatched up his hat and plopped it down over his head. "We're doin' him a favor and savin' the marshal some time."

"I'm not a part of this." The old man offered a hand up to Bert, and she stood. "Sorry, boy. I tried." He swung himself up onto his saddle. "You men ever been boys? Ever got yourself caught up in something you didn't have any business doin'? This is murder, and you know it." He headed south.

Her last hope rode away in the form of an old man named Ted. Leaving dirt clods behind him. She watched until the sound of his horse's gallop faded away along with any hope. Regret for trying to save Simon from a hanging tightened like the noose around her neck.

Leon cursed again, then made his way to his horse. He pulled a bottle from his saddlebag, untwisted the lid, and took a swallow. "We'll use the boss's horse to hang him."

Bert stole a look at the clear blue sky and the green-and-white-tipped Rockies in the distance. Her last look at anything on this earth. She inhaled the sweet scent of summer and cast her gaze toward the pink and yellow wildflowers scattered around them. As a child, she'd taken such wildflowers and woven them into crowns.

A hanging is no place for a woman.

Her brother's words raced across her mind. Would it make any difference to these ranch hands if they knew she was a female?

John Timmons didn't usually ride across his ranch without one of his brothers. But this morning was an exception. He'd saddled his chestnut stallion and left his ranch with too much on his mind to waste time talking. And with his horse's wild temperament, riding alone made sense.

He breathed in appreciation for the green, rolling land surrounding him. Cattle and horses grazed in abundance. To the west, the Rocky Mountains stood guard over the valley. Definitely a blessing in any man's vocabulary.

Four years ago, his widowed mother deeded the ranch to him and insisted their brand be changed to reflect John as the owner. Until then, the ranch was simply the ranch. He chose the name of 5T to reflect all of the Timmons brothers. The brand looked good on the livestock, and John continued to add calluses to his work-worn hands, just as he'd done since he was a fourteen-year-old.

Weeks later, the responsibility placed on his shoulders to look after his younger brothers on into manhood hit him like a bolt of lightning—there were four other Timmons boys who'd one day need a way to make a living. John woke up to the reality of what ranch ownership and a family meant and vowed to grow the 5T not only in cattle and horses, but in acreage. Since then, his Uncle Parker had sold him a bordering ranch, adding a total of a thousand acres to the 5T.

Most folks called him successful. Some called him a working fool. His brothers called him a slave driver when they thought he was out of earshot. Truth known, he claimed the title of a working fool. Ranching was all he knew, and all that mattered to keep food on the table and the cold off their backs.

He shook off the thoughts vying for the topic worrying him like a boil on his rear. He needed to add more land to the ranch.

In two weeks, Evan would be eighteen.

Aaron just had his sixteenth birthday.

Mark fell in right behind him at fourteen.

Davis, Mama's baby, turned nine in April.

Of course, that didn't mean all the boys planned on taking up ranching themselves. All the harping and preaching and lecturing about his brothers claiming an education seemed to be working. Or it might be that studyin' sounded easier than mending fences or running down stray cows.

Except Mark. The boy loved the land like he did.

Evan liked doctoring animals—wanted to take care of them for the rest of his life. Aaron claimed he'd live in the city, and Davis never wanted to leave his mama. But John had promised himself that each of his brothers would be given one hundred sixty acres when they reached their eighteenth birthday, a homestead plot like his father had purchased years before. They could sell the land back to John or start their own spread. Their choice.

John laughed at his frettin'—worse than an old woman watching for winter weather. He turned his horse northwest toward the land belonging to Victor Oberlander, the Wide O Ranch. Six hundred forty acres of Oberlander's land bordered on John's ranch—four homestead plots for four brothers. Today he planned to offer a fair price for it. Cash. With those thoughts, a northern breeze cooled his face.

For right now, John would enjoy the warm weather, clear blue skies, and solitude of his thoughts. Although his thoughts would be more pleasing once he had a firm handshake on a deal with Oberlander.

He rounded a hill about three miles from the Wide O and saw Ted Hawkins riding his way. The old ranch hand waved and spurred his horse toward John.

"How are you?" John came to a stop and leaned on his saddle horn.

"I've been better." Ted's face was flushed, what a man could see of his whiskered skin and his hat pulled down low. "But I'm sure glad I run up on you."

John's insides soured. "What's wrong? Trouble?"

"Yep. The kind a deputy like you can handle just fine. A couple of Oberlander's ranch hands have a boy they're about to hang for stealin' a horse. I tried to stop them, but—"

"A boy? What's got into them?"

"Bored, I reckon. The boy was ridin' the boss's prize mare, the one he thought got stole. But hangin' a kid isn't my way of settlin' things. Tried to talk them out of it, but Leon's mind's set."

The good Lord must have had more on His mind this morning than striking a deal for land. "A hanging of any kind without a trial is against my style. Show me where they're at."

"Sure thing, John. They're about a mile and a half back. Leon's fit to be tied about everything this mornin'. Been drinkin', and he's meaner than a wounded she-bear."

The two men rode north. Horse thieves were the sludge of the earth, but a young boy often didn't have much sense. He'd been there, and what often sounded like fun could end up being deadly. In the distance, three men gathered around a horse. On that horse sat a boy with a noose around his neck.

John lifted his rifle and fired into the air. *That ought to get their attention.* Heads and bodies snapped his way.

"That ain't gonna stop Leon," Ted shouted above the rhythmic pounding of their horses' hooves against the ground.

Although John and Ted were gaining ground, it didn't seem to deter Leon's hanging. He walked behind the horse where the kid sat.

I won't get there soon enough.

John raised his rifle again and shot through the rope.

Leon smacked the horse's rump, and the animal took off. Instead of dangling in the air, the boy was doing his best to stay atop a horse with his hands tied. Ted took out after the mare and boy as John rode up in front of the others.

Cursing broke through the morning, and Leon threw a bottle aside then jerked out his revolver. He waved his gun toward the boy.

"Pull that trigger, and I'll shoot you dead." John aimed his rifle straight at Leon's chest.

"He's a horse thief." Leon's words thundered louder than his swearin' had moments before.

"Maybe so, but you aren't a judge. And your thief looks to be around eleven years old. That makes you a big man." John pointed at the broken whiskey bottle. "So does cheap whiskey make you brave enough to kill a kid?"

The other two ranch hands backed off. Their horses had been spooked and were headed in the direction of the Oberlander barns and house. Ted had caught up with the boy and the mare, but John's stallion had noticed her too. Wonderful. Now he had one more problem to contend with.

"What about you two?" John swung his rifle toward the others.

"Leon said—" one man began.

"If you're going to follow Leon around like a puppy, maybe you'd like to follow him to jail?"

"I'm gettin' back to work," the second man said. John recognized him, but he wasn't about to call the cow pie by name.

Leon picked up his broken bottle. Most likely looking to see if any of the amber liquid in the bottom was drinkable. "Mr. Oberlander will want to know where we found his horse."

"Tell him the truth." John shot him a look meant to challenge him.

Leon raised a scraggly brow. "Some money in my pocket would keep me quiet."

John refused to let Leon see his anger. "I'll take the horse and the boy to Mr. Oberlander, since it's his property." He studied the boy while Ted cut the rope binding his hands behind him. The kid shook so that he had difficulty jumping down from Oberlander's mare. "You all right?"

The boy nodded.

"What's your name?"

The boy stared at him.

"Where you from?"

Nothing. Not even a muscle moved. His right eye was turning blue. Swollen too. John turned his attention to Leon. "Did you beat up this kid?"

"He did," the boy said.

For sure the boy wasn't older than eleven or twelve. He'd tan Davis's hide if he ever pulled a stunt like this. "Well that proves you aren't deaf and mute. Come on over here and climb up behind me. You've got a horse to return. Then we're having a long talk about taking another man's property. I have a mind to let you spend a night in jail. Might knock some sense into you."

CHAPTER 2

B ert stood beside John Timmons on the front porch of
Mr. Oberlander's house — a grand, two-story home with real
windows, a porch that wrapped around two sides, a stone front,
and fresh whitewash. She didn't know whether to run or wait it
out. She knew the man who'd saved her neck was having second
thoughts. The evidence surfaced in his frustrated explanation to
Mr. Oberlander about the return of his missing mare.

Trying to calm the turmoil in her mind, she studied the huge
ranch that sprawled over rolling green pastures with the foothills
and mountains in the distance. Everywhere she looked, cattle
and horses grazed. Even the barns looked fancy — fancier than
what she'd ever seen.

And she'd almost made it here except for those ranch
hands.

Meanwhile, Mr. Oberlander demanded payment for the months
he'd been without his horse. Like a rabbit spits out babies, the
two men tossed out dollar amounts regarding the mare she was
accused of stealing.

The ranch hands who had found her riding across the Wide
O Ranch had disappeared. All it took was Oberlander shouting a
three-word order, and they'd scattered in the direction of one of
the barns. From the sight of the grizzly looking man, she'd have
run too.

Bert studied the young man who'd saved her life. Leon
referred to him as a deputy, a title that frightened her as much
as the near hanging.

"I'm telling you, John. I need some compensation for what this kid caused me. For six months I've searched for my mare. Even considered one of my hands might have stolen her. Who is this kid, anyway?"

John breathed out a sigh and glanced her way. No doubt he regretted stopping the hanging. "He won't say."

"A no-good runaway." Oberlander eyed her. "He's bad news. I'm of a mind to make him work off the trouble he's caused. Leon would whip him into shape."

Leon would kill me. She refused to show her fear, but the notion of taking off on John's horse waved like a flag. Except he'd tied the stallion to a hitching post.

John cleared his throat. "How much?"

"Three hundred dollars."

"I could buy you six horses for that amount of money."

"This one cost me plenty. I bought her as a filly from a ranch south of Denver. Gave her the name of Queen Victoria for the queen of England, because she's royalty. None like her for miles around. You know that, John. Look at the quarter horse you're riding—the white face and feet. He's a fine stallion, and I heard what you paid for him. One I'd like to buy or breed with my mare. Or buy."

"We could work out the breeding. Both are fine horses, but he's not for sale."

"Never mind. I need three hundred dollars."

"One hundred. You have your horse, and that is more than compensation for your time."

The owner of the finest mare Bert had ever ridden or seen rubbed his chin. He leaned against a post holding up his porch. "Two hundred and let me breed my mare with your stallion."

A familiar know of fear clawed at Bert's stomach. She didn't have the money to pay either of these men.

"One hundred dollars and you bring your mare over when you're ready. This is the best deal you'll get from anyone around here."

"Two hundred."

John lifted his hands and shook his head. "I'm done. You got your horse, and now you got yourself a boy to work off his debt. I'm riding home. Got too much work of my own to do. Good day, Mr. Oberlander." He touched the brim of his hat and whirled around, taking half a dozen steps to his horse.

"Wait up. Hundred dollars cash will do and the breedin'. You take the kid."

John whipped out a money clip and counted out five twenties. She'd never seen so much money. He stared up at her. "I hope you have some muscles beneath your scrawny hide, 'cause you're going to work off every penny of this."

Mr. Oberlander laughed. "Pleasure doing business with you, John."

This isn't going to be easy.

John never thought of himself as having a temper. In fact he thought of himself as a patient man. Being big brother to four boys and facing responsibility for their welfare head-on meant using his head and heart, not his fists or his mouth.

But a twist of fate had made him madder than an agitated hornet's nest. He hadn't struck a deal with Oberlander about his land, and he'd lost one hundred dollars of his money on a no-account kid.

He looked over his shoulder at the boy riding behind him. "I want to know your name." He spoke like a man in charge, even though defeat mocked him. "I paid your debt, and you owe me a few things."

"I'll work hard."

"I guarantee it. The only thing you'll have time for stealing is a few extra hours of sleep at night. I have four younger brothers and my mother waiting at the ranch. What do you want them to call you?"

"Bert."

"Thank you. Now where are you from?"

"Not from around here."

"Where are your folks?"

"Doesn't matter."

John wanted to give the kid a generous piece of his mind, but what good would acting like Leon do? Besides, the kid had already been beaten and needed to have his eye and mouth tended to. "I bet your mama is worried sick about you."

"She's dead."

Things about Bert were becoming clearer. "Sorry to hear that."

"Happened a long time ago."

Once Bert decided to talk, he did all right. "What about the rest of your family?"

"Doesn't matter."

"Right now I figure you owe me at least four months' hard work for what you cost me. What do you know about ranching?"

"Nothing."

Make that five months. "We start before sunrise. You'll get three meals a day, and I expect you to mind your manners. Whatever I tell you to do, put some effort into it. No argument or you'll skip the next meal. There'll be no cussin', and you'll go to church on Sunday."

"Ain't never been to church."

"So along with being a horse thief, you don't follow God? Looks like you need lots of help."

"I didn't steal the horse."

"Were you riding Oberlander's horse when those ranch hands found you?"

"Didn't know they were Mr. Oberlander's men, but yes."

"That's 'Yes, sir.' I don't know where you're from, but when someone's caught riding a horse that doesn't belong to him, it's stealing. And let me make it clear, you will treat those older than you with respect. So I'd better be hearing good manners. If you don't have any, you'd better be learning some." John had a whole lecture—more like a sermon—swelling inside him. "I hope you learned your lesson today. I saved you from a hanging, and I hope I don't live to regret it."

John started to add more, but he needed to spend some time thinking about the money he'd lost and how to approach Victor Oberlander about purchasing the acreage separating the two ranches. Oberlander had always been a fair man and a shrewd businessman. John had used both tactics this morning in hopes the man would remember the generosity when it came time to discuss the selling of some of his property.

But it might not happen before Evan's birthday, and not keeping his vow worried John the most. His brothers didn't know about John's intent to provide a homestead for them. No matter. Looked like he'd failed today anyway.

Bert felt light behind him. A boy this young should have family somewhere, unless he'd been abused, or came from a bad home. Running off at his age either showed guts or stupidity. Sure hope he hadn't brought home a bad seed. Evan, Aaron, and Mark wouldn't put up with a foul mouth or sassing ways, but Davis was easily influenced.

John remembered the last time he'd brought home a stray—a mangy, flea-bitten dog. Both Bert and the dog had big brown eyes swallowing up their faces. At the time he had the same feelings about the animal as he had for this boy. Just like the dog, he'd see how the kid looked after he was cleaned up, fed, and doctored. From the looks of his clothes, Mama would be scrounging around for something for him to wear and scissors to cut the greasy hair hanging almost to his shoulders.

One more mouth to feed. One more boy to keep in line, and one more reason to stay awake at night.

CHAPTER 3

Bert clung to John Timmons's waist while the stallion flew across the field toward his ranch. The sun shone warm and glistened so bright that she squinted to see. She'd lost her hat when Leon pulled her off the mare. If not for the gut-wrenching fear for what lay ahead tearing at her insides, she might have stopped to enjoy the day laced in sparkling beauty. She could have made up a song about nature and fairies and tiny creatures that talked to each other. Those past ways of masking reality wouldn't work now. Most people were selfish takers, and no one had come along to prove otherwise.

She had a pocketful of secrets riding with her, and one of those was why she'd ridden Oberlander's mare across his own land. Two years ago, Bert had come across northern Colorado with her brothers. The rising peaks, some in variegated green and others in shades of gray rock, had held her in awe. Their magnificence stole her breath. She'd viewed Oberlander's grand ranch with her brothers on that trip. And when Simon had come back from a trip six months ago and said he'd been given the mare from the owner of the Wide O, she knew he'd stolen it. And she vowed to return the horse.

All Bert knew when she left home was the owner's name, a desire to undo Simon's thievery, and obviously not a lick of sense to go with it. Because Oberlander's ranch hands believed she'd stolen the mare. They'd tell others and the word would spread among decent folk, people she'd never be like until the past was buried.

Her plan had been to return the mare to the rightful owner, then continue the rest of the journey away from her family on foot. For certain her brothers were on her trail by now, which meant anyone who came in contact with her could be in danger. She needed to put distance between herself and what lay behind with Pa and her brothers.

Unfortunately, she couldn't tell anyone that truth.

Right now, the debt she owed John settled on her like sleeping on the hard ground in the middle of winter. Unlike her brothers, she believed in honesty. But her ideals had been sadly misplaced.

John's stallion was a handful, but his owner held a firm rein. Bert wrapped her hands around him even tighter and hoped she didn't get thrown off. She had far too many worries about how to get out of the current patch of thorns, and being tossed from a horse hadn't yet made the list.

"Where's your ranch?"

"Not too far from here."

"How large is it?"

John chuckled, a deep throaty laugh that in normal circumstances she'd have appreciated. "Oh, about twelve hundred acres, give or take a few."

She'd never dreamed a man could own that much land. "Do you have lots of livestock?"

"A few."

"How many? I mean, do you have hundreds of cattle and horses?"

John must have found her questions amusing, for his laughter rang out around them. "Is this the boy who wouldn't answer a single question? You can count them while you're working off the money you owe."

Then she remembered what she'd learned about him. "So you're a lawman and a rancher?"

"I'm a deputy when needed."

Simon hated lawmen. The thought of what her brother could do, if given the chance, made her ill.

"Are you ready to tell me why you ran away from home?"

"No sir."

"How long since you've eaten?"

She'd picked some wild berries along a patch of woods, but couldn't remember the day. The last of the fish was eaten a few days before. "I think yesterday."

"Mama will have a good spread laid out for noon." He took a look upward. "Yeah, she'll be ringing the dinner bell soon. Right now, it being summer and all, there aren't any extra ranch hands. When school starts up again, that will change. Not sure if you'll bunk down with one of my four brothers or in the bunkhouse. We'll figure out the sleeping arrangements later."

Bert nearly blurted out the truth—part of it anyway. The man who'd paid her debt had an air of decency. He *might* have mercy on her if he knew she was a girl. But she dare not give away her identity. He could decide to deliver her to the sheriff for a hanging, or he could take her back to face Leon at the Wide O. Instead he'd paid good money for a boy—who wasn't a boy—and all he asked was for her to work it off. Three meals sounded real good, even if she only stayed long enough to get her strength back and make her way to Texas.

Her whole head and face ached. Maybe she shouldn't have hit Leon when the beating began. In the past, fighting back had been her way to defend herself and survive. Simon and the others seemed to respect her spunk. Leon thought differently.

She didn't dispute owing John at least four months of work; then she'd have to move on quickly.

"Thank you." Her words seemed sparse considering her past and the uncertainty of the future.

"You're welcome. Are you feelin' poorly?"

"A bit." Weariness had taken hold of her and refused to let go. His muscled body left her feeling almost secure. But that would change once he realized she couldn't do a day's work like a half-grown boy. He'd be even madder. She could feel it in her bones.

"From the looks of you, I'd say you've been on the run for a long time."

"Yes sir."

"Did you run from trouble, or is trouble chasing you?"

Both. "I'd have to think on that."

"I'll tell you the same thing I tell my brothers. No matter what you've done, God's ready to forgive and offer you a second chance. Sometimes it takes a third or a fourth or more. You're young, and you have your whole life ahead of you. Work hard and make something of yourself. God will walk the journey with you if you let Him."

Who's God? The way her brothers used the name, she thought it was a curse word.

On the horizon she saw the outline of a house and barn. Oh my, it was almost as grand as the Oberlander ranch—only homier. The two-story cabin had a wide front porch with rocking chairs and a bench. Horses and cattle grazed in the distance. Pretty and peaceful, like a dream.

The distinct ring of a dinner bell met her ears. Dread at what she was about to face wrapped its dark paws around her and squeezed hard. At least with her brothers she knew what to expect. Even Leon hadn't surprised her with a taste of the same fury she'd endured many times before.

But this . . . Bert's mouth went dry.

"This is my home." John's voice took a reverent tone. "Soon you'll meet the rest of us. And our dog, Rowdy. While you're here, treat this land and my family as though it were your own."

Peculiar man. Who ever heard of offering a stranger—a horse thief—such hospitality?

L and sakes, John. What have you brought home this time?" Bert figured she looked bad, but this little woman made her feel like she'd been rootin' with pigs.

John leaned on the saddle horn. "A ragged boy, Mama."

Bert hoped they never learned the truth. The less they knew the better.

The small freckle-faced woman stepped down from the porch and shielded her eyes from the noon sun as she made her way to the side of John's horse. She was pretty, with light curly hair that had a nice mix of red and gold. Not at all what Bert expected of a woman with five boys to look after.

A black and white dog followed the woman, wagging his tail as friendly as could be. At least she might have one friend here who wouldn't ask questions.

"Oh, my goodness. He's been hurt."

"Yes ma'am. This is Bert. Doesn't have a last name." John glanced back at her with a threatening spark in his blue eyes.

"Good to meet you, ma'am."

The woman smiled, and a warm sensation spread through Bert, or maybe it was the hunger in her belly and the pain in her head.

"What happened to you?" The woman's eyes widened. "Never mind, let's get you cleaned up."

"I'll tell you about it later," John said.

Bert thought her heart would burst from her chest and thump into the dirt below her. This woman would not sound so caring once she learned about Oberlander's mare.

A door slammed, and four boys made their way from the house and down the steps. They were all sizes, talking and asking questions like she were the newest addition to their livestock. The tantalizing aroma of ham caused her stomach to protest its lack of food, but dizziness overcame her before she could think more about a meal that could actually fill her stomach.

John turned back to Bert. "Can you slide off?"

Bert nodded. The prancing stallion frightened her, but she didn't want to let on and swung her leg over the back of the saddle. Somewhere between mid-air and the ground, her head began to spin, and all the blinking in the world couldn't clear her vision or stop the fall.

Voices blurred. The saddle squeaked. An invisible hammer pierced her skull. She had no strength to fight whatever was pulling her into a world of blackness.

Chapter 4

John picked up the bundle of bones at his feet and carried him up the porch steps and inside the house. Regret pelted him for picking up a stray kid who was already more trouble than a twister headed straight for the house. All eighty pounds of him.

A twinge of guilt struck him—if he hadn't followed Ted, the kid would have been hanged. "Is he dying?" Davis said, on Mama's heels.

"I don't think so." John carried Bert through the big kitchen, past the long pine table, and on into the back room where Mama slept. "He's most likely hungry and feeling the results of a good beating."

"Put him on my bed," Mama called from behind him. "I'm getting hot water and ointment."

"He's dirty and smells."

"I don't care. The quilt will wash, and he'll be easier to tend to there."

John laid Bert on Mama's prettiest quilt and turned his attention to his brothers standing in the doorway, except for Davis who seemed to be tied to Mama's apron strings.

"You boys finish your dinner?"

"We'd just got started," Evan said.

When had his brother gotten so tall and lean? When had *all* of them grown so tall?

"Why don't you go back to eatin', and I'll help Mama."

"Are you thinking we aren't old enough to hear the story?" Evan turned his head and lifted a brow, reminding him of their father. His tone tossed a challenge.

It's about time you let your brothers grow up. Mama's words rang in his ears. "I'm sorry. I keep forgetting that I ran this ranch at fourteen and took over at seventeen. All of you do a man's work and deserve to be treated like men."

"Praise God," Evan said.

John grinned. He had that coming. He glanced at Davis. "Do you think you can take Racer to the barn for me?"

"Yes sir. Do you want me to rub him down?"

"You can start. One of us will come and get you in a few minutes. Don't want you eating a cold dinner."

"Oh, I don't mind. I can do a fine job. Yes siree, I can." Davis lifted his chin as though he'd been flipped a gold coin, causing his brothers to laugh. He disappeared but not without telling Mama where he was going and what he was about to do.

"John, don't start talking without me," Mama said from the kitchen. "That way you only have to tell us once. Aaron, I could use a hand here."

Bert's eyelids fluttered. He looked downright pitiful with his face a mass of dried blood and a swollen eye quickly turning black.

"Just hold on there," John said to Bert. "Once you're doctored a bit, you can eat. Aaron, bring some water for him to drink when you come."

When Mama and Aaron stepped into the bedroom, John took a deep breath. "While I was riding to see Victor Oberlander about some business, one of his ranch hands rode my way and said a hanging was about to take place. Said Leon and a couple of other ranch hands from the Wide O had found a boy riding Oberlander's prize mare. Remember when Leon rode over here a few months back and asked if we'd seen her? Anyway, Leon had been drinking and had the noose around the kid's neck. I stopped the hanging and took care of Oberlander getting his mare back. The kid looks bad 'cause Leon roughed him up a bit."

"Where's he from?" Evan said, taking a step closer to the bed. "I've never seen him around here."

"Me either," Aaron said. Mark echoed the same.

John had hoped his brothers knew the kid. "He said his name was Bert but wouldn't tell me anything else."

"Sure was stupid to steal a man's horse and then ride across his ranch with it." Evan stood beside Mama, watching every move she made.

Bert stirred. "I didn't steal it. I wouldn't take something belongin' to someone else."

John's patience was about to run out. "As I said before, if you aren't going to tell me why you were riding the mare, then don't deny stealing it."

"Give him time." Mama threw a frown John's way. "He's just a boy."

Bert winced when Mama touched a wet cloth to his face.

"Easy. You're safe here. My name's Leah Timmons, and I need to clean you up so I can see how badly you're hurt." She stiffened. "The nerve of Leon punching you like that." She flashed her anger at John. "I hope you gave him a taste of your tongue."

"I did, but I sure thought about laying a fist alongside his jaw. Guess it was enough to save this one's scrawny hide. Doesn't matter. Once he's feeling better, he's working off the hundred dollars it cost me."

Startled, Mama straightened, wet cloth in hand. "What hundred dollars?"

"Oberlander wanted compensation for being without his mare. Claimed three hundred dollars as his price, but we settled on one hundred and breeding the mare to Racer. I had the choice of either paying him or leaving the boy there for Leon to put to work."

Mama tilted her head. "You did the right thing, John. I'm sure Bert knows he owes you his life."

"More like I had too much sun and was touched in the head." John fought the urge to say a few more things but swallowed his ire. He *still* had to find a way to purchase Oberlander's land before Evan's birthday.

"I think the good Lord had you right where He needed you." Mama returned to wiping the grime from Bert's face.

John heard the chuckles behind him and leveled a seething look at his brothers. "You'll think it's funny when you're teaching him how to mend a fence."

"How about mucking stalls? Doesn't take a smart person to do that." Mark glanced at Bert. "I'll show him how to hold a shovel."

"Mark, since you have all the answers, you can brew a cup of ginger tea," Mama said. "It'll make this tiny fellow feel better."

John stuffed his hands into his jean pockets. The day had been a waste, and it was barely noon. "Why don't one of you boys fetch Davis and you get to eating? We need to finish the fence."

They shuffled out without further comment. No doubt the entertainment had worn thin in view of their stomachs. Mama continued to clean Bert up and apply witch hazel to the cuts and swollen areas. John could tell by the way she moved her mouth that she was mentally forming her words for what would come next.

"What haven't you told me about this boy?"

Looking at Bert, cut and bruised, John felt sorry for him. "I wish I had more to tell. Leaving him at the mercy of Oberlander's ranch hands was akin to murder."

"I agree."

He glanced down at Bert, wondering what filled the boy's thoughts. "I plan to talk to Marshal Culpepper about him. Other than finding an orphanage, not much else I can do."

"Except have him work off his debt."

"Right."

"John, if he didn't steal the horse and he's alone, then he needs taking care of. If he did steal, then he needs to learn there are consequences to breaking the law."

John marveled at how he could predict her words. "I did learn from the best."

She wiggled her nose at him. "Mamas do have other uses besides feeding and clothing their babies."

"You're right, and I love you for it." He bent and kissed her cheek. "Shall I fix him a plate of food?" John's stomach growled at the smell of ham and fresh peas.

"I think so. Not too much. As thin as he is, I don't want to make him sick."

"Mama, can we have the berry cobbler on the windowsill?" Mark said from the kitchen.

"No sir. It's for supper. If you're needing something sweet, grab another piece of cornbread and ladle some honey on it."

John headed for the door to get a plate of food for Bert and then himself. "What are you going to do when you don't have all of us to feed?"

"Rest. Read. And rock my grandbabies on the porch."

"That's a long time off."

She smiled down at Bert, then up at him. "You're old enough to be married, John. All we need to do is add another room onto the house or help you build your own home. I suppose the latter would suit you the most."

When would he have time for a wife? He didn't even have time to look for one. "There isn't a girl around who has my heart like you do."

She frowned and wagged a finger at him. "Then you haven't been looking at all the girls trying to catch your eye."

"The only females snatching up my attention are heifers and mares." Only to himself would he dream about a different life. But dreaming was all it would amount to.

CHAPTER 5

John stole a look toward the back of the barn where Bert had dumped another load of manure right where he'd instructed. The pile was growing, and the stalls were getting cleaned. The kid worked hard, and John hadn't heard any whining, even when Aaron and Mark teased him, which they were very good at.

Five days had passed since John brought Bert home. The notion of why the kid refused to give his full name or why he'd run away from home remained a mystery. Too much left unsaid meant a mountain of trouble. Marshal Culpepper hadn't turned up a thing, which worried John even more. He considered wiring his Uncle Parker, who represented this area of Colorado in the Denver legislature. Maybe an advertisement in the *Rocky Mountain News* might turn up something, especially if a family was looking for Bert.

John wiped the sweat from his brow and watched the boy tote the wheelbarrow back to the barn. From the kid's condition, he'd been on his own for a long while. Surprisingly, he'd survived. He ate poorly for a growing boy and looked peaked and frail. Maybe John shouldn't give him so much to do. Ease up and let him get stronger. Poor kid. He must have had a tough life.

You have too much to worry about without frettin' over a kid.

But God said to look after strangers.

The kid looked tired and hot. John made his way over to where Bert maneuvered the wheelbarrow back into the barn. "Here, let me give you a hand."

"I can do it." Bert heaved with the empty wheelbarrow.

John took over pushing it back to a far stall. "I know, but I don't want you fainting in a pile of manure."

"Hadn't thought about that."

John chuckled. "I did. And I don't like the idea of lifting you out of it."

John helped him load up two more times before the boy asked to finish the job by himself. For a skinny kid, he was strong and didn't complain about the work.

What would happen to the boy once he worked off his debt? He needed a home, a place where folks would love him and teach him how to be a man.

But not at the Timmons ranch. John had enough responsibilities without another mouth to feed and another future to consider.

Bert picked up another shovelful of horse manure and dumped it onto the pile in the wheelbarrow. At this rate, she might finish today. John had had her start at sunrise before breakfast, and now at mid-afternoon, she could see real progress. Her shoulders ached, but she'd not complain. Each time she lifted the shovel and toted the wheelbarrow to the edge of the barn, she saw more of her debt paid.

She'd never eaten this good or slept so hard. No cursing or fighting, and lots of lovin' among the Timmons family. If things had been different at home ... If Pa hadn't let Simon take over ... If she'd had a plot of ground to grow vegetables ... Oh, what was the use? The past couldn't be changed, but she could sure do something about tomorrow and the next day.

Five days had gone by since John had saved her from the hanging, and he still couldn't look at her without scowling. Oh, he had his gentle moments, but most of the time she attempted to stay clear of him. At least he hadn't blackened her other eye. She shouldn't mind he thought ill of her. Couldn't blame him either. Despite his constant frown when he came near her, she liked him . . . in an odd sort of way. She admired how he cared for his family, but he needed to laugh more. So did she.

His brothers teased her about being skinny and slow, except Davis. He was a sweet boy. And Evan really didn't pick on her as much as Aaron and Mark. So far she'd hidden her identity and had slept on a pallet in the room Davis, Mark, and Aaron shared, being careful to wait until they were in bed before she stepped in. Even then, she slept fitfully, and what if the nightmares returned? How long would she be able to conceal her identity?

What would she do when her womanly time arrived? Sometimes she skipped her monthly visitor, especially if she hadn't eaten much. One anxious thought after another made her think about running again. If she believed in the God the Timmonses spoke about at mealtimes and evening Bible readings, she'd ask Him to help her out.

A breeze swirled around her bringing the odor of what she shoveled up inside her nostrils. She smelled just as bad.

Late afternoon, Bert stood back and surveyed her work. Warmth spread through her that had nothing to do with summer's temperatures but everything to do with satisfaction of a job nearly completed. She could live like this forever.

Footsteps swished through the grass behind her. Instinctively, she panicked and swung around, certain it was Simon. Evan stood in the afternoon shadows. He must look like his pa, because he didn't share the same traits as Leah or John.

He eyed her curiously. "Didn't mean to scare you. Wanted to let you know we take a bath on Saturday night. After supper, we fill up the watering trough or head to the creek."

Apprehension raced up her spine. How could she manage a bath without one of the Timmonses learning the truth? "I don't need a bath."

Evan laughed, and his light blue eyes held a sparkle of mischief. "Take a long sniff at yourself. It's bad, just like the rest of us. No point refusing. It'll only get you tossed in with your clothes on." He anchored his thumbs on his jeans. "You're doing a fine job, Bert. We all tease you 'cause we like you. That's the way it is with the Timmons boys."

She nodded as he walked away. *Bullfrogs and black crows.* She'd gotten herself into a fine mess. She'd learned from Leah that Evan was seventeen too. This was not good. Not good at all. She turned her attention back to the job at hand while misery swirled inside her. They'd all find out this evening if she didn't come up with a plan before then. She figured John would thrash her for sure and take her back to Oberlander for Leon to teach her another lesson.

Bert ached more in her heart than in her body. Lies and more lies. She'd become as low and ugly as her brothers. One shovel after another filled the wheelbarrow until she headed out again to the manure pile. Rowdy came bounding across the pasture, his tail wagging, and a happy greeting in his step. Aaron had told her the dog was an Australian shepherd, a big help with the cattle. She patted his head and then leaned on the shovel.

"Rowdy, do you have any idea what kind of trouble I'm in?" With a sigh, she emptied the wheelbarrow onto the huge mound. "You're pretty lucky. You don't have to explain anything to folks or conjure up lies."

She massaged her back and peered up at the mountains. So beautiful, like a promise no one broke. She stared at the varying shades of silver gray rock mixed with green and snow-frosted peaks that seemed to hold up the sky. They whispered strength and a means of freedom from the old familiar fears that stalked her like a bad fever.

Her gaze swept to the fields of wildflowers, their colors prettier than anything a human could paint. Maybe someday she'd have a dress with some of those same pinks, yellows, and blues. The songbirds serenaded all around her ... comforting, peaceful. In the distance a herd of elk grazed on Timmons land. The branchlike antlers of the males gave them a noble look. The herd reminded her of small towns where everyone had a job to do. To the east of the elk, a few deer stood like statues, silhouetted against the mountains. These graceful animals held her attention the most. Perhaps their ability to take flight when startled reminded her too much of herself.

Every day brought Simon closer to finding her, and she couldn't ever stop looking over her shoulder. In the meantime, she owed John Timmons four months of hard work for what he'd done.

But what about the bath tonight?

An idea landed right smack in her brain. She'd take her bath while the others were eating their supper. She'd say she wasn't hungry. Miss Leah had already told her about a clean set of clothes. Problem solved, at least for today. Bert grinned at Rowdy, who'd turned his head sideways as if trying to figure her out. A song popped into her head.

> *I know a dog named Rowdy*
> *As fine as he could be.*
> *When he walked up, wagged his tail,*
> *I knew he was a friend to me.*

Leah straightened from removing dried clothes from the line. She stretched her back and followed Bert's lone figure pushing the wheelbarrow back to the barn. She'd walked to the garden near the manure pile to ask Bert if he wanted some water and heard every word from the boy's mouth. Bert's confession to Rowdy settled on Leah's shoulders like the threat of a summer storm. How could one so young be in trouble or have to tell lies to cover up the truth?

She decided not to ask about the water and simply take it to him once she finished pulling the clothes from the line. Still she fretted and worried about Bert as if he were one of her own. She turned her head to bathe her face with the coolness of a north wind, then swung her attention back to Bert. The longer she watched the boy, the more suspicious she became. Taking a deep breath, she reached up to remove John's shirt from the clothesline and shake it soundly before folding it. Surely her inclination had come from a part of her mind where logic had taken flight. What a far-fetched notion. Unless it was true.

Sure would make John's mood more understandable, if her poor son had any clue whatsoever about his emotions. She startled. *Oh my, Evan too, and Aaron.* What a kettle of burnt beans whipped across her motherly instincts. None of the boys had mentioned Bert's way of staying to himself. It could all be very explainable: the boy had spent a rough young life; he was afraid; he didn't trust anyone.

All very true, but ... Nonsense. Leah knew the truth about her suspicions as well as she knew her own name, and tonight was bath night. Goodness, what a dilemma, and she needed time to think. For now, she had wash to gather off the line, peas to shell, and a simmering roast to check on for supper.

Tonight could be very interesting.

CHAPTER 6

John listened to the conversation around the supper table. Someday his brothers would all be grown men, and when it happened, he hoped they remembered the lively discussions when they gathered for a meal. This is where the brothers forgot about branding time, mucking stalls, riding fence and repairing them, chasing down strays, repairing tools, curing skins and tanning hides, shoeing horses, and the countless other never-ending jobs.

"Mama, I'll never get married until I find a cook as good as you." Mark, who had dipped from the roast platter three times, rubbed his stomach.

"I thought you said cows were better company than women," Evan said.

"I did." Mark grinned. "I'll need a quiet woman who cooks like Mama."

"Impossible." John swallowed a generous bite of biscuit dripping in apple butter. "All women talk a lot and want you to tell them they're pretty."

"How would you know?" Evan reached for the honey. "I haven't ever seen you talking to any girls."

"You haven't been paying attention." John peeked at his pocket watch to see how long before Mama gave them a lecture on the virtues of a fine woman. He washed down the biscuit with a long drink of buttermilk. "You see, I'm smart. I'm observing them all so when the right time comes, I'll know who to ask."

"Whom," Mama said. "What about courting and praying for God to put the right woman in your path?"

"Oh, I'll do that." John eyed the custard pie, his favorite. "When I'm ready to settle down."

"At age one hundred," Evan said. "When your teeth are gone and you need someone to spoon food in your mouth. You're married to this ranch."

"Don't get any backtalk from cows."

"I agree," Mark said. "Me and John will run this ranch with women who don't talk, just cook."

"Mercy." Mama rose from the table. "You boys would drive a preacher to drink. A woman is not a cook or a ranch hand or a matter of a joke. She's a gift from God to help make your life's journey easier."

John hid his grin. "Yes ma'am. We'll remember that. Won't we, boys?"

His brothers echoed a "yes ma'am," even Davis. John took a passing look at Bert. No emotion on that boy's face. Didn't he know how to laugh? Bert hadn't wanted supper, but Mama insisted. She said if he still felt poorly by bedtime, she'd give him a dose of castor oil.

After supper, when the brothers were all swimming and soapin' up in the creek, the boy might relax and enjoy himself. The water rushing over the rocks always comforted John, and he hoped it would loosen up Bert too. Davis compared the air-churned bubbles to the amount of soap Mama expected them to use.

"Let's help Mama clean up and then we'll head to the creek," Evan said.

"Aaron and I tested out the new rope. We hung it over the cottonwood. Maybe this one won't break."

"Not me," Davis said. "I'll help Mama if you want to go on."

Davis didn't like heights, and he liked rope swings even less. When he was four, outlaws kidnapped him and John rode after them. Now John realized what a dumb move that had been. Uncle Parker and his wife, Sage, came to the rescue by helping to lower both boys down from a cliff. Davis needed to rid himself of the fear of heights and dangling ropes, but not tonight.

"What do you say, Bert?" Aaron said, who looked like Evan and their father. "Besides needin' a bath, you could show us how good you can swim."

"The word is 'well' not 'good'," Mama said. "You boys need to pay more attention to your grammar."

"Yes ma'am." Laughter rose from all of them—including Mama.

"Can't swim," Bert said. "I'll take my bath later."

Aaron snickered. "There's plenty of shallow spots."

The boy turned a pasty white. Obviously he was afraid of water. "Take it easy on him until he knows us better," John said. The kid asked to take his bath before supper, but John wanted him to finish mucking out the stalls. No point getting all smelly again so soon after a bath.

Aaron clasped a hand on Bert's shoulder, and Mark did the same on the other shoulder. "We'll take care of you, Bert. Don't worry about a thing."

Shortly afterward, the barefoot boys headed to the creek armed with soap, towels, clean clothes, and plenty of tricks up their sleeves for Bert. John knew their plans. Innocent fun. They'd never abuse the kid.

John followed them outside. "I'll be right there," he said. "I left the tack room in a mess and need to straighten it up."

"I'll do it." Bert's pale face indicated he didn't feel well at all.

"Thanks, but I want to check on what needs to be repaired. Why don't you get yourself clean and then head up to the house. As nasty as castor oil tastes, you might need a dose of it."

A pitiful pair of large brown eyes met him.

"You have to get a bath, Bert," he said. "There's no getting out of it."

Bert swallowed hard and lagged behind the others. Aaron turned to Mark with a grin, then snatched up Bert and swung him over his shoulder. John couldn't help but laugh at the kid kicking and hollering to be put down. Bert pounded his fists into Aaron's back as his brother hurried to the creek bank and ran in, clothes and all.

John watched to see how the kid reacted; Bert could have been abused in the past and might need some special care.

"We'll save Mama the trouble of washin' our clothes." Aaron unbuttoned his shirt and began tugging it over his arms. "Come on, Bert. Teasing aside, I'll teach you how to swim. It's not hard once you get the hang of it."

John listened and cringed at Mark's use of the word "hang." Not a good choice.

"And I'll help him get rid of those smelly clothes." Mark splashed toward him.

"No. Please no." Bert struggled to get free of Aaron. "John, help me."

The desperation in the boy's voice captured John's attention. "Bert, no one wants to hurt you."

Mark grabbed Bert's shirt, and Aaron grabbed the suspenders.

"No, please. Stop. I beg of you. I'm not a boy!" Bert's last shriek could have been heard on the other side of the Rockies, but the silence it brought left them all speechless. Aaron and Mark immediately released the kid as though they'd touched hot coals.

John moistened his lips. "What did you say?"

"I'm not a boy." Bert's voice came like a whisper.

"So you're a girl?"

She stood up to her full five feet and planted her hands on her hips. Water dripped from every inch of her. "If I'm not a boy then I reckon I'm a girl."

John started to laugh. And when he did, his brothers took to laughing too. He sat on the soft grass nursing his sides and stomach. "Poor Bert, and here I was worried about you being sick. When were you going to tell us the truth?"

When Bert didn't respond, John's mind whipped into a gallop. A girl running alone? A girl who'd deceived him? A girl who refused to give him her last name—or her first name for that matter. "What kind of trouble have you brought to my family?"

"I hope none." The fear in her eyes stopped him from saying more.

John stood from the creek bank. His troubles over one scrawny boy had just doubled. No, tripled. "I think you need to get to the house."

Bert waded out of the water. She snatched up the towel and the clean clothes on the bank. Catching her gaze, he saw the pain of something he couldn't describe in those huge brown eyes. But he wasn't about to get soft on a girl who'd lied to him and his family.

"I'm sorry."

John fished for something intelligent to say, but all of his words had drowned in the creek.

"And I didn't steal Oberlander's horse."

Then his anger kicked to the surface. "I'm supposed to believe that when nothing you've said has been true?"

She walked straight up to him, barely coming up to his chest. "Suppose not. Do you want me to leave or stay and work off my debt?"

John peered out at his brothers and caught Evan's eye. His near-man of a brother gave half a nod. "We'll talk about your future after a family meetin'."

"I can be gone before you're finished here."

John pressed his lips together and lifted her chin with a finger. "Little lady, if you aren't at the house when I get back, I'm coming after you. And that's a promise."

Leah watched Bert stomp toward the house. Curiosity moved her to the front porch with a cup of coffee in her hand.

"You've taken your bath already?"

Bert frowned. "Not exactly. I'm wet though."

Leah eyed the boy up and down. "I can see that. What happened?"

Bert ran his tongue over his lips, then stared at her. "I confessed to something."

"Then you'd better tell me." Leah sat down on the porch steps and patted the wooden plank beside her. "Sit down, Bert. We're going to have a come-to-Jesus meetin'."

"I don't understand." He hadn't moved a step. But when Leah gestured again for him to sit, he complied.

"Best begin talking because the longer you wait, the harder it'll be." Once Bert took his place beside her, she took his hand.

"I'm not a boy."

Leah had been right. "Is that so?" For a moment, she thought he, or rather she, might cry. "Anything else you want to tell me?"

Bert swallowed. "That's enough. John's real mad."

"But you're not surprised. You lied to him after he saved your life. I suspect this isn't the only thing you've lied about."

"Yes ma'am. I mean no, ma'am. I haven't lied ... just haven't told him what he wants to know." The girl's eyes pooled, and she blinked several times.

"Are you ready to tell the truth?"

Bert shook her head. "I can't."

Compassion welled up in Leah. Whatever Bert had experienced must have been a nightmare. "What are we to do with you?"

Bert glanced at the hand holding hers. "John said there'd be a family meetin' tonight. Except I'd rather leave."

"Sometimes running seems to be the best answer to hard problems. But it doesn't solve a thing. Truth is what frees us from ourselves." She squeezed Bert's hand. "Let's get your bath and help you look respectable."

CHAPTER 7

John leaned against a porch post. He'd sorted through every experience he'd ever known to come up with a solution for his problem with Bert. When his memory failed him, he prayed and thought about what his Uncle Parker might do in the same situation. Folks often said the two were alike in temperament and in the way they lassoed life. John doubted if Uncle Parker had encountered a girl with a questionable past who posed as a boy.

Uncle Parker had taught John how to live a godly life by standing up for his beliefs. He'd married a woman who'd been a bounty hunter and lived a couple of years with the Utes. That was unusual. But Aunt Sage never lied. In fact, she'd been straight up about everything in her life.

No help there, so John had gone back to praying, but his own anger seemed to drown out any guidance from the Lord. His brothers talked among themselves — Aaron and Mark laughed about something, and Evan propped Davis on his lap, no doubt a story in mind. Mama and Bert were still inside. Hopefully the girl had bathed, considering how badly she'd smelled at supper.

The door opened, and Mama walked out with Bert behind her ... in a dress. John's jaw dropped to his boots. Granted, Mama and Bert were about the same size, but Bert looked a whole lot different in Mama's blue dress. Especially since she was clean and her near-shoulder-length, honey-colored hair washed and shiny. Now why hadn't Mama given her Mark's old jeans and shirt to wear? That made more sense than ... than ... this.

"Whoa," Evan said barely above a whisper. "Guess you aren't a boy after all."

John scowled. The fears assaulting him about a female in their midst had taken physical form. Mama and Bert sat together on the porch bench. Bert's eyes were red as though she'd been crying. Women and tears were a bad combination. John wasn't about to let that weaken his resolve to find out the truth.

"We've got a decision to make here as a family." His voice lacked its usual force. "We're going to vote on whether Bert stays and completes the debt she owes, or I take her into town and let Marshal Culpepper or the preacher handle her refusal to state who she is or where she's from."

"We can ask questions?" Evan said.

John didn't like the moonfaced look on that boy's face. "In a minute. I have a few of my own. The right name sounds like a good beginning." John aimed his words at Bert with a heavy coating of sternness.

"I've always been called Bert." She glanced at Mama. When his mother gave the girl the familiar "go ahead and speak your mind" look, John's irritation changed to a twinge of jealousy. "I didn't lie about my name."

"Is your mother alive, or did you lie about that?"

Mama lifted her chin. "John, you can form your words with more kindness."

"Yes ma'am." He took a breath and Mark laughed. "Bert, is your mother living?"

"No. She died when I was born."

"Thank you."

Aaron snickered. Both he and Mark would taste his tongue later. "What about your father?"

"He's living, but we parted company."

"Any more family?"

"I'd rather not say."

So this is how she intended to play the game. "Where are you from?"

"I'd rather not say."

"Have you broken the law?"

"No. I didn't steal Oberlander's horse."

"Who are you running from?"

"I'm just on my own."

"How old are you?"

Bert looked down at her toes peeking out from under Mama's dress, then peered square into John's face. "Seventeen."

Mama gasped. Evan coughed. Aaron and Mark laughed. Davis appeared oblivious to what was going on. A hundred more questions marched across John's mind like an army headed to battle.

"You could have told us the truth about your age."

"Yes sir. I can be on my way so as not to cause any more problems. When I get to where I'm going, I'll find work and send you the money I owe." Bert gulped, and John read desperation into her words. "But I've already proved to you I can work hard."

"You did," John said. "With the garden coming in, I think you'd best help Mama. Davis can give us a hand outside." Truth was he didn't want Bert near his brothers. "That is, if we vote you should stay."

"Then let's get at it." Evan had yet to take his eyes off her.

"Don't you boys have any questions? Mama?" John didn't like the way this was heading at all.

"I don't have any questions for Bert, but I do have something to say. A few days ago, we agreed with John to let Bert work off a debt. As a boy, he'd been beaten and looked like he hadn't eaten a good meal in a long time. The only thing that's changed is Bert is a young woman—a little older than we thought. I'd welcome the help for the garden and some of the other chores inside and outside of the house that I haven't had time to do."

They all want her to stay. But how did he feel, other than frustrated and overwhelmed? Add deceived ... "Well, let's vote. Who's for Bert staying?"

Every brother raised his right hand, and so did Mama.

John's insides churned like curdled milk. "Looks like Mama has some extra help."

"What about you?" Davis's eyes were round—and far too innocent. "You didn't vote."

Wouldn't have done me any good. John smiled. "Looks like all of you decided for me." He continued to smile and focused on Bert. "Could we take a walk? Not long. The sun's setting and tomorrow is the Lord's day."

"Do you need me to accompany you?" Mama asked.

"John isn't courtin', Mama," Evan said. "He's only going to give Bert the rules."

John braced himself for the teasing to come about Bert being a girl, and his brothers did not fail him. After all, he was a grown man. But his feelings about being duped made him furious.

Still ... if he allowed himself to be completely honest, other unbidden feelings had stepped inside him and taken up residence. When he saw how different Bert looked in a dress, it reinforced a need to protect her from unscrupulous men like Leon or anyone else who'd want to abuse her. But he'd never admit that to his brothers—or Mama. He thought about taking her hand, politelike, and helping her down from the porch. Instead, he stuffed it in his jeans pocket. This little gal had a few questions to answer.

When the laughing stopped, Bert slowly stood. She trembled, and he almost felt sorry for her. Almost. She descended the porch steps, holding up her dress so as not to trip. He'd seen Mama do the same thing plenty of times. Why did Bert look, well, fetching doing the same?

The two walked toward the creek. That seemed a fittin' place since the truth came to light in those rocky waters.

"I didn't know how to tell you." Bert's voice cracked. "I was afraid. But I *am* beholdin' to you for saving my life."

Why hadn't he been able to tell that soft voice came from a female? No point dwelling on it any longer. The milk had been spilled, so all he could do was clean up the mess.

"I'm concerned about my brothers fussin' over you," he said. "They aren't used to a girl being around."

"I'll be respectful, like you said before."

John needed to know a few things to protect his family. "Is the one after you a husband?"

She shivered. "Not at all."

"A man lookin' for you to be his?"

"No sir." Her eyes widened.

I know fear when I see it. "Is the law after you?"

"I've never broken the law, at least to my knowledge. I've picked berries from other ranchers' lands, fished from the streams, and caught a rabbit or two."

"I don't call those things stealing. Some folks might, but I call it survivin'. I tell you this, if I catch you stealing anything, I'll arrest you and make sure you stand trial. Is that clearly understood?"

"Yes sir."

"How long have you been on the run?"

"Six months."

"What kind of work have you done?"

"Hard to get a job when you look like an eleven-year-old boy."

She turned her head, and he wished he could see her face. Then he'd be able to read what her words didn't say. Before her debt was paid, he'd find out about Oberlander's prize mare and the circumstances she'd left behind. "Is there anything else I should know in order to protect my family?"

She hesitated. "If I think so, I'll leave."

"I'm not an unfair man. You can talk to me."

She nodded. "I'll keep my distance from your brothers."

But who would help him stay clear of her? Even though she had made him furious. Even though she had lied to him. Even though ...

Why did she have to be so easy on the eyes?

That night, Bert should have been able to drift off to sleep. Instead she found it impossible to stop her rushing thoughts. She understood John was trying hard to be nice because she was a girl. She wished she'd known sooner how he'd react. Maybe she'd have told him the truth. Miss Leah said he had a good heart and for her not to be afraid of him. But she knew what a man could do ...

The night brought on a chill, and she shivered. Yet for the first time in longer than she could remember, Bert sensed a strange kind of peace. How very strange she felt safe within the dark confines of night when she couldn't see what was hidden outside the house. Foolishness had settled in her for sure. No one here could protect her from Simon. But the Timmonses brought out a longing and an ache for a better life. They were good people, and they believed they were doing right by her.

A feeling of something more kin to selfishness than appreciation rained over her. How many times had she been labeled a dreamer and not good enough for decent folks? She shouldn't risk this. She shouldn't risk what her staying might mean to the Timmonses. But like she told John, if she had an indication that Simon was in the area, she'd leave.

You're a stupid fool, Bert. All you're good for is doin' what you're told.

But right now the familiar condemnation seemed far away.

Simon wouldn't give up. Not with what she'd done. But surely he'd not hurt any of the Timmonses, especially with John being a deputy marshal. Would he?

For certain, during the four months it took to pay John back, she'd drink in what it meant to have a real family.

Bert rolled over onto her back and stared up at the ceiling. Sleeping arrangements had changed, and now she shared a bed with Leah. From the even breathing beside her, the dear woman lay sleeping. Tomorrow was Sunday and church. Gideon had told her once that church was not a place for their kind. Church folks spent their days being nice to each other and not looking for someone to stab them in the back.

At least Simon wouldn't show up there.

CHAPTER 8

Bert borrowed an old pair of Miss Leah's shoes for church, and she wore the dress that had shocked the Timmons boys the night before. Although she relaxed in the knowledge that her own brothers wouldn't recognize her, it didn't stop her fear of attending church. And whoever the Timmonses called God, He must be powerful and not just a name to swear by.

She sat on the front buckboard squeezed between Leah and John. Rightfully, she could have sat in the back with the brothers, but John wanted her beside him. She wasn't a fool. She knew the real reason, as though some of her bad qualities would rub off on the other boys.

John could be right. Oh, she should have run when she had the chance.

Forty-five minutes later, they entered the town of Rocky Falls. She'd ridden through it before when looking for directions to Oberlander's ranch. Another bad decision.

At the other end of the town, past the marshal's office, the saloon and hotel, the general store, undertaker, newspaper, feed store, and the telegraph office, stood a small church, built mostly of stone with a wooden steeple extending from the front portion of the roof. She sure wished she knew what to expect before she walked inside.

John pulled the team of horses to a stop.

Run now while you have the chance. But she remembered his finger pressed under her chin and his promise to come after her if she took off.

"There's Mr. Oberlander," Miss Leah said. "He doesn't miss a Sunday."

The big man rode their way on the mare Bert had tried to return. She swallowed hard.

"Mornin', Mr. Oberlander," John said.

Oberlander smiled and removed his hat, a spotless one that looked new. "Mornin', Miss Leah. You too, Miss. Don't believe we've met."

"Oh, we have." Bert took a deep breath.

John cleared his throat.

"Are we courtin', John?" Mr. Oberlander grinned.

His face turned the color of the tomatoes from Miss Leah's garden. "Not exactly."

Mr. Oberlander craned his neck and greeted the boys in the back of the wagon, his large frame lifting from the saddle. "Did the little horse thief run off?"

Davis stood. "No sir. That's her sittin' between Mama and John."

Mr. Oberlander gaped at Bert for about two seconds and then laughed until he had to wipe his eyes. His weathered face spread full, and folks turned to see what he found so funny. The boys in the back of the wagon joined him, but not John Timmons seated beside her. She felt him stiffen.

"John, you got trouble on your hands now. Better you than me."

Seemed like a lot of folks were laughin' at John's expense. Bert sighed and realized how sorry she felt for him. He'd done a good deed, and too many people were making fun of him.

John lifted his mama down from the buckboard, then reached for Bert. When his arms grabbed her waist, she sensed the heat rising in her neck and face. She must look like a tomato now too.

"I'm sorry about the teasin'," she whispered.

He frowned. But at least he didn't hit her. He drew in a long breath. "No need to be shakin'." *He noticed?* "Church isn't a place where folks will hurt you." He said it so softly that only she could hear. "People here love God and want to show it by singing about Him and listening to what the Bible says about how we should live."

She blinked and nodded. "Thanks. New things bother me."

"This is the one place you can feel safe. Preacher Waller is a good man."

She realized he'd spent too much time talking to her quiet-like, and he'd invited his brothers and anyone else to begin the teasing again.

Running was so much easier. Being hungry hurt her stomach, but it didn't make her heart ache for a life she'd never have.

"We have a few minutes," John said. "Let's take a little walk until you stop shaking."

"Your brothers and Mr. Oberlander will tease you."

His slight smile eased her. "I can handle it." He turned to Leah. "Save us a place. Bert's not doing well."

Leah tilted her head, and a curious look passed over her face. "Don't be long."

Bert walked with John across the road to a pasture where a couple of horses grazed. She appreciated that he didn't touch her, and his stride matched hers and not his. They stopped at the fence while she willed her insides to stop whirling like a twister.

"New experiences sometimes get me flustered." He stared out over the thick green pasture, just as she was doing. "But the important thing to remember is God wants us in His house, and He doesn't want us to be afraid of Him. The folks who come are good too."

She nodded, basking in his gentle tone. John Timmons didn't resemble her brothers, and she was grateful for his kindness.

"Are you going to be all right?"

"Yes sir. I won't faint."

He chuckled, and she liked the sound of it.

Inside the church, Bert sat between Leah and John on wooden benches that were carved on the ends. A large wooden cross mounted on the back wall caught her attention. Questions about what it meant and why it must be important settled on her mind.

With Miss Leah's presence, she attempted to calm herself. Her left foot tapped against the floor. Leah reached over and placed her hand on Bert's knee. She needed to simply sit quietly until church was over.

Some folks were staring. What were they thinking? Did they know Leon had tried to hang her for stealing a horse, but John stopped him? Had they figured out he regretted saving her? Did some of them assume she and John were courtin' like Mr. Oberlander had done? Oh, the questions weighing against her brain.

A woman began to play a song on the piano. Bert turned her attention to the music, allowing it to soothe her, as music always did. Leah picked up a book from the back of the bench in front of her and found a particular page. Bert pretended interest. The people around her began to sing "I Sing the Mighty Power of God," and she listened. The tune was easy to pick up, and the words were fitting for how helpless and hopeless she felt.

A man dressed in a black suit stepped up to a wooden box and smiled. "Welcome to the house of God."

The house of God? Could she endure this?

Leah wanted to glance Bert's way, but the poor girl couldn't seem to sit still. If Bert had been one of the boys, Leah would have quieted her with a mama's special look. Considering the situation, she should have thought through the seating better to make sure Bert didn't sit beside John. But she'd simply gone with the usual arrangement—making sure Mark was on one side of John and Aaron on Leah's other side with Davis. Mark and Aaron were more mischievous than a dozen boys. And it seemed like the older they got, the more they found to do to aggravate those around them.

Throughout the sermon, Leah observed Bert's uneasiness with Preacher Waller's words. The only telltale signs were the crinkle in her forehead and the earnest concentration splayed across her face. Once she whisked away a tear. Poor girl. Hearing about God for the first time had to be a shock, especially if the Holy Spirit was working in her heart. Leah had prayed for Bert to be moved toward the ways of God, but sometimes that took more than one meeting with His Word and other believers. Sometimes it took years.

Leah listened to the beginnings of another hymn, but for the life of her she couldn't concentrate on the words. Sometimes Preacher Waller chose unfamiliar hymns, claiming the words were what mattered. Of course that made them impossible to sing.

While Leah stumbled over the notes and words, her mind wandered. Seemed like John had been born age thirty. Much too serious a good amount of the time. Oh, he laughed and teased with his brothers, but he wore "head of the household" like a soldier's bandage. She wanted him to experience happiness and the satisfaction of living his life for God. Perhaps Bert could spark some life into him. He certainly had displayed a sweet spirit to her today.

Did John understand that God brought Bert into their lives for a reason?

Oh dear, should she be thinking about such things? The girl had seen abuse, and certainly more times than Leon's beating. The nightmare last night had clearly shown the girl had a troubled past.

Every time Leah reached out and reined in her wayward mind to worship God, something else entered her thoughts.

Leah thought through each one of her sons — their strengths and their weaknesses. Oh, she wanted so much for them. And Bert ... what did she see in the girl's future?

She inwardly gasped. Goodness, she was thinking of the girl as her own.

Mercy, get your mind back on God where it ought to be.

Chapter 9

Two days before Evan's birthday, John saddled up Racer to pay another visit to Victor Oberlander at the Wide O. He had a few qualms about calling on the man after the humiliation surrounding Bert and her ... identity. But if John was to give a homestead parcel of land to Evan for his birthday, he needed to swallow his pride and get the purchase made.

By now Leon had learned the boy he wanted to hang was a woman. The knowledge had either made him angrier or embarrassed. Hopefully the latter. No one needed to have a hot-tempered man as an enemy.

John rode across Oberlander land with his thoughts on the prime acreage—thick grasses and woods already thinned by nature. Most of the Wide O contained the same richness, a dream for any rancher. Pastureland for as far as the eye could see seemed to wave at a man and beckon him to enjoy what it offered. The Timmons land held the same magic—or maybe it was John's love of working with nature that sealed his heart to a slice of heaven.

He rode on up to the grand house without meeting anyone. Oberlander must have seen him coming, because he stood on the front porch and watched John make his way toward him.

"Mornin', John. I've thought about you since I saw you in church. Haven't had a good belly laugh like that in a long time." He puffed on a pipe.

"You and my brothers." Let Oberlander laugh all day as long as they agreed on a deal for the six hundred forty acres.

"What brings you here? You're not the type of man to pay a social call."

The man knew John well. "I'd like to talk business, sir."

Oberlander invited John inside to a room off the kitchen that he used as an office. The smells of fine whiskey and stale tobacco permeated the room, and the expensive furnishings made him nervous. He took a quick glance down at his boots to make sure they were clean. If his mama had a house as fine as this, his brothers would have to work real hard not to wrestle and destroy it.

While the two men settled back in plush, leather chairs, a wrinkled Mexican man brought them fresh coffee.

"What can I do for you?" the big man said. "Is your new ranch hand more than you bargained for?"

"She's helping my mother, so I don't have to keep her in tow."

Oberlander chuckled. "When did she tell you about being a female?"

Humor him. "A few days after she arrived. When my brothers told her it was time for a bath."

Oberlander enjoyed John's blunder and leaned forward, rubbing his palms. "I know you're a grown man and a smart one. Always admired how you jumped in with both feet to take over your mama's ranch, and done a better job than a lot of men. But watch out. A young woman doesn't travel alone without a past. You don't want to get tangled up in a feud. She might have slit some man's throat. And, John, don't let that pretty little lady wrap you around her finger. There might be a jealous husband looking for her."

"Yes sir." Uneasiness crept over John with a chill that raced up his spine. He'd considered the same thing about Bert several times himself. A matter he'd put off too long in discussing with his mother and Evan.

"Ever figure out why she was riding my horse?"

"Not yet. But I'm determined to find out the whole story."

Oberlander's low laugh reminded John of a bear. The man had a reputation for being rough, but in actuality Victor Oberlander was more of a shrewd businessman with a strong code of ethics — his own. The problem came when someone stepped over the line of his rules. Then he got rough — been known to bring on a fight now and then.

"When you find out the reason, I want to know. Over the years I've learned that falling for a woman has more disadvantages than advantages. Some are good women, the kind who encourage you in gentle ways to be a better man. Others spell trouble. If you need a woman, head into the saloon and get yourself fixed up there."

Not exactly a statement for a churchgoing man to make. Neither was his habit of drinking whiskey.

Oberlander leaned back in his chair. "You'd think I was your father. But I'm just looking out for you."

"I appreciate it, sir. You've given me advice over the years I should have paid for."

"Oh, you have. In sweat and an aching back." He opened a brass box on a table beside him. The moment he lifted the lid, the aroma of fine tobacco filled the room. "You smoke?"

"No sir. Never took it up. Guess when I'm ready, I'll try a pipe."

Oberlander pulled out a cigar and stroked it like it was a bar of gold. After striking a match, he stuck it in his mouth. "What brings you here today? Breeding my mare?"

"We can talk about that if you like. I'll get right to the point. What I'm wondering is if the parcel of land between our ranches is for sale. I'm ready to pay you a fair price."

"Keep it up, and your ranch will be competing with mine."

Maybe he should have laughed or grinned at what other men would have thought a joke. But John didn't imagine the 5T would ever be a threat to Oberlander's profits. At least not any time soon. "Maybe in about ten years. I promised myself when my brothers turned eighteen, I'd give them a plot of land so they can start their own ranching or do whatever they want. Evan will be of age in two days."

"Is that what brought you here last week?"

This time a smile tugged at John's mouth. "I don't normally carry that much money with me."

Oberlander removed his cigar and studied it as though his answers were written on the brown, tightly wound tobacco leaves. "I suppose we could work out something. I've got plenty of land as it is. I know we already have a deal to breed Queen Victoria to your stallion, but it would sweeten the deal if I could bring other mares."

Whatever it takes to sweeten the deal. "Bring her over whenever you're ready. And we can talk about breeding more in the future."

"Your brothers are pretty lucky to have you looking out for them."

"My pa would have wanted them to have a good start. Evan plans to be a vet so I don't know what he'll eventually do with the land."

"What if he wants to sell it back to you? Costs money to go to school."

"Then I'll buy it."

"Tough paying for land twice." Oberlander stood. "I respect what you're doing for your brothers. Let's ride over to the piece you've got your eye on. How many acres are you wanting?"

"Six hundred forty."

"If you have the money, we can make a deal."

The first thing that had gone right in two weeks.

Bert sat on the front step and listened to Davis read from the Bible. The boy knew more words than she did. In fact, her reading and writing were pitiful. Pa had seen no use in sending her to school, said she didn't need to know a thing but women chores. Gideon had taught her anyway until Pa found out and threatened to kick him out. That happened before a horse threw Pa. He couldn't walk anymore or use the leather strap on Bert, but he sure could holler and swear.

"Would you like to read from the Bible?" Miss Leah said from the rocker. "I know it's new to you, but I could pick out something easier to understand than what Davis is reading."

Heat rose up Bert's neck. "No thank you, ma'am. Listening to Davis is fine with me."

"I have other books, if you'd like to look through them."

"Don't you think Davis and I should finish picking and shelling the peas before they get too hard?"

"I'd rather read," Davis said. "Can I look through the books?"

"You know where they are under my bed." Miss Leah watched him disappear into the house, then stood and took a seat beside Bert on the porch steps. "My dear, do you have trouble reading?"

Bert inwardly moaned. No point in lying. She already had too many of those smacking her in the face. "I don't read much."

"Would you like for me to help you?"

Bert's heart thumped like a rabbit's hind foot. "I'd be embarrassed for the others to find out."

Miss Leah tilted her head and touched Bert's cheek. "Seems to me admitting those things that don't come easy would say more for your integrity than running from them."

Bert had no idea what "integrity" meant, but she did know what running was all about. "Why would you want to help me?"

"Because I see a young woman who's beautiful, and I think her beauty is inside as well as out. I also see a young woman who's frightened, and the best way to overcome fear is to face it head-on with knowledge."

Up to this moment, Bert detested being a girl—boys were able to do what they wanted with their lives. Spending time with Leah was slowly changing her thinking. Being a girl might not be so bad after all. She liked Leah, and sometimes she wondered if her own ma had been like this good woman. But Bert hoped the kindness wasn't a trick to get her to tell things she couldn't. "Picking and shelling peas I can do."

"Of all the vegetables that come on in the garden, shelling peas is my least favorite. But doing what I don't enjoy means we'll have peas when the winter winds blow. We'll get the peas done just like we'll improve your reading. With hard work, you'll soon be able to read as well as any of my boys."

"Do you really think so?"

"Of course I do." Miss Leah tapped her finger to her chin as though she was working on a plan. Such a pretty woman, and her freckles — like Bert had seen on Mark and Davis — made her look like a girl. Until Bert had met Leah, she had no idea what being a woman was all about, except getting beaten when food didn't taste good or when one of her brothers decided she needed a bruise or two.

"Miss Leah, you surely don't look old enough to be the mother of these strapping boys."

Leah laughed. "Those boys have started to give me a few gray hairs. Thank you. That was very kind of you. I'm thinking you and I could excuse ourselves earlier in the evenings for bed, and we could work on reading then."

No one would know. When the time came for her to leave, being able to read might help her stay out of Simon's path. "I'd like that."

"All right. We'll begin tonight. Hmm." She whirled around to the empty doorway. "Son, haven't you found a book?"

"No, Mama. I'm still looking," he called from inside the house.

"He's putting off helping with the peas," Miss Leah said. "But his peddlin' would give us an opportunity to look at a couple of reading primers." She nodded at Bert and called to Davis. "We're coming."

Once Davis selected a book, Leah piled the rest of the books back into a wooden box, being careful to place two primers on top. She bent to scoot the box under the bed, but it wouldn't slide underneath.

"Davis, did you move things around when you pulled this out?"

The boy, with hair the color of corn silk, frowned. "I did push a few other boxes out of the way."

Leah blew out an exasperated sigh that sounded more amused than frustrated. She lifted up the quilt covering her bed. "I do believe you shifted more than one item underneath here." She pulled out another box and an odd-shaped object wrapped in a tattered quilt. Its shape looked familiar.

"Is that a fiddle?" Bert bent to the floor.

"It is. Belonged to my Frank. He was the boys' father." She sat on the floor and pulled the quilt from the fiddle as though she were unwrapping a treasure. "We spent many an hour listening to Frank play. We'd sing. When the boys were small, they'd dance. Oh, such sweet memories." The wistfulness in Leah's voice and the way she touched the bow saddened Bert. She knew the pain of losing someone she loved.

The fiddle looked much nicer than the one Gideon used to play. "This is beautiful."

"He took good care of it — like another child." She ran her finger along the length of the fiddle. "Unfortunately I didn't realize how much I loved him until he was gone."

"Did he get sick?" Bert remembered how she'd ached for Gideon when he died. How she ached for him still.

Leah glanced at Davis, who appeared to be absorbed in a book about animals. She mouthed "Gunned down."

Bert gasped. She'd thought this good family hadn't known the ugliness of life. "I'm sorry," she whispered.

"It's been five and a half years," Leah said softly. "He'd taken a job for his brother, who was the town marshal, when a gang of outlaws shot him. Dumped his body at our front door."

"How awful." Bert had seen killing, and the sight of blood and vacant eyes stalked her sleeping hours. She'd do anything to keep from dying.

"John found him. Frank died in his arms."

"Then those outlaws kidnapped me," Davis said.

"I thought you were reading." Leah's voice lifted a notch.

"I am, but I can hear too." He stood from the opposite side of the bed. "John came after me, but they got him too. It took Uncle Parker and Aunt Sage to free us up."

Bert studied Leah's face. The woman had seen the harshness of life, but she hadn't grown bitter with it. Bert wanted to be like her someday—not twisted up in anger and lashing out at others. "Maybe we should start on those peas."

"Do you want to see the fiddle? I don't mind." Leah held it and the bow out to her.

"I can play enough to get by." Bert took the instrument and tightened the strings. She lifted it under her chin and lightly touched the bow to the strings. Closing her eyes, she played a tune that Gideon had taught her.

When she finished, she looked at Leah. The woman's eyes were filled with tears. "No one has expressed an interest in playing it until now."

"I didn't mean to disrespect your husband's memory."

"My dear girl, you honored Frank. Your playing is beautiful. Where did you learn so well?"

"My brother taught me. But mostly I hear a tune and can remember it."

Leah's eyes widened, and she turned her head as though she didn't quite believe what Bert had said.

"One of the songs at church was about a tie that binds." Bert closed her eyes and allowed her fingers to play what she remembered.

"You'd never heard the hymn before?"

"No ma'am."

"What else can you play?" Davis made his way around the bed and curled up next to Leah.

Bert shrugged. "Not sure. I make up a lot of songs."

"Then share one." Leah touched the knee of Bert's britches, a pair Mark had outgrown that Bert wore for chores.

Bert put together a few quick words, and a lively tune danced across her mind. "I'll do my best."

Leah and Davis smiled their encouragement.

I don't like to pick peas.
Don't like to shell them either,
But when my bowl is empty
I've worked into a fever.

"How grand." Leah laughed. "And that is exactly how I feel about them too. You have a remarkable talent, a real gift. You must let the other boys hear you play and sing."

Gideon used to say she had a gift too. With some gentle prodding from Leah she'd be crying. "I don't imagine they'd want to hear me play their pa's fiddle."

"Nonsense. It will be a treat for us all."

"Do you know any songs about snakes or fish or wild bears?" Davis's eyes had lit up like twinkling stars.

"I might." Not since Gideon died had anyone made her feel special. "What do you say about you and me finishing those peas and letting your ma take a rest?"

He scrunched up his face. "I already do women's work."

"I could tell you another story. And we could make up a song to go with it."

"Like the one you told me yesterday? The bear that was afraid of water was a good story. Evan tells me stories too, but he works a lot."

"Today's story could be about a wolf who forgot how to howl at the moon. And once we're done, and if your mama doesn't have anything else for us, we could fish for supper." She remembered John didn't want her around his brothers, but Davis was young and so sweet.

"Oh, I like your idea," Leah said. "The extra time this afternoon will allow me to finish a new shirt for Evan's birthday. Gracious. How very fine if you'd play the fiddle for his birthday. Miss Bert, we sure have been blessed since you came to us."

Regret wove a shameful thread through Bert's heart. She hoped they never learned about her past.

CHAPTER 10

John slammed the sledgehammer onto the top of the fence post and anchored it in place. He couldn't remember when Mama had been so happy. He should have been glad for her, but instead he was miffed.

Just admit it. All right, he had a bad case of frustration and a few other feelings he wasn't ready to put a name on yet. Why couldn't life have stayed the same as it was before Bert? For that matter, what was God thinking when He tossed a ragged, pitiful girl into his path?

Bert's huge brown eyes and silky-looking hair drove him to distraction, and he couldn't help but think she needed someone to protect her from whatever or whoever had hurt her. He hadn't forgotten Victor Oberlander's warning either. Bert might be only seventeen, but she sure had latched on to a barnload of John's attention.

He didn't have any time for a pint-size woman. She probably couldn't cook or sew or keep a house neat or help him brand horses or mend fence ... but those things didn't matter. The best thing for him to do was avoid her. In less than four months she'd have worked off her debt and be on her way.

Evan walked his way with a bail of wire. Diversion. That's what John needed. If today hadn't been Evan's birthday, he'd have ridden into town like he had deputy business.

Evan whistled. "I've waited a long time to be eighteen, and it doesn't feel any different from any other birthday."

John had watched a leggy boy turn into a man. "That's a sign you're getting old. In another year, you'll be heading off to veterinary school in Fort Collins."

"At last I'll be learning how to doctor animals properlike. I've been thinking about starting sooner."

"Sounds like a fine idea, which means you'd finish sooner."

"My idea too. Do you suppose Bert will be around then?"

John shouldn't have been surprised, the way his brother gawked at Bert at meals and in the evenings. "Who knows? She's obliged to us until mid October."

"Be nice if she'd stay on. Mama sure likes having her around. And Davis has been tied to Mama's apron strings for too long."

"I agree about our little brother. We need to have him doing more than feeding the chickens and helping around the house."

"Wonder when her birthday is?"

"Mama's is in January." John knew exactly what Evan was referring to.

"I know that. I mean Bert. Wonder when she'll be eighteen." He pressed his lips together and gazed toward the house. "I don't think she's a horse thief."

"I have my doubts. But until she feels comfortable enough to tell us what really happened, we'll have to wait for the truth."

"I'd like to think she'd feel good about telling me—"

"Any of us." If today weren't Evan's birthday, John would sit him down and talk about planning the future—without a woman.

"Sure." Evan breathed out a heavy sigh. "Have you ever felt something real special about a girl?"

How did he answer that? *Be honest.* "Yes, the beginnings of what could be called special."

"What did you do about it?"

"Prayed for God to lead me on the right path." Now that sounded like fatherly advice.

"Good advice for my birthday. I'll do the same about Bert."

Two brothers fallin' for the same girl?

No, John wasn't falling for anyone. His feelings rose out of nothing more than wanting to protect Bert—like when Leon wanted to string her up. He didn't have time for any other nonsense.

Bert thought her insides were going to burst with jumping crickets. And all because she'd agreed to play the fiddle for Evan's birthday. She'd spent the afternoon putting together a short song and hoped it was fittin'. Too many times, she'd observed Evan looking at her in a way he shouldn't. She didn't want to encourage him, especially since the time would come soon when she'd have to leave. John might skin her alive if she considered anything else.

The eldest Timmons brother puzzled her. Or rather she didn't quite understand how being around him made her feel jittery—not afraid or excited, just something in between. Goodness, what was she to do?

For Evan's birthday, Leah baked a milk cake and showed Bert how to mix the butter, flour, sugar and honey, eggs, and milk into a lovely smelling treat. From the whispers going on, the other brothers must have something special for him. How this family loved one another. Even when they bickered and exchanged punches, they always made up. So different, so very different from what she had experienced with Pa, Simon, Clint, and Lester.

Made her wonder if she'd fallen and bumped her head, and this place wasn't real at all.

"Gift time," Leah said once they'd all enjoyed huge slices of cake with wild strawberries and cream. "Let's make our way into the parlor and do this proper."

Evan sat on the sofa, which had arms artfully decorated with needlepoint cloths in pretty colors of blue, yellow, and green. The other boys gathered around on the floor and in chairs. Leah disappeared to her room and quickly returned with Evan's new white shirt all neatly folded. "I thought you might be needing this when you visit the school in Fort Collins."

Evan handled the shirt as though it were pure gold. "Thank you, Mama." He kissed her cheek. "I'll take good care of it. John and I talked about me starting school this year instead of next."

Leah smiled through her tears. "Oh, you'll be a fine veterinarian."

"I'll need to ride to Fort Collins and take the entrance exams. This shirt will make me look mighty fine."

Aaron, Mark, and Davis presented him with a new pocket-knife, and Evan made a fuss, turning it over and over in the palm of his hand. With a grin and another thanks, he stuck it in his pants pocket. This family knew what pleased each other.

John stood, then sat back down. His forehead wrinkled. Studying him caused Bert to fear the worst. What if he'd learned the truth about her and was about to tell his family? But surely he wouldn't do that on Evan's birthday.

He cleared his throat. "When I purchased Uncle Parker's ranch, I decided when each one of you became eighteen, I'd give you a homestead of your own to do whatever you like — even if it meant selling it back to me at a fair price. Evan, I'm giving you one hundred sixty acres and ten cows." He stood again and took two steps to shake Evan's hand. "Your acreage is a new piece on the northeast section of our ranch. I bought it from the Wide O."

Silence filled the room. Evan swallowed hard, no doubt to keep the tears from dripping over his cheeks. Bert glanced at Leah as the woman dabbed at the wetness beneath her own eyes. How strange, this moment. If any of Bert's brothers received a birthday gift, it was stolen.

"I don't know what to say," Evan said. "You've been more than generous by offering to help pay part of the fees for school. Thank you, John. I'll make you proud of me."

"You already have." John hugged him, and this time it was Bert who turned her head to keep the tears from dripping over her cheeks.

A few moments later, Leah asked for their attention. "Bert has something special for Evan." She nodded at Bert. "Go ahead, dear."

With numb feet and her head spinning, Bert retrieved the fiddle from atop Leah's bed. She returned, her heart pounding as hard as when she thought Leon planned to hang her.

"No one's picked that up since Pa died," Evan said.

"I can play some, and I hope none of you mind since it belonged to your pa." She tucked the fiddle under her chin and clenched her fist to stop the shaking. "Here's my gift to you. Happy birthday, Evan." Closing her eyes, Bert hoped the short song would be pleasing to all of them.

This is your birthday, and a fine one too.
It marks a time of being grown
The new things you can do.
Boyhood pranks are behind you now
But still you have your dreams,
You're one step closer to chasing them down
By crossin' life's new streams.

Once she finished and glanced at Evan, he turned bright red. "That's beautiful. Where did you learn the song?"

"She makes them up," Leah said. "I learned the other afternoon that all Bert has to do is hear a tune, and she knows how to play it. And, like Evan's birthday song, she makes up the words too."

"If I'd have known she could entertain us, I might have asked her to play in the evenings," John said. "I'd forgotten how much I missed the fiddle."

"You're welcome." Bert did her best to swallow the lump in her throat.

"I do say this is the finest birthday a fellow could ever have." Evan glanced around the parlor. "All of you have made this special. I hope when your birthdays come along, I can do the same for you."

Bert returned the fiddle to the bedroom, still nervous, but not as much since the Timmonses appeared to enjoy her song. She set the instrument on Leah's pretty blue and yellow quilt when she heard a sound. Whirling around, she saw John standing before her.

"That was a fine thing you did, Bert. I know Evan will never forget it, and I won't either."

The words to respond tried to stick in her throat, but she willed them out. "I'm beholdin' to your mama for letting me play your pa's fiddle. It's the most beautiful one I've ever seen."

"And I hope you'll play and sing for us a whole lot more. I really enjoyed it." He smiled, and she felt her insides jiggle.

"I also appreciate the way you're helping Mama. She's taken to you, and all of us like to see her happy."

"Thank you."

He moistened his lips and appeared nervous. "Just wanted you to know how we feel about your friendship and hard work."

Anything John Timmons wanted her to do, she'd gladly oblige.

You're bein' foolish girl. Simon will find you ... you know he will.

Chapter II

Bert tore out the stitches for the fourth time on the small piece of flowered fabric Leah had given her to practice sewing. While Leah's stitches looked perfect and evenly spaced on a narrow hem, Bert's looked like her needle had followed a jagged cliff.

"I don't think I'll ever learn how to sew properly."

"Yes, you will. Just like everything that's important in life, difficult things take time, practice, and lots of patience."

"I'm short on the last one."

Leah laughed softly. "Oh, we all are." She reached over and touched the ends of Bert's hair. "This is growing fast. Before long, it will be trailing down your back."

"Hasn't been long since I was a little girl."

"Did you want it shorter to make folks think you were a boy?"

The old familiar fear seized her. She remembered the last time Clint and Lester held her down and Simon chopped off her hair with his knife. "Sometimes."

"You're pale. Is there anything you want to tell me?"

The less any of them knew about her, the better. "No ma'am."

"Why? I can tell you're afraid. We can't help you if you don't tell us about yourself. John's deputy work brings him in contact with important people, and the boys' Uncle Parker in Denver knows a lot about law. He represents this area in the legislature and is highly respected."

This family had its share of law abiding people. A terrifying thought. "I'm only here until my debt is paid."

Leah stiffened. "That's ridiculous."

"What do you mean? Has John decided I'm not doing my share of work?"

"Not at all. When the boys are in school, John pays hired hands a dollar a day. My point is, he's more generous to them."

Bert had no problem with how he'd arranged for her to pay the money she owed. The deal was more than fair, considering he'd saved her from a hanging. "But I have a place to sleep and plenty of food to eat. Look at how I've already gained weight. The way I see the situation, all you have is my word that I didn't steal Mr. Oberlander's horse. I haven't explained anything about me 'cause I can't."

Leah's brow narrowed.

"Don't be upset with me, Miss Leah. Maybe someday."

"I've heard you cry out in your dreams."

Nightmares. "You shouldn't pay them no mind."

"Maybe if they only happened once."

Bert drew in a deep breath. She could not talk about the nightmares. "I do have a problem I'd like to talk to you about."

"And what's that?"

"Evan."

Leah nodded and blinked. "He does seem to be smitten."

"John will be furious. I told him I'd stay away from his brothers and now this."

"If John wants to blame anyone, it's the ways of a man. And Evan is eighteen. I was married and a mother to John at his age."

"What can I do?"

"Continue what you've been doing. I've never seen a single improper action from you. I'll talk to John and tell him about your concern."

Bert breathed a bit easier. Leah didn't blame her, and John and his mama could work out the problem with Evan, who was more like a good and decent brother to her than anything else. If she allowed her heart to walk through a field of wildflowers, she'd admit John held a tender spot in her heart. Certainly something she had to keep hidden from everyone. The truth was no man would ever want her as his wife. Not with what she'd done, but with what Simon had done to her. Yet sometimes she fancied a real home with a man who loved her.

Bert smiled at Leah. If she could, she'd reveal the past. Was there anything she could tell? She moistened her lips. "My real name is Ember. Bert's what I've been called."

A soft sigh escaped Leah. "What a beautiful name. Oh, I'll never call you Bert again."

How dear you are to me, Leah. I'll treasure you always. "No one's ever called me by my given name except Gideon, and he told me my ma liked it very much."

"I agree with your mother. Very pretty too. Who is Gideon?"

Surely one more small piece of her life would not hurt. "My oldest brother. He died some years back. Pneumonia." Perhaps she was telling too much, but Gideon had been gone over four years.

"I'm sorry."

"It was bad watching him suffer. The pneumonia started as a sore throat, and then it got worse until he couldn't breathe. His throat just kept getting more infected and finally closed up. He's the one who taught me to read some and how to play the fiddle."

"I can hear in your voice that you miss him. Could he play by ear like you?"

"Yes ma'am. If you mean he could hear a song then play it. I thought that was the only way to make the fiddle sing." Bert let her mind drift to her dear Gideon, the only one who'd never hit her. He never called her names or told her it was her fault their ma had died.

"So no one's left in your family?"

"No one to speak of." Her words were not far from the truth. *You killed Ma when she birthed you, and you couldn't tend to Gideon. Now it's your turn.*

"Ember?"

The sound of her name on Leah's lips was foreign. Gideon used to call her Ember when their brothers and pa weren't around. He'd put her middle name with it to make her feel special.

"Ember, are you all right?"

She snapped her attention back to Leah, realizing she'd slipped and gone *there*. A place where she'd promised never to venture — and with the memory came a harsh reminder that something was very wrong with her, because horrible things happened to the ones she loved. A raw ache coursed through her body, leaving her weary. For a while, she'd forgotten. She'd vowed to not grow too fond of any of the Timmonses so nothing might happen to them ... but she had. All of them.

Was it so wrong to have dreams? And hers were twofold: she craved a family, a chance to love and be loved. And she desperately needed to find a place where her pa and brothers would never find her.

"Ember?"

Bert pulled herself from her thoughts. "Did you say something?"

"Do you fear for your life?"

The memories were like a raw, bleeding wound. At times she wondered if there was a thorn in her heart. "Are you thinking Leon still wants me strung up for Mr. Oberlander's mare?"

"Are you dancing around my question?"

Bert attempted to keep her face emotionless. "Miss Leah, it's best you don't ask me any more personal questions. I have to think about some things."

"Then I'm right?"

Her temples pounded. "I mean ... I don't know. I've said far too much already."

"Any way I can persuade you otherwise?"

"Perhaps someday."

Leah tilted her head as she so often did when she had her mind on something. "Tomorrow's church day, I need to make sure the boys' shirts are ready for me to iron."

"I'd be glad to do it."

Leah blinked back tears. "Miss Ember, you can't work away your troubles. Let someone help you along the way. Someday the running and hiding will have to stop. And that means facing the problem square on and sharing what you fear with others who care about you. Let God touch you."

Bert didn't understand the latter, but she believed it was good. The problem still held her captive. No loving God would want the likes of her. She'd seen too much. Heard too much. Had been through too much.

John watched Victor Oberlander ride toward the ranch. A huge man—in size and nobility. His very countenance demanded respect. But not all of his actions. And he was right on time with his mare, a darker chestnut than Racer. John cringed at the sight of Leon accompanying him and leading the mare. Something about the foreman bothered him. He shouldn't judge a man by his looks or the way he looked at folks, but Leon had a mean streak. That was evident when he tried to hang Bert.

John opened the gate to the small corral where he'd placed Racer in anticipation of Oberlander bringing his prize mare. He waved at the two men riding in. "Mornin'."

"And a fine one it is." Oberlander grinned like a kid at Christmas.

John nodded at Leon, but the ranch hand ignored him and led Queen Victoria inside the corral. Once the gate was latched shut, Leon fixed his gaze beyond them and frowned. John knew without looking that he'd spotted Bert in the garden.

Oberlander dismounted and began to laugh. "Guess I never told you, Leon. But the boy you tried to hang for stealing my mare is a girl. A right pretty girl too."

Leon swore, and anger ripped across his face. Oberlander continued to laugh. "Enjoy the joke. We all were duped. Isn't that right, John?"

John hadn't revealed all of what happened when they learned about Bert, but he found no harm in laughing about it.

"I don't like anyone making fun of me." Leon wiped his hand across his mouth. "Least ways a horse thief and a woman."

"Easy," John said. "It's done with."

"And I'll not take lip from the likes of you either. Just 'cause you're a deputy and have a ranch, you think you're better than the rest of us."

"Leon, that's enough." Oberlander made his way to the man's side and laid a hand on his shoulder. "You'll not insult a man I'm doing business with."

Leon shrugged off the hand. "He's ..." The curses echoed around them.

"We don't talk like that around here." John would have ordered him off his land if not for Oberlander.

Fury torched Leon's eyes. "I'll talk any way I take a notion."

Oberlander stiffened. "Get back to the ranch and gather up your gear." His voice came out like a growl. "Soon as I get back, I'll get your pay. Then I don't want to lay eyes on you again. You've been given too many chances as it is, and I'm finished with you."

"You haven't seen the end of me, Timmons. None of you have." Leon stomped away without another word, swung up onto his horse, and rode out.

"Should have gotten rid of him a long time ago," Oberlander said. "Sorry you had to witness that."

"I understand. Some of our responsibilities aren't the pleasant kind." Still, threats weren't made to be ignored, and John would keep his eyes open for trouble.

"I'm thinking it won't be the last either of us see of Leon. We're smart men to take heed to a hothead."

Oberlander must have other reasons to distrust Leon. John's thoughts swept back to Bert's near hanging. Did Leon know more about the missing mare than he let on?

Did Bert fit into this?

CHAPTER 12

From the garden, Bert recognized the weasel-looking man with Mr. Oberlander and John. *Leon Wilson.* She shuddered. He'd tried to hang her and nearly succeeded. If not for the old man they called Ted, she'd be rotting in an unmarked grave. When Ted had ridden off, she believed he'd given up. But within minutes, he'd raced back with John. Like a hero in the stories Gideon used to tell her, John had shot through the rope that was tossed over a tree branch and tied around her neck. Perfect aim. If she lived one hundred years, she'd never forget what he'd done.

Leon and Simon were so much alike. Of course, her other two brothers, Clint and Lester, weren't much better. She shouldn't be thinking about the worst. Except preparing for things to go wrong was what kept a person alive. Too many times she'd been left to the mercy of her brothers who used her as a means to look good in their own eyes. Never again. She'd made it six months and somehow survived. She wasn't about to give up now.

Bending to the bushes of peas, Bert snatched up the fat pods and dropped them into the basket. What should she do? Continue living with the dear family who treated her like one of their own or leave? She could light out tonight and put a lot of distance between her and the Timmonses by morning. Leah had baked bread earlier, and a juicy ham simmered with beans. There'd be plenty left over . . .

Stealing . . . They'd all believe what Leon claimed.

No, she'd not take a thing that didn't belong to her. The Timmonses had been too kind. The only thing she'd take were the memories of how a real family was supposed to love and treat their own.

Shoving aside the depressing thoughts—and she had plenty—Bert moved down the row of peas. *Think of a song. Something to take your mind off Simon and Leon.* Escaping into her mind usually worked when she felt powerless over the circumstances around her.

Angry voices seized her attention, and she spun around to find out what was going on. Leon had let John and Mr. Oberlander know he didn't have much use for either of them. Bert held her breath. Sounded like Leon wanted to fight John, but then Mr. Oberlander fired him. Only a deaf person could have ignored Leon's final words—and threats.

One more reason to leave the Timmons ranch.

John was surprised Victor Oberlander lingered at the ranch after he sent Leon packing. Racer and Queen Victoria were getting along fine, so there wasn't any reason to stick around.

"Is Miss Leah around?" Oberlander stared at the house.

Misgiving crept across John's mind. "Yes sir. She's inside, most likely baking bread."

Oberlander had the same moonfaced look that Evan had when he looked at Bert. What was happening to this family? John had paid no mind to the many times his neighbor made a point of speaking to Mama on Sunday mornings and making sure he either sat with them in church or close by. Now it all made sense—and John didn't like it one bit.

"I'd like to say hello to your mama if you don't mind. Just to be sociable."

"She'll want to offer you a glass of cool water or fresh buttermilk." John wrestled with being hospitable or asking Oberlander about his intentions. No one had appeared interested in Mama's company since Pa died. Oh, a US Marshal had written her for a while, but his letters stopped coming about three years ago.

Oberlander seemed like a decent fellow, but this was John's mother. Earlier conversations with the rancher about women pelted his mind like fist-sized hail.

"Water sounds good." Oberlander took a few steps, then turned to John. "Your mama's a fine woman."

"That she is." Right then John decided he didn't like any man thinking about his mama in the same terms he thought about Bert.

"She shouldn't work so hard. A woman like her needs an easier life."

John sensed heat rising up his neck. "We all work together here. Bert's been a big help."

Oberlander studied him. "I don't mean any disrespect, son. Just making an observation."

I'm not your son. Neither do I have any notion to be related to you.

Oberlander tipped his hat. "I'll be greeting Miss Leah now."

John watched the big man saunter toward the front porch with feelings as varied as the different shades of rock in the distant mountains. For a moment he thought Oberlander looked skittish. Was Mama aware of the man's interest?

Evan made his way to John's side. "Is he wanting to court Mama?" The words sounded incredulous, but John knew the answer.

"Why do you say that?"

"Ever watch how he looks at her on Sundays?"

Mama seemed happy with the way life was. Didn't she? "Never paid any attention."

"That's your problem." Evan spit his answer like a man with a chaw of tobacco in his mouth. "All you think about's the ranch."

John focused his attention on Oberlander. He didn't know which was worse—Mama courtin' or Evan chasing after Bert. The two problems continued to pick at him.

He paused in his thinking when Mama opened the door and smiled at Oberlander. She was simply being neighborly. If Oberlander returned with no purpose but to call on her, then John would step in. As head of the household, he needed to protect Mama from getting hurt or letting some man take advantage of her.

"I'm going to take Bert a drink of water," Evan said. "She's been working in the garden for a long time. Wouldn't want her to get sick from the heat."

John frowned. This matter he could handle. "I've noticed you've been spending a lot of time around her."

"Maybe so. She's right pretty. Works hard too. Makes a man think about the future."

John wanted to take a swing at him. "What about your schooling? This isn't the time to worry over a girl—especially one you don't know a thing about. You have years ahead of you after schooling to consider a woman."

"I know enough about Bert to make a good decision."

John dug his fingernails into his palms. This was worse than he suspected. Much worse. "Are you two sneaking off when I'm not around?"

Evan snapped his attention John's way. "Now when would we sneak off? I happen to take what I do around here seriously, big brother. And in case you're blind, you and I work side by side."

John swallowed a shovelful of regret. "You're right. Don't know why I accused you of shirking." That wasn't what he'd insinuated, but it would do for now.

"I think you have your sights on Bert and want me to stand aside."

The comment took John aback, especially when he felt certain he'd hid his feelings. "You know better than that. How many times have you boys said I was married to the ranch?"

"I didn't say a word about getting married. But you must be thinking about it." Evan crossed his arms over his chest, his feet firmly planted on the ground. "I don't want to argue like a couple of schoolboys fussin' over who's to get the biggest piece of pie."

Whoa. What brought this on? "Neither do I. We're men, and we should be able to talk about any differences."

"So you admit to liking Bert?"

John scowled, not wanting to lie when he didn't understand his own heart, and yet not wanting to encourage Evan. Bringing up the horse thief charges or her refusal to reveal where she'd come from might drive his brother closer to her. "Like I already said, I'm concerned about your education. Becoming a veterinarian means a commitment to studying hard for a long time. It would be next to impossible while courtin'."

"Not impossible."

"Right. Remember a few years back when the McCaw gang killed Pa and then kidnapped Davis?"

"I do. Who in this family could forget?"

"Remember when I went after them alone?"

"Sure. You nearly got yourself killed."

"The reason I almost came back in a pine box was because I didn't have the knowledge to go along with my thinking. Same thing with Bert. All you've talked about for years is becoming a vet, but now you want to court Bert too. One thing at a time, Evan. That's all I'm suggesting."

"What if she feels the same way for me? Because I believe she does."

Had Bert broken her word? "If she does, I'd think she'd want you to do what's best for your future—maybe her future too. The Bible says love doesn't take. It gives."

"That's exactly what I'm talking about."

John swallowed his frustration. If he wasn't careful, they'd be scuffling in the dirt. "Why don't you slow down? Wait on speaking your mind until after she's fulfilled her obligations here." Maybe she'd leave the area, and all of John's worries about her and Evan would be for naught.

Evan leaned on one leg. "What am I supposed to do in the meantime?"

Nothing on the ranch had prepared John for this. "Be her friend. Besides, she's only seventeen."

"I could find out her birthday."

"Be careful about asking too many questions. She gets aggravated when I provoke her."

"Maybe you need to be nicer—not so surly. Mama acts like she hung the moon, and she found out her given name."

"When did this happen?"

Evan shrugged. "Davis told me yesterday."

"What is it?"

"Ember. I like it 'cause it's different. Maybe you ought to consider being nicer to her. She might tell you what you want to know about Oberlander's mare."

John refused to discuss being nice to Bert. Being around her made him jumpy, nervous. "I'll think about it. Right now, let's take a walk toward the house. I don't want Mama alone with Oberlander for very long. She might not feel comfortable around him."

"Right." Evan chuckled. "Looks to me like you want to make sure the whole family lives their lives according to your rule book."

John wanted to lecture Evan until nightfall. But that wouldn't solve a thing. Perhaps Bert would show a side of herself that wasn't appealing, and all of John's concerns would fade.

Ember? Strange name. Pretty too.

A short while later, Bert heard the pounding of horse hooves and stood from her crouched position among the rows of pea bushes to watch Mr. Oberlander ride off. She must have caught John's attention because he waved and walked toward the garden. At the sight of him, her heart hammered against her chest. He was a fine looking man, and she'd never forget his kindness.

"Need some help?" he said, once he was a few feet from her.

She glanced up into his blue eyes, like a piece of the sky. "My basket is nearly full." She hesitated. "I heard what went on with Leon."

John's face clouded. "Be careful. He has a quick temper."

She nodded. "I never meant to bring trouble on your family."

He studied her, and she longed to press him for his thoughts. "I don't imagine you'd ever want to see anyone hurt."

His words warmed her, as though she might be a good person. "Thank you. I've never been happier since I came here."

"Even with all the work?" His eyes sparkled.

"It's not work at all when you're with folks you care about. But John, I can leave anytime if you're fretting about your family."

His face etched with something she couldn't read. "I don't want you to leave." He paused. "I don't know why."

Silence filled the air, and she wasn't sure how to respond.

"I think you've got enough peas there," he said. "Let me take the basket."

She held it out to him, and their fingers brushed ever so lightly, and for the first time in her life, she didn't flinch at the touch of a man.

CHAPTER 13

Storms blew across the 5T Ranch Saturday night. Each time Bert considered sneaking out of bed and taking out into the darkness, a flash of lightning and a roar of thunder shook the house, and another storm stampeded in. The streaks and crashes grew closer together until they followed each other without giving her a moment to breathe. Bert remembered the times her brothers had locked her outside their crude cabin during a storm. They'd laughed while she tried to be brave.

The old emptiness crept unbidden into her, a narrowing dark hole that seemed to suffocate her. Here she'd felt safe with a real family until reality nipped at her heels. The idea of running had persisted with her all day and night, refusing to let her go. She longed to disappear into the night, not for herself, but for those who lived within these four walls. The storm's insistent raging sounded like demons daring her to flee so they could throw bolts of lightning her way. The viciousness of nature gripped her attention. Oh, to not be afraid of so many things.

Bert didn't want to leave the 5T for all the reasons that gave her comfort and a sense of belonging, but wanting and needing were two different sides of the coin. A part of her believed Simon would be glad she was gone, and another part believed he'd come after her simply because he could. She lay beside Leah in the early dawn trying to figure out if she should simply get up and take her chances or wait for it all to end.

"This will have to let up before we head to church," Leah whispered.

Bert had waited too long to leave. Now she must live with her decision one more day. "Maybe it will end soon."

"You and I both know that Colorado storms can last hours. We'll have church here this morning."

Bert had seen the result of storms too many times not to understand. Man and animals often fell prey to a death-bolt. "How will we do that?"

Leah turned over onto her side just as lightning lit up the room, followed by thunder so loud it pierced Bert's eardrums. Rain splashed against the window and pummeled the roof. "We'll pray, read God's Word, talk about what He's done for us, and have a little singing." She laughed softly. "If you would consider playing the fiddle, we could sing hymns. Would you mind?"

Music, the gentle poultice of her heart. "Not at all—"

Davis burst into the room.

Leah rose up on one elbow. "I wondered how long it would take before you scrambled this way."

He crawled into bed on Leah's side. "John said I needed to grow up some, so I waited as long as I could."

Leah combed her fingers through his corn-silk hair just as lightning made the room as clear as day. "I've noticed you've been spending more time with your brothers. I'm proud of you."

"Yes ma'am. I'm going to be helping them bring in the cattle from the higher pastures in the fall."

"You are?"

Bert heard the catch in Leah's words.

"Yes, and I'll spend the nights away from you. Will you be all right?"

Leah sighed. "I'll try my best."

The sound of voices from the kitchen made their way into the bedroom. Leah threw back the thin coverlet and stood. "John Parker Timmons, don't you dare go out in this weather until the storm calms down."

"Mama, Evan and I have things to do." Irritation edged John's tone, and Bert hoped he and Evan didn't make their way into their mama's room too.

"You heard me."

"If the good Lord says it's my time to go, there's not a thing I can do."

"But there's no point in shaking your fist and defying Him."

Bert hid her laughter. Leah would win out. She always did. She seldom raised her voice at her sons. Instead she spoke with a firmness that demanded obedience. Thunder shook the house again and caused Davis to startle.

"There went a tree in the corral," John said. "Right over the fence. I'm heading out there."

"John!" Leah grabbed her robe.

"Yes ma'am."

"Uprooted quick as you please," Evan added. "Good thing it's raining. The spark could have caused a lot of damage."

"That means we'll need to ride to the higher pastures and check on the cattle," John said. "Not exactly how I planned to spend my Sunday morning."

"Not until the storm stops and we have church," Leah said.

John chuckled. "Yes ma'am."

"At least Oberlander's mare and Racer are in the barn." Evan's words caused Bert to breathe easier. That mare had been the cause of a lot of discontent.

Another jagged sword crossed the sky with thunder resounding from its blade. A light from the kitchen revealed one of the boys had lit the lantern.

"I'm chasing Davis out of here right now so Ember and I can get dressed. Some hot coffee and breakfast would taste real good."

"Ember?" John said. "When did you start calling Bert by another name?"

"Since I learned her mother named her Ember." Leah gently coaxed Davis to his feet, and the boy scurried out of the room.

"How about a last name?" John said.

Bert looked over at Leah. "That's my secret. But I could be related to Billy the Kid or the James Brothers or the Dalton Gang. Do you really want to know?" The truth sent a shiver up her spine, but she refused to acknowledge it.

"You've been around Mama too long and picking up her wit," John said.

"I'll take that as a compliment, John Timmons." Bert started to laugh. Amidst the storm capable of waking the dead, they all took to laughing like crazy folks.

While she dressed, she comprehended that real families laughed together a lot. It felt good, real good. Almost like she belonged.

But she didn't.

Ember. John rolled the name around in his head. Bert was a better name. Safer. Now how was Mama able to learn her name when he'd about run out of ways to persuade Bert to tell him a thing?

He shoved another dry log into the stove and poured himself a second cup of coffee. He wanted to get outside and check on the fence and the livestock, but not until the storm died down along with the wind. Truth be known, Mama's wrath, if he ignored her orders of staying out of the weather, outdid any storm. When Pa was alive and Mama was unhappy, he used to say dynamite came in small sticks.

Next to him Bert peeled potatoes for breakfast while Mama rolled out biscuits. Evan had sliced bacon, no doubt so he could be closer to Bert, and Aaron beat a bowlful of eggs.

Mark had already set the table and was pacing the kitchen. A wildcat could be kept in a box easier than Mark inside the house. John caught his eye and winked; he and Mark were so much alike. Except that John had work outside bearing down on his mind, while Mark needed the outside to make him feel whole.

John stole a look at Bert. His big brother talk with Evan had been as successful as spitting into the wind. John had not accomplished a thing except to learn Evan was thinking about a future with Bert. He was still uncomfortable with how that made him feel. Uncle Parker had told him once that how a man felt about a woman was a powerful emotion. Love could cause a man to be more than he ever dreamed possible or do things so evil that only the devil would have him for company. Thank goodness John wasn't in love.

A small cry escaped Bert's lips and jolted John back to the present. He glanced her way and saw the blood dripping down her finger into the bucket of potato peelings. Moving quickly, he reached for a towel and wrapped it around her finger.

"Are you all right?"

"Oh my, yes. Just cut my finger. I should be more careful." Her face turned a soft shade of pink. He'd seen the same color in wildflowers.

"Mama has some small strips of cloth we can wrap around it, even some medicine if it's cut deep."

"I'm sure it'll be fine." She peered into the bowl of potatoes soaking in saltwater. "Good, there's no blood on them, but I'll rinse those potatoes again to make sure."

John glanced down and saw he still held her fingers wrapped with the towel. Swallowing hard, he dropped her hand as though he'd been burned. When he stepped back, he saw Evan glaring at him, and his brothers watching on. Snatching up his hat and poncho from a wooden peg near the door, he stepped out onto the porch with the thunder and lightning shaking the earth while rain formed huge puddles between the house and barn.

He'd made a complete fool out of himself in front of his whole family. For the first time, he considered calling Bert's debt paid and allowing her to go free. At least he and Evan wouldn't be at each other's throats over the same girl.

My mind should be on ranching. His efforts needed to be on the land and all the work required to support his family. Anything else was pure foolishness. All he needed do was believe it. Instead he seemed to be split in two like the uprooted cottonwood in the corral.

He snorted. It was a cottonwood that had introduced him to Bert.

The door opened, and Mama joined him, closing the door behind her. "You've been out here a good thirty minutes."

He didn't want to talk to anyone right now. "I'm watching the storm."

"You could get struck by lightning."

Odd, he hadn't noticed the storm outside for the one inside of him. "So could you."

"Love means you take a few risks."

Now what did she mean?

"Breakfast's ready," Mama said. "Then we'll have church. Would you read from Luke 15 this morning?"

That's just dandy. The prodigal son. Which one of us is she thinking needs the reminder the most?

CHAPTER 14

M onday morning, Leah fretted with the wagonload of trouble that had been dumped in the middle of the Timmonses' household. And the pile kept getting bigger. The animosity between John and Evan had extended beyond boyhood squabbles to serious problems, which had the potential of destroying their relationship. And she was at her wits' end to figure out how to deal with the whole situation.

The boys' simmering anger reminded her of when she, Frank, and Parker were young people living in Virginia. She and Parker were two fifteen-year-olds when sweet love attached itself to them. Then Parker's older brother Frank moved into the picture and swept her off her feet. She loved Frank and never regretted marrying him, but she regretted hurting Parker. The rift between the brothers took two decades to heal, and Leah would not let that happen in her household.

Merciful beans and cornbread. What was she to do? If Frank were alive, he'd sit those boys down and explain the powers and dangers a woman possessed over a man. John and Evan, as different as night and day. Both falling for the same sweet-faced woman—a woman with a shadowed past. A woman who could hurt them, could separate them as brothers.

Since the afternoon she first realized Bert was a girl, she rubbed calluses on her knees praying for her sons and Bert.

She'd picked everything in the garden and preserved all she could find.

She'd pulled weeds.

She'd scrubbed the house until not a speck of dirt could be found.

She'd beaten her scant rugs and then beaten them some more.

Not a sock needed darned or a hole sewn.

The washing was done—for now.

Taking a deep breath, she walked out onto the front porch. The temperatures were scorching, adding heat to her mounting anxiety. Sighing, she chose to visit the small corral where Racer and Victor Oberlander's mare were courting.

Courtin'. Leah wished she'd never heard the word. John and Evan vied for Ember's attention. Praise God the girl had the sense to ignore both of them.

Victor Oberlander and his request the other day had amused and perplexed her. She had no use for a man when she had five boys to rear. Why add number six? To think he wanted to come courtin'. Lands, she was forty-one years old, and the beauty of youth had slipped by. Either Oberlander was blind, or he hadn't looked around Rocky Falls for a single woman without children.

I'd be honored if you'd let me take you for a buggy ride on Sunday afternoon.

Leah had sensed his interest in the past, but she'd avoided him. She had too many disruptions in her life without adding another one. But Victor refused to let it rest. Mr. Charm had pushed away her polite refusal as though she were a ... child who didn't know what she needed. He could view her as a challenge or a burr under his saddle. No matter, he could take his fascination elsewhere.

Should I ask John for permission?

Leah hadn't considered a buggy ride or asking John if he minded. She'd smiled and thanked Victor, making certain he understood she had obligations and responsibilities right there without adding more.

I'm not giving up so easily, Miss Leah. I've thought about this for a long time.

Victor could go on thinking about it from now until the good Lord returned. She had plenty of other problems to hold her interest—like keeping John and Evan from going to blows over Ember.

Ember ... How could one pint-size woman cause so much agitation? Had she stolen Mr. Oberlander's horse? What lay in her past that gave her nightmares? And what could Leah do to keep her sons from fighting over her? John was the levelheaded one, but Evan was sensitive. Both boys—rather, men—were tasting first love with a young woman who might hand them a kiss of poison.

All of that, and Leah liked Ember. Felt sorry for her and often saw the hurt in her eyes. Leah wanted a peaceful and satisfying life for the young woman. But a mama's loyalty clung to her sons, and she'd do anything to protect them.

Orange and purple streaks of daylight had barely met Tuesday morning when John stepped from the campsite along the northern section of Evan's acreage and watched a rider approach them in the distance. John grabbed his rifle and studied the man, then relaxed. The steel-gray gelding, the high brimmed hat with a single center crease, and the way he sat tall in the saddle could be only one man—Bob Culpepper, Rocky Falls' marshal and undertaker.

And yet, for Bob to ride all this way so early in the morning meant trouble.

"Looks like me and Evan will be working alone." Mark stepped into the rising sunlight, drinking a mug of coffee that he'd made with enough grounds to cover a creek bottom.

John nodded. "Evan doesn't mind since we're campin' on his land."

Yesterday morning, the three had checked on the cattle grazing near the upper free range. After rounding up a few strays and driving them back into the herd, they rode to Evan's land to build fence. John had the deed granting Evan the acreage, but a fence separating Evan's land from the Wide O made sense.

The three took turns cooking and cleaning up, always working hard and enjoying each other's company. These were the times all of them would no doubt remember in years to come when they had families of their own.

Thank goodness Mark had enough sense not to bring up the subject of Bert. Evan and John had an unspoken truce with the matter. But it was hard, real hard, not to persuade Evan to forget her and remember his future of becoming a veterinarian.

"Mama hates it when you're busy with deputy work," Mark said. "I don't like it either."

"We haven't had any serious crimes for nearly five years since the McCaw gang tore through here. Could be Bob is taking the missus for a trip and needs me to fill in for him."

"Not this early in the mornin'." Evan made his way beside John and Mark. "We might be younger, big brother, but we aren't stupid. This means stealin' or a murder. I can feel it in my bones. And Mama will be horrible to live with until you return."

Evan's most likely right. "You can ease her mind by keeping the others from fussin' and fightin'." John clamped a hand on Mark's shoulder. "You and Aaron need to ease up — not just while I'm gone but permanent-like."

Mark frowned. "I thought we were doing a good job."

John laughed. "You are. But a reminder never hurts."

"Who's going to watch after Ember?"

The sound of Evan's voice when he mentioned her name cut through John's heart. *I can't let him think his feelings aren't real.* "She'll be fine. Mama talks to her, and that's probably all she needs. I want you two to hear exactly what the marshal has to say, so when Mama asks, you have the right answers. No surprises or exaggerations of the truth."

Bob rode up and dismounted. After exchanging "Mornin's" and Mark getting him a mug of coffee, he eyed John. "We got trouble."

"Figured as much. What's happened?"

"Possible cattle thieves." Bob took a gulp of the coffee. As strong as Mark made it, the brew would part his hair—what he had left. "Two ranchers have missin' cattle. About fifty head total."

John remembered Leon's threats and wondered if any Oberlander cattle were missing. He didn't want to consider Leon, but he had to. "What are the plans?"

"Question the ranchers involved again. Call on some of the other ranchers to see if they have the same problem. Check out a few nearby canyons cattle and horse thieves have used in the past."

John nodded. "Who reported the stolen cattle?"

"Sparky McBride and Walt Breacher."

Neither one had large ranches. "That's a lot of livestock for them to lose. Did either see anything unusual? And did either of them question if the missing cattle were due to Sunday's storm?"

"Both ranchers made the discovery on Sunday after the storm. Breacher sent ranch hands out looking, but horse tracks indicated they were rounded up and driven south. Then it rained again, and they lost the trail. McBride reported the same kind of thing."

"But somewhere in the canyons south of here?" Which could be in a number of secluded areas. "Unless the thieves are driving them to Denver."

"Chances are they haven't had time to change the brand. Any of yours missing?"

"Not to my knowledge." John moistened his lips. *Bert.* Surely she wasn't involved in this. He hated to accuse anyone without proof ... but she had been caught riding Oberlander's mare. "I'll ride back to the ranch and then head to Rocky Falls. I'd like to talk to Victor Oberlander. See if his place is all right. He fired one of his hands, and that man could be behind this."

Bob rubbed his chin with his knuckle. "I'll ride with you as far as your place. I'd like to talk to the boy you saved from a hanging a few weeks ago."

"How'd you know about that?"

"Word gets around. He might know something."

Evan cleared his throat, but John refused to look his way. "The boy was a girl, and she's been right here ever since," John said. "We can both talk to her."

"Where'd she come from?"

"She hasn't said, and I don't have a last name either."

Bob stared out toward the snow-capped mountains as though pondering John's information. "Sounds suspicious to me. Could be she's working with somebody."

"She said she didn't steal the horse." Evan's shaky voice gave away his loyalty.

"They all say they're innocent, son," Bob said. "If you're looking down a hangman's noose, you'll say anything to save your neck."

John silently agreed with Bob. He cared for Bert, but he wasn't naïve enough to believe she couldn't be involved in illegal activity. Could things get worse? "I'm ready to ride. We can talk to Bert, then I'll get my gear." He swung his attention to Evan. "You're in charge. You and Mark check on the cattle again before riding back to the house. If any are missing or you see something suspicious, send Mark or Aaron into town. Don't get involved in a shootout. Once the job here is finished, head home. I shouldn't be gone but a day or so."

Within the hour, John and Bob stood on the front porch while Mama and Bert sat on the rocking chairs. The girl's face blanched, and she refused to answer most of Bob's questions.

"I hope you realize you're putting yourself at the top of the list of suspects." Bob leaned against the porch post. "Missy, folks don't take to cattle and horse thieves. You were lucky once. You might not get a second chance."

"Yes sir." She glanced at Mama and then at John. "I could lie, but that's not right."

"Then give me your name, where you came from, and why you were riding Victor Oberlander's mare."

Bert stiffened. "Can't do that. All I can say is I've never had a hand in stealing horses or cattle."

John bent down and took her hand. She trembled. "I don't believe you had a thing to do with this. But Marshal Culpepper and I need a few answers."

Bert glanced down at the hand around hers. "I can't tell you my last name or where I'm from. If it wasn't for owing John money, I'd not be around here."

"Or hanged."

She startled. "Yes sir. You're right."

"Whoever you're protecting isn't worth it. Looks to me like they left you to take a hangman's noose."

Bob spoke the words that had rolled around in John's head for days. More than once he'd considered talking to Mama about it, but why cause her to fret? Sometimes his mama spent more time worrying about one of them than she did breathing. Yet he knew Bert was afraid of something or someone — and she was ready to die for him. Who could have such a hold on a person? *Another man?* John would be a fool to think otherwise.

Still on one knee and holding her hand, John faced her squarely. "Bert, any man who'd let another person die for him is dirt. I don't care who he is or what he means to you."

Bert swallowed hard and shook her head. "You don't know what you're sayin'."

"So you're protecting another man?"

"I don't know a thing about the stolen cattle."

"Looks like I'm right, you—"

"John, I swear I don't know a thing about the cattle."

He pressed his lips together while noting the fear in her eyes. Had this man she protected ever held her or told her she was beautiful? Had anyone ever told her not to be afraid? Given the right circumstances, he'd welcome the chance to protect her. And with no logic or proof to back up her innocence, John believed Bert wasn't a part of the thievery. But he also realized with every bit of strength in him that she knew who was behind the missing cattle.

"You're lying to me." His voice sounded gentle even to him. "At this point, *we* don't have missing cattle. What do you think the other ranchers will say about the 5T cattle being safe and accounted for? What will it take to break through your stubborn head? I hope it's not someone getting shot or killed."

The fear in her eyes changed to terror. What thoughts kept her paralyzed?

John released her hand and stood. His mother whisked away a tear. "I'm leaving with Bob, and I'll be gone a few days. Send one of the boys into town if you need me." He swung his attention back to Bert. "Don't leave the ranch. As I've said before, if you leave, I'll come after you. Not for what you owe me, but because Bob and I are sure you know something about what's going on."

CHAPTER 15

Leah forced a shaky smile for John. If she protested his leaving with Marshal Culpepper, then bad feelings were sure to simmer between them until he returned. She remembered sending Frank off to Rocky Falls the day he was killed. She didn't want to think about it, but the memory hammered against her thoughts every time John rode off to help the marshal. Her heart felt like it would break at the slightest hint of turmoil. Cattle thieves were deadly, just like the outlaws who had gunned down Frank. She believed God had all of her sons safely tucked in his arms. Trust was such an expensive commodity. It took her body and soul to hold her faith together.

She believed her oldest son—the rock of the family—had sincere affection for Ember, and his attempt to prod the truth from her in a gentle fashion proved it so.

Evan and Mark knew about the cattle rustling too, and they were out riding the range. Oh, dear, her worries kept mounting.

The entire Timmons family could be foolish to believe in Bert's innocence when she'd been found atop Queen Victoria's back. No reason to be riding the mare. No explanation as to where she'd come from. They wanted to believe her because they'd all grown to care for her. So why didn't Ember see fit to tell Bob and John what they needed to know? Her silence made her look guilty, and maybe she was.

When Leah pondered what had happened since the girl had arrived, she failed to remember any time when John had openly stated he believed in her innocence. Oh, her poor boy. His heart had been plucked away while his mind fought to maintain reason.

And Evan ... Aaron, Mark, and sweet Davis. If anything happened to one of her dear sons because of Ember, Leah would tear her apart with her bare hands.

Leah startled. Her emotions were as torn and varied as her sons' temperaments. She glanced at Ember, wanting to reassure her, but she couldn't smile at the girl. With the truth holding her in a staggering hold, she wished she'd never set eyes on her.

If Leah felt this confused, how must John feel?

The girl kept her life private except when she relaxed and talked about her brother Gideon. How much should Leah reveal to John about those conversations? Yet Gideon might not be her deceased brother's real name. And he might not be dead. Or he might not have been a brother.

Would any of them ever find the answers? Leah prayed the truth about the mare and the current missing cattle didn't lead back to Ember.

Frank, I need you!

"Do you want me to help you put a few things together?" Leah stood from the rocking chair.

Her gaze met John's, and she saw his perplexed emotions. "No thanks. I'll only be a minute. I'm in a hurry to get this handled." He glanced at Bert, his features stoic as though some inner resolve had given him strength. Lifting the latch, he marched inside.

Within a few minutes, John joined Leah, Bert, and Bob on the front porch. He slung his saddlebag over his shoulder.

"Take care, son. And Godspeed." Leah would not cry. She'd see him off just as she'd done the other times—wishing him well and being brave. "We'll all be praying for you."

John hugged her and planted a kiss on her cheek. "Appreciate it. I'll be home as quick as I can. Bob's riding back to town, but I plan to visit a few ranchers first." He narrowed his gaze at Bert, then nodded.

What was her boy thinking? Regret for allowing his heart to overrule common sense? Leah watched Bob and John ride off, her emotions threatening to crash in around her ... remembering again when Frank wore a deputy's badge and paid for it with his blood. At that moment, her heart felt like it would break. She eased onto a porch step and emptied her heart through a flood of tears.

All the way to the Wide O, crossing over his newly purchased land, John fumed at the thought of cattle stolen. The business with cattle thieves had brought Bert's possible horse thievery to the forefront again. Just when he thought the summer would trickle by like the summers before, a pint-size bundle of trouble had landed on his front porch. Now one of his brothers thought he was falling in love, and two ranchers were missing cattle.

John believed the good Lord never handed out more than a man could bear. Perhaps He needed a reminder that John Timmons had requested it all to end.

John found Victor Oberlander at home reading the latest cattle prices in the *Rocky Mountain News* and drinking coffee mixed with brandy. The bottle sat beside a silver coffeepot. Mama did not need this kind of man in her life, especially when whiskey had dealt their pa a raw hand. Oberlander could take his "need" to town, just like he'd advised John.

"What brings you to see me?" Oberlander laid aside his paper. "Or did you read my mind?"

John sat in Oberlander's parlor with the distinct odors of money and liquor swirling around him. "If you have missing cattle, then we need to talk."

Oberlander lifted a brow and poured a jigger of brandy into his cup—minus the coffee. "How'd you find out?"

"Marshal Culpepper paid me a visit this morning. Sparky McBride and Walt Breacher reported missing cattle. Breacher trailed them until rain washed away the tracks. How many of yours are gone?"

"About fifty head. Discovered it this morning."

That meant at least a hundred stolen so far. "Have any idea who's behind it?"

Oberlander took a healthy drink from his cup. "I think we both know the answer to that."

"Leon Wilson didn't take too kindly to you firing him."

"It got worse. We had more words, and he knows better than to ever come near my property again." He set the cup on a small table. "Any of yours gone?"

"Not to my knowledge. I'm having my brothers check the summer pastures."

The look on Oberlander's face revealed the same thing John suspected. "We got ourselves two possible thieves—Leon and that gal staying at your place. Since Leon tried to hang her, I don't think the two would be working together. He's most likely out for revenge since I fired him, and he decided to add a few heads to his herd." Oberlander added coffee to his cup. "Not sure Leon's part makes sense with cattle missing from different ranchers. Have you learned anything about Bert?"

"Nothing. She refuses to talk about herself. Culpepper questioned her too." John's thoughts stayed fixed on the possibility of Bert's involvement. If she was in custody, Evan might think twice about his feelings. But that was wrong—John didn't have evidence to arrest her. Neither did he want to. If only life were simple. If only the sight of her didn't cause him to think about a family of his own. "She's been at the house the whole time. Works hard too."

"Never met a lawbreaker yet who didn't try to outsmart his— or her—victims." Oberlander stared into his cup. "I'll show you where the cattle disappeared. Some of my men are out looking for those—" He stood. "I know you disapprove of cursing, and most times I do too unless there's a no good thief taking what belongs to someone else. You have my word on this. When they're caught, I'll hold the hangman's noose myself."

John wasn't about to lecture about cursing or the law. Victor Oberlander knew the difference between right and wrong.

The two men rode out across the Wide O's acreage, through a sprinkling of pine, and on through more green pasture, steadily climbing to higher ground where the trees grew thicker. Their horses picked over the brush and the stones of a clear gurgling stream. Chipmunks scampered and birds flew from the treetops as though they sensed trouble on the horizon. In the distance, the variegated shades of green led on to the foothills, but that wouldn't be where the thieves had taken the cattle. They'd have driven the livestock to where the cattle could be hidden in canyons.

Oberlander drew in his reins. He pointed to the northeast parcel of land that now belonged to the 5T. "That's where they drove the cattle across."

"Right after the storm," John said. "Looks like they were waiting for just the right time." He pondered a moment on the situation. "If the thieves were looking to cast the blame on someone like Bert, seems to me they'd leave my ranch alone."

"Makes sense. For that matter, someone could accuse you or Evan." He wiped the sweat beading on his forehead. "Let's keep our eyes and ears open to see if that rumor starts. If the rustler is local, he'd start the talk."

"Right. Do you know where Leon is? Or if he has family in these parts?" John wanted to talk to him in a bad way.

"He's from down near Silverton. If he knows what's good for him, he'll disappear. By the time I'd gotten back from delivering the mare, he was drunk—mean drunk."

"I'll send a wire. He has it in for both of us." John considered Leon seizing the opportunity to take his vengeance out on the 5T ... his family ... or Bert. He couldn't ignore the likelihood. Neither could he run scared. He had a job to do.

With John gone, Bert was free to run. The thought ate at her like varmints picking at Miss Leah's garden. For her own good, Bert needed to hightail it out of Colorado and head south to Texas where she wouldn't need to worry so much when winter blew its cold winds.

Every time she remembered the agony in Leah's weeping when John left, Bert wanted to break down too. Leah ... the strong mother who raised her boys with a mixture of love and real life had been devastated. Bert had started the trouble in this family, and she must be the one to make sure it stopped.

She stared up from breaking green beans to the small corral where Racer and Queen Victoria kept company. The mare was a constant reminder as to why she had weeks left to work out her indebtedness. She paused to calculate how far she'd get before John came after her. And she had no doubt he'd ride night and day until he caught up to her. He'd be terribly angry.

Aaron talked nonstop about the cattle thieves, and he blamed Leon, reminding them of the greasy man's threat. Aaron also wondered why their ranch had been spared. The longer Aaron talked, the more nervous Bert grew.

According to Marshal Culpepper, other ranchers hadn't reported missing cattle. Aaron didn't know for sure; he'd wait for Evan and Mark to report back. The 5T could be minus a few head too.

If the culprit had been Simon and he knew Bert was staying with the Timmons family, he'd have taken their livestock before the other ranchers'. Surely her worries about her brothers' involvement were unfounded. She'd seen the results when Simon got even with a person, and his vengeance meant a dead body. And in this case, it would be hers.

She dropped a handful of crisp broken green beans into a huge crock. If she left now, John might be too busy to come after all. She relaxed a bit. That made sense. She had to get away before Simon found her, before—

"What are you thinking about?" Miss Leah reached for a handful of fresh beans from the basket and placed them in her lap to trim and break.

"Nothing really. Why?"

"You've sighed a few times, and I wondered what was ailing you."

Bert felt Leah's intense gaze. She'd been under that scrutiny more than once today. She couldn't blame Leah for being distrustful. The woman had been so kind to her. "I was thinking on what I'd do after I'm finished here."

"It'll be nearly winter."

Freezing to death didn't sound like a good way to die, and she wasn't ready to simply give up without a fight. "I understand a body just goes to sleep."

Leah blanched. "When you freeze to death?"

Bert shuddered. "Yes."

"I've been thinking you might find a job in Rocky Falls. Possibly earn some money to help you make your way in the spring."

If Simon hasn't found me by then. But the winter snows would stop him too. She shook her head.

"Why not?"

Bert tossed a questioning look. "I'm sorry. I wasn't listening."

"I suggested working in Rocky Falls until spring. Then you could plan your future."

"Sounds like a good idea." Bert let her thoughts end there. She had to leave. No matter how much she wanted to be a part of this dear family, her dreams also had her far beyond her brothers' reach. Too many times she'd postponed the journey, but her selfish ways could get someone hurt.

CHAPTER 16

John left the Wide O near twilight. Urgency filled his gut to find the cattle thieves before the ranchers found them and had a lynching. He wondered if his brothers had discovered some of their own cattle missing. Being a part of the problem cast the blame on someone other than Bert. He never thought he'd wish some of his livestock gone. For all he knew, Bert could be a part of a gang. If he had his doubts about her, then what would a crowd do once they had a reminder she was caught riding Oberlander's mare?

John understood the way men reacted when they'd been wronged. He couldn't think of anything worse than trying to stand down angry men with retribution on their minds and a noose dangling from a tree. God-fearing men who lost control were just as deadly as a gang of outlaws.

His ponderings came full circle back to Bert. John could handle bad news and deal with the fact he might have grown fond of a woman set up to deceive him, but what about Mama and Evan and his other brothers? Who was he trying to fool with his bravado? Bert made his knees weak and his mouth dry. How could a man let a woman get under his skin in three weeks and one day?

He patted the gelding's neck. At least his horse didn't have woman problems or lawbreakers or family responsibilities. *Sure would be nice to talk to Uncle Parker and have a little help sorting out this mess.* John didn't have the time to travel to Denver. But he did have time to talk to God. Sure would be nice if God would send him a telegram.

He rode into Rocky Falls. The town looked peaceful, a quiet community. Since Bob Culpepper had been elected marshal over four years ago, he'd handled the rare problems with a firm hand. Being the town's undertaker gave those who chose to break the law something more to think about. He had a way of reminding law-breakers about the coffins stored in the back room of the funeral home that scared them straight. John found the marshal's threats amusing, but reality worked. Maybe Bob should run for judge too. A man who served as town marshal, a judge, and an undertaker ought to eliminate any problems in and around Rocky Falls.

Dark shadows lingered by the time John tied his horse to the hitching post in front of the marshal's office. Weariness bore down on him before he'd begun the search for the cattle rustlers. Bob had indicated the need to form a posse, but first the men needed a trail to follow. After Saturday night's gulley washer, the tracks had vanished. Maybe the thieves would get cocky and try adding to their herd. Ranch hands would be armed and wait-ing. Blood would flow, and unfortunately the innocent would fall along with the guilty.

A lantern shone through the window indicating Bob labored over a mound of work, rubbing his chest. John opened the door to find him studying a hand-drawn map of the ranches in the area. He glanced up and greeted John, then motioned for him to sit down. "You look as tired as I feel."

"Then we both need to get some rest soon."

"You sound like my wife. She brought me supper and pro-ceeded to tell me I wouldn't be losing so much hair and com-plaining about my aching bones if I'd give up being the town's marshal."

"What did you tell her?"

He grinned, and the lines lifted around his eyes. "That being an undertaker taxed a man's view of age too."

John enjoyed a good belly laugh. "Learn anything about the rustlers?"

"Widow Bess told me Leon Wilson showed up at the saloon the evening Oberlander fired him. Made some strong threats. Wish she would have gotten word to me then so I could have talked to him."

John slid a chair across the wooden floor and positioned it across from Bob's desk. "Oberlander has around fifty head missing, bringing the total to around a hundred. Just like McBride's and Breacher's losses, the rain washed away the tracks. Frankly, I think we could still pick up a trail." He took in a deep breath in hopes his body would stop screaming out for rest. "Oberlander told me Leon Wilson's people are from Silverton. That's worth a wire in case he shows up there."

"We'll handle sending it first thing in the morning. According to McBride and Breacher, the cattle seemed to disappear."

"What else did you learn?"

"The *Rocky Mountain News* claims a gang of brothers have been stealing cattle in the southern part of the state. Could be the gang's moved this way. I've been studying a map to see if there's a pattern. Looks varied to me at this point." Bob sat back in his chair and ran his fingers over the top of his balding head. He looked like ten hours of sleep would do him good. "Could be Leon. Could be any number of gangs."

"Anyone killed?"

"A ranch hand and a few others. Blamed on the gang of brothers."

Not since Uncle Parker and Aunt Sage took out over the Rockies to free him and Davis from the McCaw gang had John felt serious trouble from the top of his head to the tips of his toes. He'd been eighteen when the outlaws hit the area, and now he was twenty-three. Same time of year as then too. No wonder he sweated during the summer months. The uneasiness had more to do with the memory of a murdering gang than the hot sun. The summer his father was murdered hadn't left him; the pain was merely masked with work and responsibility.

"Who's leading the gang of brothers?" John already had an idea about writing Uncle Parker. His state contacts would aid them in getting federal marshals to Rocky Falls.

"A man by the name of Simon Farrar. Supposed to be three of them. However, the newspaper claimed five men were involved in one of the incidents."

John groaned and studied the bullet hole on the top of Bob's desk. "Do you mind if I contact Uncle Parker for a US Marshal? I know the last time we got a man who wasn't much help, but if my uncle is making the request, we'll get an experienced lawman."

"My thoughts too." Bob winced. He brought his hand to the left side of his chest. "Even after five years, the McCaw brothers are still fresh in our minds."

"I'd take a horsewhip to one of my brothers if they even hinted of taking what wasn't theirs."

"Sometimes all it takes is a hungry belly and the oldest promising a better life—just like the problem we had here five years ago. Those cattle rustlers plaguing our community are no doubt following the same kind of man—clever and able to manipulate others. Hope for a better tomorrow has a powerful hold."

Wisdom had spoken, and Bob had much of it to give.

"Ever been hungry, John? I mean so hungry you'd eat the bark off a tree?"

"No sir."

"I was nearly thirty years old when I fought in the Civil War. Hunger for food—or whatever it is that makes a person desperate—moves a man to do things he's never thought of doing before. Sometimes it makes a man a hero. Sometimes it makes him an outlaw."

"Like my pa. Whatever happened to him in the war drove him to drink. And, come to think of it, the McCaw brothers came out of the war as killers seeking revenge for what happened to their families and homes."

"Hard times affect men in different ways."

John took a moment to chew on what Bob had said. "Stands to reason if you can figure out what makes a man behave a particular way, you'd have a lot less lawbreakers." He hesitated. "I'd like to study law someday."

"Sounds like something your Uncle Parker would say."

John missed his uncle. "He probably has, and it's finally sunk into my stubborn brain."

"Right now, we need to find these cattle thieves. Every day that goes by will make the local ranchers restless and trigger-happy."

"Where do we begin?"

"I've been thinking about the best way to outsmart them. One is to search every canyon large enough to hold over one hundred fifty head or more of cattle, which could take a long time. The other is to deputize a couple of good men, send them out to the ranchers, and offer a reward for information leading to the rustlers. We could distribute posters around town and have the same announcement written up in the paper."

John stood and paced the wooden floor, his thoughts weighing each idea. "Let's do it all. Something's bound to turn up. The people of Rocky Falls need to know we're doing the best we can. If they think we're shirking, someone's going to get hurt." When Bob didn't respond, John studied his weathered face. "Are you thinking we need to go see Bess?"

"Wouldn't be the first time Widow Bess helped us. She might have already heard something else we could use. And we both could use some supper."

"I thought your wife brought you food?"

Bob stood from his chair. "She did, but after we got over our fussin' about me being town marshal, it got cold." He nodded toward the back door of the jail. "My wife is a good woman, but some of her cookin' needs help. Cold liver and onions with dry cornbread is one of them. God forgive me, but I had to toss it out to the dog."

John laughed at the pitiful expression on Bob's face, but a man needed good food to keep him going. *Could Bert cook?* John took a moment to reflect on the young woman's abilities in the kitchen. A few tasty meals came to mind. Why was he thinking about Bert ... in that way ... when he didn't know if he could trust her?

The two men strode out of the marshal's office and down the darkened street to the building that housed a hotel on one side and a saloon on the other. Quite handy for the soiled doves of Rocky Falls. Widow Bess had worked the hotel for years, mothering the girls employed there and urging them to leave their livelihood. If she didn't own a stake in both businesses with a shrewd man, she'd have been fired years ago. As it was, the two owners barely spoke, each trying to buy out the other.

The portly woman waved from behind the registration desk. "Evening Bob, John. You two hungry?"

"We sure are," Bob said.

John swallowed a laugh and smelled the roast and potatoes. Liver and onions, whether hot or cold, weren't his favorite. His stomach growled, and his mouth watered at the same time.

"Have a seat, and I'll be right with you. Just made fresh coffee, so I'll get a couple of cups." She made her way toward the kitchen, then swung around. "I bet you two are here on business."

"That we are," Bob said. "Can you spare a few minutes?"

She glanced around the dining area. A couple sat at one table and three men talked at another. "I'll see what I can do. Heard something interesting since we talked about Leon."

Shortly thereafter, Bess waddled toward them with two steaming mugs of coffee and wearing a smile that would open the gates of heaven. "This must be about the cattle rustlin'," she said. "The place was buzzing like bees on rotten apples last night with all the talk."

John chuckled. Leave it to Bess to find something amusing about a dire situation. "Did you hear anything we can use?"

She sobered. "Heard some talk about the boy you stopped from being hanged. A couple of men think he might be a diversion for rustlers."

John wished there was a way to free Bert from the list of suspects. "He's a she, and she's been at the ranch helping Mama."

Bess's eyes widened. "That's a twist of fate if I ever heard one."

John frowned, the reminder of the whole mess worsening his day. "I've made better decisions than bringing home a girl."

"I think it's sad a little girl's on her own." Bess shook her head. "That's how some of the women here ended up working at the saloon."

"She's not a little girl," John said. "Seventeen."

Bess blinked. "Ouch. Sounds like a sore subject, John Timmons. From the frown you're wearing, I'd say you've seen happier days."

"Twenty-three years of 'em."

Bob tried to disguise his laugh with a cough. "So what else have you heard?"

Bess appeared to ponder the question. "Oh, the typical. Blaming ghosts, Indians, town drunk, various outlaws. Sounds like speculation to me."

"Nothing to hang your hat on, huh?" Bob rubbed his whiskered jaw.

"One of the Wide O hands brought up Leon Wilson again."

"Maybe so." John focused on reading Bess's eyes. "He didn't have time to put together a clever plan unless he had help."

She stared at him, then at Bob. "Help? As in a seventeen-year-old girl?"

"If he and Bert were working together," Bob said, "hanging her would have made him look good until he was ready to do something with the cattle."

John hadn't considered that aspect. "Except he was fired. Was most of the talk about Leon and who might be working with him?"

Bess nodded. "So the girl's name is Bert?"

"Yes ma'am." John needed to get Bert off his ranch—away from those he loved. Or did he? "I'm wondering if my family's safe. I need to make a few decisions about her."

"Get some food in your belly first," Bess said. "Hard to figure out what's the right thing to do when your stomach is protesting."

John and Bob talked through supper, tossing out suggestions about how best to proceed. Their ideas were as varied as how to pitch horseshoes at a church social. They paid their bill and thanked Bess for her help. Once they were outside the hotel, John felt his exhaustion clear through to his bones. But concern for his family weighed him down more. "I'm going back home tonight."

"I understand," Bob said. "And in your boots, I'd feel the same. You don't know if those cattle thieves are taking advantage of your being gone or if that gal is in the thick of it all. But you're tuckered out. Why don't you get a good night's sleep and ride home tomorrow?"

Loud voices rose from inside the saloon, and both men turned to check on the source. When nothing else was said, they walked toward the office. "You can bring her back here where we can keep an eye on her. Not sure where she'll stay, but at least you won't need to fret about your mama and brothers. In the morning I'll send a telegram to Parker about needin' a US Marshal. I'll also pay a visit to the newspaper office about asking the community to help us find those thieves."

Bob's suggestion sounded good enough to accept, but—"I wouldn't be able to sleep. I'll bring Bert with me in the morning. I'm hoping Bess can take her in. Before I get here, I'll stop at the Wide O again. Oberlander and I talked today about deputizing a few of his ranch hands, and I'd like to take him up on the offer. I really want him to see that Bert's no longer staying at the 5T."

Bob clamped a hand on his shoulder. "Parker would be proud of you. You think before you act."

Not always. Going to be hard not to see her every day. Harder yet to arrest her if she's behind something illegal.

CHAPTER 17

B ert listened to Leah's deep, even breathing. The day had been long and disturbing. Every inch of her loathed the past she could not change. Six months ago, she'd wanted to start fresh, run free with hope for a new future. And yet her prospects of a better tomorrow looked impossible. Fleeing Simon had been so much easier before she met the Timmons family. If she cared so much for these loving people, why had she put them in possible danger? Every one of them held a special spot in her heart—John, Evan, Aaron, Mark, Davis, and Leah. Sweet Leah who had worked with Bert late into many a night in a painstaking effort to teach her how to read. The encouragement gave her confidence. Her reading improved, and the new words opened her mind to an exciting world.

In a precious few weeks' time, she'd found herself caring for a man and affection for an entire family.

Cattle rustlers roamed the area, and dread filled her that the thieves might be Simon, Clint, and Lester. The lump in her throat rose. Surely Simon would not have talked her brothers into working this far north? And if they were in this area, did they know she was here too?

One thought after another darted in and out of her mind. Maybe the thieves weren't her brothers after all. Maybe it was Leon, the man who'd tried to hang her. After all, he made his anger clear when Mr. Oberlander fired him.

The marshal from Rocky Falls had done a good job digging for the truth. She trembled still. Bert thought the man could read her mind, as though he knew she was an affliction to anyone who befriended her.

Bert's hand covered her mouth. She'd nearly moaned aloud. Misery did that to a person, made them hurt inside and out. The time had come to leave the 5T, and she needed to do it now. Maybe someday she'd meet another man as fine as John Timmons, a man who caused music in her heart and her fingers to dance on the strings of a fiddle.

She remembered the other night when she'd been playing the fiddle. Leah began to sing "Shoo Fly Shoo," when John took the fiddle from her.

"Let Mama sing, and let's dance," he'd said.

Shocked at his request, Bert simply stared until John laughed and pulled her to the center of the parlor. "Line up boys, we're having a party."

The other boys joined Leah in the singing, but they all took turns swinging Bert and Leah around the floor.

Bert cringed at first, especially when Evan held her a little tighter than she wanted, but it had nothing to do with the dancing.

Shaking the memory aside, she eased from the bed and grabbed her roll of clothes from beneath it. Earlier she'd placed them within easy reach where she could change in the barn and leave Leah's nightgown for her to find. She'd not take food. Again, she reinforced her belief that stealing made her no better than her brothers. Well, not all of them. Clint and Lester didn't brag about what they did with Simon. Neither of them would be breaking the law if not for Simon pushing them. When he wanted one of them to do something, he could turn a phrase and make the vilest idea look like the proper thing to do.

She inwardly gasped, for she was no better than Simon. She'd taken twenty dollars of his money in the name of needing it for herself. Still had five of it hidden away. Between the money and Oberlander's mare, Simon did have reason to be angry. This time when she ran, she'd have to find a way to get to a town big enough where she could find work. Change her name and become respectable. She'd learn more about readin' and writin' and doing figures. No one would call her stupid again. Neither would she ever allow a man to hit her or—

In the blackness, she allowed one quick glance at Leah sleeping peacefully. Even though she couldn't see the dear woman, she'd never forget her kindness. Later she'd reflect more about John and the things about him sealed in her memory. But not now when her heart wanted to stay in the warm bed beside Leah with her dreams to keep her company.

Bert snatched up her boots and tiptoed across the floor and through the kitchen. The smells of fried chicken from supper and the cinnamon apples with sweet cream wafted about the room. The homey smells of food made with love were treasures to be remembered during the lonely days ahead. Someday she'd have a home like this.

Crazy thought. *Who would ever want me?*

Sweeping aside her silly notions, she concentrated on what must be done. A couple of times today, she'd practiced opening the front door without making a sound. Holding her breath, she lifted the latch and crept out onto the front porch. The stars were like a million candles lighting up the dark night, and the half moon would help her find the way south beyond the 5T, beyond Rocky Falls. She didn't like traveling at night, but what choice did she have? At least John wouldn't be after her in the morning, and she hoped he stayed gone for a long while. However, Evan might attempt to trail her.

Rowdy nudged against her leg. She smiled. What a friendly dog. Together they stepped down from the porch and made their way to the barn. Rowdy couldn't go with her, even if she wanted his company. The boys loved the dog, their dog, not hers. Bert stopped in front of the barn door. She could change into her britches and shirt out here, but she needed to put Rowdy in a stall.

A figure stepped in front of her. She sucked in a breath and nearly screamed.

"Just where do you think you're going?"

John wanted to grab Bert by the shoulders and shake some sense into her head. All of his suspicions about her were true. He'd been tricked, fooled, and lied to. Angry didn't begin to describe the fury racing through his veins. He wished she were a boy 'cause then he'd escort him to the woodshed.

"I said, just where do you think you're going?"

"John . . . I thought you were in Rocky Falls." Her voice broke. Good. She ought to be shaking in her bare feet. "I . . . couldn't sleep, so I was taking a walk."

"Carrying your clothes?" John grabbed her shoulders. "And your boots?"

"Please—"

"Please what? Step aside so you can run off? Steal one of my horses? Meet up with whoever's rustlin' cattle? What else do you have wrapped up in that bundle?"

"Nothing. Just my clothes."

"Right. I want to take a look."

"I have to leave."

She was crying; he could hear her sob. But he wouldn't back down from what he needed to do. "Why? What are you hiding? Who are you hiding from?"

"I've told you over and over. I can't tell you."

John was tempted to swear like a drunk denied another bottle. He'd been in gun fights, gotten himself beaten, gone after a gang who murdered his father and kidnapped Davis, and gone against odds alongside Bob Culpepper to uphold the law. But never had he been provoked to lose his temper like now.

"I think you'd better do some explaining, or I'm going to arrest you."

She gasped. "For what?"

"Holding back information that could lead to finding cattle rustlers."

"I don't know who's stolen the cattle."

"What about Oberlander's mare?"

Her silence ground at his nerves. "So what's it going to be, Bert? Are you going to tell me about yourself, or am I forced to take you into Rocky Falls and have you face questioning again and possible arrest?"

"I haven't broken any laws."

"Do you expect me to believe that?"

"I suppose not. But it *is* the truth."

"Ever spent a night in jail?" John couldn't remember a woman ever spending a night in Rocky Falls' jail, and he didn't want to think about locking up Bert in there either. Unless he slept in Bob's chair to watch over her.

She stiffened. "No, but I'm sure a jail's not any worse than sleeping in the rain or snow."

"I'm not feeling sorry for you. Leave those sentiments for Mama or Evan." John released her shoulders. His head pounded with the exasperation of finding Bert ready to take off. He'd try Mama's way. Be gentle. "I'm sorry if I hurt you. Please, why won't you tell me the truth?"

"I don't want anyone else hurt."

"Have you witnessed a murder?" When she didn't respond, he realized he'd inched closer to the truth. "I'm a deputy. I can help you."

"It's too muddy. Too many people involved. Can you be with your mama and your brothers every minute?"

"My brothers know how to use a rifle."

"Maybe on a wolf or a bear, but what about another man? I've heard the story about what happened to Davis. Do you want that scare repeated?"

It was John's turn not to respond as he took time to contemplate her words.

"Let me leave," she whispered. "I care too much for all of you to risk anyone getting hurt."

The front door of the house closed, and John jerked his attention to the porch. "Who's there?"

"Me. Evan. I thought you were in town."

Could things get any worse? No point in holding back why he was there. "I had to take care of things here first."

"Like what?"

"I have to take Bert to town."

Evan stomped down the porch toward them. "For what?" His voice thundered through the darkness.

"Keep your voice down. You'll have everyone up." John blew out an exasperated sigh. "I'm taking her in for her own safety. Talk in town has her part of the cattle rustling."

"Because of Oberlander's mare?"

"What do you think? And none of our livestock is missing. Or is it?"

"Nah. We have them all." Evan stood before them. John could feel the animosity seeping from the pores of his brother's skin. He didn't want an argument or a fight. On the ride back from town, he'd thought through Evan's feelings for Bert and how best to persuade him that this was the best way to protect her.

John reached down inside him for what had to be said. "We don't want a mob riding out here. You know what could happen, and our brothers would see it all."

"Where will she stay?" Evan's soft voice revealed his heart. John hated this. Why had God shoved Bert into their lives? What good reason could cause all of this turmoil?

"I'm thinking Widow Bess might take her in. Maybe give her a job at the hotel."

"I'm not so sure I like Bert being around those women at the saloon."

"Do I have a say in this?" Bert said. "Since you two are deciding my future."

"No." John had no problem adding firmness to his words. "Little lady, you cost me money, time, and the safety of my family. You have no say in anything until this is resolved."

"Don't you think you're being hard on her?" Evan's voice rose.

"Not at all. She refuses to talk about where she came from, and that spells trouble. Sometimes I'd like to ring her pretty neck." John caught his own words. He'd actually said "pretty."

"Just leave me alone," Bert said. "Fighting among brothers isn't right. I'd rather take my chances on my own. I'll send you the money I owe once I get settled."

"I don't care about the money, and the answer is still no." John would tie her up if she tried to take off. He lifted the bundle of clothes and boots from her arms. "You can go back inside and get some sleep, or we can ride back to Rocky Falls tonight." The latter would make him one tired man, but he'd do it.

Irritating silence met him.

"Tonight or in the morning?" he said.

"John, quit badgering her." Evan's tone had reached fighting level. John had heard it enough through the years.

"In the morning," Bert said.

"I want your word you won't try to run off," John said. "And think about this while you're scheming to get away. If you leave, the other ranchers are going to blame me and my family for harboring a cattle thief. And if you have any feelings for Mama and my brothers, then you'd be wise to think twice before putting them in danger."

"I'll not run off." Her passive voice indicated her resignation.

"Thank you. Now go on to bed. You've been enough trouble for one night."

Bert turned and walked back to the house. She didn't ask for her clothes. Neither would he have given them to her. Now he had Evan to deal with. Would this night ever end?

"You can't believe she's a cattle rustler," Evan finally said.

"Have you forgotten she was caught as a horse thief?"

"You and I know there's a reason. You and I also know she's running from somebody who's trying to hurt her. She's too good and kind to be on the other side of the law."

"Evan, please. I'm tired, and I don't want to argue. This situation is beyond us. It's the law."

"Sounds like an excuse to get her off the ranch so you can court her yourself."

John rubbed his face with the sleeve of his shirt in an attempt to wipe the exhaustion, frustration, and all of the other things plaguing him from his mind. "Evan, my family and the law come first. It's my responsibility. I don't want to keep you from a girl you care about, but I do want to keep you safe. And her too. I'm done talking tonight."

He left Evan standing alone in the barn in hopes his brother would listen to reason. But after a few steps he swung back around. "I've got her clothes in case you two have any ideas."

CHAPTER 18

Leah heard Bert slip back into the dark room, just as she'd heard Evan shouting at John outside. The other boys probably knew more about the details of the argument than she did. Leah wrestled with getting up to find out the problem or allowing her sons to settle their differences like grown men. Except sometimes they acted more like scraping toddler boys fussin' over a toy. But this time the object was not an item to tug back and forth with a shout of "mine" but a seventeen-year-old girl.

Obviously John had returned from Rocky Falls.

Obviously he and Bert were discussing something outside. And why was she out there in her nightgown? *Mercy, do I even want to contemplate such a scandal?*

Obviously Evan had walked into whatever had compelled them to meet at midnight.

And obviously her sons had argued about Bert.

Dear Lord, can this get any worse? The words barely left her mind before she realized that yes, a whole lot more things could go wrong. And she'd better be prepared for it. Might as well begin now. If only she could see Bert's face, but that couldn't be helped unless she got up and lit the lantern. Sometimes a person could talk easier in the dark.

"Did John and Evan get into a fight?"

Bert climbed into bed and released a sigh. "Almost."

"Do I want to know why?"

"You probably already do. Part of it anyway."

Keep going. The situation would eat at her until she did. "What were you doing out there in your nightgown?"

"I ... I wanted to leave. Didn't expect John to be there."

"Do you have feelings for either of my sons?" Silence. Bert was so good at saying everything with nothing. "I assume the answer is yes. And I think I know which one."

"Yes ma'am."

"He's a hard man to understand."

"Yes ma'am."

"And he hides his feelings. Instead of voicing them."

"Yes ma'am."

Leah took a deep breath and realized the burden of guilt she carried because of John's temperament. "And he's eaten up with a worm called responsibility."

"Yes ma'am."

"He'd do anything for us. He was born with a purpose of caring for his family. Even before his father died, he looked after his brothers and me. But no one's ever done it for him. He won't allow anyone to wait on him. Says he doesn't need lookin' after."

"Yes ma'am."

"Does John have any idea how you feel about him?"

Silence. Poor Evan was about to get hurt. Maybe John too.

"How could I tell him in one breath and not give him my last name in the next?"

Oh, my dear girl. What stalked her like a grizzly?

"There's more and it's not good," Bert said.

"I figured as such. You could make life easier on yourself and those who care about you by telling what you know."

"That's what I was trying to do tonight."

"By running?"

"By maybe saving their lives."

Leah moaned. "I'd kill anyone who tried to hurt my sons." She caught her breath. "I—"

"I feel the same way. John's taking me to town in the morning to stay with someone until this is over."

Leah swallowed her relief. "Do you think all of us will be safe then?"

"You will be."

"Ember, will you be safe?"

Silence, and Leah chose not to prod any more tonight.

Chapter 19

John dressed the following morning feeling more tired than when he'd lain down on his bed. Last night, while riding back from Rocky Falls, he believed he'd be asleep the moment he pulled off his boots. But the worries marching across his mind made rest impossible. One conversation after another had taken root in his thoughts and kept his mind racing. Until the cattle thieves were found, the folks around him would be pointing fingers and accusing anyone and everyone.

Evan's bed had groaned with his restlessness until the wee hours of the morning. But John knew better than to question what bothered him. Now his brother slept, and John hoped he finally got some much-needed rest. Aaron and Mark could do chores, and it gave John time to rouse Bert and leave for town.

John gathered up his boots and the roll containing Bert's clothes and made his way downstairs. He couldn't smell breakfast yet, which meant Mama was still in bed. Good. He could leave without having another confrontation with any of his family.

He made his way to Mama's door. In the past he wouldn't have gone into her room with Bert sleeping beside her. Last night changed things. He slipped into the bedroom and in the darkness, he touched Bert's arm. Instantly she jerked, as though seared with a hot branding iron.

John touched a finger to his lips, and she nodded. He guessed she didn't want a show of her leaving either. He handed her the bundle of clothes and made his way to the door.

"You two need breakfast," Mama whispered.

What did she know?

"We need an early start," he said. "Bob and I have lots of work to do."

The bed creaked, and Mama stood in the shadows. Her silhouette and Bert's nearly matched. Two tiny women who held his heart; two tiny women who could be so stubborn.

Mama walked past him and into the kitchen where he heard her pick up a splint from the kindling box. Lighting it from the hot coals of the cookstove, she carried the burning stick into the bedroom. He couldn't think of a single thing to say to her or Bert. Must be the weariness tugging at his eyelids. Mama lifted the glass chimney of the lantern and raised the wick slightly. Soon the lantern on her night table flickered, sending dancing flames around the room.

Mama would not let them leave for Rocky Falls without breakfast. But he had been born with her determination and refused to waste one minute of daylight.

From the doorway, he glanced at Bert, who stood in her nightgown clutching her clothes. A fragile-looking girl who held too much power over him. In the dim light, her face etched a map that led to fear and doubt. Normally, he'd have felt some kind of compassion, but the events of yesterday and last night, along with the lack of sleep, made him irritable.

"I'm not hungry," Bert said.

"I'll get breakfast for both of us at the hotel," John said. "I promise. Right now, we need to ride."

Mama pressed her lips together, then sighed. "Be careful." She studied Bert. "No matter what the future holds for you, for this family, I'm praying God's will is clear to all of us."

"I'm sure Evan will tell you what's going on." He walked over and kissed his mother's cheek and gestured to Bert. "Time's wasting. Your boots are on the front porch." He whirled around to head outside and saddle up the gelding. Bert could ride behind him.

By the time he led his horse from the barn, Bert was waiting beside the corral. She reminded him of a schoolgirl who'd gotten into trouble. *I'm doing the right thing for my family and the good of the community.* Without a word, he mounted and pulled her up behind him. She sobbed, and the sound bothered him more than he'd ever admit to anyone. But her arms wrapped around his waist gave him a strange sense of comfort.

A mile from the ranch, they still hadn't spoken. The only sound was the creak of his saddle and the steady rhythm of horse hooves. Birds sang rather mournfully, like a funeral dirge, or so John thought. Normally he enjoyed the birds and insects greeting the day. But not this morning. He had an uneasy feeling in the pit of his stomach that refused to go away.

"I don't like this anymore than you do."

She continued to sob.

"Wish you wouldn't do that."

"I . . . can't stop."

"Bert, why did God put you in my life?"

She sucked in a breath. "How would I know?"

"Well, I've never met anyone who aggravated me like you do."

"I'm sorry." She loosened her grip from around him.

But he liked her holding on to him. "Best not let go. In the dark, you could fall and I'd never find you."

"That might be a blessing."

John didn't think losing Bert could ever be for his own good.

In the east, the sun slid over the horizon in a thin arc of orange and yellow. Tonight it would dip down over the mountains. Always the same. Only man and his schemes changed. John wished he had a plan of sorts instead of the gut-wrenching notion that the terror from the McCaw gang five years ago had come calling again.

His first stop was at the Wide O, and he heard her gasp when they turned toward Oberlander's ranch. "I want him to see you with me," he said.

"Like I can't be stealing cattle if I'm in jail?"

"I'm not putting you in jail. It's house arrest."

"Same thing." She relaxed against him. "I understand, though. I really do."

Her tiny body against his back continued to do strange things to him. Things he shouldn't be thinking about. "I also want to see if any of his ranch hands can be deputized. If any of them are working with Leon, they'll not want to volunteer."

"Makes sense. John ... I never led Evan to believe I was interested in him."

"I believe you."

"Thanks. That's important to me."

It's important to me too.

At the Wide O, John left Bert sitting on his horse to show her he trusted her. Hopefully that wasn't a mistake. He knocked on the door and waited until the Mexican man greeted him.

"I'd like to see Mr. Oberlander outside," John said. "It won't take long."

A few moments later, Oberlander joined him and the two stepped onto the front porch. "What brings you out here so early in the morning?" He glanced up at Bert. "Trouble?"

"I'm trying to prevent any. Taking Bert into town where Marshal Culpepper can keep an eye on her. A lot of talk going on and I don't want folks taking the law into their own hands."

"Smart man." He waved at Bert. "Mornin', Miss."

"Good mornin' to you, Mr. Oberlander."

Wonderful. She knew when to use manners. "I have a favor to ask of you. Are you willing for any of your ranch hands to be deputized in the search for the missing cattle and rustlers?"

"Sounds like a good idea. I'll walk down to the bunkhouse now and ask them."

"Thanks. I know Bob is getting some men together, and I'll have him stop here first later on this morning. We're putting together a reward too. Won't be a lot but it might cause a man to volunteer."

"Appreciate it. I'll kick in a few dollars." The two shook hands, and John climbed back on his horse—a bit of a maneuver with Bert behind him.

"I'm telling you, John," Oberlander said. "If the rustlers aren't caught, I'm arming my ranch hands."

What could John say? The Wide O had issued a challenge, and he could do nothing if Oberlander chose to protect his own property.

John and Bert rode into Rocky Falls with the hustle and bustle of morning bringing the town to life. Bob hadn't gotten to the marshal's office yet, so John decided to take Bert to breakfast like he'd told Mama. He wasn't hungry, but if he didn't get some food in his stomach, he'd be weak before the day was over. And for sure, it would be a long one.

"Where are we going?" Her first words since leaving the Wide O.

"Breakfast. Then we'll find the marshal."

She stiffened against him. "Nothing's changed. I can't tell you what you want to know, because I have no idea who's behind the cattle rustling."

"I've heard it before." He refused to put any emotion in his words. She might learn how he felt about her and use it against him. "But I'll find you a decent place to stay."

"I heard you mention Bess. Who's she?"

"You'll meet her at the hotel. A good woman. Her lot in life seems to be taking care of soiled doves and cooking fine meals."

Bert didn't respond. He started to add he wasn't accusing her of earning a living like them. But she could have. He shoved away the thought, not wanting to think of her as a woman who used her body to earn her keep. Right now he was convinced God must have played a joke on him by having him fall for a woman he knew nothing about.

"How long will I have to stay in Rocky Falls?"

"Until this blows over."

"I want to finish paying you back. Either working it out at your ranch or sending you the money from somewhere else."

"The money no longer has any importance. Other things have taken over." And that was all he intended to say about the matter until he sorted out the problems in his life.

Once inside the hotel, Bess caught his eye. She greeted him and pointed to a round table covered with a blue-flowered cloth. He had his speech all prepared about Bert, and he should have felt good about getting rid of her. His heart said no to abandoning her, but reason said he needed to keep her and his family safe.

Bess brought two mugs of coffee and set them in front of John and Bert. "Is this the little lady Bob was telling me about?"

"Yes ma'am. Miss Bess, this is Bert—no last name. Oh, her first name is really Ember."

Bess patted Bert's arm. "I've known lots of girls with no last names. Do you prefer Bert or Ember?"

"I'll answer to either." She glanced at John, and he read the sadness.

"Well, I like Ember. I'll get you both a plate of breakfast, and then we can talk."

Good, Bess must have been agreeable to the idea of Bert living there.

Within thirty minutes, Bert had a small room near the kitchen and a job keeping things clean. John figured if he had to entrust his charge to anyone, Bess was the person. He was hungrier than he thought, but Bert picked at her food like a chicken pecking at pieces of grain.

"We'll be back later," John said when he paid the bill. "Thank you for helping us." He turned to Bert, prompting her to show some gratitude. She said the right words, but misery cloaked her voice and eyes.

Once they began their walk to the marshal's office, John considered voicing his thoughts while he still had Bert alone. "I appreciate the fact you didn't ask Evan to help you get away."

"I wouldn't put him in danger or take advantage of his affections."

"Then I'm going to ask you to continue by staying with Widow Bess. She'll be good to you."

"Ugly things could happen whether I'm here or at your ranch."

John stopped and studied her again. Unless he was a fool, she was more scared than trying to cover up a crime. He sure wished she didn't have such big brown eyes and smooth skin. Her lips reminded him of flower buds, and her hair ... "When are you going to trust anyone?"

Tears welled her eyes. "If I could, John Timmons, it would be you."

Now why did she have to say that?

CHAPTER 20

That afternoon Bert swept out the dining room of the hotel, wishing hard she had the means to leave town. But Marshal Culpepper told her she'd be thrown in jail if she so much as visited the outhouse without letting Widow Bess know. She'd rather be at the 5T helping Leah, but she didn't have a choice there either. In fact, nothing was her choice.

Make up a song. That would capture her worries. Except neither the words nor the joy of a tune comforted her.

Bess stepped from the kitchen, her swishing skirts announcing her arrival. She busied herself behind the registration desk that faced the dining area. Bert pretended to ignore her, when in fact the woman made her feel uncomfortable. Seemed like Bess saw right through her, and some things Bert chose to keep private. Maybe some of the girls who worked at the saloon had been hurt too.

Bess planted her hands on her ample hips and stared at Bert. "Can you cook?"

Bert swallowed a sigh. "I've done some cooking."

"Good. I need help tonight with supper. Need some chickens plucked for dumplings."

Bert nodded. She'd finished sweeping and could use anything to keep her mind from mulling over her predicament. "Whereabouts outside do I pluck them?"

"I'll show you. Come on. We can do it together."

Misery clung to Bert. She'd prefer to handle those chickens by herself. Talking to a woman who was friends with Marshal Culpepper didn't settle well.

"You look real happy about being here, Miss Ember." Bess chuckled.

"I appreciate what you're doing, ma'am."

"What is it then? I understand John needs you here to keep you safe and make sure you're not involved with cattle rustlers."

Bert stiffened. "Do I look like a cattle thief?"

"What about Oberlander's mare?"

One more person knew about her near-hanging. Bert shook her head. "It's all complicated. But I didn't steal the horse, and I had nothing to do with the cattle rustlers." That much was true.

Bess pointed toward the kitchen. Bert followed her out onto the back porch where the smell of blood from the chickens met her nostrils. Bess picked up a large bucket of steaming water and grabbed the two beheaded and gutted chickens by the feet and plunged them into the steaming water. Three other chickens draped over the porch rail, their guts spilling out onto the ground where a couple of cats enjoyed a feast.

"If you'll start pulling out those feathers, I can clean these others." Bess picked up a large knife and waved it. "Mind you get all of those pin feathers. Burn them out of their behinds. Make 'em as smooth as a baby's rear. Our guests deserve the best."

"Yes ma'am."

"This afternoon's prayer meetin'. We have it about four o'clock before supper guests, and the girls have to go to work."

Bert weighed the words, trying to figure out what she was supposed to do.

"I can't leave to go to church, so I hold it right here on the back porch with a couple of the girls from the saloon," Bess said. "That means we need to get these chickens done and the mess cleaned up. Hard to talk to Jesus when cats and birds are picking at the chicken guts. Hopefully a breeze will carry off the smell."

What had John gotten her into?

"Are you a believer?"

"In what?"

"God."

"Sorta," Bert said.

"Honey, you either believe in Jesus or you don't. Which is it?" Bess wielded the knife again, and with her size, Bert knew better than to rile her.

"Girl, don't look at me like I'm going to whittle on you. I simply asked a question."

"I went to church a couple of times with the Timmonses."

"Bein' in a building doesn't make you a believer."

What does? "Ma'am, I'm confused as to your meaning."

"Thought so." Bess split the chicken right down its belly. "From the talk around town, you need Jesus in your life. Especially if you're about to get hanged as a cattle thief."

Bert's eyes widened and her stomach churned. She yanked out a handful of feathers, burning her hands in the hot water.

"No need to fear dying if you have Jesus." Bess shooed away a cat that had gotten too close to the chickens.

Bert tossed a handful of feathers into a gathering pile on the ground. For sure she wasn't ready to die. "Where do I find Him?"

Bess stood and grinned. "Thought you'd never ask."

CHAPTER 21

John and Bob rode out of Rocky Falls with three of Oberlander's men and four volunteers, following up on a lead that Bess had heard the night before. One of the ranchers riding with them stated he'd seen Leon Wilson southeast of town near Sparky McBride's ranch, the High Plains. A deserted cattle camp bordered McBride's land and the 5T, and Leon could be holed up there. Farther south led to deep canyons, which was a smart place to keep stolen cattle and a prime area to hide from the law. But to get there, he'd have to cross the High Plains and a long strip of land owned by Victor Oberlander. Hard to drive cattle over either of those areas without being spotted.

Leon might be looking for work, or maybe he had plans to rustle cattle. In any event, he needed to be questioned, to find out where he'd been when the cattle turned up missing. Sure would be nice if Leon could supply more answers than Bert.

As the men made their way closer to the small deserted cabin, the sound of gurgling water from a white-churned mountain stream drowned out their arrival. The nine men spread out around a grove of juniper and pinion trees in case Leon decided to make a run for it.

"Don't open fire," Bob said for the third time. "Leon Wilson, you in there?"

John studied the brush leading up to the cabin. Broken sticks and boot prints showed two men had come and gone.

"We need to ask you a few questions," Bob continued. "No need to get alarmed. Just come out peaceful like so we can talk."

Empty moments ticked by.

The bubbling stream didn't miss a beat. Neither did the birds.

A hawk flew overhead, reminding John of Sage's red-tailed pet, a bird of prey that had saved her life before she and Parker were married. She and Parker's experience with a gang reminded John too much of what was happening around him.

An elk tramped through the woods.

A marmot dashed from the brush.

"I'm going in." John leaned on his saddle horn. "Don't think anyone's there anyway."

Bob raised his rifle to signal the others to keep John covered. "Leon's not happy with you. Be careful."

"Yer right about that." John recognized Leon's voice. "I ain't hangin' for something I didn't do."

Surprised to learn the man was actually inside the cabin, John made his way to the door. "Leon, we're not here for a hanging. You already know how I feel about upholding the law. Marshal Culpepper feels the same."

"He's right," Bob said. "All we want to do is ask a few questions."

"I'm no fool. Seems to me a marshal who's a undertaker is an enemy."

John dismounted and stole closer to the back of the small dilapidated cabin. No windows revealed his whereabouts, unless Leon could see through the cracks in the logs.

"Then let's talk about it," Bob said. "I'm not making an accusation."

"I'm supposed to believe you? Oberlander fired me, and his ranch hands are ridin' with you. Timmons is chapped 'cause I tried to hang that gal for stealing a horse."

"I'm here to uphold the law. Like John said." Bob's voice thundered above the sounds of nature.

"Bull. You won't take me alive."

The sound of gunfire pierced the air, and a sharp sting dug into John's upper left arm. He dove onto the ground while rifle fire exploded around him.

Bert had just removed an apron and draped a wet towel over the back porch rail, opposite of where the chickens had been cleaned, when Bess called for her. Every muscle in Bert's body ached for rest. She'd not slept last night or for the past several nights worrying about what was going on with Simon. Surely Bess didn't have another chore for her before the prayer meetin'. Any other time, Bert would have welcomed the work to occupy her thoughts, but not today.

Bess stood in the doorway leading inside to the hotel's kitchen. "Got some bad news. Thought you should know about John."

Bert's gaze flew to the woman's face. Her heart plummeted to her feet, shaking her body in the fall. "What about him?"

"He's been shot in the arm. Not bad, and the doc's treating him now."

Bert's stomach sickened. Too many scenarios raced through her mind. "How did it happen?"

"The marshal, John, and some deputized men rode out to find Leon Wilson. He refused to come out and opened fire. John was in the way."

Bert gasped. "But he's going to be fine?"

Bess nodded. "That's what one of the deputies said. We could walk down to Doc's and see for ourselves."

"Yes. I'm ready." The two hurried inside, through the kitchen, the entrance of the hotel, and on outside to the boardwalk. Bert's head whirled with the thought of John being wounded. "At least they got Leon."

Bess didn't answer right away, and Bert studied her as they kept up a good stride. "He's dead," the older woman said. "Hate to see a man end his life in violence, but the local ranchers can relax 'cause the cattle rustlin' is over."

Bert didn't know how to feel about Leon's death. Although he'd tried to hang her, she didn't want him dead. And she was relieved he'd stolen the cattle and not Simon and her brothers. "Did they find the cattle?"

"No, but a couple of the men are looking for them. He most likely wasn't working alone."

Bert refused to dwell on the missing cattle. The livestock would be found and returned … soon. Her thoughts focused on John and how badly he might be wounded. Had anyone ridden to tell Leah? She remembered the distraught look on Leah's face when John rode off with Marshal Culpepper and then with her this morning. And the tears. The poor woman would be devastated.

I'd kill anyone who tried to hurt one of my sons.

"If he was hurt real bad, I would have been told." Bess puffed at their fast pace. She pointed farther down the street. "The doc's house is on the edge of town."

They couldn't get there fast enough to suit Bert, and she wanted to run. Goodness, she'd had enough practice with that. *God, if You're really there, make sure John's all right.* Strange. She had no idea if anyone heard. Maybe some of Bess's talk had rubbed off.

CHAPTER 22

John hated the fuss being made over him. He'd been hurt worse wrestling with his brothers. But there he was with Doc Slader, and his left arm stinging worse than the time he broke it crossing the St. Vrain on slippery rocks. Evan could have bandaged him up just fine — just like he did for hurt animals on the ranch. "Aren't you done?"

Doc chuckled. "I don't want any infection setting in. Modern medicine says wounds must be cleaned. Unless you want to risk losing your arm."

"Very funny."

"You sure are in a good mood."

John closed his eyes. "A man's dead, and I'm not going to be much use to Bob or my brothers for a while."

"If I didn't know better, I'd swear I was talking to Parker."

John felt a smile tug at his lips. "Thanks. Those are hard boots to fill."

Doc wiped his hands on a blood-stained towel. "You're doing a fine job for this town. Always have. I think you were born all grown up."

He'd heard that before. Mama had always said his middle name was "responsibility." Actually his middle name was Parker.

A knock on the door seized John's attention. Must be Bob since he said he'd be right back.

"Come in," Doc said.

The door opened and Bert, pale and trembling, walked in with Widow Bess right behind her. John wanted to see the young woman ... and he didn't. She looked upset. Was it because Leon was dead? Or because he'd been hurt? "Evenin'."

Bert wrung her hands. "Are ... are you going to be all right?"

He forced another smile through the pain in his upper arm. "Sure. Isn't much at all. A scratch. But Bob insisted I see the doc."

She took a step closer. "Did anyone ride out to tell Miss Leah and your brothers?"

"No need. This is nothing. Really." Why didn't Bess say something? He nodded at the older woman. "I appreciate your keeping Bert busy and giving her a place to stay."

"You already told me those same words once today. Ah, Ember's a hard worker. I can use her help for as long as she needs food and a bed."

John realized Bert *could* return to the ranch. But he wasn't sure how he felt about the constant friction between him and Evan with her there. Grimacing, he chose to consider it all later when he was able to think straight.

"When do you think you'll be able to ride home?" Bert said.

"As soon as Doc's done."

"I'll hog-tie you to the bed if I have to." Doc's tone left no room for argument. "You're bone tired, and there's nothing going on that can't be taken care of in the morning."

"Yes sir." John felt like one of Doc's nine boys. He swung a look at Bert. Oh, he could get lost in those eyes. "Looks like I don't have much choice but to wait until morning to ride home."

"Supper and breakfast are on me," Bess said. "Whew, John. You gave us a scare."

"Gave myself one too." He tried to sit up. When the agony in his arm forced him back down, he mentally conceded to Doc's request. "Thought I was on the road to meet my Maker."

"I thought you said it was a scratch." Bess clicked her tongue. "By the way, one of Oberlander's men plans to stop at your ranch."

John didn't want Mama finding out about the shooting from anyone but himself. "Has he already left town?"

Bess nodded. "Right after he stopped into the saloon for a drink."

"Mama will be as flustered as a stirred up snake pit."

"Probably so," Bess said. "Speaking of our Maker. Bert and I were discussing that topic earlier. She's going to be a part of my prayer meetin' after bit."

Bert shifted from one foot to the other. John had heard of Bess's fire and brimstone sermons, and no doubt Bert had been the recipient of one.

"We ought to be going now," Bert said.

The girl could not learn how much her presence affected him.

"Reckon so," Bess said. "John, I'll send supper down to you."

"The Missus has plenty," Doc said.

"Supplying supper makes me feel like I'm helping the local law. And I'm having John's favorite—chicken 'n' dumplings."

"Thank you, ma'am." Would she send Bert? An awkward silence passed between him and Bert. How strange she didn't know what to say either.

"Glad you're not hurt too bad," she finally whispered, as though emotion had crawled up into her throat.

After all, he had saved her from a hanging. "This should take the blame off you."

"Hope so. What does this mean for—" Bert didn't finish her words, and John knew exactly what she was about to say.

"We'll talk later."

Bess chuckled. Doc Slader cleared his throat and joined in the laughter. What was so funny?

Leah realized when John was a baby that a mother had premonitions when something was wrong with her children. As sons were added to her family, she studied their eyes to see if they were sick, like a farmer observed the weather. The moments came and went with children—black eyes, skinned knees and elbows, bruised feelings, and an aching in her heart without visible proof that one of her sons was hurtin'. The feelings she had about Frank prior to his murder had been nightmares and headaches.

She was in the same place now.

Her head throbbed. And like a mother hen, she wanted her babies gathered close to her. Evan and Mark hadn't returned, and John was helping Marshal Culpepper find cattle thieves. They'd all been together early this morning, and now they were scattered.

Leah gathered up her skirts and marched out onto the front porch. Not a cloud in the sky to indicate a change in weather, to which she'd gladly attribute her peculiar feelings. Her stomach flitted as though a dozen caterpillars had burst into butterflies. Not good. Not good at all.

"Aaron," she called.

He stepped from the barn into scattered western sunlight. Goodness, he looked like his father. "Would you ride out and make sure Evan and Mark are all right?"

He cocked a hip. "John said I wasn't supposed to leave you and Davis alone."

"John's not here."

"Yes ma'am. What's wrong?"

"I hope nothing. But I have a feeling."

"Yes ma'am. I'll saddle up now."

She waited while he prepared his horse and then watched him ride away. Aaron understood her feelings, and they'd not failed her yet—unfortunately.

After dusk, Leah and Davis ate alone. Or rather, Davis ate and she listened for the sound of riders.

"If Bert were here, we'd not be lonesome," he said.

Leah missed Ember too and wished she was there. Although the confusion about the girl made Leah want to shake her. Could her sense of dread have something to do with the bit of a girl who had stolen all of their hearts? If only Ember—

The sound of a rider seized her attention. Leah scraped the chair leg across the wooden floor and walked to the door in an effort to hide her apprehension.

"Mama, John always says not to open up the house until you know who it is."

"John's not here." Hadn't she responded to Aaron the same way earlier in the evening?

She flung open the door to Victor Oberlander.

CHAPTER 23

Freedom. Sweet freedom.

Bert could run now. Nothing really stopped her.

John wouldn't be riding after anyone with his arm bandaged and the fear of Doc Slader breathing down his neck. She could make her way to Texas and hide out forever from Simon and her brothers. But here she was sitting on the back porch with Widow Bess and two other ladies who were dressed like they were ready for bed. They exposed parts of their delicate flesh that she'd never show. But they were friendly. One of them had a mole on her cheek — looked like it had been drawn on with a piece of coal.

"Did you girls read the book of James?" Bess used her ample lap as a table to place the Bible. Until a few weeks ago, Bert had no idea what a Bible was.

One of the women responded she had, but the one with the mole said she'd been too busy. She also said this time was prayer meetin', and Bess hadn't said a word about reading.

"You're right about prayin'. We'll talk about what James has to say a few verses at a time."

"Goodness, Miss Bess. We might be here all night, and I have work to do," said the mole woman.

"Just an hour, sweet girl. I'll read and then we can discuss our findings."

For the next hour, Bert actually paid attention to what Bess had to say. What she read made sense. If a person was to believe in God and all those things He said, then they needed to act like it. At least, that's the way Miss Bess explained what Mr. James had written.

Leah acted like a real believer. So did her sons. They didn't swear and try to hurt each other. She was used to plain mean and spiteful like her brothers and pa. Except Gideon. She sure missed him—the sparkle in his earth-colored eyes and the way his lips turned up when he smiled. The goodness in him was what killed him. If he hadn't tried to help her, he'd be alive today.

Did she carry something inside her that brought evil to others? She wanted to believe it was another one of Simon's lies.

"The point of what James is telling us is we need to back up our faith with good works. Like showing folks we're believers without telling them. They should be able to tell we love Jesus just by listening and watching us." Bess smiled, and for a moment Bert could see the young girl in her. "Think of it this way. We can't cook on a cold stove. We fill it up with wood, drop in some kindling, light a fire, and wait for it to get hot. We don't have to ask if the stove's fit for cookin'; we just know it."

Maybe if Bert's life had been filled with people who cooked on a hot stove, she'd not be in such a fix today.

Bess finished with a prayer, and Bert did her best to pay attention. But it was hard, especially when she had to be thinking how to get away from Rocky Falls. She made her way back to the kitchen for her next job.

"Ember, I'd like for you to take John his supper."

Looks like she'd be leaving later on tonight than what she intended.

John's stomach had growled for most of the afternoon, and as much as he wanted supper, he fretted over who would bring it. Widow Bess suited him fine. He was becoming as fickle as a woman. Staring into Bert's eyes would be his demise. Besides, more important matters needed his attention. For starters, where were the stolen cattle? Leon must have hid them near the cattle camp, and John could have found them if not for the bullet ripping off a piece of his arm. Leon couldn't have stolen the livestock and driven them somewhere alone. So who'd joined up with him? The two ranch hands who'd conspired with Leon to hang Bert rode with the posse.

Tomorrow the pain in his arm would subside, and he'd be useful ... but for what?

Who am I kidding? The only role he'd be playing as deputy amounted to paperwork. He'd rather ride back home and see what he could do there. Horses needed to be shod. The barn needed some loose boards nailed down—and the repairs only took one hand. He could ride out looking for strays. Yes, he had plenty to do at home. Unless Bob needed him to let ranchers know Leon had been found, and hopefully the rustled cattle would turn up.

When thinking about Mama's reaction to his arm, he realized the importance of him telling her. Ever since Pa died, she fretted every bump, bruise, and potential bully.

John glanced out the window of his room. Darkness had set in about thirty minutes ago. Mrs. Slader had lit the lantern so he didn't lie there like a corpse. He was such a miserable and angry creature, flat on his back and waiting for his supper. Bess probably had a dining room full of customers while his stomach protested and the gash in his arm hurt like ...

If he didn't know better, he'd swear self-pity had set in. Which sounded as bad as an infection.

But he knew the problem and it had nothing to do with the burning in his arm. A knock at the door interrupted his woebegone thinking.

"Come in."

The door slowly opened, and there before him stood the object of most of his turmoil.

John observed Bert holding a cloth-covered plateful of what his nose detected as chicken 'n' dumplings, and it shook like it was alive. If she didn't set the plate down soon, she was going to drop his food. He hadn't seen her so nervous since the night of the family meetin', after they learned she was a girl. The smell of chicken 'n' dumplings caused his stomach to complain. Of course, Bert being there made the moment uncomfortable— and well, pleasant. She couldn't be mixed up in this rustlin'.

"Thanks for bringing me supper. Why don't you put it on the table here by the lantern?"

She obliged and reached inside her dress pocket for a fork and spoon. "You're welcome."

"Widow Bess is a good woman." He took the utensils with his right hand. She handed him a blue checkered cloth, but when he attempted to spread it over the quilt, she took the cloth and smoothed it over him. Her touch felt strangely intimate. Now *he* was shaking. "Were you busy this afternoon?"

"Yes. Bess had lots of chores, but she's the caring type. Kind … and blunt."

He chuckled and took a bite of a tender dumpling. "She doesn't hold back anything. How was prayer meetin'?" The food melted in his mouth. Oh, these were good.

"Interesting."

He grinned but she didn't appear to calm down in the least. "Did she do the prayin'?"

"A lot at the end. She talked about a passage in James."

John studied her. Her gaze darted like a scared animal. "Why don't you sit down and tell me what's bothering you?"

She stiffened. "Nothing."

Her speech had improved. When Bert first came, her grammar needed help. That must be what Mama was doing when they went to bed early.

"I can't remember if you heard what happened. But it looks like Leon's the one who's been rustling cattle, and now he's gone." John paused. "I don't relish the idea of any man dying, especially the way he did. He lived hard and died hard. My point is your name will be cleared as soon as the cattle are found along with whoever was working with him."

She nodded and wrung her hands in her lap. "I'm relieved."

"I suppose I can take you back to the ranch." He hadn't resolved the issue of how he and Evan could be civil to each other with her there. "Unless you'd rather work for Bess and live here in town."

"Living in town might be easier for all of us." She stood. "I'll be going now."

"So soon? I'm not running you off. You could wait until I'm finished and take the plate back with you."

"With your wounded arm, you need your rest."

"I'm fine, and rest to me is anything that doesn't require work."

Bert looked at everything in the room but him. "Bess has things for me to do."

"I see. Thanks for bringing me supper. Tell Bess the chicken 'n' dumplin's were tasty."

"I'll pass it on." She grasped the doorknob. "I hope you heal fast. In case I've never thanked you proper, I'm doing so now. You saved my life and introduced me to your family. Miss Leah and your brothers are wonderful. I'll never forget any of you. It's been like a real family."

"You're ... unforgettable too." He allowed his mind to trail backward to the moment on the riverbank when he learned she was a girl.

She smiled a good-bye, and in the lantern light playing off the walls, she looked sweet, pretty. Her light brown hair reminded him of fresh honey, and she wore a green dress no doubt borrowed from one of Bess's girls. But decent in its ... coverage. He remembered when Sage was shot, and Bess found a dress for her. Five years, and a lot of history was repeating itself. Except this time he and Bert wrestled with their feelings for each other, not Uncle Parker and Aunt Sage.

"If you're living at the hotel, I'll have to bring Pa's fiddle for you to play and sing."

She glanced back from the doorway, with sadness clearly spreading over her face. "You're a good man, John Timmons."

Once the door closed, John lowered the wick until the light disappeared. Weariness slammed against his eyelids. The past two days had kept him in the saddle and craving a bed. For sure he'd sleep past dawn and give his arm a chance to heal. He yawned, feeling his whole body give in to sleep.

Bert . . . she hadn't wanted to be here, but Bess had given her the food to deliver. Yet she'd had a rough time saying good-bye tonight and mustering the words to say thanks for a deed she'd already thanked him for.

John's eyes flew open in the darkness. Bert had been telling him good-bye, not good night. His pint-size imp planned to light out of here. He threw back the thin quilt covering him and reached for his britches in the dark.

Doggone her hide. That woman was more trouble than a pack of coyotes in a chicken house. He fumbled with the buttons on his shirt and did a slow job of putting on his boots with one hand. What was she running from? Obviously she hadn't figured out he could help her—wanted to help her. This time when he found her, he'd make sure she told him the truth. Every word of it.

Snatching up his rifle, he quietly opened the door. Doc Slader sat in a chair in the parlor reading a thick-bound book. Most likely something about medicine. His wife claimed he read those books more than the Bible. Doc glanced up; his spectacles perched on his nose like a bird on a fence post.

"John Timmons, where are you going?"

Caught. "Sorry, Doc. A matter has come to my attention, and I need to handle it."

"It can wait till morning."

John wasn't one of his nine boys. "No, it won't."

Doc wagged a finger at him. "Go on then. But when you take to bleeding again, you're going to get a lecture so bad that you'll wish I'd taken you behind the woodshed."

"Yes sir."

"I hope the little lady is worth the delay in your arm healing."

"I—"

Doc waved him away. "As I said, you and Parker are cut from the same tough piece of leather. Get your courtin' done and get back here, or I'm coming down to Bess's after you."

Courtin'. He was beginning to despise that word.

CHAPTER 24

"M r. Oberlander." Leah sized up the lines fanning from the man's eyes, and fear rippled through her heart. "Won't you come in?"

"Evening, Leah." He stepped inside, hat in hand. "Are the other boys here?"

"Only Davis. What's wrong?" She took a breath to gain control. "Please, sit down." She motioned to a chair at the table. "This is about John, isn't it?"

"Yes ma'am. That's why I'm here. But he's going to be all right."

She touched her chest as though she could slow her heart's incessant beating. "I've had a bad feeling all day."

"I'm sure it's difficult having him work as a deputy during hard times. One of my hands who rode with John and Marshal Culpepper returned a bit ago, and I thought you should be aware of what happened."

She trembled. "Tell me, Victor. All I can think about is when Frank was shot."

"The posse found Leon Wilson in an old cabin. From what my ranch hand said, there were nine men who surrounded the place. John attempted to go in after Leon, but he was shot in the arm—just a flesh wound. Nothing serious." Victor touched her shoulders. "He's all right. Doc Slader treated him and thought it best for John to spend the night at his home. Mind you, Miss Leah, your son wanted to ride back tonight, but Doc wanted to keep an eye on him."

Leah nodded, biting into her lower lip to keep from crying. "Thank God, he's all right."

"John's a strong young man. My hand said he was attempting to bring Leon in for questioning without using force."

She sniffed. "My son, the hero."

"Yes ma'am." Victor looked around. "Where are the other boys?"

"Out checking on the cattle. I've been expecting them."

"If you don't mind, I'd like to stay until they get here."

She smiled and let relief flow through her. "I appreciate your kindness. Excuse my poor manners. Can I get you something?"

"I'm fine. I'll just sit here with Davis until your sons ride in."

For once Leah was glad to have Victor Oberlander for company.

John didn't realize how much his left arm hurt until he stepped out onto the dark street and attempted to take his usual stride toward the hotel. The laughter of those who chose to solve life's problems with whiskey and gambling, and in the arms of paid women, resounded from the saloon. His father had used the diversion of strong drink and gambling as an ointment from Civil War memories. But he'd been faithful to his wife. Because of Frank Timmons's weakness, John kept a watchful eye on his brothers. They remembered how their father coped with his demons, and John didn't want them indulging in the same.

He moaned with the sharp stab of pain, a reminder of what had happened to him in an effort to question Leon. The man's body had reeked of alcohol. If he'd not been drinking, maybe he would have listened to Bob. Instead he lay dead. Sad to see a man's life wasted. Made him more determined to find out who was working with him.

But what about Bert? At times John feared she'd end up the same way. So much he didn't know. What he did know was she'd been hurt and was scared. She had a kind heart and didn't mind work ... Music seemed to be a part of her, like a fire inside her. He marveled at the way she could pick up the fiddle and play like it was second nature. And when she sang, her clear voice reminded him of an angel.

The day would come when he'd be able to say her real name, but not yet. Right now he had to stop her from running again.

The reality of her leaving hit him in the gut, and anger seemed to make the throb in his arm hurt even more. Were his actions tonight merely concern for a lost and lonely girl? Or was it a nagging suspicion that she was playing some kind of a game, and her sweetness was a cover-up for something else? He stomped onto the boardwalk in front of the hotel with the awareness that fury didn't solve a thing. Easier to give out advice than it was to follow it.

He stepped inside and glanced about, hoping to see Bert working. Bess bustled about the dining area, smoothing out tablecloths and placing silverware to the right and left of where a plate would be set. She glanced toward the door at him. If her glare had been a bayonet, he'd have been a dead man.

"What are you doing out of bed?" Her tone should have startled him, but he was a man on a mission.

"I need to see Bert."

"She's in bed. I worked her pretty hard today."

"Check on her for me, will you? If she's there, ask her to meet me out here."

"What do you mean 'if'? I saw her go to bed."

John had no intention of explaining the situation to Bess. "I want to make sure she's all right."

Bess shook her head and disappeared into the kitchen. A few minutes later she approached him with quickness in her step. Was that a new line on her face?

"John, she's not here. I'm sorry. No one saw her leave. She must have climbed out the window."

"Thanks. I'll see if I can find her. She couldn't have gone far on foot."

Bess frowned. "Unless she stole a horse."

A queasy sensation in his stomach once more churned doubt about the girl. "Let's hope not, but I'll start at the livery."

John hurried toward the livery, not knowing if he wanted to find her there. Sure would reinforce the accusations flying around if she was caught with a horse. A stable boy sat by a bale of hay reading a dime novel by lantern light.

"Anyone show up tonight wanting a horse?"

The boy's head jerked to attention. He must have been knee-deep into the story. "No sir. Haven't seen anyone."

"Are all of your horses here?"

Confusion etched into his young face. "I reckon. Would you like for me to check, Mr. Timmons?"

"I'd appreciate it."

The boy rushed to his feet, novel in one hand and a lantern in the other. "They're all here," he said from the back of the livery.

"Thanks." John glanced out into the street, realizing Bert could have taken only one way out of town. And she was on foot. "I'll take my horse. Can you saddle it for me? My arm is paining me a bit."

"Yes sir. I heard you were shot while going after cattle rustlers." Already the boy had made his way to John's gelding in a rear stall.

"Yeah, got in the way of a bullet."

A few moments later, the boy led the horse to John. He tossed him a nickel and swung up into the saddle as awkward as a city slicker. A deep groan escaped his lips, and he felt embarrassed. Grown men, especially those who uphold the law, were supposed to be tough.

Touching his heels to the gelding's flanks, he set his sights on finding one girl on a dark road.

Lord, I need help. Where would she have headed?

When he found her, they were going to finish the discussion they should have finished the day he brought her home.

CHAPTER 25

Bert followed the road out of Rocky Falls southeast in the direction of Denver. Ordinarily, she'd cut across fields and keep moving, but no one would be looking for her tonight. The new moon lit a faint silvery trail and stars dotted the clear night. As much as she hated that John had been wounded, the situation allowed her to leave town undetected.

Still, she hurried. The five-dollar gold piece tucked into her britches would have to be rationed out if she were to make it to Denver and then on to Texas. She'd run for six months before, and she could walk even longer to keep all of the Timmonses safe.

She wore the same clothes she'd worn the day Leon tried to hang her, except they were clean. But she'd remember wearing a dress—and so much more.

The terrain heading to Denver was rolling, easy to walk, not like heading north into the foothills and then the mountains. However, she fretted about taking the flatlands, even though they were easier to walk; folks could see a lone figure for miles on those stretches.

Heading west and north had its own share of danger. The mountains offered a reprieve from anyone trailing her, but the ability to hide came with a price. Narrow, rocky trails and dangerous ledges could send her to her death. And the higher she climbed, the more she risked colder temperatures. She'd made the right decision by heading south. Maybe in Denver she'd find work—change her name so Simon wouldn't be able to find her. And then on to Texas.

Better yet, maybe he'd given up trying to find her. Figured she wasn't worth it. He'd never believe she wanted to return Oberlander's mare. Instead he'd think she rode the horse to wherever she was going.

A plan ... she needed a better plan and needed to stick to it.

Bert yawned. The chores from today had made her more tired than usual. She'd sleep at daylight until about noon before moving on. Already loneliness had crept inside, leaving her cold and empty. The sound of hoofbeats seized her attention. She swung around, realizing she didn't have a weapon and she couldn't see well in the dark.

"Bert, you have become worse than a case of chiggers."

John. Defeat caused tears to form in her eyes. Why wouldn't he leave her alone? She turned back around and continued to walk.

"You can keep on walking, but I'm riding beside you."

"Please leave me alone. I don't know how else to make you see that it's better this way."

"Try me. I might understand."

She read the hopeful lift in his voice. "There is nothing I can do."

"Why not tell me the truth about yourself?"

Her shoulders slumped as the impossibility of what he asked coursed through her weary body.

"Well?"

"I'd be better off if you'd shoot me right now."

"That's rather pathetic for a gal with spunk."

"The spunk's all gone. Not so sure I ever had any."

"I think you're feeling sorry for yourself."

"And what if I am?"

"It doesn't solve anything, Ember."

Ember. He'd not used her given name before. "I've told you all I can. I'm not running from the law or a husband."

"Fine."

What did he mean by that? "So you're letting me go?"

"Nope. Are you tired of walking yet?"

"I'm not tired at all."

"How about running?"

She was plenty tired of sores on her feet and a hungry belly, but she'd not admit it. "For a man who has a ranch as big as yours, you sure are hurtin' for money to chase me down for less than one hundred dollars."

"It's not the money."

First he called her Ember, then he told her it wasn't the money. "Then what is it?"

"A woman who needs help."

Now he called her a woman. "I can manage on my own."

"If I can catch you, so can whoever is after you."

John was right, but she'd not give him the satisfaction of confirming it. "I'm not one of your brothers for you to look after."

He chuckled. "I've noticed. You've noticed me too. That's why we fuss so much."

Bert's heart leaped. Had she heard right? "I have no idea what you're talking about."

"Yes, you do. Remember the time I reached for the basket of peas and our fingers touched? We both felt a jolt of lightning then."

"John, I'm not good for you."

"You haven't convinced me about that. Climb up behind me and let's get back to town. I'm hurtin' and you need sleep. I want to know the truth, but I'm too tired to get it out of you. We'll sort this out in the morning." He sighed, and she assumed he was talking out of his head. "We can start by being friends and planting a seed of trust."

She knew exactly what he meant, and a part of her really wanted what he offered. "You were right the first time you sized me up. I'm trouble."

"Nothing new there."

Bert allowed the quiet sounds of night to keep her company while she pondered what to say. John deserved to know what he was up against in order to protect those he loved. Yet the thought of reaching out and grasping a day brimming with hope sounded nearly impossible. And she wanted to believe John could stop Simon, but John was good and cared about folks. Simon cared about no one but himself. "These men are not afraid to use their guns. And I'm worried about what they might do to you or your family."

"We can talk about all of it."

If only she could believe for just a little while—like a child's fantasy where the world was perfect. Yet in the darkness with the bright stars and the sliver of a moon, she'd believe until sunlight brought her back to reality. "What about Evan?"

"We'll work it out."

Bert stopped and reached for the saddle, knowing he couldn't help her up with his wounded arm. "I don't understand any of this."

"Neither do I."

Somehow his admission comforted her, and she allowed herself to lean slightly closer into him. If only for tonight.

John laughed into the black corners of his room at Doc Slader's home. When he'd returned from chasing down Bert and delivering her back to Bess, the man was asleep in his chair with a book on his lap. The moment the door closed behind him, Doc jumped and snorted. He called every one of his nine sons' names, demanding what was going on.

"It's me, John Timmons," he said. "I'm back and going to finish the night here."

"Night, my eye. It's nearly dawn."

"Sorry to waken you."

"That's all right. Are you bleedin'?"

John's bandage was not spotted with fresh blood, but it sure felt like someone had lit a match to it. "No sir."

"Do you need a cup of yarrow tea for the pain?"

John wasn't about to bother a man who needed to be in bed. Besides, the pain had grown worse because of his insistence on going after Bert. "No sir. I'll be fine."

"I know better. But suit yourself."

John bid him good night and made his way into the room that doubled as a patient and guest room. He figured tonight he was both. He laid down, too exhausted to sleep. His mind focused on the shooting and every detail surrounding the unfortunate circumstances that left Leon Wilson in a pool of blood. The posse reacted with no sense at all once John was hit. And yet the idea that Leon had stolen cattle on his own, especially over one hundred head, didn't seem credible. He lacked the intelligence to put together a clever plan—no disrespect for the man's intelligence intended. Leon had been working with someone, but who? And the "who" was holed up somewhere with stolen cattle.

The scene just prior to the shooting played out before him. John had crept behind the small cabin, and Leon shot him from inside. *Whoa.* How did Leon know where he was standing when a window didn't exist in the cabin? Through the cabin's cracks? Or a lucky shot? Or was a second man involved? John considered the direction of the weapon in relation to where he'd been wounded. The bullet had entered the back of his upper left arm and gone out the other side. *Impossible for Leon.* Why hadn't he realized this sooner? The shooter had to come from the grove of trees behind the men. He needed to tell Bob, and he wasn't going to wait until morning.

Pulling himself from the bed, he once more fought with his boots while his arm ached. He touched it and realized the wetness on his fingers was blood. He could only imagine Doc's lecture.

CHAPTER 26

The following day, John didn't waken until nearly noon. For certain, he must have been beaten and left for dead, because every muscle in his body screamed for mercy, and his arm throbbed every time his heart beat. For once he wished he was a drinking man so he could allow the whiskey to numb him all over. Coward's way out, but oh so tempting.

Last night and early this morning clearly indicated John's stupidity. When he returned from talking to Bob Culpepper and crept inside Doc's house, he was certain the family would be asleep. Instead Doc was again snoozing in his chair by a dim lantern. John thought he'd gotten by with his second exit of the evening, but when he turned the doorknob to the bedroom, Doc startled. He lectured him for nearly fifteen minutes.

"John, do you have scrambled eggs for brains?" Doc struggled to his feet. "Look at that arm. I can tell from here it's bleeding again." The words of wisdom flowed freely, with John being compared to a mule, his Uncle Parker, and a few animals' posteriors.

With fresh bandages, Doc ordered him to bed with the threat of hog-tying him there. Maybe John wouldn't have felt so bad this morning if he'd listened last night. But if he hadn't gone after Bert, she'd have been long gone by now. He'd come as close as a man could to telling her how he felt. When this cattle rustlin' business was over, he and Bert had plenty to talk about.

John had needed to tell Bob what he'd surmised about the shooting. Bob hadn't appreciated being wakened before dawn until John explained why he'd come.

" … So Leon couldn't have shot you. Another man in the woods behind us had to have pulled the trigger. Any idea who?"

"Not at all. Thought you might have an answer. The shooter must have wanted Leon dead. Which leads me to believe the cattle rustlin' isn't over yet."

"You're probably right. Glad I wired Denver for help." Bob rubbed his face and yawned. "I'm up now. Guess I'll get an early start on the day." He peered at John's arm. "You're bleeding."

John cringed. "Figured so."

"Best get back to Doc Slader. He won't be happy about you slipping off."

Again.

All of the thoughts swirling around in John's head brought him back to the present. He'd wasted daylight sleeping, and with all of the happenings in the last day—or did staying up all night mean two days? Didn't matter, he had work to do. Mama would be worried sick about him, and he had to let her know he was fine. Then there was Bert. And Evan.

The door opened before he had a chance to swing his legs onto the wooden floor. Mama stepped in with Victor Oberlander. Seeing those two together changed his mood from anxious to surly, but he vowed not to show it.

Mama rushed to his side with tears spilling over her cheeks. "I'm fine, Mama. Don't get yourself all worked up over nothing."

Her lips quivered. "You were shot. Could have been killed."

"But I wasn't. I knew I should have ridden home last night."

"Nonsense, but I'm here to take you home now. Victor was kind enough to drive me here in his wagon. We have blankets in the back so you'll be comfortable."

We have blankets? John bit back his first initial response. "I'm not ready to go home yet."

"Why?" She startled. "I can take care of you."

"I have a few things to talk over with Bob, then I'll ride home. Is everything at the ranch all right?"

She nodded, while another tear fell. He hated to see her cry. "The boys are working close to home today."

John glanced up at Mr. Oberlander. "Thank you, sir, for bringing Mama into town. I'm sorry I won't be joining you. But I promise I'll be home this evenin'."

"We can wait."

Between his battered body and a hundred other pressing matters, John was about to forget his manners. He took in a deep breath.

"Are you in pain?" Mama touched his cheek.

"Of course not. But I have matters to tend to."

Mama lifted her chin. "Victor said we'd wait, and that's exactly what we'll do."

John believed if he were thirty years old, his mama would still think she could treat him like a boy.

"I have to talk to Bob. I'm also expecting a telegram, and I have to check on Bert at the hotel."

"Ember. Her name is Ember. I can call on her while you're taking care of other things."

No point in arguing. Her mind was set. "I need for you to step out so I can get dressed."

"By yourself? How can you manage?"

He shook his head and realized the motion made it hurt worse. "I learned how to dress myself a long time ago. Nothing's changed."

Leah's shoes tapped in rhythm against the boardwalk all the way to the hotel. While she pacified John's absurd whim to talk to Bob, she'd check on Ember and make sure the girl was all right. Bess would take good care of her, and staying at the hotel where John and Evan wouldn't see her every day made sense. But Leah longed for the girl — her sweet temperament and gentle ways with all of them. Davis loved her stories, and the whole family adored her singing and playing. Leah loved her despite all the problems and rough waters between John and Evan. The caring had nothing to do with pity but everything to do with the pain in Ember's eyes and the deep need for love.

The first glimpse of John this afternoon had brought back the nightmare of what happened to his father. Last night Victor had insisted John would be fine, even offered to check on him and report promptly to her. But she had to see for herself. Leah swallowed a lump of emotion. She was made of stronger earth than this.

She saw the glossy tolerance of pain in John's eyes. Doc Slader said he'd been traipsing around all night and not getting the rest he needed. The wound had taken to bleeding again, which required more bandaging. Leah trusted Doc and the herbs and medicines he prescribed, but John needed his mama, and she was going to make sure he healed proper. While he rested in her care, she'd talk to him about tossing that deputy job like sour milk. She'd never approved. Outlaws had killed his father, endangered Parker and Sage, and now this. About time someone listened to her.

Leah walked into the hotel and immediately saw Ember sweeping the floor. The girl leaned the broom against the wall and rushed into Leah's arms. And Leah welcomed her. They both clung to each other as though they hadn't seen each other for years.

"You know about John?" Ember said, stepping back from Leah and wiping the wetness from her cheeks.

Leah pressed her lips together and nodded. "I came to take him home where he belongs.

"Is he better this morning?"

"Looks to me like his arm is hurting him and he's incredibly tired."

"He should have stayed at Doc's last night instead of—"

So John was with Ember. Goodness, do I want to know more?

"Doc said he didn't get much sleep. But he'll rest at home. However, I hear he's not a good patient."

"I suppose not. Do you have any help in gettin' him to the ranch?"

"Victor Oberlander drove me in. In fact he was the one who told me last night about John being shot." Leah took a breath. Exhaustion had settled on her too. "Right now Victor is getting supplies at the general store."

"Are the other boys all right?"

Is she concerned about Evan? "They're all worried about John. None were too happy about Victor driving me into town, but his actions were simply a neighborly gesture."

"Miss Leah, I think he likes you."

Leah frowned. "Neighbor to neighbor, that's all. I'd have been in town sooner, but Davis got sick in the middle of the night and didn't stop until mid-morning."

"I'm so sorry." Ember shook her head. "If only I could help."

"Taking care of sick children is one of those parts of motherhood. Davis seemed to be fine when I left. I hope the other boys don't get it, especially with John needing my attention." She paused and touched Ember's face. "Sweet girl, do you want to come back too?"

A single tear slipped from her eye. "It's best I stay here with Bess. She has a job for me, and I can pay John back with my earnings."

"But I missed you as soon as you left."

"Miss Leah, neither you nor I want John and Evan fussin' over me. This is better."

"Doesn't mean I like the arrangement."

"Why must men be so difficult?"

"I have no idea," Leah said. "But they certainly are a handful."

Bess called out a greeting. "Do you have time for some fresh coffee? No charge."

"No, thank you. I need to hurry back to Doc Slader's and get John home. But it smells good. Is that potatoes and ham?"

Bess beamed, her face red from being in the hot kitchen. "Your nose tells you right. Is John better?"

"He's a bit disagreeable."

Bess laughed. "He'll be up and about in no time. I want to thank you for sending Ember my way. My, but she's a hard worker."

Leah wrapped her arm around Ember's waist. "She's a fine one. Don't be motherin' her too much. I'm rather partial to her."

Another tear slipped down Ember's cheek. Hadn't anyone ever told her how special she was?

CHAPTER 27

A week had slipped by since John was shot, and Bert thought about him every moment of the day. The words he'd spoken when he chased her down that night repeated in her mind. They had feelings for each other, and the thought warmed her and alarmed her at the same time. He said the situation with Evan would work out. But what about Simon? Dwelling on how her heart swelled with the memories marked a foolish road. She and John could never be together.

Bert hurried down the street to get the flour and sugar Bess needed from the General Store before the afternoon cooking and baking began. She'd struggled with Leah's invitation to live at the ranch again. The woman knew the source of problems between John and Evan, and yet she wanted Bert at the ranch. How very dear of Leah. If Bert was ever to escape Simon, she'd welcome a home and a family. She'd tell her husband and her children every day how much she loved them.

A dream ... how sweet a life with John would be. Ah, the child in her still lived in a fantasy world.

Bert stared up at the sun directly overhead and shielded her eyes beneath her bonnet. The brilliant light blinded her, but she liked the heat. She'd spent most of her life cold, and the hot days of summer had quickly become her favorite.

"Excuse me, Miss," a man said.

Bert gasped and held her breath. The sound of the familiar voice made her dizzy with terror. She whirled around. *Simon!*

"I bet you didn't think you'd see me today."

Her chest hurt from its rapid pounding. "What do you want from me?"

He leaned on one leg. "The twenty dollars you took and my mare. A few other things would be nice." He sneered.

"You stole the horse," she said, too frightened to speak above a whisper. "I'll get the money back to you."

"I've added interest." His gold-brown eyes glared, reminding her of a mountain cat.

"Leave me be, Simon. Please."

"You owe me, little sister. And I've been watching you."

An eerie chill crept up her neck. His threats had haunted her for six months. She wanted to get as far away from him as possible. She wanted to scream. But would anyone help her escape her cruel brother? If only she could gather the courage to bury her fists into his callused flesh.

He was still her brother. Gideon had said families stick together 'cause they had no one else. But now she had the Timmonses, Bess, even Marshal Culpepper, and Doc Slader. They'd been kind, caring.

Simon laughed. "Since you don't have anything to say, let me tell you what you're going to do."

"No." Her voice sounded flat and ragged, but she'd not be bullied. Not this time. "I will not help you steal or set up someone to kill."

"Yes, you will. If you refuse me, I'll make sure John Timmons and his family are laid in a pool of blood at your feet. I shot him once, and the next time my bullet will take off his head. And do you really want to know what I'd do to his mother and that old woman at the hotel?"

Bert trembled. She fought the dizziness threatening to overcome her and the sudden throbbing in her temples. "No," she whispered.

"No, you aren't going to do what I say? Or no, you wanna see your new friends dead?"

She didn't have a choice ... None at all. "What do you want?"

"I'll be in touch. Don't try runnin' or I'll leave a trail of blood behind you."

"Why?" she said. "Even before I ran off, you did this to me."

Simon's loathing stare chilled her. "We were happy until you came along. You killed the only two good people in this lousy world—Ma and Gideon. You'll pay until the day you die."

Simon turned and walked toward the hotel and saloon, his stride long and determined. No doubt he'd soon be drinking and mean as ever. Acid rose in her throat. Memories from the past darted in and out of her mind. She needed help. But who?

Gideon had told her she was a good girl; that it was Simon's way of bullying her. But at times she wondered if Simon was right.

J ohn's first day back in Rocky Falls after letting his mother wait on him for a week, and already he faced bad news. Stepping into the marshal's office, he tossed a telegram onto Bob's desk. "I'm ready to ride to Denver and give my uncle a piece of my mind—a big piece."

Bob glanced up and his spectacles dropped onto the desk. "Good to see you too. I take it your mama cut you loose."

"Very funny." The news of Mama's march into town like a military general must have spread like wildfire. It would take a long time to live this one down. "I'd have been here sooner, but work at the ranch kept me busy."

Bob chuckled. "I'm sure that was the reason. What's going on? You're red from the neck up."

John slumped onto a chair across from Bob. Nothing seemed to go right lately, and this was proof of one more thing. "Read the telegram from Uncle Parker. I'm hoping he's not serious."

Bob perched his spectacles on his nose and unfolded the piece of paper. "Sending US Marshal to help with cattle rustlers. *Stop*. Wirt Zimmerman is on his way. *Stop*." He lifted his bushy eyebrows. "Wirt Zimmerman? That's the same US Marshal who was sent to help us five years ago. He was greener than grass."

"My point." John sensed his annoyance seeping through the pores of his skin. "He didn't know anything about tracking or bringing in outlaws. In fact, he was quite a dandy." He started to mention Wirt had written his mother for two years afterward, but thought better of it.

"I don't think Parker is teasing."

John blew out a sigh. "Trouble is, I don't think he is either. Is Rocky Falls training ground for US Marshals?"

"I bet he's changed," Bob said. "Wirt's had five years of experience since he last set foot in our town. Parker cares too much for the people here to send grief upon us."

"Wirt could have had five years to become more arrogant. We'd be better off to handle things ourselves."

Bob handed the telegram back to John. "But we haven't. That's why we need help. Evan came in to see me a couple of days ago."

John frowned. "He was supposed to be staying at the cattle camp. What did he want?"

"He wanted me to deputize him."

John's stomach did a flip. "He's just a boy."

"Ah, you were eighteen when we went after the McCaw gang, and soon after, Parker deputized you."

Evan didn't have the maturity at eighteen that John had back then. "What did you tell him?"

"Told him he needed to be twenty. Of course he pointed out you were eighteen when you took an oath to uphold the law." Bob leaned across the desk. "I told him Colorado's laws have changed."

John forced a grin. "Thanks. I appreciate it." He rested against the back of the chair. "I need to get home after I check to see if Oberlander has any more missing cattle. And I need time to figure out what I'm going to say to Wirt after five years."

"If he rides up all decked out like the man we remember, we'll tell him we don't need him."

Best news John had heard all day. "Well, I'll be headin' back soon. Anything you need?"

"Just a report from Oberlander. Sure hope his men have located their cattle. But I'm sure he'd have contacted me if that were the case."

"Makes me wonder when the rustlers will strike again."

Bob rubbed his face. "Does look like we're in for more stealing."

"And why didn't the shooter who grazed my arm finish me off?"

Bob appeared to study John's face. "Good question. And I don't have an answer."

"I can't believe it was a lucky miss." John stood and refused to think about Bert and her possible involvement. No, he refused to give in to his own suspicions.

CHAPTER 28

All Bert could think about was her morning's encounter with Simon. She tried to push it from her mind, knowing she couldn't do a thing about his demands, but the nightmare still plagued her. The old sensation of a heavy weight bearing down on her shoulders had returned.

Late in the afternoon, she helped Bess roll out pie dough for berry and custard pies. Her thoughts continued to race about Simon ... what he could do ... what he'd planned for her.

Bess was in her preachin' mood, at least that's what Bert called it. And she did attempt to pay attention, if for no more reason than the things about God were important to the Timmonses and Miss Bess. But Bert's problems were far more serious than what any God could handle. God would have to write a new book just for her.

"I sure like the Proverbs," Bess said, breaking eggs into a bowl.

"Why?" Bert measured sugar into a cup and poured it into Bess's bowl.

"It's filled with wise sayings telling us how to live. I like the no-nonsense language. It's blunt. Just the way I am. One says there's a friend who sticks closer than a brother, a brother who loves you no matter what you've done or will do."

Gideon's words repeated in Bert's mind. He didn't believe in God. He said a person lived and died. Nothing more. Whom did she believe? Gideon had been the only one who cared for her, the only brother who'd protected her.

"What if you have a brother, a good brother, who isn't God-fearin'?"

"Same thing. God sticks close to those who trust Him. Better than a brother, who might be good or bad. But what the writer is talking about is a good brother."

Could Gideon have been wrong? Bert let the words swim through her mind. She needed a friend she could trust, someone who'd not abandon her when the going got hard. He'd not be afraid of Simon, and he'd be bigger and more powerful.

"What if I wanted this friend?"

"God's more than that, but you have to ask Him. He doesn't come without an invitation."

Bert carried those words inside her for the remainder of the afternoon and on into the evening. In the quiet of her room, she tried to remember what Leah, Bess, and Preacher Waller had said about trusting God. Leah said having God walk with her didn't mean hard times wouldn't come. It meant Bert didn't have to walk the road alone. All the lonely nights while she shivered in the cold and listened for wolves filled her with an intense longing for a better life.

An incident with Davis came to mind. The boy had repeated a story Evan had told him. A mule wanted to be a horse in a bad way. He hated his ears and the way he had to work hard, when all he really wanted to do was run like the wind with the horses on the ranch. One day he refused to be hitched up to a plow. So the rancher couldn't work the soil to plant wheat. When the winter winds blew and the cattle and horses weren't able to graze, the animals had no grain to eat. The cattle, horses, and the mule grew very thin. Some even died. The farmer couldn't take lean cattle to market. And the horses were too weak to run. The mule realized if he'd done his job, his friends would not be starving. He loved all the animals on the farm and considered running away. The rancher looked at all of the animals and told them how much he valued them. The mule vowed right then to always do his job. Every animal had a special purpose on the ranch, and if one failed to work, the others would suffer.

Bert understood every person had a purpose, but did she have one apart from Simon?

Davis's story continued to repeat in her mind. The child's story gave her fresh hope that life could get better.

So far Bert had made a mess of things, and the situation wasn't getting any better. With Simon admitting he'd shot John and her knowing what he'd done to other folks, she assumed he'd been the one working with Leon to rustle cattle. She needed help ... answers now before anyone else got hurt.

Don't try runnin' or I'll leave a trail of blood behind you.

Bert had a choice to start trusting God or to fall prey to whatever Simon planned. The old way had filled her with grief and shame—often made her wish she was dead. She didn't want to die or be filled with sorrow one more day. She wanted to live.

Lord, I'm trusting You with my life. Help me to never let go.

Leah had been up most of the night. And in the predawn hours, she made a decision: Ember belonged at their home, not at the hotel. Although Bess was a fine woman, Leah had seen Ember first. She'd never had a girl, and Ember was her chance to be a mama to a girl who'd never known that special kind of relationship. No matter that Ember was full grown. Mothering didn't begin and end with age.

She finished turning the bacon and checked on the biscuits. Aaron stacked plates on the table—his turn this week to help her with breakfast. With Ember gone, she needed help inside so she could tend to the garden and other chores outside. And Davis needed to be independent from her.

"Aaron," she began, "as soon as breakfast is over, I want you to get the wagon hitched up for me. I'm riding into Rocky Falls and getting Ember."

Aaron laughed. "I've missed her too."

"Then don't be teasing her so much."

"Ah, Mama. We only tease her because we like her."

Leah remembered how Parker and Frank used to tease their sisters. "She is like a sister to you."

"I don't think John and Evan would agree."

Leah shot him a silent warning. "You didn't have to remind me."

"What are you going to do when they're fightin' in the dirt over her?"

She wagged a fork at him. "Your brothers have more sense than that, and I won't allow it."

Aaron took on a serious look. "Mama, I'm not a boy anymore. Both of them have feelin's for Bert."

"Do you think I should leave her in town?"

Aaron crossed his arms over his chest. How many times had she seen his father do the same thing? *Frank, are you lookin' down at your sons?* "If you leave Bert in town, then John and Evan will continue talking about everything but what is wrong between them. If you bring her back, then it will force them to deal with it."

When had Aaron gotten so wise? "Then I guess I'd better make sure I have a talk with both of them before the trip to town." She stood on tiptoe and kissed his cheek. "If they take to fighting at the breakfast table, you reach for Evan and I'll reach for John. In the meantime, we'd better pray."

Footsteps thumped on the porch steps, and Aaron grinned. "I'd better make sure there's plenty of honey for the biscuits."

Soon John and Evan had finished breakfast, and Leah still hadn't brought up the subject of Ember. She inwardly told her galloping pulse to slow down. These were her sons, and she had no reason to think her discussion with them would end badly.

"I have something to discuss with all of you," she said. "It won't take long, but it's important."

Five pairs of blue eyes peered back at her.

"I'm going into town this morning and bringing Ember back here. I feel it's the right thing to do, but there are a few matters we all need to talk about first."

John's face revealed no signs of emotion.

Evan smiled from ear to ear.

Aaron played the part of the surprised brother.

Mark's eyes sparkled like the mischievous boy she knew him to be.

Davis looked just plain happy.

Leah directed her attention to each boy. "Davis, you took advantage of Ember before. Although you need to be helping your brothers, I do expect you to maintain a few of your own chores, like feeding Rowdy. Mark, teasin' is a sign of caring, and I know that's your way. But too much is aggravating. Aaron, you don't need to be teasin' so much either. Evan ... and John, both of you have indicated a fondness for Ember. To the best of my knowledge, you two have not talked this through. I will not have you two fighting and fussing over her. If, and I say if, she has any caring for one of you, let her make that decision. I'd prefer you think of her as a sister, but if you can't, at least be sensitive to the awkwardness it places on her — and the rest of us."

She could have heard a biscuit crumb fall to the floor. "I guess I owe all of you an apology. Bringing Ember into our home means we all need to take a vote." Leah caught her breath. "I'll abide by your decision." She turned her attention back to Davis. "What is your vote?"

"I like Bert. And she plays Pa's fiddle real nice."

Leah focused on Mark.

"I'd like to see her again too."

On to Aaron.

"I miss her, Mama. And I know you enjoy her playin' and singin'."

Leah nodded and moved on to Evan.

"Of course I'd like to see her here again." He looked into John's face. "You and I have always gotten along. Since it's no secret that both of us care for Bert, I'm willing to stand aside and be her friend while she decides which one of us she prefers."

"She may not be interested in either of you," Leah said. "Be prepared for that."

John nodded and reached across the table to shake Evan's hand. "I'll do the same."

Leah swiped at a tear. "Do you know how proud I am of you two? There are many grown men who would be tearing into each other right now."

John laughed. "Now, Mama, you have no idea what we'll be doin' when you're not around."

All she could do was pray her older sons would be able to keep their word.

Chapter 29

Bert tapped her foot against the buckboard floor and silently urged Aaron to hurry the horse along. For a moment she considered jumping from the wagon and running the rest of the way to the 5T. But that would have made her look like a child, and she was full grown. Ever since Leah had walked into the hotel this morning and announced the time had come for Bert to return home, she'd felt like dancing—and for certain singing.

"I need to bring our Ember home," Leah had said. "We all miss her too much."

"How can I argue with you?" Bess said. "I see the love you have for that girl, and as much as I'd like to stomp my feet and demand she stays, I can't do it." She tilted her head at Bert. "If things don't work out, you have a place here to live and work."

"Thank you for taking me in." She turned her attention to Leah. "What about—" She couldn't bring herself to say John and Evan in front of Bess.

Leah waved away her concern. "We had a family meeting this morning. Any problems at home have been talked through."

However, the problem with Simon would not go away. Bert clung to the belief that it made little difference if she lived at the hotel or at the Timmons ranch. When her brother was ready to strike, God would provide a way to make things right. Trust. She had to believe in the God of her new faith.

"It won't take long to put my things together," Bert said. "In fact, less than five minutes."

"Don't forget the Bible I gave you." Bess planted her hands on her hips and nodded at Leah. "We have a new believer."

Leah gasped. "Oh my. On the way home, you'll have to tell me all about it."

"I'll sing it," Bert called over her shoulder.

Once they were on the road, Bert had a moment of hesitation. Surely Simon wouldn't stop them as they traveled.

"Leah, I am so happy about being a believer. I'm still fearful about things—things I can't talk about. But I'm happy for the first time in my life." Could God take care of Simon so Bert would never have to deal with him again? She wanted to believe, and from what she'd read, God could do anything. But He might choose not to. She breathed in deeply. Whatever happened, He'd be there with her. That *should* be enough. If only the terror of what Simon might do would leave her alone.

Leah patted her knee. "When troubles come along, remember the joy you feel now."

"Someday I want to be just like you."

"Now I'm going to cry. But Ember, be yourself." Leah swiped at a tear. "I'm waiting for your new song."

"All right. This one came to me this morning. Hope you like it.

> *I thought the river far too wide*
> *The chasm much too deep,*
> *Until I took the leap toward grace*
> *And fell at Jesus' feet.*
> *I heard the rushing waterfall*
> *The white-churned roar of time,*
> *And plunged into its endless depths*
> *And let His breath be mine.*

"My dear child," Leah's voice cracked. "You have such a passion for life. I hear it in your soul."

While Aaron drove Mama into town to fetch Bert, John kept himself busy all morning making shingles to repair the roof of the house and barn. Mark worked alongside him, lending a good hand since John's bandaged arm slowed him down. Evan had fired up the blacksmith forge. He had a talent for hammering and bending iron to form tools and horseshoes and repairing wagon wheels.

Excitement and longing wove through John at the thought of Bert coming home. *Home.* A good place for all of them to be.

But John had other problems occupying his mind. Victor Oberlander had another twenty head of cattle missing. He needed to be helping Bob, and the work on the ranch didn't get done by itself. Evan was more than capable, but John hated to rely on him when he planned to leave soon for school. The clang of the hammer hitting the anvil reinforced his confidence in Evan's abilities. John *had* to sidestep his big-brother attitude and let his brothers be their own men.

Laying aside the saw, he made his way to the small three-sided shed where Evan worked. Davis sat on a stool watching his brother.

"Can you spare a few minutes? I'd like to talk," John said. His brother nodded, and it occurred to John that Evan might think this was about Bert. "It's not about Bert."

Evan offered a grim smile. At least they were keeping their truce. "That's good to know. I'd hate for Mama to get back and find you all bruised up worse than what you already are."

"Yeah. She'd have us cut our own switches and then march us to the woodshed."

Evan wiped the sweat from his face with the back of his shirtsleeve. "Been a long time since we've gotten ourselves into that much trouble. Even then we were bigger than she is. Pa always said messin' with Mama was like getting stung by a bee—small but mighty. What's on your mind?"

"Cattle rustlers. Leon wasn't working alone. In fact—" He glanced at Davis. "Would you fetch a bucket of water from the well? All of us could use a cool drink."

Davis jumped down from the stool and was gone without a word.

John turned back to Evan and noted Mark stood in the shadows of the shed. "I haven't told Mama this, but Leon couldn't have been the one who shot me."

Evan frowned and stepped from behind the hot forge. "I don't understand. Weren't there other riders who witnessed it?"

"Leon was inside the shack and did open fire, but he couldn't have shot me." John drew a line in the dirt with his boot. "I was here at the corner of the cabin. The bullet had to have been fired from the woods to get me at this angle."

"Sounds like whoever shot you wanted it to look like Leon did it," Evan said. "That tells me Leon was working with at least one other man, or maybe Leon had nothing to do with the rustlin' at all."

"I think the real shooter wanted Leon to take the blame for everything. As jumpy as the men in the posse were, anything resembling gunfire would have caused them to pull the trigger." John resisted the urge to massage his wounded arm for fear one of them would tell Mama.

Mark stepped up to his brothers. "Sounds like the shooter wanted to show you he could shoot you and get away with it. Have you made anybody mad?"

John studied Mark, who seemed to grow faster than Aaron, and took a moment to consider his response to the fourteen-year-old. "I don't know of anyone who's mad enough to shoot me. I make a few enemies now and then but not the murderin' kind. If you're right, then we have a dangerous man out there—one who isn't afraid to take chances."

"And he's still stealin' cattle," Evan added.

John carefully chose his words. "That brings me to what I wanted to talk to you about. I need to be helping Bob bring this to an end. Would you handle things around here while I'm gone?"

"Of course. What about your arm?" Evan said.

"I'll be fine. Praise God it's my left and not my right." He captured Evan's gaze. "You need to have a loaded rifle with you at all times—Mark and Aaron too."

"Maybe I should put off visitin' the school in Fort Collins until things settle down."

John shook his head. "No sir. I want you continuing with your life plans. Just be careful."

"Are you thinkin' if the shooter missed you once, he might aim for one of us?" Mark said.

With those words, the air grew heavy, almost stifling. One of John's brothers being the next victim hadn't entered his mind. "I hope not. Pray not. All of you need to be alert for trouble. Watch the house. I'll talk to Mama about keeping her rifle loaded too."

Davis walked toward them with a sloshing bucket of water and two ladles. His small frame made him look younger, and with his freckles and strawberry blond hair, he looked a lot like Mama.

"How much do we say to Davis?" Evan said. "Not so sure he ever got over those outlaws nabbing him five years ago."

As much as John wanted to keep his youngest brother free from worries and let him remain a boy, the coddling wouldn't mold him into a man. "You were quick." He took the bucket from Davis. "We've been talking about avoiding trouble and the cattle thieves. You need to hear this too. I plan to ride into town tomorrow, and while I'm gone Evan is in charge. Your brothers are going to keep their rifles loaded in case of trouble. So will Mama. I need you to keep your eyes and ears open."

"I'll do whatever you say," Davis said. "Just like Mama says. She's not raising boys, she's raising men."

CHAPTER 30

John thought he'd never seen a sight so pretty as when Aaron returned from Rocky Falls with Mama ... and Bert stepped down from the wagon. Her honey-colored hair clung to her shoulders, and she wore a dress he hadn't seen before. Maybe Widow Bess had gotten it for her from one of the women at the hotel and saloon.

His insides flipped when she smiled at him and waved. Come to think of it, the last time he'd seen her was in the dark hours of the morning when she ran off. Now she looked rested, and her cheeks had a pink tinge to them. He could barely suppress an all-out grin.

Is this what love is all about? He felt like staring at her forever. Quickly he glanced to Mama, who wore a smile too. His weak knees and the foolish inclinations of his heart nearly gave him away.

All the boys stopped their chores and made their way to the wagon, gathering around Mama and Bert. He made sure he was the last one to state his welcome. No point in everyone finding out how his insides tossed back and forth like a canoe jumping over rapids.

This had to stop. Grown men didn't behave like this. "Glad you're back," he said as calmly as he could.

Bert blushed as red as his face felt. "Thank you. I ... I'm grateful to all of you."

"We voted," Davis said. "And Mama said John and Evan couldn't be fussin' over you. But I don't know what that means."

He peered up at Bert with one eye shut to block the sun. "Do you, Bert?"

She grew redder, and John probably did too. Mark snickered.

"I'm sure it was nothing," Bert said.

John walked to the other side of the wagon. "I'll take care of the wagon. Davis, why don't you help me?"

John worked on the shingles with Mark the rest of the afternoon. While he hammered and sawed with one arm, he recalled the circumstances surrounding the shooting that left him wounded and Leon Wilson dead. What had he missed? Once he was back in Rocky Falls, he'd ride out to the abandoned cabin to see if he could find any evidence the shooter might have left behind. The last time John was there, he'd seen two sets of tracks leading to and from the cabin. Those boot prints had to be the shooter's.

Every time his thoughts moved to Bert, he attempted to push them away. How could one man's mind be fixed on so many things?

The hours rushed by until suppertime. Mama and Bert had prepared thick slabs of beef fried up tender and juicy and lots of vegetables from the garden. This winter, they'd still be enjoying the vegetables Mama was canning and drying today. The cornbread melted in his mouth, but then again, Bert had baked it.

"So there's no changing your mind about helping Bob look for the rustlers?" Mama hadn't eaten much, and the color of her face had faded to white.

"I've talked to everyone except Bert about taking precautions while I'm gone. I could be back day after tomorrow or in a week. There're a few things I need to see for myself."

"All right. But I'm not happy," Mama said.

"That's real plain." Evan rested his forearms on the table. "But John has a job to do. Just like the rest of us. I'd be going with him if he didn't need me here."

John remembered Evan tried to get Bob to deputize him, but he'd keep that information to himself.

"Don't even think about it, Evan Frank Timmons." Mama's eyes flashed a rare display of anger.

Evan held up his hands. "Calm down. I have plenty of tools to mend in the next few days, and a letter to write to the Colorado State Veterinary Association."

John wanted to stand up and cheer. "Are you working on the admission papers?"

"Oh, I've already completed those. Looks to me like I need to get started on my education as soon as possible."

Misgivings crawled through John's mind, and he hoped Evan's eagerness had nothing to do with Bert. The two would have plenty of time to be together while he was gone.

"I want to check on Oberlander's mare before it gets dark," John said. "I think he can pick her up anytime. I could probably deliver her in the morning on my way to Rocky Falls."

Mama smiled. "That's a good idea. Victor won't need to make an extra trip here to get her."

Good. She isn't fond of Oberlander. John scooted his chair back from the table and noted Bert had finished her supper too. "Bert, would you mind joining me? I need to talk to you about what to do if you see someone strange. Everyone here has a rifle but you."

Bert moistened her lips and glanced at Mama.

"Go ahead. This is important. We'll have you sing and play for us later, if you don't mind."

"Yes ma'am. We won't be long."

John avoided Evan's eyes and made his way to the door with Bert behind him. One of the boys laughed, and John figured it was Mark or Aaron. Stepping outside onto the porch, he breathed in the fresh air. He had Bert to himself, and he didn't care if it was selfish.

They walked side by side to the corral. She stood almost to his shoulder. How could one so small have such power over him?

Concentrate on the horses. Racer and Queen Victoria had become cozy, which would help John stay in the rancher's good graces. He could talk to Bert about horses and not get so flustered.

"Look at the sunset," Bert said. "I love those soft colors of yellow, orange, and purple. God painted it very nicely."

"Is this your way of telling me God's now a part of your life?"

She laughed softly. "Yes, it is. I'm very new, a brand new Christian, you might say."

Thank You. The news spread through him like warm syrup. "I'm real happy for you. When I was about twelve, I thought following God was the coward's way out. Then I grew close to my Uncle Parker and realized a real man understood where his brave heart comes from."

She was quiet, but he'd not pry. He'd learned that much about her. "Be careful while I'm gone. If you sense anything strange, let Mama or Evan know. My pa's rifle is under Mama's bed. I'll make sure it's cleaned and loaded."

She nodded. "I hope you catch him before then."

Him? What did she know?

"How did you get your name?" John said. "Not the nickname, but Ember. It's unusual."

"My mother gave it to me just before she died."

"I'd like to hear the story."

She hesitated, as though thinking through her words. "My mother birthed me and knew she was dying. According to my brother Gideon, she fought desperately to name me while life slipped away. She was staring into the fire as the last log fell apart into ashes, sending sparks everywhere. That's when she said for my pa to call me Ember. She said my life was beginning while hers was ending. She died shortly afterward."

He pictured a woman who looked like Bert holding on to life until she'd given her baby girl a name. "That's a beautiful story. Do you have a second name?"

She took a deep breath. "Rose. Gideon gave it to me because it belonged to my mother."

"Ember Rose. Fits together real nice." How could he ever call her Bert again? Maybe when the time was right ...

"Thank you. Gideon was the only one who ever called me by my rightful names. My pa and my brothers always called me Bert."

Relief swept through him. She did have someone good in her life. "Where is Gideon now?"

"He died of pneumonia four years ago."

The thought hit John that those who'd loved her had died. "I'm sorry. I can tell you miss him. You already told me your father is alive. Whereabouts are you from?"

She glanced away.

He'd gone too far into her private world. "You aren't going to tell me any more, are you?"

"I can't, John. It's too dangerous."

He refused to make her feel bad. Not today. "Maybe another time. Right now I want to be your friend and earn your trust. Like I told you the night on the road. I appreciate your telling me how you got your name. I haven't pried like I set out to do because I want you to tell me the truth when you're comfortable."

She nodded and from the way she stared out into the corral, she must have wondered if she'd done the right thing by telling him how she got her name.

"Telling me about yourself is not a thing to fear."

"But I'm afraid, and I can't tell you why."

"I'm trying to understand."

"Why?"

How much more could he reveal about himself than what he'd done on the starlit night? "I think you already know."

She rested her arms on the corral fence and leaned into it. "When I'm here and with you, I feel safe."

"That's the way I want it always to be."

She continued to gaze out at the horses. "But it's impossible. Someone's bound to get hurt again. And I don't mean just Evan and breaking his heart. I'm talking about blood."

A chill rose on his arms. "The cattle rustlers?"

She shook her head. "Stealin' and killin' is all he's ever known, and he has a way of dragging others into the mud with him."

"Do you know where this 'he' is?"

"No. He's like a snake, slithering under rocks and striking when a person least expects."

"Would you give me information about him if you thought someone might get hurt?"

Bert continued to stare out at the horses. She slowly turned to face him. "When I decided my life needed God, I also decided I would do whatever I could to stop any more bloodshed." She touched his arm. "I'd rather die myself than see any of you hurt."

John didn't like the finality of her words. Neither did he like what they meant. Weariness had taken a toll on John's heart, and he wanted answers now. "How long is a man supposed to wait for a woman to trust him?"

She shook her head and walked away.

John had his answer.

CHAPTER 31

Two days later, Leah found herself alone during the afternoon. Ember had taken Davis fishing while the other boys were off looking for strays and making sure their own cattle were intact. Leah hated that they were gone. Their absence worried her. And she was afraid they'd run into rustlers. Her sons carried rifles, and the weapons were a constant reminder of what had happened to John—and could happen again.

"We have our rifles with us all the time," Evan had said when she voiced her fears. "Nothing's changed."

"I'm no fool. But you normally carry your weapons to protect yourself from wild animals, not armed men."

Aaron leaned on his saddle horn and reached out to take her hand. Mercy, the boy could charm just like his father. "There will always be wild animals and men who want to take what we have. Totin' guns means we have a chance against them."

Leah had no answer for him.

Now she realized her best pondering and prayer time came when she washed clothes. Something about scrubbing the dirt from her sons' britches and shirts, rinsing out the soap and hanging them on the line to dry, seemed to bring answers to problems. But not today.

Rowdy's barking brought Leah's attention to the road leading back to the 5T. A lone rider headed toward the house. *Lord, haven't we had enough strangers?* She gave the man a second scrutiny, and when she didn't recognize the horse, she dropped the clothes into the basket and hurried to the porch to fetch her rifle. With all the talk of rustlers and missing cattle, she'd not hesitate to send a no-good man to meet his Maker.

Leah lifted the heavy weapon to her shoulders. Sometimes she wished she were twice her size. The man waved as though he knew her. She squinted. Surely not.

"Miss Leah." Wirt Zimmerman rode right up to the front steps. "You're as pretty as I remember." The same pale gray eyes and smooth skin. A few lines had formed from the corners of his eyes, but the easy smile drew her to him.

He hadn't changed. "Afternoon, Wirt. It's been a long time. What brings you all the way out here?"

"Business. Parker sent me. Said you folks needed help with cattle rustlers."

Then why did he send you? "We've had problems."

Wirt pushed his hat back. "I'm not the same man, Miss Leah. I've worked hard with the US Marshals and learned a lot. I can imagine what you're thinking, but I'll not disappoint you or anyone else in this community."

Leah had given Bert a second chance. She could give Wirt one too—at least a partial one. "Would you like some cool water?" She rested her rifle against the side of the porch.

"I would." He dismounted, and she caught the familiar sparkle in his eyes.

She wondered about those eyes more than she cared to admit. *Gray.* A mix of black and white. Her daddy back in Virginia said a man with gray eyes could never be trusted—never knew whose side he was on. Of course her daddy had chased Parker and Frank off with a shotgun.

"Won't be taking up much of your time," Wirt said. "I need to ride on into Rocky Falls, but I was anxious to see you. How are the boys?"

"They're fine. Growing like weeds. John's still in charge of the ranch and doing deputy work. In fact, he's in town working with Marshal Bob Culpepper."

"I'm not surprised. The boy I remember must be a man now. He did have a heart for justice."

"Would you like to come inside?"

"No thanks. I'd rather wait on the porch here. Seems more fittin'. And I do need to help bring in those cattle rustlers."

Maybe he *had* grown into a US Marshal. She left the door open while she dipped a ladle of cool water into a glass. "Not sure you'd recognize the boys."

"Five years is a long time. I was thinking John's about twenty-three."

"Right."

"And that makes Evan eighteen, Aaron sixteen, Mark fourteen, and Davis is nine."

She smiled and handed him the glass of water. "Your memory serves you well, Wirt."

"For some things, yes."

His tender look told her the words he'd written in his letters were still on his heart. "Have a seat. Did you visit your family?"

Wirt sat on the bench by the front door, and Leah slid onto a rocking chair. "I did. The Quaker life isn't for me, but I respect their beliefs. And I felt a need to make some sort of reconciliation with my folks."

"Were you well received?"

He glanced toward the barn, then back to her. "As I expected. But I tried, and that's all God requires of me. I write them and hope they read the letters."

Guilt assailed Leah. "Sorry I stopped writing. I was confused with what you asked, and I didn't know for sure how I felt."

"I understand. I was pushing you too soon after Frank had died, not thinking about the worries of raising those boys. While I'm here, I hope you'll see my dandy days are over."

Leah rubbed the palms of her hands together. Victor and Wirt. Good heavens. Now she knew how Ember felt.

"No need to say a word. I'll prove myself. I've had five years to think about you—about your sons—and what God has purposed for me." He stood and handed her the empty glass. "Unless you tell me you have another suitor, I'd like to call on you."

Was Victor a suitor or simply an interested man? "I don't know what to say."

"Good. That's not a no." He righted his hat. "I'll be leaving now."

She watched him mount his horse while curiosity picked at her. "When did you become a Christian?"

He smiled. "When you quit writing. Guess that makes it three years, four months, and two days."

Leah laughed. "I'm glad to know my refusal to marry you went for God's glory."

He sat straight in the saddle, looking far too appealing. "But you see I'm back and even more determined."

Wirt rode away at a fast pace, not giving her a moment to refuse him. She wrapped her arms around her chest and wondered what he'd say if he knew she'd kept his letters.

CHAPTER 32

John rode into the dusty streets of Rocky Falls late in the afternoon, tired and tasting a mouthful of dirt. For two days, he'd ridden hard to talk to folks about the cattle rustlin', but no one had a thing to report. He reached for his canteen and finished up the water, washing down the dirt and grit—enough to grow potatoes. The number of missing cattle had risen to two hundred head. He told himself and the angry ranchers that plenty of cattle grazed in the higher summer pastures, but not two hundred of them. The cattle must have been driven farther south, which meant the rustlers were well on their way to Denver.

He knew many of the ranchers suspected Bert having a part in the thievery, so he offered to turn in his deputy badge. Not one man took him up on it.

No one had better break the law today, 'cause he wasn't in the mood to hear any excuses.

Truth was, he fretted about a wagon load—no, two wagon loads—of burdens that weighed hard on his mind. He understood the importance of bringing his problems to the Lord, but it didn't stop the anxiety raging through him. The rustlers were growing bolder, as though daring him and Bob to discover their identity. The instructions he'd given his brothers and Mama to keep a loaded rifle close by as a precaution gave him some peace of mind. But just some. He feared for them, especially if the rustlers got wind of him not being around.

Another matter tearing through him was Bert. As much as he wanted to believe she cared for him, the idea of her and Evan keeping company in his absence sent a green streak up his spine. John's feelings were new and fragile, and he wanted to trust her. But Evan might not be ready to concede. One couldn't help but see the caring in Evan's eyes. And why couldn't she confide in him about her past?

Lately Oberlander found excuses to come by the ranch. Another reason for John to examine his feelings. Shouldn't he want Mama to be happy? Except he didn't think Victor Oberlander measured up to what he figured she deserved. There, he'd admitted it, if to no one else but himself. Oberlander had plenty of money, and Mama worked much too hard. But she never complained.

Another troublesome notion was John didn't think Oberlander had a close relationship with the Lord. The language he used and his actions often pointed to the condition of his heart.

I won't figure any of this out today.

He tied his horse to the hitching post outside the marshal's office and studied another horse tied there too. John frowned. The painted gelding didn't look familiar. *Sure hope it isn't more trouble.* Fine looking saddle and saddle bags ... Certainly not a drifter.

John stepped onto the boardwalk and turned the knob into the marshal's office. The aroma of fresh coffee and the not-so-pleasant smells of the jail met him. Wirt Zimmerman rose from the chair across from Bob's desk. A smile spread over the man's face, and he reached out to shake John's hand.

"Good to see you," Wirt said. "You've grown into a fine lookin' man."

Wirt Zimmerman was not what he and Bob needed. But John shook the man's hand anyway as a gesture of good manners. Maybe the US Marshal had gained some valuable experience — or maybe he hadn't. John realized he needed to rein in his surly mood. "Parker wired us and said you were coming. Good to see you."

"I imagine I'm not what you or Bob wanted, but I've learned a lot over the past five years. A good US Marshal decided to make a man out of me, and I did my best to live up to his expectations."

"We all need someone to show us the ropes." John had learned a lot in five years too, and he needed to give Wirt the same credit. "I hope I'm not the same hot-headed kid who took after a whole gang of outlaws by myself." He captured Wirt's gaze and offered silent respect. They both grinned.

"That arm of yours all right?"

John refused to look at the bandage and admit it still bothered him once in a while. Mostly stiff. "Yeah. I'm ready to get rid of the bandage. Makes me feel like a helpless old man."

Wirt chuckled. "Between the three of us, we should be able to figure out who's behind the cattle rustlin'. Like you, I hope we can find the livestock before the thieves make their way to Denver. The stockyards are aware of stolen cattle, but not much anyone can do if the brands are changed."

"I agree, and we're ready to do whatever it takes to stop them," Bob said. "The ranchers here are edgy and nervous. John and I spend as much time tryin' to calm them down as tryin' to stop any more trouble." He nodded at John to pull up an extra chair to the desk.

"Parker tells me the problem started about a month ago," Wirt said. "Do you mind filling me in on what's been going on?"

"Be glad to." Bob pointed to the coffeepot on the small stove. "I made coffee less than an hour ago. Grab a mug from my desk. I've drunk plenty for the day."

Wirt immediately snatched up two mugs. "John, you want some?"

The Wirt John remembered would have thought only about himself. "Sure thing. Thanks."

Bob cleared his throat. "We may have caught one of the thieves, a man by the name of Leon Wilson. He worked for one of the ranchers, Victor Oberlander. Wilson got himself fired and bragged about what he was going to do to Oberlander. Then cattle turned up missing."

Wirt glanced at the empty cell. "Where is he now?"

"John and I, along with some other men, rode out to where we heard he was hidin' out. He opened fire and was killed."

Wirt gave John a calculated stare, as though he knew just the right moment to peer into John's soul. "So that's how you were wounded?"

"It is." John turned his attention back to Bob. He still felt stupid about not listening to him the day Leon shot him.

"While John was recovering, he figured out Leon couldn't have shot him from inside the cabin due to the angle the bullet entered his left arm."

"That was a sure way to shut Leon up." Wirt paused. "What did Oberlander's ranch hands have to say about it?"

"A couple of them rode with us. None of them cared for Leon. Claimed he was a loner, drank too much, and liked to fight. I asked them if Leon mentioned another man or men working with him to get even with Oberlander, but they believed he worked alone."

"Which he obviously didn't." Wirt poured the coffee into two mugs. "Do you trust those hands?"

Bob shrugged and shifted his huge frame in the small chair. "Don't have a reason not to. One of them opened fire when John was shot. None of them have ever been in trouble. John here can tell you more about Leon, since he had dealings with him that led up to him getting fired."

John inwardly moaned. But if they were going to catch the cattle rustlers, then Wirt needed to know about Bert. Not a subject he felt comfortable discussing. But he must. "Just before the rustlin' started, I was riding over to see Oberlander when one of his hands stopped me. Leon and two other Oberlander men were going to hang a boy for stealing a mare. The horse happened to be a prize mare belonging to Oberlander. I stopped the hanging and later took the boy to my ranch. A few days later, Oberlander and Leon brought the mare to the 5T to breed with my stallion. Leon still smarted from our dealings, and when he learned the boy he'd tried to hang was really a girl, he got even madder. His reaction is what got him fired. He rode off and threatened both of us."

Wirt set the coffee in front of John and sat down. "Where is the girl now?"

"At my ranch. She claims to have been traveling for about six months. Won't tell any of us where she came from, but someone's chasing her. Whoever he is has her scared to death. She told me a few nights ago that 'he' has stolen and killed. She called him a snake."

Wirt toyed with the handle of his cup, his attention obviously focused on John's words. "How old is this girl?"

"Seventeen. She claims the one following her is not a husband or a man wanting her for those reasons."

"Hard to believe she was working with Leon when he tried to hang her. Unless he planned to double-cross her."

"Could be." John recognized his own defensive attitude about Bert. "By the time I got there, he'd beaten her pretty bad."

"What's her name?"

"She goes by Bert—no last name. Her given name is Ember Rose. I had Bob check around the area to see if anyone knew her, and I wired Parker for the same."

"Anything turned up yet?" Wirt glanced at Bob.

"Nope. John here doesn't think she's involved, but I have my suspicions. When I questioned her, she acted like a scared rabbit. That could have been an act, but the fella she's tryin' to avoid is probably our thief."

"Do you mind if I talk to her?" Wirt swung his attention between both men, then back to John.

"Guess not." John's insides swirled. "On the way, we could stop at Victor Oberlander's ranch, the Wide O."

"Good. I have a couple of other questions before we ride. Could I have a list of those ranchers who've reported stolen cattle?"

"Got it right here." Bob pulled a piece of paper from his drawer. "We've looked for a pattern. Nothing. And the tracks always indicate the cattle were driven toward Denver. But that's it. A lot of canyons between here and there." Bob handed the list to Wirt.

"What about those ranchers who haven't had problems?" Wirt glanced down at the names.

"Are you thinking the thief might be someone we know?" Bob's brow arched, and John saw the challenge. "We've talked to ranchers and hands and everyone else in between."

"I'm sure you have." Wirt's calm, in-control tone was a new trait that John respected. "Later when I'm thinking through all the things you've told me, I want to be sure I've asked all the right questions. I know you've done your job."

Tension hung in the air like a pendulum that had forgotten how to swing. Bob finally nodded. "At the bottom of the list of names are those ranchers who haven't lost any cattle. All the ranchers have taken into account the open range and summer pastures."

"Do you have any idea why these ranches haven't been hit?"

"The thieves would have to ride over open range south. Too easy to detect." Bob tipped his chair back and grabbed the coffeepot on the stove. After pouring a mug of strong brew, one he'd declared a few moments before he didn't want, he pulled a map from his stuffed desk drawer. "John or I can show you where the ranches are located."

"Thanks. I'd like to talk to all of them," Wirt said. "I'd prefer meeting them face to face. Would one of you have time to ride with me tomorrow and get started on this?"

Bob smiled at John. "Do you mind?"

John hid a smirk, knowing Bob didn't want the job of showing Wirt around. "No problem. I could introduce you."

"Can we get started early in the morning?"

"Just name the time. I'm not expected home for a few days."

"Six o'clock? I plan to stay at the hotel. Is Widow Bess still there?"

"She is," John said. "Feisty as ever."

"Oh, I remember." Wirt finished his coffee. "I'd like to take my horse to the livery and see about a room at the hotel."

The men stepped outside into the brilliant sunlight. Bob rubbed the left side of his chest, something John had noticed a lot of late. He followed them out onto the boardwalk and tossed a grin John's way. That lopsided smile meant the joke was on John. He'd have to put up with Wirt Zimmerman until the man proved his mettle.

Bob Culpepper was the stabilizer here, since he seemed as timeless as the mountains. What a threesome. For sure, working with Wirt Zimmerman would be interesting.

John swung up onto his saddle, still feeling the awkwardness of grabbing the saddle horn with his right hand. But this time he had a better attitude.

Soon they'd have those thieves and murderers behind bars.

Soon he'd convince Mama she didn't need Victor Oberlander.

And soon he'd get the truth out of Bert, and Evan would back down from pursuing her.

"I saw your mama earlier today," Wirt said as the horses trotted toward the livery. "She looks as pretty as a picture. Just like I remember."

John gritted his teeth.

CHAPTER 33

L eah sensed heat rising up her neck and flooding her face. Drowning sounded like a sweet escape from two of the men seated around her table. Why ever did John bring Wirt and Victor to the 5T? Just like hungry boys who picked and teased at each other, Wirt and Victor talked and joked, each attempting to secure her attention while she and Ember dished up berry cobbler and poured fresh coffee.

She sensed their intense study of her, as though she were some filly. Make that a mare. In any event, she didn't welcome their gawking. What did they want her to do? Open her mouth so they could check her teeth? Mercy, grown men could be so bothersome.

Smoothing her apron and slipping one of her many wayward curls behind her ear, she handed Ember a bowl of cobbler to set before one of the men. The girl looked as ready to crumble as a brittle leaf in fall. Every man in the room had questioned her about the cattle rustling. Maybe later they could both laugh about this humiliating situation.

Mercy, why couldn't they have discussed their business at Victor's? The Wide O had a much bigger and fancier parlor, with a servant. Leah had seen the fancy dishes that had been Victor's grandmother's from Germany.

Victor sat the closest to her — the man who never ceased to voice his devotion and his desire to court her. At his right sat Wirt, whose marriage proposal she refused three years ago because of his dandy ways. And poor John, who was dancing to the tune of protecting his mama from both men and holding down a discussion about the best way to catch the cattle rustlers and clear Ember's name.

If adversity bred character, then she and John already had their mansions in heaven.

"Miss Ember, are you sure you can't help us?" Wirt said, after thanking her for his cobbler.

Ember stared straight at him, with no looks of helplessness cast at Leah or John. "Sir, I have no idea where the cattle are or where to find the rustlers."

"What about who's behind the stealing?" Wirt stood, and Bert took a step back. "Miss, you're shaking. I didn't set out to frighten you, only to see if you might know something that would help us. Why not sit here before you fall. Are you ill?" He pointed to his chair. "I'll help Miss Leah with the cobbler and coffee."

Leah caught a granitelike stare from John.

Ember took the offered chair. "If I could answer your questions, I would."

John reached over to take Ember's hand, and this time Leah nearly gasped. Lord help them all if Evan walked in.

"I know you're afraid of a man. I know that person is capable of some bad things. I know you're too scared to give us his name, but we're your friends. And we'll protect you."

Ember continued to tremble, but her gaze focused on John. Leah could see she did care about him very much. If the girl could tell any of them what she knew, it would be John.

"I can't," she whispered. "He and those with him would find a way to kill all of you."

"You don't think the men of this town could stop them?"

"I'm afraid who'd be killed. Maybe he's gone since you can't find the cattle."

"Do you really think that?"

Ember sighed. "I'd like to believe he'd never strike here again."

The door opened and Evan stepped in with Aaron. He nodded at Bob. "Marshal Culpepper, I'm glad you're here. You too, Mr. Oberlander. Aaron and I found a body on the land John bought from you. It's one of your hands — Ted Hawkins." He shifted and his gaze took in John and Ember's hands woven together like two fishing worms. "A horse was grazing close by, and I assume it was his. Has the Wide O brand. So I have Mr. Hawkins and the horse."

Victor's face wore the lines of hard work and worry. "Any idea what happened?"

"Bullet in the head, sir. In fact, Aaron and I heard the gunfire and rode to investigate."

B ert stood on the front porch beside Leah while the men lifted Ted Hawkins' body from his horse. Numbness swept over her, and all she could feel was the agony of what Simon had done to others, and the pounding question in her brain about whether he had done this too.

She remembered the old man who'd done his best to talk Leon out of hanging her. If Leon were not dead, she'd assume he'd shot Mr. Hawkins.

The sensation of being in a fog vanished, and in its wake came a throbbing in her temples and pain that swept throughout her body. Tears filled her eyes, not only for Mr. Hawkins, but for others who had befriended her before their lives ended.

"He tried to save my life." She folded her arms over her chest. "In fact he did, since he found John. If not for Mr. Hawkins, I'd be cold in an unmarked grave."

Leah wrapped her arm around Bert's waist. "Those men out there will find who is threatening our lives. I have faith in their abilities and know that God is a God of justice."

Bert nodded and wiped away the wetness on her cheeks. "I wish my faith were stronger. But this — " She pointed to those gathered around Mr. Hawkins' body " — proves what was often said to me."

"What, Ember?"

"I destroy everything I touch or care about. I can't stay here, no matter how much I want to or how much I owe John." She started to say "love John" but to voice it meant her feelings were real.

"Look at me." Leah touched her cheek.

Bert hesitated before she complied. At times she feared Leah or John could see to the depths of her soul.

Leah caught her gaze. "You called on the name of Jesus and stepped into eternal life—a life now and forever that is blessed. Anyone who said this to you lied to manipulate and control you."

Bert admitted Simon's words and actions had done those very things. She shivered in the late afternoon heat. From her earliest memories, Simon had lashed out at her with his fists and his tongue. Only Gideon had stepped in to stop him. Then he died. Mr. Hawkins stepped in, and now he was dead. What about John? Leah? And the other Timmons boys?

"I want to believe you. And from what you and Miss Bess have told me about God, I know He's supposed to be looking after me. But who will look after those who try to help me?"

"Pray for God to protect your loved ones. Ask Him to stop the man who holds you captive."

"I am," Bert whispered. "And I will continue. I ... I have no choice."

Leah kissed her cheek. "You can't carry this burden yourself. All of us here want to help."

"I know. Perhaps I should pray for courage."

"An excellent idea." Leah smiled. "We will weather this."

But Bert was not so sure. Had Simon killed Mr. Hawkins, and if he did, why?

CHAPTER 34

John pulled the rope taut, securing a dead tree to a pair of mules. Now he and his brothers would take the walk back to the house where they'd chop it up for wood. The long cold months ahead weren't far away, and he wanted more than an ample supply. Heavy blizzards would blow in from the mountains and keep them inside for a few days or a week at a time. The tree had fallen some years before and had reached its prime for burning. It would keep them warm and provide many a good cook fire.

Two weeks had passed since Ted Hawkins' murder and not one incident of cattle rustling had occurred. Neither had Ted Hawkins' killer surfaced. Some folks claimed he was involved with the rustling, but John knew better. Ted Hawkins lived the difference between right and wrong. The man had the respect of Oberlander and the other ranch hands of the Wide O. Hawkins had no doubt been privy to information that would put the guilty thief in a bad position.

John refused to believe the lawbreakers had escaped capture. He spent a few days with Bob and Wirt scouting for missing cattle and searching out remote areas of the foothills and beyond for the thieves. Nothing. The rustlers and the cattle had seemingly disappeared.

A man or men had lined their pockets with money from stolen livestock.

Wirt wired Denver and alerted authorities to be looking for cattle carrying many of the ranchers' brands. Of course, the thieves could have already changed the brands before driving the herd to market.

John massaged his arm. Although he'd tossed the bandage protecting his arm, it didn't take much work to get it sore and aching again. His constant striving to make sure every chore and responsibility around the farm was completed to perfection had slid downhill while he mended.

"Let me lead the horse," Mark said. "Give that arm a chance to rest."

"It's healing fine." But John stepped back and allowed Mark to take over. "You're probably right. It won't heal as long as I work it."

"Yeah, we need you with two good arms." Mark grinned, always the happiest when he was outside working.

Evan tightened the rope on a second dead tree. He motioned for Aaron to take the bridle and lead the horse toward home. "You sure it'll be all right for me to leave for a couple of days?"

"Yes sir." John said, more than anxious for his brother to start his studies.

"I'm kinda excited about visiting the school," Evan continued. "But I'm nervous about the entrance exams."

Mark pretended to choke. "You who had perfect marks in school? The school will be asking you to teach."

Hold on to these times. Someday we'll all be grown men.

The walk home would take an hour, but the time allowed all of them to talk. Davis raced up beside Evan, no doubt wanting the older brother to tell a story. While Evan's voice raised and lowered with the familiar tale about a bear who could not find a home for the winter, John's thoughts trailed in another direction. He had a new situation to consider, and he refused to call it a problem—yet. Wirt Zimmerman and Victor Oberlander vied for Mama's attention. Fortunately, she wasn't giving in to either of their pursuits. But John saw the look in her eyes when Wirt came calling. She'd invited him to supper a few times for the sake of friendship, and she hadn't extended the invitation to Victor Oberlander. At least Wirt hadn't asked John for permission to court. If John pondered the possibility of Wirt and Mama finding love, he welcomed that union before a relationship with the owner of the Wide O. A fine house and fancy clothes made life comfortable, but he wanted Mama to love a man who loved God more than anything else.

Sometimes John's desire to pursue his own dreams floated to the top. Thoughts of a life with Ember stayed with him. But what if he learned things that turned him against her? He shoved away the rising number of questions with no answers, realizing the futility of it all.

Sometimes he believed God didn't want to answer him, so why continue to ask for direction?

"Then the bear stood on his haunches and saw a cave far off in the mountains—beyond the foothills of Rocky Falls and beyond the mountains outside of Estes Park. There, when his belly was full of nuts, berries, and fresh fish from the streams and rivers, he'd sleep the whole winter. No one would tease him about being a small bear, because when spring came again and melted the snow, he'd be the biggest bear of all."

"Like me?" Davis said.

"Like you. You'll be as tall as the rest of us soon. Maybe taller."

John laughed. "Let's hear another one." He never grew tired of Evan telling stories. He was a good brother with a kind heart for young and old, while John sometimes became grouchy when things didn't suit him. Guilt assaulted him. Bert deserved a kind man, not a man who had sour moments. Maybe Evan would be a better choice.

An unselfish man would stand aside and let Evan and Bert find happiness. The selfish side of him shouted "no," that he'd worked hard all of his life for his family, and he deserved to be happy with Bert—Ember Rose. But could those ambitions be wrong, and was Evan the better man for her?

Evan laughed. The familiar jolly sound caused John to feel envious of his brother's easygoing temperament. Again, John was wrong. He'd learned long ago God created each man for a purpose and gave him the tools to perform it. John's lot must be to work like a fool so others could have an easier life.

John hated his fickle thoughts. He either believed Bert wasn't involved with the thieves, or he didn't. He either loved her or he didn't. He either trusted God or he didn't. No wonder he was a grump.

God and John needed a long talk where he would do the listening and not the complaining.

Bert finished shoveling the ashes from the fireplace, a dirty job, but she was glad to be useful. The boys had been busy all day dragging dead trees back for firewood. She stood and surveyed the clean cookstove and now the fireplace. This was a sight easier than mucking stalls.

A lively tune came to her, and she hummed it before the words sprang to her lips.

> *Feels like I'm breathin' air so pure and real,*
> *Feels like I'm livin' and startin' to feel.*
> *For the first time in my life, my heart has a song.*
> *The wind whispers Your name,*
> *I'll never be the same.*

She finished sweeping the remaining ashes into a small shovel and poured them into a bucket.

> *For the first time in my life, my heart has a song*
> *For the wind whispers Your name,*
> *I'll never be the same.*

A shadow in the doorway caused her to spin around. Evan stood motionless. Not a smile. Not a frown.

"Is something wrong?" she said, while a dozen fears rushed through her.

He pressed his lips together and shook his head. "I was listening to your song. So sweet and pretty."

"Thank you. But I don't understand."

Evan walked to her side, and she hoped he didn't plan to try to touch or even kiss her. She'd allowed John in, but anyone else was forbidden. Evan's eyes were liquid, and she saw pain. "I'd like to think your song was for me, but I'd be a fool."

"Oh, Evan." Her heart fluttered for the agony clouding his eyes.

"Hush." He held up his hand. "Let me say this before I change my mind. John loves you, and I can tell you have feelings for him too. He's a special man, and I think it's time he started thinking about himself instead of the rest of us. I won't be causing any more problems."

Bert held her breath. How was she to react—to show Evan she valued his gift to his brother? Compassion rushed through her. She reached out with her hand, and Evan grasped it.

"What is this?" John stood in the open doorway, his hands on his hips and his face blood-red.

Bert's gaze flew to his face. She stepped back. He'd never believe what had happened between her and Evan.

"I just made a confession to Bert." Evan shoved his hands in his pockets.

No, Evan. He won't understand.

"I can only guess." John growled his words. "Look, I have work to do. Couldn't find you and thought you might be here."

"It's not what you think." Evan took two steps toward his brother. "I came looking for Mama, not Bert."

"So where's Mama?"

"She's in the garden." Bert's voice sounded weak to her ears, as though she should be ashamed of talking to Evan.

"Why didn't you say so?"

"I never gave her a chance."

Bert inwardly cringed. Now she looked like she'd encouraged Evan—what she'd promised John she'd never do.

"How good of you to take the blame."

Fury rose inside her. Evan meant well. The words were coming out wrong, but he'd sacrificed his heart for John, and now John was accusing him—them—of something not true. Bert snatched up the bucket of ashes. "I'm not listening to this. John Timmons, you have no idea what happened here. Neither do I have the desire to explain it. You wouldn't believe me anyway, not that I've given you much of a reason. But I won't stand and listen to two men I care about fuss like two little boys."

Bert stomped down the steps and hurried toward the barn where she'd dump the ashes behind it. John knew how she felt about him. Why would she behave differently?

CHAPTER 35

Two days crept by and John still couldn't approach Bert to apologize. She avoided him like he had cholera. And as he went about the ranch pondering over his stupidity, how he'd met her, her silent strength, and her stubborn nature to keep her past to herself, he realized that the problems of her life and his needed to be settled before he could speak his heart. But he still owed her an apology, and she refused to talk to him.

Once Evan returned from his visit to Fort Collins, John needed to apologize to him too. John had shaken his hand the morning he rode out with a feeble "I'm sorry" on his lips and remorse in his heart. But more needed to be done to make up for his jealous streak.

He'd like to release Bert from her debt. Frankly, he'd long since put aside why she owed him. Now she'd become his first thought in the morning, a sense of hope for the future. But her past ... He was a fool just like Evan said, but for more reasons than John cared to list.

A fool.

He loved her, but he wished he didn't.

A fool.

The cattle rustlers had successfully gotten away with stolen livestock, making him and Bob look bad.

A fool.

Leon had been killed because the posse thought he'd shot John.

A fool.

Ted's murder lay unsolved.

Bert as good as stated that those behind the crimes were not to be reckoned with. John could feel the evil in his bones. He should be spending time prying information from her, not dwelling on this strange attraction. At times he questioned if he had any control over his feelings at all.

The same accusations repeated—

A fool.

He loved her, but he wished he didn't.

He wanted to ask God for help, but why should God lend a hand when John hadn't listened in the past?

Leah led her sorrel mare from the barn, saddled and ready to ride. John and Mark rode with her. She preferred to have John alone to encourage him to talk. She had surmised enough to know the problem existed between him, Evan, and Ember. Hearts were often shattered and feelings often hurt by words spoken in vain.

Evan had returned from Fort Collins full of enthusiasm, his mind opened to life beyond the 5T and Rocky Falls. He loved every square inch of the school and had taken the entrance exams. They would send a letter informing him of his acceptance or denial of his application. Her entire household sensed Evan's anxiety.

Racer pranced, always in the mood to run—or other things—as she reined her mare away from the magnificent stallion. Mark rode a gelding. No trouble there. But this adventurous son much preferred a stallion of his own. He'd be taking a ride soon on the open range to catch a mustang as wild as the streak running through him. His love for the outdoors reminded her that this son was her mustang. Mercy, however would she keep her impulsive son in a bit and bridle?

"Won't be long before Evan leaves for school," Mark said, climbing onto the saddle. "Then it's more chores for the rest of us."

Leah stiffened. "I just want him to receive his acceptance letter."

"Now, Mama, Evan's so smart he makes the rest of us look like mules."

"He'll be here on holidays and during the summer." No sooner than Leah had spoken the words than she peered at John for a reaction. He looked troubled. Trying to get that boy to talk was like trying to get water out of a dry well.

"I'm going to miss having him around," John said. "And I realize this is just the beginning of each of us going our own way. Rankles me a bit, and I should be happy for him, but I know it's the way of families."

"You've got me." Mark laughed. "I'll be here to help until you kick me off the ranch — or when I'm eighteen and have a homestead of my own. But I agree. Evan is a good brother."

The three rode out along the St. Vrain River and on toward the foothills. Leah urged her mare beside John. "Make sure Evan knows how you feel."

"He does," John said. "I want so much for him. Almost makes me hurt."

"Did that come before or after you two went to wrestling in the dirt?" Mark said from behind them.

Calm down and listen or you'll never learn a thing.

"We didn't wrestle in the dirt." John turned in the saddle and glared at his brother. "And thank you for letting Mama know about it."

Mark laughed. "No matter. You two talked about whatever got you riled up."

Leah fumed. She didn't know any more than before. "Should I know about any of what happened between you two?"

"Nope," John said. "Just brother stuff."

Then why won't Ember look at or talk to you?

John stretched in his saddle and peered ahead of them. "Is that Wirt heading this way?"

Leah's heart did a flip, and she stared toward the lone rider on the painted gelding. She recognized the horse, and she sure recognized the rider.

"Wonder what he wants?" Mark said. "Hope there isn't trouble again."

Leah hadn't considered trouble, only that Wirt might be on his way to see her. Once he made his way to them, he greeted her but nothing more.

"What brings you to the 5T?" John said.

Wirt leaned on his saddle horn. He sure had a grand way of carrying himself. At that thought, she sensed color rising in her cheeks. One would think she had been touched in the head.

"I wanted to talk to you about a few things." He glanced at Leah then back to John. "Not exactly anything I'd want to discuss in front of Miss Leah. When would be a good time to come back?"

"Nonsense," Leah said. "Mark and I can ride on together."

"Are you sure you don't mind?" John said.

Leah nodded at Mark. "I'll race you to the river."

"And you've already lost." Mark dug his heels into the gelding's flanks and took off with Leah right behind him.

"My horse is faster than yours."

They raced over the pastureland alongside tall spindly bushes of wildflowers, yellow daises with black centers. This was another part of being a mama that she'd one day relive in memories. But for now, she'd leave John and Wirt alone and hope it didn't mean trouble.

CHAPTER 36

John and Wirt watched Mama and Mark leave clods of dirt in their wake. The two men walked their horses back toward the ranch.

"What's going on?" John said. "Can't believe you'd ride all this way for a social call." He paused. "Well, yeah, you would." Granted, he didn't mind Wirt showing up at the ranch, but how did he feel about him courting Mama?

"Partly. I have something else to talk about, but not at the moment. I wanted to tell you what I learned from Victor Oberlander."

John didn't like the sound of those words. Every day that had gone by without an incident from the cattle ranchers made John more nervous. He'd seen too much to think trouble had ridden off.

"Do you remember when we took Hawkins' body to the Wide O and questioned the whereabouts of a couple of his ranch hands?" Wirt said.

"Right, I was curious about where they were since they rode with Leon the day I stopped Bert's hanging. Those two had motive to kill Hawkins since he and I humiliated them. But Oberlander claimed they were with cattle on the free range."

Wirt scratched his jaw where stubble covered his normally shaven face. "I stopped by earlier today to see if they'd returned or if there was a way to talk to either of them. Oberlander tells me both men have disappeared, and about twenty more head are missing."

John's suspicions had surfaced. "The rustlers saw they'd gotten away with stealin', and now they're back to make more money. So it looks like the three men involved in the attempted hanging got into the cattle rustlin' business." Did Bert know the three who tried to hang her? "And one of the missing ranch hands was the first to open fire on Leon."

"Possibly four men are involved."

"And one of them decided to eliminate Leon. But——"

"What?"

John thought through the rest of his suspicions. "I'd like to find them, either alive or dead."

"So would Oberlander."

"Let's ride over to the Wide O and see if he'll accompany us on a search party." John's mind spun with more of what he'd been thinking. "Neither of those ranch hands acted smart enough to pull off this big of an operation."

Wirt took a deep breath. "Ever think about being a US Marshal?"

Close thought. "A few times. Mainly I'm interested in law." He chuckled, but nothing was really funny. "Odd, I've never admitted that to anyone. I'd be obliged if you'd keep it to yourself. Folks around here think I'm a born and bred rancher."

"Don't wait too long to pursue what you really want. I did, and now I wonder if it's too late."

John had another crawly feelin' about where this conversation was going.

"I think you have a good idea why else I'm here."

"Most likely so," John said.

Silence hung between them. A mockingbird flew over. Crickets chirped. And John waited.

"Five years ago, I met Leah and made a fool of myself in everything I did—not only with her but with Parker and those involved in bringing in the McCaw gang. Since then, I've become a believer and learned all I could about following the Lord and doing the best job possible as a US Marshal. I'm still working hard on both of these."

John waited while Wirt must have been garnering the courage to say why else he'd come.

"Before becoming a believer, I wrote Leah for a few years. Even asked her to marry me. She had the sense to stop writing. But I never forgot about her. Coming here was important to me on two counts—redeeming myself to the people of Rocky Falls and to Leah. John, I'm asking permission to court your mama proper. Victor Oberlander cares for her too, but I don't give a lick. If the good Lord intends for Leah and me to spend the rest of our lives together, then it will happen." Wirt blew out a long sigh. "So do I have your permission?"

John considered every word from Wirt, the way the man spoke his heart, the honesty, and what John wanted for Mama. A quick prayer filled his thoughts. What he said next to Wirt had to come from God, not from John's selfishness of making sure Mama was always there for him. "Who am I to get in the way of a man who's in love?"

Wirt stopped in his tracks and reached out to shake John's hand. "If she'll have me, I'll take care of her for the rest of my life. I'll love her and treat her like the most precious woman on the face of the earth."

John laughed. "Maybe you should write that down. Sounds like a marriage proposal."

"Maybe so."

"What about the age difference? You're a good eight years younger than Mama."

"Makes no difference to me."

John kept his gaze fixed on the man who claimed to love his mama. "What about children of your own? Mama might not be able to have more. "

"Looks to me like we'd have ourselves five boys."

"All right, Wirt. Hope you know what you're takin' on."

"A journey with Leah and wherever the road takes us."

Listening to Wirt made him wonder if he should be talking to Ember about their future. Could he make her happy? More so, could he make her forget the past stalking her like a mountain lion?

Bert stirred together sugar cookies just the way Leah had showed her. As soon as she popped them into the oven, she'd cut huge slices of beef for tonight's supper. While Leah, John, and Mark rode across the ranch, Bert wanted to prepare a fine meal. Evan, Aaron, and Davis were busy cleaning out streams that flowed from the St. Vrain's, so the animals would have fresh water. She appreciated the time alone to think and do something special for the family she so dearly loved. How her heart ached to love John and have him love her ...

There she was again, living in a fantasy world. She shoved away the melancholy thoughts with a prayer for God to make things right. A song rose to her lips, one she'd been humming all afternoon.

I saw a bright blue birdie
A sittin' in a tree,
It sang so sweet, it made me cry
And brought me to my knees.
Keep on singin', sweet birdie
Make me happy with your song.
Fill my heart with your music
Lastin' all the day long.

A knock at the door startled her. The old fears of who stood on the porch raced through her. She dug her fingers into her palms and walked across the room.

"Who's there?"

"Your brother."

Her temples began to throb. "I'm not opening the door."

"Do you want me to kick it in?" He lifted the latch and stepped inside. She'd forgotten to lock it when the others left. The rifle leaning against the wall by the fireplace caught her attention. *Can I turn a gun on my own brother?*

"Don't go near that rifle, or I'll use it on you."

Bert's gaze slowly lifted to his. Simon grabbed her arm and pulled her to him. His wide eyes burrowed deep into hers. "I oughta throttle you good for all the trouble you've caused me. But you'd have to explain to John Timmons what happened. Can't risk you spillin' your guts."

"Where are Clint and Lester?"

"None of your business."

"Are they even alive?"

Simon buried his fingers into her flesh. "Bein' sassy won't save you, so you best shut up. I did good by you, and you owe me."

"How did you ever do 'good' by me?"

"Made sure you had food in your belly."

"But you stole and killed people to get it," she said, sounding braver than she thought. "I'd rather have died."

"Don't think I didn't want that to happen. Having you gone would have meant more for the rest of us."

"Then leave me alone."

"Brave talk for a stupid fool."

I'm not a fool, and I'm not stupid. A burst of courage swept through her. "What about Lizbeth? Why didn't you settle down with her?" She'd heard Clint and Lester laughing about him sneaking over to Lizbeth's when her husband was gone. Lizbeth's husband liked to hunt more than he cared for his wife, so Simon took care of what she needed. At least Simon claimed so.

"I got tired of her."

"You killed her husband and abandoned her with your baby. Explain that to me."

He sneered, and the pressure increased on her arm. One more bruise to remind her of what he could do if he put his mind to it.

"Why didn't you put that life behind you and work at being respectable?"

"You mean livin' poor while other folks did good? No thanks."

"Lizbeth didn't care about money. She cared for you. Told me so."

"She killed any feelings I could have had for her," he said. "When I shot her old man, she acted like I was an animal. I did what was best for her and the baby. But she didn't look at it that way. The look in her eyes made me sick. Come to think of it, she looked at me the same way you do."

"Have you beaten her too?"

He released his hand from her arm and shoved her across the room and onto the floor. Her head hit the table leg. Simon stood over her, his legs spread on each side of her body. For a moment she thought she'd black out completely. A vigorous throbbing in the back of her skull threatened to make her ill. Simon's silence meant his anger was about to explode. She knew well. Some scars never healed.

She and Lizbeth did have one thing in common—a loathing for a man that they'd once tried to love.

"Mind you, girl. You owe me. I have a job for you, so don't try runnin'." He kicked her in the ribs and left her. His boots thudded across the porch and down the steps.

She took a sharp breath praying her ribs weren't broken. When the pain slowly equaled the hammering on the back of her head, she prayed Simon, Clint, and Lester were stopped. She didn't understand any of her brothers, but she didn't want them dead … just stopped.

CHAPTER 37

I'd hoped to find signs of your ranch hands." John swung his leg over his horse and walked to the edge of a rocky peak. From there, a man could see for miles. He lifted binoculars to his eyes. "They hid their trail pretty good."

"No sign of them at all." Oberlander wiped the sweat streaming down his brow and joined John. "All we have is a string of unanswered questions, dead bodies, and rustled cattle." He swore.

Sure glad Wirt will be courtin' Mama instead of Victor Oberlander.

Wirt took a long drink from his canteen. "John here thinks those two weren't smart enough to steal cattle and drive them out of the area."

"Good point," Oberlander said. "I always thought they were two knots short of a noose." He laughed. "Didn't even know how to count their pay."

"Somebody could have been using them. But unless we can locate their bodies or bring them in for questioning, we have nothing." Wirt dismounted and joined John and Oberlander.

John continued to scan the area with his binoculars. Elk, long-horned sheep, and cattle roamed the free range area.

"Do me a favor and tell me you see those two. Or at least the cattle," Wirt said.

John handed him the binoculars. "See for yourself. Not a sign."

Wirt sighed. "I may need to wire for help."

"I'm against that," Oberlander said. "US Marshals don't have a stake in what's been stolen like us ranchers who've lost valuable property. We're mad and want this stopped. Deputize us and we'll find the thieves and string them up."

John wanted the rustlers caught, but he wasn't about to organize a group of vigilantes. "Deputies don't hang lawbreakers. They bring them in to stand trial."

"Right," Wirt said. "Neither Bob, John, nor I will put up with a hanging party."

"I'll make a deal with you." Oberlander adjusted his hat. "Whoever finds those thieves first gets to choose how to deal with them."

Wirt shook his head. "I don't make deals like that."

"Neither do I."

John read the challenge in Oberlander's eyes, a trait he'd seen in him before. "I'm asking you real politelike not to take the law into your own hands," John said. "I'd welcome men who'd be willing to ride with us, but not on your terms."

"And I'm telling you that I've put up with your law-abiding ways long enough." Oberlander walked to his horse and grabbed the reins. "No man's going to rustle my cattle and get away with it. I'll pick my men, and you pick yours."

"Don't do anything you'll regret," Wirt said.

"No chance of that. One more thing, Zimmerman. Stay away from Leah. You're not good enough for her."

Wirt squared off with Oberlander, eye to eye, shoulder to shoulder. "Miss Leah is quite capable of choosing which man she wants — if she wants either of us. I don't cower to a threat. Neither do I run. Stick that in a piece of cornbread and swallow it."

John stood back and attempted to dispel his own aggravation at Oberlander. Mama might not have all the things Oberlander had to offer, but the price she'd pay for his disrespect of the law and his temperament weren't worth it. Yet Wirt had handled himself well, and John was pleased. Could probably take a few lessons himself since John still fumed with the arrogant owner of the Wide O.

"John, you could ride with me," Oberlander said. "No need wasting your time with the local law and a coward of a US Marshal. You're good with a gun, and I need men who aren't afraid to bring a man down."

"I believe in enforcing the law." John put his heart behind his words. "If a man takes the law into his own hands, then he isn't any better than those rustlers."

"I take that as an insult."

"Take it any way you like, Mr. Oberlander. I'm committed to the law." John breathed in satisfaction for standing up to the man. But this wasn't over yet. In fact, the problem had just grown worse.

CHAPTER 38

Leah stole a glance at Ember while the girl finished setting the table for supper. With the knives, forks, and spoons in place and the plates directly in front of the chairs, Leah fretted over what must be bothering Ember. Ever since Leah and Mark had returned from their afternoon ride, the girl looked pale, and her brows knit together as though she were in pain.

"Are you feeling all right?" Leah whispered.

"I'm fine." Ember smiled, but Leah could tell it was forced.

"I don't believe that."

"My side's bothering me." She avoided Leah's gaze.

"Ah, I see. I can fix you a cup of ginger tea to ease the cramping."

"Thank you. I'd appreciate the relief."

Leah wrapped an arm around Bert's waist, and she winced. "I'm sorry. Sometimes my womanly time pains me too. The supper you've fixed here is wonderful. Almost like a celebration."

Ember shrugged. "I wanted to show you how much you all mean to me."

"Oh, we know, sweet girl. All any of us need do is look at your face." She stroked Ember's hair, which had continued to grow and taken on the look of spun honey.

The door creaked open, and John and Wirt stepped inside. Leah sensed her insides bouncing as if she were a silly girl. Mercy, Wirt seemed to get more handsome every day, his shoulders broader.

"Mama, I asked Wirt for supper. Hope you don't mind," John said.

Leah laughed. "Ember has quite a feast for us tonight. And of course I don't mind."

Wirt lifted his chin. "Smells wonderful."

Was it Leah's wishful thoughts? Or did he seem nervous? Of late, her words twisted and stuttered until she found herself embarrassed. "I'm going to ring the dinner bell. Ember has everything done but pulling it off the stove."

John cleared his throat. "Wirt, why don't you give Mama a hand with the dinner bell? Sometimes it's a bit of a chore since she's short." He peered at the platter of tomatoes and cucumbers on the table. "I'll help Bert if you two will bring another tomato from the garden. I've got a real taste for fresh tomatoes. Could eat two of them by myself."

Leah stared at her oldest son. Why did he want her and Wirt alone? Understanding flashed. John wanted to spend a few minutes with Ember. She snatched up the garden bucket. "I'll make sure there are plenty."

John and Evan must have talked about Ember. She loved it when her sons behaved like grown men.

Once outside, Wirt rang the dinner bell and carried the bucket. Together they walked toward the garden. "Thank you for allowing those two to spend time alone," she said. "Looks like John has decided to get to know Ember better."

"What?" Wirt's widened eyes caused her to laugh.

"John and Ember. He must want to talk to her privately." She gasped. "I hope he hasn't discovered bad news."

"The only bad news I know about is Oberlander has decided to form his own posse to find the cattle thieves."

Trouble always came in threes, but lately it came in fours and fives. "Is there anything you can do?"

"Free country, Leah. Victor Oberlander has the right to meet like the rest of us. Only when he breaks the law can one of us step in. But Bob told me something this morning that might help. One of those ranch hands has a sister who lives in Estes Park. She might know his whereabouts."

Leah nodded. "I wish John wasn't a deputy, but that's like asking the sun not to shine." She glanced back at the house, and a shiver rose on her arms. "Is John questioning Ember again?"

Wirt coughed. "No. Not to my knowledge. He's giving me time to talk to you."

Leah stopped at the beginning of the row of tomatoes. "Talk to me?" But she knew. She really did.

"I asked him if I could come calling on you. If you don't mind."

Leah's gaze flew to his face. Oh, such a finely chiseled one too. He had the grayest eyes and a dimpled smile. She shivered again. Heat raced up her throat. "Wirt, I'm forty-one years old with five sons. You've never been married."

Wirt set the bucket down onto the ground and took both her hands into his. "Leah, you know I care about you. I want to court you proper. I want us to be married." He pressed his lips together. "I'm not saying this right. I love you, Leah. I want to marry you and take care of you for as long as God keeps me on this earth."

Leah's heart fluttered, and for a moment she thought it might burst from her chest. "Wirt, are you sure? I'm not sure I can give you children, and you—"

"I can think of nothing finer than helping you with your sons."

She wanted to scream yes, but was it possible to have a life with Wirt? What if God said no? "I suppose I should pray about this."

He smiled, a sweet caring upturn of his lips. "I'd expect you to."

She wanted him to kiss her. Years had passed since Frank had sealed his love on her lips. Was she betraying him?

No, she thought not. Leah stood on tiptoe and brushed a kiss across Wirt's mouth.

A grown woman of forty-one had every right to steal a kiss from the man she loved.

John believed if a stone wall stood between him and Bert, he could break his way through. But the problems separating them were thicker than a mountain of rock. He'd set out to earn her trust, and he'd done a fine job of ruining any hope of having her confide in him. He wanted to end her fears of whoever had frightened her, but how could he when she avoided him?

"What can I do to help you with your fine supper?"

She peeked inside the oven. "Nothing. I'll finish up as soon as everyone gets inside."

He propped his weight on one leg and then the other. "I'm really sorry for the way I acted ... when you were with Evan."

"I haven't thought any more about it."

He wanted to think that she had fretted about his accusations. "Guess I'm a jealous fool."

Bert straightened, and he noted her pale face. "What did you say?"

He swallowed hard and stepped closer. "I said I acted like a jealous fool."

"You don't know what you're sayin'. There are too many bad things you don't know about me. I tried to get you to listen the night you decided to chase me down."

"Anything you might have done was taken care of when you became a believer."

"But the past doesn't disappear. We both know that."

John found himself swimming in the depths of her brown eyes. "I want to earn your trust ... be your friend ... build a future together."

Tears pooled her eyes, and he ached to hold her. "John, we have no future until those who chase me are gone. Maybe not even then."

He gathered her into his arms. She winced, and he wished he could eliminate the fear in her eyes. "Let me help you. No man should have that much power over a woman. Who is he? Who are they?"

At first she trembled and buried her face into his chest. Her quiet sobbing was all he could hear. He refused to let her go, and slowly she relaxed. "This is where you belong, Ember. Not running. Not hiding. You belong right here beside me."

"Everything I touch or care about is destroyed."

"Someone has filled you with lies. Trust me, please. Tell me who is after you."

She lifted her tear-stained face from his chest. "I can't," she whispered. "Because all of you will be killed. You have no idea the people he's killed ... they've killed. I should leave, but I can't. Am I weak? Am I selfish for wanting to stay with you and your family?"

John could only draw her closer to him. He had no answers. He'd prayed for guidance but God hadn't responded. Or maybe John wasn't listening hard enough.

She pulled herself away from him and stepped back. "You'd best tend to things outside. I need to finish supper, and I can't do that with you here."

John noted her stubborn stance, how her jaw tightened and the way she pressed her lips together. "All right. I'll leave you alone. But someday we're going to talk about us—you and me." He reached out and rubbed her shoulders, wanting to draw her into his arms but knowing he needed to abide by her wishes.

Her stoic look didn't match the pleading in her eyes. But what did that mean? He shouldn't push her because she might run like before. Taking a deep breath, he turned and forced one foot in front of the other to the door. He grasped the latch and watched his knuckles turn white while the ache inside him for the woman he loved increased. As selfish as it sounded, he was tired of always doing things for everyone else and not following his own dreams. God help him if his thoughts were wrong, but he couldn't let this moment pass without speaking his heart.

John whirled around and captured her gaze. "I can't go."

"What do you mean?" She glanced at the stove and wrung her hands. "I have things to do."

Courage rose stronger than anything he'd ever imagined. "Nothing could be more important than what I feel for you."

She gasped and he took quick steps back to her. Taking her into his arms, he let his thoughts find their way to his lips.

"I love you, Ember Rose. I can't imagine another day of my life without you. Guess I've known it all along. Tell me we have a future together. I need to know now."

Her pale face might have stopped other men, but not John Parker Timmons. He waited. Her body finally relaxed against him.

"I'm not sure I can answer you."

He rested his chin atop her head. "I need to know." His heart continued to pound against his chest, and he waited.

"I do love you, John. I have nothing to offer you but a horrible past, but I do love you."

She trembled in his arms, and he held her until she calmed again. "Your love is all I need, all I ever need."

She lifted her head, and he could resist no longer. He found her lips and drank deeply, firmly committing his love to the tiny woman in his arms. Whatever the future held, they'd face it together. Nothing could come between them. Nothing.

CHAPTER 39

John and Wirt rode up to a small stone house on the narrow road leading out of Estes Park into the Rockies. Bob had given them the name of Aggie Hanson, the sister of Ralph Hanson, who was one of the missing ranch hands from the Wide O.

John noted the blue columbines—one of Mama's favorite wildflowers—blooming in the front of the house, and a rocker on the porch. A calico cat sat on a rag rug. Homey. It looked like a place where folks could be happy. Not a place where two potential cattle thieves might be hiding.

The two men dismounted and tied their horses to a hitching post. Revolver in hand, they scanned the area for signs of an ambush. The blood in John's veins flowed like a flash flood. Mixed emotions always accompanied him with deputy work. He enjoyed the excitement of the chase, but he dreaded the possibility of spilled blood.

Wirt nodded and John crept around to the back of the house in case the two suspects decided to make a run for it. Chickens pecked at a sprinkling of corn on the ground. Birds sang. A butterfly fluttered past. But no sounds from inside the house. Memories of Leon's demise filled John's thoughts. He wasn't about to get shot this time. Neither did he want to turn his gun on another man, unless he had to.

A small dilapidated barn stood about forty feet from the house, a good place to hide. He crouched low and hurried across the yard separating him from the barn. He waited outside and listened.

Wirt pounded on the front door of the house. "Miss Hanson, this is US Marshal Wirt Zimmerman. Ma'am, I'd like to speak to you, if you don't mind." The man's booming voice could wake the dead. "Ma'am, if you're here, I'd like to talk to you. The marshal told me you live alone, and I assure you I only want to ask a few questions about your brother Ralph."

John glanced about. A fence needed mending. The house and barn roofs were in sad repair. A window on the side of the barn caught his attention, but he'd stay put until he heard from Wirt.

"Ma'am," Wirt said. "I'm asking you one last time to open the door. If not, I'm coming inside."

A few moments later, Wirt appeared from around the house. "The door's locked." He turned the knob to the backdoor, and it creaked open. He nodded for John to join him.

John clenched the handle of the weapon in his hand. Lingering smells of bacon and eggs from breakfast clung to the air. Wirt motioned for John to cover him before he stepped inside. In the kitchen, a small table covered with a blue and yellow tablecloth sat under a yellow curtained window. The curtains were drawn, decreasing the men's view in the small shadowed house. Gun positioned, John scanned every corner while Wirt moved on to a bedroom. A single bed and trunk filled the area, definitely a woman's quarters with a quilt and what looked like embroidered pillowcases—hard for John to discern in the dark shadows.

"Miss Hanson. Don't be afraid. We only want to talk to you." Wirt kneeled and looked under the bed. No one hid from them there.

The men made their way into the parlor with its sparse furnishings. The only sound came from a mantle clock above the fireplace.

"Odd she'd leave the backdoor unlocked," John said. "Let's check the barn. I didn't hear anything when I was out there, but a window facing the back side of the house would give somebody a clear shot."

Wirt shrugged. "Then we'll go out the front and circle around."

A short while later, they slipped up to the barn door. This time John lifted the latch while Wirt covered him. The latch lifted and dropped with a dull thud. Sunlight lit a golden path down the middle of the neatly kept barn. A cow was tied on the left side and a swaybacked mare stood beside her. Both animals had fresh hay. A person could hide here but not for long.

Wirt pointed to the hayloft. John started up the ladder, tucking his boot into each wrung without a sound.

"We might as well give up and head on back to Rocky Falls," Wirt said. "This place is deserted, and we've got plenty of work to do. What's wrong with Miss Hanson that she won't answer the door to a couple of US Marshals?"

By then John had climbed to the loft. The wound to his shoulder was still sore enough to breathe caution into every step. Wirt stood below with his revolver poised, but he didn't stand beside John. He peered over the top. The loft had a small pile of hay in the far corner. No one cowered in the corners. A rustle in the pile caught John's attention. He crept over the top of the loft and made his way to the hay.

"I've got my gun aimed at you," John said. "Come on out of there, or I'm opening fire."

The rustling increased, and a gray-haired woman crawled out of the hay with a rifle in her hand. "Please, mister, don't shoot me. I don't know where Ralph is."

John took her rifle, then helped her to her feet. "If you have nothing to tell me, why are you hiding?"

Her eyes widened. "Because I was afraid."

"Of what?"

"Are you one of them?" Her lips quivered.

"You heard the US Marshal. We're here on law business."

Her eyes darted back and forth across the loft like a frightened animal.

"Ma'am, let's climb down the ladder so we can talk. We're not here to hurt you but to find out information on Ralph's whereabouts." He took her hand and led her to the ladder.

The woman didn't look over ninety pounds. She picked at the pieces of hay sticking to her faded brown dress. With a sigh she followed John to the ladder. Once she was near the barn floor, Wirt helped her the rest of the way.

"Miss Hanson, I'm US Marshal Wirt Zimmerman, and the young man climbing down the ladder is the deputy from Rocky Falls. Your brother is missing, and we have reasons to believe he's a part of a cattle rustlin' gang."

Her eyes pooled. "I haven't seen him."

"When did you see him last?"

She moistened her lips.

"Miss Hanson." Wirt's voice softened. "Is Ralph running from the law or someone else? Or both?"

John thought how much Wirt's questioning sounded like the unanswered questions he'd posed to Ember.

"Ralph is my only brother."

"Yes ma'am. Has he been here?"

She hesitated and looked from Wirt to John and back again. "I know my brother has broken the law, but I don't know what he's done. He said if I told anyone he'd been here, we'd both be killed."

The similarities between Miss Hanson's and Ember's circumstances reinforced John's thoughts about the thieves. The connections ... the man or men who used manipulation and fear to accomplish what was needed. Granted, most lawbreakers used clever tactics to outsmart the law. But what Ember refused to state was linked to fear, not only for herself but for the entire Timmons family. "Who would kill you?" John said.

"I don't know who they are. Ralph said he had a job to do for them; then he would have enough money to leave the territory. But if he made a mistake or if I told, those men would kill us." Her voice cracked, and she sucked in a sob.

In his gut, John knew she spoke the truth. He'd seen the same terror in Ember's eyes. "Miss Hanson, I believe you."

"I'm weary of watching the road and not lighting the lantern at night and hiding in the hayloft." She lifted her chin. "I'd rather be dead than be a prisoner in my own home."

John breathed in regret for the woman. Once he helped bring in the rustlers, he was devoting his time to Ember. If she didn't tell him what and whom she feared, someday, someone would be pulling her down from a hayloft. And she'd be a frightened old woman who'd rather be dead than live another day looking over her shoulder. John turned his attention to Wirt.

"Ma'am," Wirt said, "did Ralph tell you what he was doing? Or the names of who might harm you?"

She shook her head. "I'm so afraid."

"Is there a place where you can go until this is over?" Wirt said. "A relative or friend?"

"My ... my niece lives in Nebraska."

Wirt smiled. "I understand you don't trust us, but John and I would like to help you find safety."

"I don't have any money."

"I'll pay for it," Wirt said. "You pack your things, and we'll take you to the marshal to make arrangements."

She gasped. "Why would you do that for me? I could be lying."

"If you're deceiving us, one day it'll catch up to you. But what I see is a woman who wants to live free from the bondage of fear."

She began to weep, and Wirt wrapped his arm around her shoulders.

"Thank you, sir. I'll never forget you. My brother has broken the law and still you are looking out for me." She lifted her weathered face to him. "Even if you pay for my traveling, I can't tell you more about Ralph."

"John and I are determined to find who's behind the cattle rustlin' and murders. We think Ralph is involved. Understand I can't guarantee what will happen to him."

"Yes sir."

John admired and respected what he'd just witnessed in Wirt. Mama had a good man. From this moment on, he'd never worry about Wirt Zimmerman and his mother.

CHAPTER 40

Dead ends. John had seen enough of them. The ranches around Rocky Falls had not reported stolen cattle in two weeks. And like before, the folks were spooked. He held his breath and waited. Meanwhile, the weather for mid-August had stayed warm, but soon the days would drift into autumn, and that meant winter would soon be knocking on their door. Tomorrow all of the boys would haul more dead trees from higher ground for firewood. Mark had cured hides to tan. John always felt anxious this time of year with winter on their heels and so much to do.

He leaned on the corral fence and watched Racer pick up his head as a northern wind blew across the pasture. This afternoon they'd take a ride to check on the cattle.

"You feel it too?" he said to his stallion. "Soon the leaves will fall and snow will fly. Then we'll be stuck mending bridles and harnesses instead of spending so many hours on the range."

"And we'll all be shivering," Ember said.

He whirled around and smiled at the young woman who had stolen his heart. She handed him a cup of coffee. "Supper is about ready."

"I'm on my way. Heard the dinner bell and wanted to enjoy a few more minutes of the sunset." He took a sip. "How's my girl?"

"Very happy."

"Hope I can take the credit."

"You can, especially today."

"Why's that?"

"It's my birthday."

"Wonderful!" John scanned the area to see if any of his brothers could see from the house. Satisfied they were alone, he planted a kiss on her full lips. "Happy birthday."

"Thank you, Mr. Timmons. Even if it wasn't my birthday, I'd still be incredibly happy, and you can take all of the credit." She touched her finger to her chin. "God takes the credit first."

John warmed from the inside out, while affection for her caused him to think things he dare not say or do.

"If you could be anything in this great wide country, what would it be?" she said.

"Strange question for you to ask."

"It's my birthday, so I'm asking." She gestured all around them. "I already believe you are the best rancher in the country. But I imagine there's more."

Did she know him that well? "I've told only one other person this."

She tilted her head, and he thought about kissing her again. "So it's a secret?"

"Guess you'd say so." He shook his head. "Not sure I can say it aloud again. A dream is rather personal. Although I did mention it to Wirt after he told me how he felt about Mama."

She nodded. "A bigger ranch? Fine horse stock? A thousand head of cattle?"

"None of those things."

"I have no idea. To me, you could do anything you set your mind to."

He lifted his hat and raked his fingers through his hair. "I'd like to go to law school and help Rocky Falls grow into a fine city. The railroad line hauls sandstone from the quarry, and we've drawn in a few folks because of their health and the benefits of the mountain air. But businesses here can only grow with the expansion of the railroad."

"What about ranching?"

"I love the land and cattle, but it's been a means of taking care of my family. There's a law school in Austin, Texas, and in a few years Denver may have one too."

She gave him a special smile, one he'd come to recognize as reserved for him. "You'd make a fine lawyer, John. You listen and you're fair." She pointed to the top rail of the fence. "See how straight this is? It's you."

He gazed into the brown eyes he'd grown to love. "I'd like to think so."

"With the coming months, you'd have time to read up on schools. I'm sure your Uncle Parker would help."

He smiled and watched Racer trot toward them. "How could I ever leave with the ranch to run?"

She patted the stallion. "You were younger than Aaron and Mark when you took over."

"But it was real hard. Not so sure I'd want my brothers to give up their boyhood for hard work."

"What if they'd like a chance to prove themselves? To be men of purpose like you?"

He touched her nose and grinned. "Are you always going to challenge me?"

"Always."

"And you'll stay until this is over."

She blinked and nodded. "I don't want to leave you."

Winter could not come soon enough. A hope for the future . . .

Early Tuesday morning, right after sun-up, John walked through the barn and admired the mucked out stalls. The barn hadn't looked better since Davis took on the job.

John heard a rider and walked out into the sunlight to see a stranger riding toward the house. His rifle leaned against the side of the barn. This time of the day, his arm often stiffened, but he could shoot straight and to its mark. Cattle rustlers might still be combing the area, and he'd be a fool to trust a man he didn't know.

He scrutinized the rider. The man looked like he'd been traveling for a while—dusty clothes, shaggy beard, lean. But his rifle lay horizontal on the right side of his saddle instead of across his lap. One hand rested on his thigh, opposite the rifle and the other hand held the reins. Good sign. But John had to invoke caution.

"Mornin'," John said. "What can I do for you?"

The stranger stayed on his horse. "The name's Steven Lockhart. Lookin' for work."

The boys were heading back to school soon, and he needed help, especially with Evan leaving. "Where you from?"

"Wyoming. Gets mighty cold up there."

"Does here too."

"Can't be any worse. All I know is ranchin'. Can you use me? I work cheap."

John smiled. "My brothers help out during the summer months. Right now I don't have much work until they get back to school in September."

"I'd be willing to work for room and board until then."

John continued to study the young man before him. Caution jumped into his bones. "Do you have anyone I can wire in Wyoming about you?"

"Sure do. I even have a letter in my saddlebag from the last ranch where I worked."

With all the rustling of late, John's nature refused to take the word of a stranger. "I'd prefer wiring myself."

"I understand. A man has to be careful. I'd do the same. Once you get a good word about me, how long before you'd need an extra hand?"

"Not for about five weeks." John thought by then he'd be able to do Evan's chores plus his own without his arm paining him. "I do have fence to build and cattle to drive back from summer pastures."

"Do we have a deal?"

"Let me send a wire and talk it over with my family."

"All right. Mind if I camp on your land tonight?"

John had been hungry and tired many a time, but those times built character. "Why don't you have breakfast with us, and I'll make arrangements for you to stay at a hotel tonight in Rocky Falls?"

"Couldn't I camp on your land after I check a couple of other ranches to see if they need help?"

"We've had some problems with cattle rustlers. I need to be mindful of you and those looking out for their own cattle."

"What about the local law?"

John chuckled. "I'm Rocky Falls' deputy. We thought we found the rustler, but more livestock are missing. Folks are edgy."

"Thanks for the warnin'. I'd enjoy breakfast with your family, but I'd like to help with chores. Never been one to take charity."

"I respect a man who wants to work for his keep."

"Thanks." Steven swung down from his horse. "What can I do to help you until breakfast?"

John pointed to where a couple of trees needed to be chopped. "I was about to chop wood until then."

"Let's get at it."

About thirty minutes later, with another cord of wood ready for winter, John showed Steven where to wash up at the well. His brothers were curious and introduced themselves. Evan studied him but said nothing. The stranger had worked hard and been good company. John listened to every word he said. Many a man with bad intentions knew how to befriend his prey. Steven could be what he claimed, or he could be a man looking for something to steal. Still, he didn't carry a hand gun and seemed content to leave his rifle with his horse.

"I like that you're protective of your family," Steven said. "Shows you're a smart man. Of course you bein' a deputy and all shows you know how to use a gun."

"I'd like to think so, but life can deal us a hard blow if we're not careful."

"What happened to your arm?"

"Got shot trying to bring in a cattle rustler. Probably not one of my smart moves." John handed Steven a towel to dry his face, hands, and neck. "Mama's a good cook, and there's always plenty."

"Bert baked the biscuits," Davis said.

Steven laughed. "You have a brother who bakes bread?"

"No sir. Bert's a girl. She helps Mama in the kitchen and stuff. I used to help, but now I'm too big."

Steven eyed Davis appreciatively. "I can see you're about ready to bring in wild mustangs. I bet you could break them too."

The group made their way to the front door. His brothers joked and talked to Steven as though they'd known him all their lives. Maybe since John couldn't do much with his bandaged arm, Steven might be an answer to a prayer for help.

The door opened and Ember walked out onto the porch. "Your mama and I thought we might have to go round you all up. Breakfast is—" She blanched.

"We've been talking to Steven," Davis said. "He helped John chop firewood while I did my chores in the barn."

"Ember, this is Steven Lockhart," John said. "Thought there'd be enough breakfast for him this morning. He's new to Rocky Falls. Lookin' for work."

"Mornin', miss," Steven removed his hat. "If the food inside tastes half as good as it smells, I'll be one happy man."

Ember seemed glued to the porch. "It's a . . . pleasure, Mr. Lockhart."

"Come on in," Mama called. "I've set an extra plate."

John studied Ember. Something about Steven bothered her. Frightened her. Did she know Steven? One way to find out.

CHAPTER 41

Leah liked Steven the moment he smiled and thanked her for allowing him to have breakfast with her family. The least they could do was feed him and hope he found work. John could have given him plenty of chores for the day, but she respected his decision. Couldn't be too careful. However, the Bible did speak clearly about taking care of the homeless and feeding the hungry.

"These are the best biscuits," Steven said. "My own sister couldn't have made better. Miss Bert, I thank you for these."

"Where's home?" Ember stared at the man. Belligerence sparked from her voice and eyes.

Why doesn't she like Steven? Does she know him?

"Missouri. I hired on to a rancher in Wyoming, but the winters are too cold. I plan to earn some money and head home. Gotta girl waitin' for me there."

"I'm sure those at home are missing you," Ember continued. "Do you have any brothers?"

Steven smiled, revealing a few missing teeth. "Two brothers younger than me." He jabbed a slice of apple with his fork. "The apples are right tasty."

"Ember takes the credit for those," Leah said.

"Thank you, miss. Now is your name Bert or Ember?"

Ember stared at Steven. She hadn't touched a thing on her plate. "I answer to both." She turned to Leah. "Is Mr. Zimmerman stopping by this evenin'?"

"Not tonight. He rode into Denver."

"When will he return?"

Odd that Ember was interested in when Wirt planned to visit them. "Less than a week. He promised to stop here on his way back." She paused for a moment to consider how God had blessed her with such a fine man who never tired of demonstrating his love and devotion for her. She missed him whenever he was gone, but he was always in her heart.

She sighed. How could a US Marshal and a widow with five sons form a family? Wirt said for her not to worry. She inwardly smiled. Worry was a woman's lot in life.

The boys talked noisily—as usual—each one vying for Steven's time. And he did not fail them. A good-mannered young man. He did his parents proud. Yet, it bothered her about Ember, and she promised herself to find out why.

The next morning, John walked to the barn to hitch up the wagon. His brothers gathered up the tools they'd need to mend fence, and Ember was packing them a noon meal. Steven rode up about the same time as the previous day.

"Mornin'," Steven said. "I'm like an old flea-bitten dog. I'm back to see if you'd sent that wire to Wyoming and if your brothers had made a decision about takin' me on as a ranch hand."

John shook his head, never liking to be the one to give bad news. "I'm sorry. I can't afford to pay you until Aaron, Mark, and Davis are back in school. Evan plans to leave for university training shortly after. Then I'll need to hire help."

Steven slowly shook his head. "What about the option of helping out for a bunk and food for a little while? I'm powerful tired of an empty belly. I like the stars as a roof over my head but not in the rain and snow. I didn't ride out to those other ranchers you told me about. Didn't want any of them thinking I was up to no good."

Compassion touched John. Never be it said that he let a man go hungry. But he hadn't ridden into town to send the wire. A lot of work had beset them of late. John inhaled deeply. "I'll go in and talk it over with Mama and Evan."

"I'll wait."

John hesitated while his thoughts raced. Might be nice to have Steven here when he had to do deputy work, especially when Evan left. All Steven claimed he wanted was food and a place to sleep. Since he'd offered information for John to wire the ranch in Wyoming and his parents' home in Missouri, he surely wasn't a rustler. And none of them could spare the time today to ride into Rocky Falls to send the wires.

John refused to give in to pressure and then realize he'd made a dangerous mistake. Being head of the household seemed to get harder instead of easier. He walked to the barn and searched for his brother. "Evan, can I see you in the house for a minute?"

Evan obliged. He waved at Steven and pushed a shovel onto the wagon before following John to the house.

"What does Steven want now?" Evan said.

Alarm raced through John. "I take it you think there's a problem with him."

Evan shrugged. "Too mannerly for me. Like he's hiding something."

"He wants to work for food and a bunk."

"Sounds like he's hungry and tired of sleeping outside."

"I can tell him no," John said. "Remind him we need to hear from the ranch in Wyoming or his folks in order to verify what he told us."

Evan stopped on the porch and stared at the man still mounted on his horse. "Seems to me a man wouldn't offer that information if he was up to no good."

"My thoughts too. I want to ask Mama's opinion."

Inside the house, he flashed Ember a smile, and she returned it—along with a strange look he had no idea how to decipher. Women ... so hard to figure out. He wanted to ask her about Steven last night, but she'd gone to bed early.

The moment Evan closed the door behind them, he turned to Mama and Evan. "Steven's back. He wants to know if he can work for food and a bunk until I can bring him on."

"I'll wait outside while you discuss this," Bert said.

"No need," Mama said.

"Uh, I think so." Without another word, Bert stepped onto the porch.

She must be sick. Or possibly Ember didn't feel like she should be present during family discussions. Later he'd discuss the matter with her.

Mama peered up at Evan. "What do you think, son?"

Evan hesitated and John gave him time to form his words. "Do you think it's wise with the cattle rustlin' going on?"

John studied his brother's face before he responded. "You told me outside that you thought he was too mannerly. Do you have doubts about the man's character?"

"It's probably me," Evan said. "Puts me in mind of a bully."

Mama looked at the door, and John wished he could read her thoughts. "I watched him with the same concern as Evan, and I know you were sizing him up too. Did Ember recognize him?"

"She hasn't said a word." John turned to Evan. "Has she talked to you about him?"

"Nothing. And she'd give that kind of information to you, brother."

"I failed to see anything to be leery of," Mama said. "In fact I like him."

John weighed Mama's and Evan's words. He hoped he wasn't making a mistake. Offering Christian hospitality was one consideration. Opening up his home to a thief or a murderer was another. "Trust for me can be hard to come by. But we could give him a chance today. If we see anything that makes us uncomfortable, then I'll ask him to leave right then."

"Sounds fair enough," Evan said.

"I agree," Mama chimed in.

Two voices out of three made sense. He'd put Steven to work for the day.

Bert couldn't tell what was being said inside the house. She wanted to know, but she didn't. For sure the topic had something to do with Simon. She'd fought hard to get the courage to tell John about her brother, but her dearly loved family could be murdered in their sleep.

How could Simon have such a powerful hold on her? *Because I've seen him kill without blinking an eye.*

Simon dismounted his horse — one she hadn't seen before and probably stolen. Davis had managed to make his way to Simon, and the child's position frightened her. She'd heard the tale more than once about how outlaws had kidnapped the boy when he was a four-year-old. Davis had to be kept safe.

Bert clenched her fists. If she were strong enough, she'd shoot him herself. But Gideon's words echoed in her mind. *Families must stick together.* Oh, the horrible confusion.

She didn't love Simon; she despised him. He pretended to be a ranch hand who wanted a job. He'd taken a gamble by giving John two places to wire about his "trustworthiness." If she didn't help Simon, he'd kill the Timmonses. And if she did, then she'd be stealing from those she loved. How did one choose between two horrible wrongs? Her insides ached.

Bert wanted to bury herself in a remote place where no one could ever find her. She'd never thought things could get this bad. Simon had done all he'd ever threatened, and she feared what would come next. He'd shot John and probably Leon and Mr. Hawkins. Now he wanted to work for John. All the while he was planning something terrible. Where was God when she needed Him? How could He view this nightmare and do nothing?

"Mornin', Miss Bert." Simon touched the brim of his tattered hat. "Sure is a right pretty day."

Could John or Marshal Culpepper or Wirt or even God stop a killer?

"John Timmons and his family have a handsome ranch. I see all of you work good together."

Gut-wrenching hate whirled through her. Where were Clint and Lester? Were they waiting for orders from Simon as they always did? Trapped and cornered, and she saw no way out.

CHAPTER 42

John and Steven rode fence along the northern parcel of the 5T. John noted more broken fencing, an endless job. Later in the week, they'd get the repairs made. The rest of the boys were felling trees, which suited John fine since he wanted time alone with Steven to make sure he was a fitting man to be around his family. *His family. And that meant Ember Rose.* He'd never felt so certain about anything in his life than wanting a future with her.

"That is some horseflesh." Steven sent an admiring glance at Racer.

John grinned and patted the stallion's neck. "He's a champion. I bought him on a whim a couple of years ago when cattle prices were up. Never regretted it. There's a powerful feeling sitting atop him when he's racing with the wind."

"Must be where you got the name."

"You bet."

"Have you bred him?"

John nodded. "The owner of the Wide O—Victor Oberlander—bred Racer to his prize mare. I'm real curious to see the colt once it's here next spring." John wasn't about to give the circumstances surrounding Ember.

"The Wide O, you say. I was going to stop by there to see about work. Like I said earlier, I figured other ranchers are skittish, like you, because of trouble with cattle rustlers."

John nodded. "A man can't afford to make mistakes when his family and his means of earning a living are at stake."

"Oh, I understand. My folks would feel the same."

John breathed in relief. The concerns he had for acting foolishly may not have substance. Steven talked a lot about his family and the girl waiting for him in Missouri. Evan's reservations were unfounded.

Four days later, Bert realized she had to find a way to turn the Timmonses against Simon without telling them the truth. The thought occupied her waking and sleeping hours. Leah and John suspected she was ill, and that was fine with her. Anything but the struggle within her to protect those she loved from evil—the worst imaginable.

She remembered reading in the Bible about the truth setting a person free. But free from what? Telling anyone about Simon invited her brother to start a killing spree. From the past, she knew his vengeance could be taken out on anyone who got in his way.

While she drew water from the well, she heard Simon talking to Davis—an innocent child who'd seen enough tragedy in his life.

"I brought you something." Simon dipped into his pocket and pulled out a peppermint stick. He bent down and presented it to Davis. "I went with your brother into Rocky Falls. Saw this and thought you might like it."

Could it be that John had finally sent those telegrams?

Davis beamed. "Thank you, Steven. Peppermint's my favorite."

"Good. I thought so. And I brought one for Miss Leah and Miss Bert." Steven pulled out two more candies from his pocket.

How would Simon explain the money to buy penny candy? He thought through everything he said, and this would be no exception.

"I'd be glad to give it to them," Davis said.

Simon patted Davis on the back. "Someday I hope to have a son as fine as you are."

Bert wanted to scratch his eyes out—take his rifle and blow a hole through him. *What can I do?*

"Where did you get the money to buy candy?" Evan said as the two washed up for supper.

"I had a few dollars. Didn't want to spend them unless I had to. A few pennies for candy are the least I can do for all your family has done for me."

Bert lifted the bucket from the well while she fought the urge to be sick. Simon was close enough for her to smell him. Normally she walked to the stream where cool, fresh water tasted the best, but she feared Simon might find her alone. Glancing toward Evan, she caught his attention. *He's the only member of the family who doesn't trust Simon.*

A gasp nearly escaped her lips. She must act soon. Keep an eye on Simon and follow him when the others were asleep.

Davis reached out to give her a peppermint. "No, thank you. Why don't you save it for yourself?" The child's eyes sparkled.

Bert had to find a way to end this. If only she knew what Simon planned. If only she could figure out how to get all three of her brothers together so the law could make an arrest. They'd hang for sure.

How could she live with herself after that? The Bible didn't say a thing about what to do when families were killers. At least she hadn't read anything about it yet.

Bert carried the bucket of water inside the house and set it on the table. Leah kneaded bread, and Bert could feel her friend's gaze.

"I thought perhaps you were sick," Leah said. "But now I sense something else."

"I feel fine," Bert said. "Would you like for me to take the ham off the stove?"

"Not yet."

Bert recognized Leah's motherly tone of voice, and there was no escaping it. And she'd pry until Bert told her something that satisfied her.

"You don't like Steven, do you?" Leah continued to knead the bread.

Bert picked up the broom and swept an already clean floor. "Why would you ask me such a question?"

"Because when you're upset, you stay to yourself. You talk, but you don't add anything to the conversation. You're with us, but you're not. Excuse me for putting the situation this way, but the lantern is lit except no one's minding the house."

Please, Leah. "I've had much on my mind lately."

"Are you jealous because John spends a lot of time with Steven?"

Tears filled Bert's eyes. If only the truth of her feelings could be explained so easily. "No ma'am. Watch him, Leah. He's only out for himself."

"Do you know him?"

How could Bert answer the question? She was a child of God. Lying was wrong. But Simon would kill all of them. "I have to make a choice, Leah. And no matter which way I decide, something horrible is going to happen."

"Choices are usually right or wrong."

"Leah, you are so dear to me, but in this instance you're wrong." She glanced toward the door, her thoughts filled with the wickedness of her brothers. "I'll place the ham on a platter now." Without another word and feeling the intensity of Leah's gaze, she smiled all the love in her heart. "I may be a new believer, but I know God is watching out for those who love Him."

The answer to the nightmare frightened her, the choice that would change the lives of all of them. But when she weighed the magnitude of all Simon and her brothers had done and all they were capable of doing, she knew she must commit herself to the task.

Clint and Lester allowed Simon to give them orders. When he wasn't around, they didn't hurt or steal from others. Without Simon, her brothers lacked a leader. If she knew where her brothers were camped, then she could lead Mr. Zimmerman, Mr. Culpepper, and John to them. Since that seemed impossible, she'd have to expose Simon and pray her brothers left the area and rode back to Idaho.

The whole nightmare would be over. Gideon's words about families sticking together no longer meant anything to her. Gideon may have been the only member of the family who'd protected her, but his kindness didn't make him always right. In the last several weeks, she'd learned what it meant to live and love according to the Word. God had laws about how people should treat each other, and those who chose to commit crimes still needed to answer for what they'd done. Even if they were family.

She had to do this. Her life had been filled with turning her eyes away from unspeakable things. But no more, and she had to do her part. Mr. Zimmerman could return as early as tonight. Lately her songs had been influenced by the Bible and Leah's hymnal. This one seemed to come from God Himself.

In Your hands I place my trust
In Your hands I find righteousness
In Your hands all fear is gone
And by Your Spirit I find rest.

CHAPTER 43

The following day, Sunday afternoon, Leah strode into the barn where she knew John was brushing down Racer. She made her way to his side and admired the sleek stallion's glossy coat.

"I need to have a word with you."

"Sure." He grinned. "I can tell by the look on your face something's on your mind. No one's here in the barn."

"I want Steven gone."

He startled. "Why? He's been a big help and a friend to all of us."

"I don't trust him."

John ceased the brushing. "What's happened to make you think this? You know how I feel about keeping the family safe."

How did a woman explain feelings to a man? "The way he looks at us. The way he glares at Ember. The way he never slips and shouts or says something improper. It's not real."

"I disagree, Mama. I need something I can see and hear to discard a new friend. Do you want me to tell him that you don't trust him?"

Leah stiffened. She felt certain her inclinations were right. "All right. I'll find the proof. In the meantime, I don't want him alone with Davis or Ember."

"Maybe you're just missing Wirt."

A flash of fury swept through her. "I *am* missing Wirt, but not for the reasons you may think. Steven is dangerous." She lifted her chin. "Have you checked to see if the rancher in Wyoming or anyone from Missouri has responded to your telegrams?"

"Haven't been in town except the day I rode in to get feed. Then I was in a hurry to get back. So, no, I haven't checked for a wire." He went back to brushing Racer, and Leah remained by his side with her arms folded across her chest. She had no intentions of leaving the barn until she received the response she needed from John.

"Ember doesn't trust him."

"Why? She hasn't said a word to me."

"Maybe she's afraid to."

John turned to her, his gaze troubled. "All right, Mama. I'll tell him tonight after supper that it's time for him to go. And tomorrow, when he leaves, I'll send Mark or Aaron into town to see about those wires."

Every portion of her heart eased with John's words, but she didn't know why.

Bert shucked corn for supper, adding two more to the huge pile in hopes Mr. Zimmerman would return. Simon's mission of spying on the Timmonses for whatever wickedness he had in mind was running short on time. He could disappear or pull out a revolver.

Lord, please. If You have a better way, tell me.

As though her prayers had been answered, she glanced up and saw a familiar painted horse and rider heading toward the house.

Thank You. I'll do my part.

With the boys working late in anticipation of Evan moving to Fort Collins soon and the younger boys heading back to school, supper came later than usual. All of them were tired.

Earlier in the day, Leah told her John had agreed to let Steven go and planned to tell him tonight after supper. Bert considered more than once the idea of pulling John and Mr. Zimmerman aside, but too many people were crowded into the house. She didn't dare let Simon suspect a thing. Every word and move must be done according to her feeble plan.

Hungry boys and men crowded around the table, filling and refilling their plates. Bert waited for the right moment to expose Simon. He wasn't wearing a gun, but he normally carried a knife in his boot. John sat on one side of him and Mark on the other. Wirt sat at the end of the table nearest the door with his rifle propped against the wall. Bert prayed no one would be hurt.

"What did you learn in Denver?" John said to Wirt.

"The cattle's probably been sold. And you know how I feel about rustlers." Wirt picked up a glass of water, staring at the clear liquid as though it held the answers to his problems. "We can talk later. I saw Parker and talked to the marshal there. I'll tell you what they think."

"Sure," John said.

"I'd like to volunteer to help in any way I can," Simon said. "Haven't any experience as a deputy. But in a short time, this area has come to mean a lot to me."

"Thanks," Wirt said. "I'll let you know. A man needs experience to ride as a deputy. John here remembers when I rode out to help capture some outlaws, and I was green as grass. Nearly got us all killed."

"I understand, but I'm willing to learn." Simon finished his coffee. "I believe a man has to stand up for what he believes."

Bert swallowed the acid rising in her throat.

"This country needs more men who stand up for what's right." Wirt nodded as though he agreed.

"If it wasn't for this gal waiting for me, I would have joined the army."

Liar. Simon, you don't know the truth.

"An admirable career," John said.

"Thanks. I may enlist yet." Simon smiled at Leah. "Think I'll turn in. Thank you, Miss Leah, for a fine supper. You too, Miss Bert."

"Steven, I need to talk to you," John said. "I can follow you out there or—"

"Just come on out to the barn," Simon said. "I have a few things to do first."

"I'd forgotten you wanted to clean your rifle," John said.

The thought soured Bert's stomach. She forced herself back from the table and stood. "Simon, why do you need to clean your rifle?"

"Simon?" Confusion etched John's face.

"Yes, Simon Farrar, my brother. He's behind the cattle rustlin' and the murderin'." Bert grabbed the rifle behind her and lifted it to her shoulder.

Chairs crashed to the floor, and Wirt headed for his rifle. Simon rushed to his feet, throwing his chair back.

With her finger near the trigger, Bert aimed at his cold, black heart. "I saw you kill enough men to know how to use this."

John grabbed Simon and pinned his arms behind him, and Wirt jammed his rifle into Simon's back.

"What's this all about?" Simon appeared to startle. "I don't understand this crazy girl."

Bert's courage grew. "I could start with you braggin' about stealing Mr. Oberlander's mare and how I tried to return it. What about how many men you've killed? Or the woman in Durango? Or the way you said you'd kill this family if I refused to help you?"

"You don't know what you're talking about." Simon struggled against John's hold.

"Then why are you fightin'?" She pressed her finger against the trigger, knowing it was wrong to kill him, but she couldn't help herself. "You and I both know there isn't a rancher in Wyoming who would vouch for you—unless you paid a man to say so. The only person in Idaho, not Missouri, who misses you, is Pa, and you two are alike."

"What do you have to say for yourself?" John's face hardened, and he tightened his grip on Simon.

Mark drew back his fist. Aaron clutched a wicked looking knife, and Evan held a rope from the front porch while Leah positioned Davis behind her.

"Ember, you don't have to kill him." Leah's gentle voice reached deep into Bert's soul.

"The man's not worth you being his judge and executor," John said. "Let the law handle this."

Bert swallowed a rock-size lump in her throat. No doubt all of the Timmonses despised her for not telling them sooner about Simon's deception. She watched Evan step behind Simon and wrap a rope around his wrists.

"Move away," Bert said. "He doesn't deserve to live."

"Put the rifle down." Leah touched her back, a comfort while her heart twisted with revenge.

Was she no better than her brothers?

Slowly she lowered the rifle and handed it to Leah. Simon stared at Bert with the rabid, murderous stare she'd come to recognize. "You heard me that day in Rocky Falls and again here. No matter what happens to me, hell is going to burst open. You're cursed, little sister."

"You've gotten too cocky, too greedy," she said. "The stealing is over. The murdering is over. You're wanted throughout the state for what you've done to folks, and I will tell every lawman I meet what I know. Including all about Clint and Lester. And I'm not cursed."

"The Farrar brothers," Wirt said. "Heard about you boys some time ago. Makes me real proud to be a part of bringing you in."

Bert stared at John until she captured his attention. "I'm … I'm sorry I couldn't tell you before."

"You're so stupid." Simon continued to struggle against John's hold and the rope tying his wrists. "I'll slit your throat myself."

John whirled Simon around and laid a fist into his jaw. "Only a coward picks on a woman." He grabbed Simon by the shirt collar and hit him again, sending the man sprawling to the floor. Mark jerked Simon to his feet, and John raised his fist again.

"Enough, John," Wirt called. "He's only trying to prove he's in control by aggravating you. We'll see how much he brags sittin' in jail."

Bert didn't realize she was shaking until dizziness threatened to overtake her. She slid back onto a chair. Leah bent and placed an arm around her shoulder. The touch meant so much, and she nearly gave in to a wave of tears. Simon would never hurt anyone again.

Not even her.

CHAPTER 44

John rode back home close to midnight. Simon Farrar was locked in jail, and he hadn't stopped cussing and threatening. The whereabouts of Clint and Lester Farrar remained a mystery, but Simon might talk another tune in the morning. Obviously he'd evaded the law for so long that he thought the law owed him. The situation reminded John of the desperation he'd seen a few years ago in the McCaw gang. The longer John pondered the matter, the more he believed some folks felt like they were entitled to what they hadn't worked for.

John also suspected another kind of abuse, and the thought made him want to kill Simon with his bare hands. He remembered when Ember flinched at his touch.

Why hadn't he seen Simon's treachery? The circumstances filled him with anger and contempt for himself. There he was, the one in charge of protecting his family, and he'd been blind. Never again.

Studying law entered his thoughts. Having the cattle rustlers and murders handled had taken a load off his mountain of worries, but his and Ember's future, possibly law school, and the responsibility he felt toward Mama and his brothers still seemed overwhelming. Wirt and Mama would marry for sure, but seeing John's younger brothers through school was John's job.

He took a deep breath and stared up at the star-studded sky. How long had he yearned for someone to talk to, and God had been there all along? He'd been stubborn, praying but not listening.

Riding closer to home, he asked God to forgive him for trying to solve his problems alone instead of asking for help. His unanswered questions had more to do with pride than anything else.

Back at the ranch, he unsaddled Racer and felt the ache of strained muscles. Tomorrow would come much too early for his liking. Once he started to the house and saw the lit lantern shining in the window, he thought about the risk Ember had taken to expose her brothers. Blinking, he saw the object of his musings sitting on the step.

"Can't sleep, or did you wait up for me?"

"I wanted to see you before you went to bed, and I doubt if I could have slept."

The sound of her sweet voice soothed his weary heart and mind. He sat beside her and took her hand. "What you did tonight took a lot of courage."

"No, John. I'm a coward. I couldn't tell you the truth until I simply had no choice. Simon approached me in Rocky Falls and once here at the ranch. He wanted me to help him or he'd kill all of you. I believed him instead of trusting God."

"That's easy considering he'd broken the law before. When you feel comfortable, I want to know all about home."

"I'll tell you. But I need to sort out bad memories." She shrugged. "Leah always says the truth is what frees people, so I may need for someone to listen to my ramblings. Actually my past is vile." She paused. "When I came here and Miss Leah discovered my poor reading, she began to teach me in the evenings. I've learned so many new words that express the thoughts in my head. I'm … I'm so grateful for all this family has done for me. I hope I can someday repay all of you."

"None of us have done things for you in order to be repaid."

She laughed, and he remembered her original debt to him. "All right, I'm the guilty one. Seriously, I'm wide awake if you want to talk."

She leaned against him, her small body warm and frail. Although exhaustion invaded John, he was one content man.

"Are you sure?" she said.

He draped his arm around her. "We can talk 'til daylight." She sighed, and then trembled. Oh, for the day when fear vanished, and she could trust him. He longed to see her completely at peace. A side of her he'd never seen. A part of her she might not have experienced without embracing belief in God. "Start at the beginning. The best way for you to deal with the past is to talk about all those things that hurt you."

A few moments passed, and he tucked her closer to him.

"I never lied to you," she said. "But it was wrong not to tell you who I suspected was behind the cattle rustling and killings. Then when Simon approached me in Rocky Falls, I was so afraid for all of you. I should have trusted. For that I'm sorry."

"I know you are. From what I can figure out, Simon used his fists to make sure you saw things his way."

She stiffened and pulled away. "John, I know you care for me. And because of how good you are and what you deserve in a woman, I have to tell you something."

"I'm listening."

"Beating me isn't all Simon did."

John's throat ached to release his tears. How could a man do such a thing to his sister—or any woman? While on the way back from town when he pondered the tragedies of Ember's life, he'd considered Simon might have abused her. "I figured as such. I'm sorry."

"So I understand I need to leave here and Rocky Falls."

"Why? Because the man is an animal? What he did to you doesn't change how I feel. We'll work through this."

Her sobs broke the silence around them. "You don't know what you're sayin'. A man like you deserves a woman who is ... pure. I've been living a fairy tale by wanting to be a part of this family ... wanting your love but not deserving it."

"Purity is a state of the heart, Ember."

"Not sure I can ever look at it that way. Guilt and shame settle on me when I least expect it."

"You might want to consider telling Mama. She won't judge you, and talking woman to woman would probably help."

"I'm so ashamed."

John had to ask what weighed heavily on his heart. A reality he might have to face and handle. "Are there any children?"

She stiffened again. "No. I would never desert a child, no matter who was the father."

He sensed relief and then questioned his love for her. What would he have said or done if she'd responded affirmatively? He wanted to believe he'd have done right by her, but the thought of a child as a result of Simon's cruelty rattled him. Right now he could only praise God she had survived. "Seems like all I can say is I'm sorry. No wonder you ran off."

She said nothing for several seconds, but her body still nestled against his, where she belonged. Where he could always take care of her and protect her. But she'd proven her courage with Simon, and he'd never forget her selfless act. "My brothers are all so different, but then again so are yours." She touched the top of his hand. "My mother died when I was born, just like I told you. My oldest brother Gideon was twelve years old at the time. If not for him, I would have died. He took care of me like a parent. Taught me things like how to play the fiddle." She sighed, a sad lonesome sound that spoke more than words could convey. "But, John, he didn't know God, and Gideon's reasoning for family loyalty was wrong. He died of pneumonia about five years ago. That's when Simon started breaking the law even worse than before." She breathed in deeply. "He was always wild, but after then he added killing—and other things."

"Were Gideon and Simon close?"

"They were opposites. Gideon liked music and taking long walks. Simon wanted to hunt and looked for reasons to fight." She tilted her head. "Sorta like Jacob and Esau from the Bible."

"That's what I was thinking. I just wondered since you said they didn't share common interests."

"I do know he blamed me for family misfortunes. I tried to look at things the way he did. His ma died giving birth to me, and his brother died when I was supposed to be taking care of him."

You're cursed, little sister. John remembered Simon's words spoken earlier this evening.

"Just before Gideon took sick, Pa got thrown from his horse and couldn't walk anymore. Simon took over our dirt patch of a farm in Idaho. Like you, he had a sense of wanting to take care of everyone. But unlike you with your love for your family and respect for others, Simon took to breaking the law. I helped our other brothers hunt and fish for food while Simon rode out and returned with money, horses, cattle—whatever he'd stolen. Soon he got my other two brothers to join up with him. Things got worse after that. At times when I look at all the evil he led them to do, I wonder if a devil got into him. He always said the hard times were because everything I touched spoiled or died."

"You know better, right? We've been blessed since the day you arrived."

"Depends on how you look at it. Simon shot you. He told me so. Leon and Mr. Hawkins are dead, and ranchers are missing livestock. Who knows what happened to Mr. Oberlander's missing ranch hands?"

"Simon and your brothers choose what they do. So did Leon and those ranch hands. You have no reason to blame yourself."

Again silence fell between them.

"I don't think Clint and Lester will attempt any crimes without Simon," she finally said.

"So you think they'll leave the area?"

"There's no reason for them to stay." She turned to face him. "They're a bad lot, but I never wanted to see any of them hanged."

"Family loyalty has always come easy to me. It pains me to hear what yours have done."

"I've never broken the law like my brothers."

He smiled in the darkness. "Thank you. Sure would hate to take another trip into Rocky Falls tonight to put your scrawny hide in jail."

"So now I can expect more teasing?"

"Will the sun rise in the morning?"

A chilling wind blew around them, and she snuggled closer. "I don't care if you do tease me. Coming from you, I like it. Goodness, I think I said too much."

He kissed the top of her head, and the gesture felt natural. "I'm about to say too much. And most likely too soon, but I don't care either. The future is like being lost in a cornfield, except I don't want to take the journey without you. I'm not sure if God wants me here running this ranch or if He wants me in the city studyin' law. But I do know I want to be with you, Ember Rose. Never been so sure about anything in my life."

Soft sobs and a gentle shudder caused him to wonder if he'd spoken too much too soon. Or if she had plans for her future that didn't include him.

"I'm sorry to upset you." John did his best to sound strong when inside his heart lay open.

"You haven't made me sad, but happy. I love you—have for a long time." Her stammered words served to enforce what was written in her eyes. "I've had feelings for you since you blew a hole through Leon's hangman's noose."

"And I thought you were a boy." He laughed. "Strange how one scraggly boy could blossom into one beautiful woman."

"I think you're wearing blinders, but I appreciate your words just the same."

"They're true." He squeezed her lightly. "I'm looking forward to the long months of winter when we can get to know each other better."

"Are you sure I should continue to stay here? Shouldn't you take a family vote?"

"No one will want you to leave, especially me." John resolved to make sure no one ever hurt his Ember Rose again.

CHAPTER 45

John made the early morning trek to the barn while Ember started breakfast. Since they'd talked three nights ago after Simon's arrest, they'd grown closer. For the past few mornings, she'd risen from Mama's room when she heard him in the kitchen. Together they read a passage from the Bible and prayed for each other and those they loved. John made a point to pray for Simon, Clint, and Lester; however, Ember hadn't been able to mention her brothers. John silently prayed for the day when she could forgive them. He knew leaving the past behind was hard, especially when he was having a difficult time himself. Their early morning moments with God were special, a precious glimpse of what life with Ember could be like, and John didn't care if his choice of words to describe it sounded poetic or like a moonstruck calf.

He entered the barn with a lantern in hand. Davis kept the stalls sweet smelling, always taking pride with his chores. Hard to tell what the future held for Davis, but he was young with lots of experiences ahead to form him into a man.

Last night, John kept Racer inside since he had a morning ride into Rocky Falls. He and Wirt planned to escort Simon to Denver. After the news about the man's capture had reached the US Marshal's office in Denver, several other warrants for his arrest mandated that he be taken to the state's capital to stand trial. Warrants for the arrest of Clint and Lester circulated not only in Colorado but in neighboring states. John wanted them caught. They'd willfully broken the law and needed to face justice.

John whistled for Racer, but the horse didn't respond with the familiar whinny. "Hey, boy. Are you ready for a ride this morning?"

He lifted the lantern and walked back through the barn to the far left corner. The stall door stood open, and Racer was gone. Rowdy lay on a pile of straw where the stallion had stood.

"Rowdy?" When the dog failed to respond, a feral groan escaped John's lips while a mixture of grief, anger, and alarm consumed him.

John knelt at the dog's side and tried to rouse him. When the dog didn't respond, he bent his ear to his heart. A faint beat gave him hope. He eased his arms under Rowdy and felt for blood. Nothing. As he gently worked his hands around the dog's body, he felt a huge knot on the back of his head.

Dear God, please let this poor animal recover. He's never done a thing to deserve this.

He scooped Rowdy up into his arms and grabbed the lantern. Remembering his rifle propped against the porch wall, he felt defenseless against anyone who still might be lurking in the barn. He knew better than to be without his weapon, and his stupidity could get him—and his family killed.

But the horse thief was long gone, and Rowdy needed attention. A frightening thought passed through him. If someone had stolen Racer and hurt Rowdy, then he could have gotten into the house and hurt his family.

John took off on a run. He had to make sure Mama and his brothers were all right. He raced through the barn carrying Rowdy to the house.

Simon might be in custody, but he could have left standing orders.

Bert leveled a cup of flour with a table knife and dumped it into a bowl for the morning biscuits. A smoked ham sat on the sideboard for her to slice for breakfast. Peace flowed through her. No fears. No looking over her shoulder for a hand to clamp down on her body and spin her around. The nightmares of the past might always be with her, but they would not plague her future.

The door flew open, and John rushed in carrying Rowdy. One glance and she saw the family pet wasn't moving. He laid the dog on the rug in front of the hearth and hurried back onto the porch. A second later the door slammed, and John's ashen face greeted her, while his hand gripped his rifle.

Alarm took over. "What happened to Rowdy?"

John's gaze darted first to her and Leah's bedroom and then the loft. "Was Mama all right when you left her?"

What's wrong? "I think so. She didn't say anything or stir."

"John, I'm fine," Leah called from the bedroom. "What's wrong?"

Without responding, he handed Bert the rifle. "Don't hesitate to use this." He hurried up the steep stairway that led to the loft, calling out his brothers' names.

Leah appeared in the doorway with sleep still evident on her face. Her friend appeared as confused—and frightened—as Bert.

"I have no idea what John found or saw outside. But Rowdy's hurt."

Leah rushed to the dog's side. "He's breathing." She looked to the stairway leading to the loft. "John, what's going on?"

"In a minute," he said.

"We're fine," Evan called. "We're all here. Awake. What's going on?"

"Racer's gone, and whoever took him hurt Rowdy. He's still alive, but he has a big knot on his head."

"I'll tend to him," Evan said.

Bert gasped. Who would do such a thing? Couldn't be Simon. Would Clint and Lester steal a horse?

Of course they would.

Carrying the rifle, she raced out the front door to the barn, ignoring Leah's cries to be careful. She refused to stop until she reached Racer's stall. In the darkness she sobbed. This *was* Simon's doing. She recognized her brother's vengeance and spite. He must have managed to leave orders with a man or men who feared Simon more than the law.

"Ember." John's voice rang from the rafters.

"I'm here. In Racer's stall." She heard his footsteps, but she couldn't bear to face him, even in the dark. His arm wrapped around her shoulders. "I'm so sorry." She longed to weep, but emotion would not bring Racer back. "Who do you think did this?"

"I have no idea," John whispered. "As soon as daylight hits, I'll ask Mark to look for tracks while I ride over to the Wide O. I want to see if Oberlander has his mare."

"It's a warning," she said. "Meant to frighten us because of Simon."

"You may be right. I can't ride to Denver this morning with this going on."

"That's what they want. If you don't go, then those out there have you right where they want."

"You can't mean I should leave all of you alone?"

"John, every one of us knows how to use a gun. Do your job, and let us mind the ranch."

"What if something happens to one of you?"

"We could be hurt regardless of where you are."

His arm tightened around her shoulder. "I've faced danger many a time, but I've never felt as helpless as I do right now. So many crimes, and just when I thought our troubles were over."

A black picture of the past slipped into her memory. She understood what it meant to be helpless and afraid. "When Simon used to … I lived with this dark, empty feeling deep inside me. I wanted to be dead, fearing everyone knew my shame. Somebody stealing Racer and hurting Rowdy while we slept makes me feel the same way. Except this time I'm angry, and I'll do anything to stop Clint and Lester — or whoever is behind this. No one is going to hurt those I love. Not as long as I have life and breath."

CHAPTER 46

John arrived at the Wide O just as sunrise lit the horizon. He grieved for Racer, and fury had him locked outside of good sense. Deep-rooted bitterness for the unfairness dealt his family and friends was about to wipe out his control. During the ride, he'd attempted to force logic to rule his tongue and actions instead of the desire to render his own judgment for those responsible.

He blew out his anger in a heavy sigh. He had no idea who'd taken Racer, but he'd find out. The suspects—Clint and Lester Farrar—were nowhere to be found. The only other men who might have been a part of the lawbreaking were the Wide O's two missing ranch hands.

Tying his horse to a hitching post, John mounted the steps to Oberlander's front door and knocked hard. He remembered the harsh words that had passed between them in the ongoing struggle to find the cattle thieves. For a moment he believed all of his rage about Racer went into his fist.

The door flung open. Oberlander's face registered surprise. "John, your knocking could have raised the dead."

"With the mood I'm in, I could wake a graveyard."

Oberlander's brows narrowed. "This isn't a social call, is it?"

"No sir. We need to talk."

"Come on in, then." Oberlander stepped back from the door.

"I'd rather find Queen Victoria."

"Why? Do you have reason to believe my mare's been stolen again?"

"Yes." John summoned a calm composure, realizing the man before him valued his horses more than people. "Someone stole Racer last night, and if my suspicions are right, your mare may not be in her stall either."

Oberlander rushed out the door to his stables with John beside him. The man hurried inside the building toward a rear stall. Flinging open a stall door, he uttered a deep guttural grief that John recognized as how he'd felt when he discovered Racer was missing.

Victor Oberlander swore. John stepped out of the stall and allowed the man his ranting. He'd considered using the same language — as heathen as it sounded.

When Oberlander emerged from the stall, hatred burned from the pores of his skin. "Any idea who's stolen our horses?"

"I have a few suspects."

"My missing ranch hands are at the top of my list."

"Add Clint and Lester Farrar. Bob, Wirt, and I wanted to believe they'd left the territory. But that's changed."

"Stealing a man's property is worth a hanging," Oberlander said. "And I'd welcome the chance to do it. Queen Victoria's been stolen twice, and she's the finest horseflesh I've ever owned."

John wanted to agree, except he valued a man's life more than an animal's. He had a feeling more men would die before this ended.

Leah stood on the porch while Evan coaxed Rowdy to open his eyes. Aaron, Mark, Davis, and Ember knelt beside the dog as the solemn scene unfolded in front of her. She'd shed more tears this morning than she'd done for a long time. Racer's disappearance and Rowdy's condition were like more bruises to a battered family. Right now all she could do was pray for Rowdy to fully recover and pray for Racer to be found.

This morning, John feared his family could have been harmed. When she thought about it, she realized the improbability of such a thing happening. But John had much on his mind. He'd been wild, frantic with the realization someone had stolen valuable property while the family slept.

How much could John handle with the evil surrounding them? They'd all thought it was over with Simon's arrest. Now the situation had grown worse. She thought of how a cat played with a mouse before killing it ... and the gut-wrenching fear accompanying those emotions made her physically sick.

She stared at the rifles lined up by the barn within easy reach. Glancing behind her, she viewed her own borrowed weapon close by. *Oh, Lord, watch over my family. Help John, Bob, and Wirt find who is doing this. Please.*

"Come on, Rowdy." Davis stroked the dog's side. "I know you can do it."

A tear slipped from Leah's eyes. Her baby boy loved that dog.

"Maybe he needs to sleep some more," Mark said.

Evan nodded. "I'll carry him back inside and keep watch. He took a nasty blow to the head, and it may take awhile for him to wake up."

"Let's feed the animals and do a few chores while we wait." Aaron stood and caught Leah's eye. "The time will pass quicker if we're doing something."

Good. They could work off their angst. Hopefully they'd talk and help each other. She grabbed her rifle and walked toward her family.

"Did you boys pray again for Rowdy and John?" she said.

They nodded.

"And I prayed John or Marshal Culpepper or Mr. Zimmerman finds Racer." Davis's young voice filled with conviction. "John loves Racer. He told me when Jesus comes again, He'll be riding a horse like Racer, 'cept that horse will be white."

Had it been just the other night when they'd gathered in the parlor after supper? They'd laughed and enjoyed apple cobbler.

Later Ember sang a new song. Taking a deep breath, Leah remembered the words.

Where do I go when life's unfair,
When my heart aches
And the world's cold?
Where do I hide from sin and shame,
When my heart aches
And the world's cold?
Where do I go when life's unfair?
I bathe my soul
In love and prayer.

Leah's oldest son often refused the help of others, thinking he had to handle life all by himself. In many respects he was getting better. Ember's presence had helped him understand that love was giving and receiving. But today, all of his family longed to help ease his sorrow, and she hoped he knew how very much they loved him.

CHAPTER 47

John couldn't recall a time when Bob Culpepper had ever displayed anger, but when he heard what happened to John's and Victor Oberlander's horses, he rushed to his feet and stomped over to Simon's cell. "Who else is behind this?"

Simon sneered. "Told you all hell was gonna burst open."

Bob pointed a finger at Simon. "Shut up. Wirt and John can't get you out of here fast enough."

"I say hang him," Oberlander said. "Why go through the formalities of a trial when we know he's guilty?"

"Can't do that," Bob said. "But it's tempting."

Oberlander slumped in a chair across from Bob's desk, red-faced and grim. Deep signs of an explosive temper were etched across his features. At least when the man shouted with language that belonged in the outhouse, John could read his feelings.

"I thought this had all been settled." Bob's words spat like sparks from a forest fire.

"I did too," John said. "I found one set of boot prints and horse tracks, which means we're looking at one more man."

"A dead man," Oberlander added. "Who's out to get us, John? When I think about the cattle rustlings, killings, and now this, I wonder what we can expect next. Here I was ready to offer you a good price for your ranch."

Strange. "I just bought land from you."

"I know, but with all that's been going on, I thought you might want to sell out and move to Denver near your Uncle Parker."

"The 5T is not for sale." John wanted to focus on the law-breakers, not on selling land. "In my way of thinking, the Farrar brothers and possibly your missing ranch hands are continuing without Simon." John could almost read Oberlander's mind from the way his eyes hardened.

"Trouble started when that gal rode through on my horse." Oberlander nodded at Simon. "His sister."

"So you're going to blame Ember for running away from her brothers and attempting to return your mare?" John swallowed his ire, realizing exchanging barbs wouldn't solve the problem.

"You don't know for sure. Odd, how she's still here and troubles keep mounting. You ought to think about where your fondness for her leads."

John clenched his fists. *Easy.* "She's been at my ranch, except for a couple of days spent with Miss Bess. Unless she can be at two or three places at one time, you need to back off your accusations."

"She ain't worth it." Simon laughed. "Can't trust her either. How do you know we didn't plan for me to get arrested?"

"You—" Oberlander pointed his finger at John—"had better open your eyes to a gal who's out to steal from all of us. What happens when she pulls the trigger on someone in your family? Is that what it will take to prove me right?"

John took a step forward. He'd taken enough threats and bad-mouthing.

"Slow down, John," Bob said. "Fighting won't solve this mess." He glared at Oberlander. "Even if the man is talking through his rear."

John turned heel and headed for the door.

"Where are you going?" Bob said.

"To find Wirt and tell him I'm ready to take the prisoner to Denver. We'll be back in a couple of days."

"Why's he coming back once Farrar's been delivered?" Oberlander's face had reddened even more. John almost told him about Wirt and Mama. Almost. Except Oberlander's next stop would be to convince Mama to marry him instead of Wirt.

"Unfinished business," John said. "I suppose he'll be here a while longer with what we found this morning."

Oberlander's features hardened. "We don't need a US Marshal or any of their kind. I'll pay men to chase down our stolen livestock."

"Last time you said that, Leon Wilson ended up dead, and I was shot. No thanks. I'll take my chances on those trained on how to find lawbreakers."

Bob cleared his throat. "We need to find out if any of the other ranchers have been hit."

John thought about the never-ending chores at the ranch, but he was needed more right there wearing a deputy's badge and escorting the murdering cattle rustler to the proper authorities. The idea of his brothers and Mama and Ember carrying a rifle sat like a rock in his stomach. Being armed for impending danger because lawbreakers were on the loose was the difference between civilization and two-legged animals. If he thought about it long enough, worry would drive him crazy.

"On the way back from Denver, Wirt and I can call on a few ranchers who had missing cattle in the past," John said.

"Wait for me to ride with you on those calls," Bob said.

"I don't need a bodyguard."

"Right. You can protect me."

John shook his head. A town marshal and undertaker who had a sense of humor. And Bob was a crack shot.

"I'm taking care of this my way." Oberlander swung a look at Simon. "Be glad you're leaving because someone could put a bullet in your head."

"Word of advice," Bob said. "Break the law, and you're under arrest. Think about that."

Oberlander flashed him a look of contempt and stomped out onto the boardwalk.

With Simon Farrar delivered to the US Marshal's office in Denver, Wirt stayed behind for a few days while John rode back to Rocky Falls. He and Bob checked with other ranchers about their cattle, but no one had experienced any more problems. John pondered riding home. His family could take care of themselves, but no doubt his ranch and the Wide O had been singled out. He assumed Clint and Lester were taking revenge for Simon's arrest.

John and Bob rode onto Sparky McBride's High Plains Ranch in brilliant sunshine, not at all the kind of day a man would expect crime to burst from unexpected places. Four more stops after this, and if no problems were reported, John would check back with his family.

Sparky's wife said her husband had left early that morning with their son to cut a few trees to add another room to their house before winter. They'd be on the northeast portion of their property. John knew the location, which would make them easy to find.

"Do you mind if we take a look in your barn?" Bob said. "A couple of ranchers found their horses missing this morning, and we're making sure the other ranches are all right."

"Go right ahead." Sparky's wife walked their way, a robust woman who could hold her own in any brawl. "I just came from the barn about two hours ago. Everything looked fine."

"Then no need for us to see your barn." Bob leaned toward her on his saddle, his tone soft.

From beneath her bonnet, she shielded her eyes from the dazzling sunlight. "Sparky said you'd caught the cattle rustler."

"Thought we did," Bob said, "until this morning."

John noted the casual way Bob stated the announcement about more trouble. Folks were jumpy, quick to press the triggers on their rifles.

"None of us can handle losing any more of our cattle — or our friends." Her gaze moved to the east. "The barn's empty."

"We'll be going then, ma'am," Bob said.

"After you talk to Sparky, would you stop back and let me know he's all right. All this makes me nervous. Our oldest boy is with him, and he's only eight years old."

Bob tipped his hat. "Sure thing, Mrs. McBride. I understand your apprehension."

They left her standing in the barnyard, her arms crossed over her chest like a soldier on guard duty. Although Mrs. McBride and Mama didn't share the same size, they shared the same fears for their families and the same stubborn courage. He'd seen it in Ember too. Those qualities were what counted when adversity stood on its haunches, bared its teeth, and growled.

John led the way to where he believed Sparky McBride was cutting timber. As the two men neared the area, a tree crashed to the ground. The two sunk their heels into the sides of their mounts and headed toward the fallen tree in the foothills.

They found Sparky and his young son, who had carrot-colored hair like his father, tightening rope around a previously downed tree and hitching it to the wagon.

"What brings you up here?" Sparky said, with a firm grip on the horse's bridle. "Don't suppose you found my cattle."

"Wish we had good news," Bob said. "But looks like trouble is trailing some of us."

"Who?"

John took heed of what he said in front of Sparky's young son.

"Someone stole my stallion and Victor Oberlander's prize mare. Have you had any more problems?"

"Not at all."

John pointed to the tree he and Bob had heard crash against the earth's floor a few moments before. "Want some help, trimming some of the branches and hooking it up to your wagon?"

Sparky nodded. "I never turn away another pair of arms."

Bob and John dismounted and walked with Sparky and his son toward the tree. Any other time, he and Bob would be on their way, but John sensed in Sparky what they'd seen all morning—folks needed reassurance that Bob and John were there to establish order. And if calming a family's fears meant taking time to help a father and son, then so be it.

"Who do you think is behind all the trouble?" Sparky said, his tone hushed while his son walked several feet ahead of them.

"Oh, John and I think Simon Farrar's brothers are still working the area and possibly the ranch hands from the Wide O who disappeared weeks ago."

"Makes me wonder if the fellow in custody is the one leading the gang."

John hadn't considered another gang leader before. What would it take for Simon to take orders from someone else?

Sparky glanced ahead at his son, who'd stopped in his tracks. "What is it?"

John followed the rancher's gaze and gripped his rifle. Could be a bear ... a wolf ... or a man.

"Poppy, the tree fell on a man. He don't look so good." The boy swung his attention back to Sparky. "A skunk must have been here too, 'cause the smell is awful."

Hours after John had left, sadness still settled like a heavy blanket upon Bert and those she loved. Rowdy had yet to regain full consciousness. Bert thought she understood the grim feelings. Perhaps a person might have a chance to defend himself, but a horse and a dog depended on man to do the caring. At least, that's the way she felt, as though she were somehow responsible.

She hadn't thought Clint or Lester could stoop as low as Simon, but their involvement made sense. In the past, she'd been consumed with staying out of Simon's way. While she avoided her older brother, had she ignored Clint's and Lester's decay?

"What do your brothers look like?" Evan said. He'd announced earlier they'd all stay home today and work on last minute tool and building repairs before school started.

Bert questioned the logic of talking about her brothers ... But like Simon, they could ride onto the ranch and deceive any of the boys. "Clint's the shorter one, and he's not as tall as Mark. He has broad shoulders, and he's strong. Never says much. Lester took after Simon. He's thinner, taller."

Talking about Clint and Lester dredged up old memories, but in forcing herself to relive them, she might think of something that could help the law. "Guess I've been stupid thinking they weren't smart enough to carry on after Simon was gone. But if Simon was riding with someone else, then who? Hard for me to believe Simon would take orders from any man."

Aaron studied a huge wasp's nest attached to the stone by Leah and Bert's bedroom window. "John says a man who breaks the law does so for money or power or both. Which would it be for your brothers?"

Good question. "I never thought about it."

"Power could mean they break the law to show they can," Aaron continued. "And that means they get more pleasure out of getting away with something than whatever's stolen or done."

Bert recalled her childhood. "We grew up hungry, always wanting food in our bellies. Made my brothers mean and want to fight. Pa said his boys were like lean wolves. They made him proud." *Made me sick.*

"But you escaped." Evan's voice gave away his longing, and she refused to look at him.

"I could have been just like them. God must have had His hand on my life." Was God there when Simon ... "Simon did the talking and the planning and gave the orders. He got Clint and Lester to do what he wanted by reminding them other folks looked down on us. He said they turned their heads when we walked by 'cause we were poor. Laughed at our dirty and torn clothes. He told them he brought self-respect back to the family and took care of them like they deserved." She paused while the sound of Simon's voice haunted her. "Odd how they believed him, but I knew he lied."

"How's come you're different?" Davis said.

Goodness, Davis didn't need to hear this conversation. She tossed her best stern look at the other boys that meant to hush them. She'd seen it from Leah many a time. "I'd like to think God smiled on me and pulled me out of the snake pit."

"Yep. Me too," the boy said.

"You've just heard grown-up talk," she said. "Promise me you won't be telling any of your friends at school about my brothers or what your brothers have said."

His eyes widened. "No ma'am. I mean, yes, ma'am."

"Thank you. Your friends will find out about bad men soon enough. You don't need to be telling them before they're ready."

"You sound like Mama." Mark laughed.

First good thing she'd heard all day. "I'll take that as a compliment."

"Maybe you're practicing for when you and John get married," Mark said.

Ouch. Evan shouldn't have heard that.

"Yeah, John may find he has a bossy wife." Evan laughed, and when she whirled around to see if his words were sincere, she saw a sparkle in his eyes.

Relief swept over her. She smiled at him and brushed the hair from her eyes. She turned toward the wasp nest and where they all were standing. Making her way to Davis's side, she took his hand and led him away. The boy stood much too close to the nest. "Wait until tonight to knock it down," Bert said to the two pranksters. "No point in any of us getting stung because you two want to have fun at our expense."

"See, I told you," Mark said. "She's practicing on us for when she's married. Poor John. He'll never have a minute of rest."

She began to laugh, and it felt like all the worries of the day had been lifted. Leah peeked around the front porch, and from the look on her face she'd heard every word. And she was laughing too.

"I have great news," Leah said. "Rowdy is awake, and he's acting fine. Of course, he can't tell us his head hurts. But he's alive."

Now if only John were here, so Bert would know he was all right.

CHAPTER 48

Ralph Hanson had been dead for about a week when Sparky McBride's young son found him. John and Wirt wrapped his body in an old blanket from Mrs. McBride and borrowed a wagon from Sparky to take the body back to town.

John thought about Ralph's sister. He'd write her a letter tonight and explain the circumstances as delicately as possible and ensure her that Ralph would receive a proper burial. Now he wondered if Oberlander's other ranch hand was dead too. He and Wirt had combed the area and found nothing. So many questions and no answers.

Sure hated the boy had found the body. John had done the best he could to shelter Davis from the harsh realities of life. He'd be introduced to it soon enough.

One more reason to find out who was behind the crimes in Rocky Falls. A past conversation repeated itself in John's mind. He tossed it aside, attributing it to sheer absurdity. But the notion still stuck like a tick to a dog's hide.

A few days after they found Ralph Hanson's body, Wirt joined the Timmonses for supper. John could read nervousness in a man, and tonight Wirt looked like a hen ready to hatch her eggs. Once supper was over, Wirt cleared his throat. Twice. John figured he'd have some fun and make his future stepfather sweat.

"I'd like a word with you, if you don't mind," Wirt said. "Can we take a walk?"

John figured he and Mama had set a date for their weddin', and out of respect, Wirt wanted to make sure John approved. "Sure. Grab your coffee."

Outside, in the coolness of evening, John walked toward the corral. For a moment he expected Racer to join them. Deep longing coupled with fury bubbled up inside him. Justice would find its way to those who stalked their community.

"Leah and I would like to get married soon," Wirt said.

"When are you thinking? Tomorrow? Next Sunday?" John chuckled.

"You know how hard this is for me, and you're not making it any easier." Wirt laughed too, but it sounded weak. "We're thinking about Thanksgiving. Sort of fittin'."

John let the reality of Mama and Wirt marrying sink in. He'd thought about the situation for weeks, and Wirt Zimmerman was a fine man. He'd loved Mama for a long time, and she deserved to be happy. Life had been hard on her after the Civil War, dealing with the move from Virginia to Colorado, mothering five boys, and the problems with Pa's drinking.

"Wish you'd say something," Wirt said. "Is the date not agreeable to you?"

John clasped his hand on Wirt's shoulder. "Nope. The date's fine. I'm thinking you and Mama make a fine pair. I'm glad for both of you."

"Good." The word breathed out like a sigh.

John thought for a minute about his dream to study law. He'd need to toss it aside since Wirt would be busy with his job as a US Marshal. The 5T couldn't run by itself, even if Mark welcomed the opportunity to show his mettle. He and Ember could build a cabin nearby, leaving Mama and Wirt to their own home.

"I want to make you an offer," Wirt said.

"I'm listening."

"I'd like to buy the 5T. I have the cash, and I'd also make sure Aaron, Mark, and Davis received their homestead parcels when they turn eighteen. We could work out the details, put it all in writing, note acreage you'd want to keep for yourself, and I'll help your brothers with their education. Like you, I believe they should have a stake in it, but I don't want you to worry about a thing. And Mrs. Felter and her children are fine living in Parker's cabin. I wouldn't want to interfere there."

Shocked best described John, as though a mountain stream had frozen solid in summer. "How are you going to keep your job as a US Marshal and work a ranch?"

"I'm going to resign. You see, I don't want to put Leah through the worries of another husband working for the law. It's not fair, and I've always wanted a ranch of my own. This may come as a surprise, but I even know how it's done. Grew up on a ranch."

Could this be God's way of clearing a path for him to study law?

"The last thing I want is for you to think I'm trying to take over your ranch. This is an offer, an idea. Because—"

"And a fine one." John spoke before Wirt could say another word. "I'd welcome the opportunity to put some figures together and see what we can do. I'd want to present it to the other boys. Make sure everyone is in agreement. Until then, I'd rather they not know about our discussion. And let's hope we don't lose any more cattle." He remembered a recent conversation. "Victor Oberlander offered to buy the 5T. But I told him I wasn't interested. I'd rather keep the land in the family."

"Are you sure, John? This ranch has been your whole life since you were fourteen years old."

"Sometimes a man has to move on."

CHAPTER 49

The following evening, John helped Ember finish the dishes after supper, giving Mama a little rest and his brothers something to snicker about. While Davis showed the rest of the family his lasso trick, John needed to ask Bert a few questions about Simon.

Ember cast her big brown eyes his way. "Now, why did you offer to dry dishes?"

"I wanted to talk."

"We could have taken a walk once Leah and I were finished."

"But then you might have been tired or the other boys would want to join us."

She studied him for a few moments. "This has to do with finding the lawbreakers, right?"

He nodded. "I have a few questions about Simon, because I'm beginning to think he was taking orders from someone else."

She handed him a wet plate. "Not Simon. He wouldn't take orders from anyone."

"Would he pretend to if enough money was involved?"

She hesitated and tilted her head. "Possibly. What are you thinking?"

"Let me ask you a few questions first, then I'll explain myself."

She smiled, and his knees felt like jelly. "But then I want to see Davis lasso a fence post."

"All right," he began. "Remember when you said you rode with your brothers up through this area some time back?"

"Yes. It was almost two years ago. Simon had me ride along in case I decided to take off."

"Do you know why he came to this part of Colorado?"

"He had business with a man here. But I never heard the man's name." She handed him another wet plate. "I figured he lied about it."

John couldn't get the timeline in his head straight. "Simon must have made a second trip here to steal Oberlander's mare."

"Right," she said. "Sorry I didn't make myself clear. When I asked him about stealing the horse, he said the owner gave it to him. As if I'd believe him."

He allowed her final words to sink deep into his mind. "Anything else he might have said that you found unusual?"

She appeared to be thinking through her answer. "Simon always bragged about getting rich and folks respecting him. Honestly, John, I never paid much attention. His bragging got old."

He brushed a kiss across her cheek. "For sure he won't bother you again."

"Right. Now all I'll have to contend with is you. And I love it."

He frowned but couldn't hide the smile. "Don't forget it either."

As they returned to the dishes, John couldn't let go of a gnawing notion.

Will you sing at my wedding?" Leah scrubbed a pair of jeans on the washboard.

Bert startled. "Are you sure?"

"I am," she said in a matter-of-fact tone. "I'd like it even more if you'd write Wirt and me a special song."

Bert had already been forming words for a song ever since she learned the two planned to marry at Thanksgiving. "All right, since I have a few months to work on it."

"Oh, a song from you would be a wonderful gift." Leah giggled, reminding Bert of a schoolgirl. "Unless you and John want to make this a double wedding."

"Leah!"

Leah's eyes widened, accenting her freckles. "Don't tell me you and John haven't talked about marriage."

"He's not asked. We ... we haven't gotten to that point."

"Mind you, he's thinking about it. Knowing John, he'll want a house built and a garden dug and a barn raised, then expect you to say 'yes' without hesitation."

Bert raised her chin and nodded. "You're probably right."

Leah tossed the jeans into a barrel of rinse water. "I still like the idea of a double wedding at Thanksgiving." She picked up one of Davis's shirts. "Wirt said he had a surprise for me. Wouldn't say what or when."

"Knowing Mr. Zimmerman, he's probably got a half dozen orphan kids on their way here, all of them dirty, hungry, and crying for a mama."

"Merciful beans and cornbread, Ember. We have fallen in love with two men who'll make sure we never have a dull moment."

Ember Rose Timmons. The name had a pretty ring. John hadn't asked her officially, but he'd said he wanted her in his future. And he loved her. And he never said anything he didn't mean.

She felt like a princess in a child's story.

CHAPTER 50

On Thursday evening, John sat near the middle of the crowded church between Bob and Wirt, and Mama sat on the other side of Wirt. Victor Oberlander had called a town meeting about the cattle rustlers and killings. Only the church could hold that many men and women.

John figured Oberlander planned to point out the inability of the local law and a US Marshal to find the culprits and protect the ranchers. Curiosity had drawn John here. The other folks were likely here for the same reason.

Mixed into the crowd were a few storekeepers and business owners. Rocky Falls hadn't grown as much as other towns, but John believed their isolated status would change once the narrow-gauge railroad line grew to a standard gauge. Timber and the stone quarries were bound to draw the attention of huge railroad conglomerates who had roared through from the east, developing areas and providing jobs wherever they laid down track. All of this confirmed the town's need of a lawyer ... possibly a future position for John.

Oberlander slowly walked to the front of the church, his boots tapping along the wooden floor. The man had sat in the back, and John figured his march down the aisle was so everyone would take note that the largest landowner in the area had come to address them. The move accentuated the man's pride— something John disagreed with. Even if half of Colorado belonged to John, he'd still remember who'd provided it for him and not have people look up to him like he was a god.

Oberlander stood behind Preacher Waller's pulpit bearing the commanding stance of a military leader. "Folks, I want to thank you for coming out tonight. I won't take up much of your time. We've had trouble in our area, and although our marshal and deputy along with a US Marshal have worked hard and caught one of the lawbreakers, more are still on the loose. This meeting is not about our lawmen, because I think they're doing a fine job. This meeting is about how I can help some of you who are struggling with loss of livestock."

He took a step down from the raised pulpit and unbuttoned his coat. "We're a community, and although I've had my losses, it's a drop compared to the devastation some of you have experienced. The idea of a man worrying about keeping his land or putting food in his children's bellies doesn't sit well with me. That's not how a Christian man is supposed to live."

John maintained a stoic composure. He chose not to look at Bob or Wirt beside him. Oberlander was laying the groundwork for something sure to benefit himself.

"All of my ranch hands have been ordered to shoot anyone who rides across our land. I'm sorry if some of you take my measures personal, but I'm not losing one more cow or horse to a thief. If you have business with me, come to the house. I won't be held responsible otherwise."

He paused and looked out into the crowd. "A few of you have indicated your losses have ruined you financially, and I hate to hear some of you have chosen to leave our area. I'd like to help in one of two ways. I can offer you cash loans with the same interest rate as a bank, even sell you some cattle, or I can buy you out at a fair market price."

John's insides twisted. At this rate, Oberlander would end up owning most of the land around Rocky Falls. A hard and devious man preyed on those who were down on their luck. He paused in his thinking. Perhaps he hadn't given Oberlander a chance. Maybe the man meant well.

But the longer he observed Oberlander and his pompous ways, the more something didn't sit right with him.

I know I'm right. I just need to find a way to prove it.

Some folks might think Oberlander's offer was an answer to prayer—a way for them to start all over again, whether they chose here or somewhere else. But not John. And the longer the cattle baron talked about hard times and opportunities closer to Denver where the law could keep their families and property safe, the more his mind swayed toward what he felt in his gut.

After the meeting, several men and women crowded around Oberlander. He joked and complimented the women like a politician who was only interested in votes and not the real problems and concerns of the people. John had never seen this type of behavior in his Uncle Parker, and it sent a ripple of doubt through him about every good and decent thing Oberlander had ever done.

John left the church with Bob, Wirt, and Mama. No one said a word until they reached the road.

"I could use some coffee and pie from the hotel," John said. "Haven't seen Bess in a while either."

Bob chuckled. "I have a few ideas about why this meetin' was called too. What about you, Wirt?"

"Let me form my thoughts before I say anything."

Mama remained quiet as the group made their way toward the hotel. John wished Ember was walking beside him. But she'd stayed at the 5T where she'd be safe.

At the hotel, they talked to Bess and ordered pie and coffee. John studied Bob's and Wirt's faces. He hesitated to speak his mind without evidence.

"John, something's eating you," Bob said. "I want to hear it."

John leaned in closer. "Oberlander offered me a generous price for the ranch." He nodded at Wirt. "Anyway, I turned him down. But his interest in the ranch after I'd just purchased acreage from him got me to thinking. Then I learned a few things from Ember about Simon." He shook his head. "Is it me, or does it seem suspicious that Oberlander suddenly has a generous heart?"

Bess returned with cups and a fresh pot of coffee. "Here, now I won't be bothering you folks by filling cups. Your pie comes next."

John smiled up at Bess and watched her swish back to the kitchen while he waited for one of the others to comment.

"I heard in Denver the railroad will be expanding out here more than what the folks here have seen." Wirt lifted the steamy brew to his lips.

"Is that so?" Bob said, barely above a whisper. "Are you saying my partial homestead will be worth a lot more money than it is now?" Sarcasm topped his words.

Mama gasped and touched her lips. "Are you men suggesting Mr. Oberlander is taking advantage of these people?"

John leaned back in his chair and juggled the thoughts burning into his mind. "What if he is behind all the cattle rustlin' and murder?"

Bob shook his head. "I don't think so, John. You're climbing your own mountain with this one. I wouldn't put it past him to buy up land so he can make a fistful of money when the railroad brings more business to Rocky Falls. And I've heard rumors that more gold ore's been discovered. But Victor Oberlander is not a killer."

"I have to agree," Wirt said. "Look at what happened to his mare. And he had more cattle stolen than the other ranchers, and ..."

"My point," John said. "Does it matter how many of his cattle were rustled or his mare stolen if he knew where they were?"

"But not murder," Bob said. "He may be a horse's a—" He glanced at Mama.

"John, you're wrong," she said. "Not murder. Why, he's been in church ever since he moved here."

"What if," John began, "he was trying to court you to get his hands on our ranch?"

Bess approached them with a tray of pie slices.

"Think about it." John reached up to take a generous slice of custard pie from Bess's tray. If he was wrong, he'd gladly concede to Bob, Wirt, and Mama. But if he was right, then all the problems, questions, and suspicions made sense.

"What did Ember tell you about Simon?" Wirt sliced his fork into the pie and popped it into his mouth.

"He made two trips here. One was business and when he returned from the second trip, he rode Oberlander's mare. He told Ember the horse was a gift."

Wirt studied a second bite on his fork. "And what are you thinking?"

"I'm only relaying what she told me." John needed to find proof for what he guessed those sharing pie and coffee with him would call folly.

Over three weeks passed, and school started for Aaron, Mark, and Davis. Evan would be leaving at the end of the week for Fort Collins to begin his studies. Bert scattered feed around the barnyard and watched the chickens flock around her skirts. A chilling wind that matched her mood made her wish she had her shawl. The last of September should not be chilly, and she realized the cold inside her was from the unrest in the community. The mountains were alive with color. The deep reds and golds and oranges held their own beauty, even though they'd be covered in snow in short order.

Her attention swung to the road. She longed for John to return home from town. He said he had business, but she assumed it had to do with his worries. The past few days had worn on all of them. The cattle rustlers were like ghosts who herded up cattle and caused them to disappear. More ranchers had reported stolen cattle. One rancher's barn burned to the ground. Poor John. He seldom slept, and he frowned more than he smiled.

Leah fretted about him too, and when the boys left for school each morning, the quiet gave both of them more time to think ...

and worry . . . and pray. John tried to be friendly, but Bert understood him enough to know he'd not rest until justice was served.

As though her wishes for John to return had been a prayer, she saw him riding in with another man who wore a black duster. Finished with feeding the chickens, she left them alone to pick at the corn. An instant later, Leah burst through the door and down the steps, waving and laughing at the same time.

"Parker Timmons, how dare you not let me know you were coming!" she said to the man who jumped from the saddle and caught Leah by the waist.

"I wanted to surprise you."

"And where is Sage?"

"Mornings aren't agreeing with her."

Leah laughed again. "And will this one be another boy?"

"I wanted eight girls, and so far I have two boys who are as ornery as I ever was."

"Serves you right." Leah whirled around to Bert. "I'm forgetting my manners. Parker, this is Ember Farrar."

He reached out and took her hand. The moment he faced her, Bert saw the startling resemblance between him and John. The same blue eyes that rivaled the sky sparkled back at her. The same broad shoulders too, and the way they leaned on their right leg. "So this is the woman who has stolen John's heart. I can see why."

She felt herself grow warm and glanced at John, who slid his hand around her waist. "And I've heard much about you—all wonderful," she managed.

Leah wagged her finger at John. "Why didn't you tell me Parker was coming?"

"Just like he said—a surprise."

Leah's eyes narrowed. "This is all about the trouble we're having, isn't it?"

"Yes ma'am."

"And your ridiculous suspicions?"

"Yes ma'am."

"John's filled me in on what's been happening. And Wirt and I spent time together when he was in Denver. I've been doing some digging on my own. So we'll see what turns up."

"You and John are so much alike. You deserve each other for a few days. But the rest of us will enjoy your time here in the evenings."

Bert peered up at John. *He's already told his uncle about me? He does love me. He truly does.*

As though reading her thoughts, his hand tightened around her waist. *I love you too.* She sensed his determination to end the law breaking, as he exchanged glances with his uncle. Hope rose in her too.

With Parker Timmons here, the mystery of who was behind the crimes of Rocky Falls would soon be over.

CHAPTER 51

J ohn and Parker rode into Rocky Falls. The chill of autumn seemed to give their horses an extra lift in their step, and the gold and scarlet leaves added a splash of color to the landscape. The trees had turned early this year, and he assumed everyone was in for a hard winter.

John's gaze lifted to the mountains. He never grew tired of their splendor or feeling powerless when peering up at them. The Indians revered them as sacred. Some folks claimed they were God's throne. John viewed them as majestic proof of God's hand in creating the world, and like all of nature around him, he respected the lofty peaks.

"Tell me what you've learned about what's going on," John said. "Curiosity is eating at me."

Parker laughed, the familiar rumble that John missed. Oh, how he ached for the days when Parker and Sage had lived in Rocky Falls. "If Victor Oberlander is a friend, you're going to be disappointed."

"The man has a temper, and in my opinion he'd do whatever it takes to get a job done."

"Tell me what you've experienced. Hard to read between the lines in a telegram. He's expanded considerably since I lived here, and he's ambitious. Never had a problem with him. Seemed congenial and interested in growing the community."

John considered his words before speaking. "He's the largest rancher in the area, which makes him the wealthiest. He's offered advice to me on several occasions. In fact, he's gone out of his way to treat me well. But that was before Wirt started courtin' Mama."

"He was interested in Leah?"

"Oh, yeah. Like a backwoods fool, I didn't take note of it for a long time."

"Sounds like you believe his befriending you was due to his interest in your ma."

"I do. And a few other things too, which I mentioned earlier."

Parker pulled in the reins of his horse, and John did the same. "I think you're right."

John nodded. "Makes sense, doesn't it?"

"Especially with what I learned. Rocky Falls is on target to grow, bringing business folks from all over. Land prices are going to jump."

"When I think of all that's happened, it makes me mad enough to ride over there and confront him. But I don't have anything to go on but the feeling in my gut."

Parker urged his horse on. "Can't fault a man for buying up land. We've got to catch him negotiating."

"Nice way to say hirin' a gun. Did you have any luck with Simon?"

"He refuses to talk. Most likely his brothers are still working for whoever's behind this."

"When I asked Ember about the trip she made here with her brothers nearly two years ago, she said Simon claimed to have business with a man living in this area. No name. Then Simon made a trip back alone. That's when he returned riding Oberlander's mare. He said the owner gave him the horse. I mentioned this to Wirt and Bob, but neither of them thought it was reason to suspect him."

Parker nodded. "I'd like to pay the Wide O a social call once we finish in Rocky Falls. Nothing like saying hello to an old friend. You know, most folks would think Simon Farrar meant he stole the mare, but you and I think differently."

"I wonder if Oberlander gave him the horse to seal the deal and make himself look innocent. It would also pave the way for what would happen to other ranchers by being the first victim. And—" John hesitated.

"Speak your mind."

John thought a minute longer. "My other thought is Simon did steal the horse to make sure Oberlander kept his side of the bargain."

Parker grinned. "A man who thinks like me. But we still have to prove it."

"Wirt may have a few ideas. Now that you think I may be on to something, he and Bob might listen."

"They didn't always agree with me either."

"It's the Timmons in us." A memory of his Uncle Parker's trials and triumphs flashed in his mind. "I've thought of keeping a vigil on the Wide O. Might have to dodge his ranch hands since all of them have orders to shoot trespassers on sight."

"Could be a long process."

"If we can—"

"We?"

John ignored the sarcasm. "As I said, if we can get Bob and Wirt to help, the job wouldn't be so taxing on a single man."

"Single as in one man doing all the work, or single as in a man who'd rather be spending his time courtin'?"

"Does Sage take this from you?"

"What do you think?"

"You probably give her no choice. But she does have her pet hawk to protect her."

Parker laughed. "That's exactly why I've been storing it all up for you."

"You can spread it out among my brothers."

"Oh, I will. Are you reading the law books I sent?"

"Reread a few of them. Another topic I want to discuss with you."

"And here I thought you wanted to invite me and my family to another wedding."

"Soon, I hope." John relished this time with his uncle. Here he could be himself—not have to worry about appearing brave or sounding logical. The prospect of marrying Ember pleased him. Pleased him a lot. "You and I may be talking all day and night. But first tell me about Sage and the boys."

During the rest of the way into town, Parker told one story after another about his family. He and Sage had weathered a rough start with her job as a bounty hunter and his position as Rocky Falls' marshal. Neither one of them liked the other until they realized love didn't always beckon a man and a woman who have everything in common. The differences were what made them one. John wanted a marriage with Ember like that one day.

"Tell you what," Parker said. "I have a few connections in Austin. I'll contact the law school on your behalf and see what I can find out about entrance requirements. It'll be a couple of years before Denver has a law school."

"I'd appreciate it. Not sure how I'd repay you."

"I may need a good lawyer one day. Sure would like to use one who's in the family."

Life was going to work out … Dreams had a way of making a man wear a smile. The fight to find the lawbreakers in the community hadn't ended, but the road at the end sure had a sweeter look. At least Simon was in jail, which meant Ember was safe.

Bert walked through what was left of the garden, searching for a single tomato or cucumber. Most everything had withered or gone to seed, except for the root vegetables. With winter knocking at their door, she was glad to have been able to help Leah with all the vegetables. When the snow piled high, the canned and dried vegetables would taste fine.

Next spring, the process would start all over again. By then, she and John might have their own home. He longed to study law, and she longed to be right there beside him, even if it meant leaving Rocky Falls. She fancied a job for herself to help with expenses. This could be an opportunity to show him how much she loved him and wanted him to succeed. And she'd add more arithmetic and history to her reading and writing skills. John deserved a wife who would do him proud when they were with educated people. The thought both thrilled and startled her. A new life ... God was indeed good.

A raven flew overhead, and she lifted her gaze. The bird's *croak* and *caw* didn't have the pretty song of other birds, but she enjoyed the response of another raven hidden from view. Gidéon used to say a raven could laugh, but she'd always thought their calls were harsh.

"Well, if it isn't my little sister."

Bert froze. *Clint.* She whirled around. "Why are you here?"

"That's a fine welcome."

"You're not welcome." She planted her hands on her hips, not even recognizing her own response to a man who could lay his fists into her as harsh as Simon.

"Doesn't matter. I'm here, and you're going with me."

"No. I'm not." Her heart hammered into her chest until it hurt.

Clint sneered. "You've gotten brave since you ran off. I'll have to take care of that."

She recognized the same bullying traits as Simon. "Do what you want, but I'm not going anywhere with you."

Clint's hard glint reminded her of the many times he'd stood by when Simon beat her and turned his head when other vile things were happening. He nodded toward the house. "You know, John Timmons has a fine looking ma. And all four of his brothers look like hard working boys. Would be a shame if anything happened to them."

A rock slide of fear crashed around her. "Leave them out of this. I'd think you'd be glad I'm gone."

"You're too valuable to let you run off."

God, help me. "For what? You've stolen cattle and horses, and murder is pinned on all of you. I'd think you'd be long gone before the law catches up."

"Not yet. Got to make sure Simon is let go. And that means one more job before we leave."

"What kind of a job?"

"Clearin' out the 5T of its cattle and horses."

Losing all John and his family had worked for would destroy all of them. "Can't you just take what you already have and move on?"

Clint sneered. His greasy hair hung to his shoulders, and he stank of the weeks without bathing. "What's it gonna be, little sister? Leave with me now, or do I start target practice on your fancy friends?"

Do I pretend to cooperate?

"I need an answer!"

"I'll go." She'd find a way to escape and get word to John. God would help her fix this, make it right for John and his family. "What will you have me do?"

"You'll see. Lester and I found out you told the law about Simon. Gotta pay for betraying the family. It's your fault this ranch will have nothing but empty pastures."

How did they get the information about Simon so quickly? Someone in the area must be supplying them with it.

Bert refused to be defeated. Her brothers would not win. Not this time. By going along with Clint's demands, he'd think she was the sister he knew before God entered her life. But she'd find a way to show them that good and right would win over their evil ways.

CHAPTER 52

Leah lifted her skirts and stepped down from the porch. On this Saturday morning, with a vibrant display of fall colors, came the promise of winter. A cool breeze greeted her face, a pleasant touch to a day spent baking bread, which had heated the kitchen far hotter than she liked. Now the loaves sat cooling on the table. Their pleasant aroma tickling her nose and stomach. She shielded her eyes from the sun and scanned the area for Ember.

"Ember, where are you?"

No sign of the tiny woman with the big heart.

Strange. Leah walked to the barn and peered inside. Only quiet greeted her.

The young woman had gone to the garden for any late ripening tomatoes. By the time Leah made the trek to the garden and saw the boot prints of a man and Ember leaving in the direction of the river, she wanted to scream. She knew this was not what Ember would have done of her own volition.

Leah followed the tracks to the river where two horses and another person must have awaited them. She raced all the way back to the ranch. Panic and near hysteria swept through her.

Who could she get to help? John had ridden off early that morning with a refusal to tell any of them where he was going. He said Wirt would be checking in on things this evening, which meant only God knew when John would return.

She hurried back to the house and pulled out pen and paper from her dresser drawer. Carefully penning a note about not being able to find Ember, she left it on the kitchen table in case someone stopped by the ranch.

Visions of what Ember's two brothers might have done to her sickened Leah. She snatched up her rifle and ran to the barn to saddle her horse. Hopefully Wirt or Bob or Parker was in Rocky Falls. She prayed so. But not John. If Ember were ... Leah refused to think about the awful possibilities.

John raised the binoculars to his eyes one more time. Besides being bored as the time crawled by, he'd seen nothing to indicate Victor Oberlander was involved with the cattle rustling or murders. Parker had been right; this might take days. He could have brought a book to read, but then he couldn't keep his sights fixed on the Wide O.

His stomach protested the lack of food. But he didn't think he'd get hungry before supper just sitting and watching the comings and goings at the Wide O. He hadn't decided what he'd do come nightfall, when he couldn't see a thing. Exasperation nipped at his heels. What a stupid idea.

Grass rustled behind him, and he whirled around with his rifle.

"Easy," Parker said.

"Did you come to keep me company?"

"Not exactly."

John didn't like the tone in his uncle's voice. "What's going on?"

"Ember's missing. Leah went looking for her when she didn't return from the garden. And Leah saw Ember's and a man's tracks leading from the garden to the river. There were tracks of a second man and two horses headed west into the foothills."

"Clint and Lester Farrar," John whispered. "I'm heading to my place."

"Do you want me to go with you or stay here?"

Strange Parker would ask John what he wanted him to do. John swung a glance at the Wide O ranch house and shook his head. "Ember means more than spying on Oberlander. I can't lose her."

Bert rode behind Clint on the back of his horse. She wished she'd fall ... wished John, his Uncle Parker, Mr. Zimmerman, or Mr. Culpepper would ambush them ... wished her brothers would change their minds about forcing her to hurt John and his family. Which could be worse, destroying a life or destroying property? Clearly, Bert had no choice, for life was more precious. But she despised herself for what lay ahead. More so, she despised her brothers for the power they held over her.

"Where are we going?"

"Doesn't matter," Clint said. "Tonight we have a job to finish, and you're going to help us."

Her heart plummeted. Evan and the other boys had left to drive the cattle closer to the 5T. "Must it be tonight?"

"That's the plan. You don't have a choice."

"I don't want to go with you."

"You don't have a say. We're headin' home once we're done here."

Her mind pushed Pa and his fiery temper to a faraway place she hoped never to venture again. If she couldn't have a life with those she loved, she wanted no life at all.

"How is stealing the Timmonses' cattle going to free Simon?"

"We're guaranteed a lawyer to get him out."

John wouldn't even be around to protect his family or his livestock. He'd believe she had betrayed all of them and used them for her own gain. Her stomach twisted. He'd think she'd lied about her love for him.

Dear God, if You love my adopted family as I know You do, help them. I don't care what happens to me. But help John and his family. Please.

CHAPTER 53

John and Parker spurred their horses toward the 5T. Mama should be there with Wirt, then the four of them could try to make some sense of Ember's disappearance. Each time an image of Clint and Lester hurting her entered his mind, John pushed it away. Crazy ideas made a man forget his good sense, and he was nearly there. Other thoughts fed on his worries—like what Simon had done to Ember and what her brothers were capable of doing.

At the 5T, Wirt's painted horse hitched to the post out front told him Mama did not have to pass the time alone. For the first time, he wished Davis was there too.

If only he'd open the door and find Ember inside, smiling up at him with a sparkle in her eyes meant only for him. She'd have a reason why Mama couldn't find her and an explanation for the two men at the river. They'd take a walk and plan the future.

Foolish man. Accept it. You may never see her again—alive.

Wirt sat at the kitchen table with Mama. Both had full cups of coffee in front of them, and John failed to see any steam rising from the tops. Mama's eyes were red, and if he weren't a full grown man, he'd cry on her shoulder. Fear ... a formidable thing.

"She hasn't returned," Mama said. "I keep waiting."

John gave her a grim smile meant to reassure her and nodded at Wirt. "Parker told me what happened. I'm going to follow the tracks."

"I'm going too," Parker said. "Are any of the boys here?"

Mama shook her head. "They all went to drive the cattle back. I don't expect them before tomorrow."

"I'll head their way," Wirt said. "Hopefully I can find them in case ... Perhaps hurry things along. I can find them in the dark."

John understood what Wirt meant. Concern for his brothers also plagued his mind. He leaned on the table. "Mama, this means you're going to be alone for a while. We'll all do our best to get back here soon. In the meantime, keep the door locked and the rifle with you."

She nodded. "Seems like I'm praying as much as I'm breathing."

Wirt picked up Mama's hand. "Without your prayers, none of us have a chance of finding Ember."

With nightfall creeping in, Wirt left for the free range and summer pastures, and John and Parker led their horses to the garden to pick up Ember's trail from the river.

Parker bent to the ground to study the tracks. "Doesn't look like she struggled. Of course, he probably had a gun pointed at her." He stood. "There's where they crossed the river."

Another thought crawled up John's spine. *Would she have gone willingly?* But he shook it off. The two followed the trail until darkness stopped them, noting the men wasted no time in riding west toward the mountains.

Parker reined in his horse as the shadows danced off the rocky peaks. "We're going to lose them."

"I'll start fresh in the morning."

"We'll both start fresh then. What are you thinking?"

John twisted in the saddle for a panoramic view of the countryside. Fall glistened all around them, the end of harvest and the steady march of winter. Some folks called winter the death season. Lifting his binoculars to his eyes, he searched for a sign of any man. But just like the past miles had indicated, the riders had seemingly disappeared into the foothills.

"I love her," John said. "No point denying it. Except right now I'm helpless in finding her." Without a word, he turned his horse southeast toward home.

At home, a light in the kitchen window showed Mama moving about. She'd faced enough heartache alone. Since John realized his love for Ember, he understood the love between a man and a woman was different from love for family. He'd been told that before, but he had to experience the consuming emotions to understand what love for a woman did to a man.

He wished he had good news for Mama. He wished he had good news for himself.

When Clint and Lester rode toward the mountains, veering away from where Evan and the others were driving the cattle back from summer pastures, Bert had hoped her brothers might have changed their minds about stealing the Timmonses' cattle. But as dusk was beginning to settle, they turned abruptly to where she feared the boys were camped. They dismounted and waited. Perhaps they couldn't find the cattle.

Hours later Clint and Lester mounted their horses again, with Bert in tow, and rode, seemingly knowing where to go.

"Get down from the horse," Clint whispered. "If you want those kids to stay alive, then keep quiet."

The midnight darkness around them should have given her a moment to get away. She might be able to outrun a bullet. Except Clint and Lester held the ace—they'd shoot the Timmons brothers for spite.

Bert slipped off the horse. Another sound met her ears. The cattle were closer than what she originally thought. Darkness had always disoriented her, and the night sky had few stars to guide her.

Clint and Lester slipped to the ground. A rifle barrel pushed her along toward the herd.

"Hold up," Lester said. "I don't trust her." He made his way to her side and wrapped a dirty bandana across her mouth.

Her last hope of alerting Evan and the others vanished. She prayed for their safety—to stay asleep until it was too late to grab their rifles. They walked closer to the animals ... She could smell them, almost hear them breathe.

"Stay here," Lester said. "I'll scout out the area and get back to you. One of those boys might be watching the cattle from this side, and I'm not ready to get shot."

She waited with the understanding her footprints sealed her guilt. Having John and the others confirm her betrayal in this way felt worse than anything she'd ever endured.

"This herd will bring us a fine price. Even with splitting the money, we're doing good. We'll get Simon out of jail and head back home."

She wanted to tell him Simon would hang. No fancy lawyer could pay off a judge and jury, especially for a man convicted of murder and stealing.

Lester returned within the hour. "One of them boys was keeping watch. He ain't dead, but he's gonna have a bad headache. The other fellas are waiting for us to signal."

Bert cringed. Hot tears scalded her eyes. More men helped Clint and Lester?

"Let's get us a few cows," Clint said. "Our last job for a while."

One more time, she rode behind Clint. One more time, she wished she could stop them. One more time, all she could do was pray for whoever had been hurt and those asleep.

Rifle fire pierced the air. Frightened cattle fell prey to thieves and began to move.

John couldn't sleep. He'd been up and down the loft and inside and outside of the house, noting the steadily colder temperatures. The frosty air matched his mood filled with fear and doubt. Yes, doubt about Ember's disappearance. He tried to shake off the suspicions, but they were vivid and alive. She wouldn't have used John ... no, of course not.

Parker slept, and John wondered how the man could relax with so much to think about. But reality proved John had more at stake … more to lose. The days ahead filled him with dread. The cold and snow could hold a man prisoner. He'd envisioned those times with his Ember and making plans for the future. Now those dreams were as cold and lifeless as the coming months.

He wanted to be riding into the mountains after Ember, and light could not come soon enough. He wondered how his brothers were faring and if they were warm enough tonight. He should try to sleep. No, pray. Those he loved needed shelter from possible harm.

Ember, where are you?

Throwing back the quilt, he carried his boots down the loft for the last time. No point disturbing Parker with his tossing and turning on a creaky mattress. He might as well stay up and keep thinking and praying through the worries—oh the worries.

The enormity of trouble besetting Rocky Falls needled him, and it didn't make him feel any better about Oberlander claiming Ember was working with the cattle rustlers. Leon's death, followed by Ted's and the ranch hand's from the Wide O were reasons for every rancher to get trigger happy. John had almost been number four in the killings. Some folks were taking advantage of Oberlander's offer and were selling out to him. The idea of someone capitalizing on a man's loss sent a hollow feeling to the core of John's soul. He still believed Oberlander had a hand in the misfortune.

While he sat on the porch steps with only his thoughts and his coat for company, the sound of horse hooves drew his attention. He wrapped his fingers around the rifle beside him and waited until he heard Wirt's voice.

"Davis, you run and get your mama," Wirt said. "We'll help Mark down from his horse."

Alarm jolted John, and he rose to his feet. "What's wrong with Mark?"

"I'm fine. Just a bad headache. When I get my hands—"

"Hush," Evan said. "Someone hit him in the back of the head. He's got a nasty cut and a lump."

"I—"

"Quiet," Wirt said. "Listen to your brother." He jumped down from his horse. "John, I'm sorry. I didn't get there in time to help."

John hurried to help Wirt and his brothers with Mark. "What happened?"

"Rustlers hit him in the head just before they run off with all of our cattle." Evan's words ripped through John. Ember gone and now this?

"All of our cattle? Did you see any of the men?"

Mark moaned. "Just before I got hit, a man said this was from Bert."

Bert? "You must have heard wrong."

"Then where is she? My guess is she's gone. Joined up with her no-good brothers," Aaron said, his voice resounding against the night. "Sure would like to ask her a few things. She's behind this. I'm sure of it. What kind of person uses others and then betrays them? Tell me, John. Does she care about you or is she using you?"

"Calm down. We'll wake her and see what she knows," Evan said.

"No, you won't," John said, his voice brimming with anger at what this meant. "She's been missing all day. We've tried to find her—"

"What?" Evan said. "What do you mean she's 'missing'?"

"Gone. Not here." John swung Mark's arm over his shoulder. "I tried to follow the tracks of two horses that were involved, but they rode into the mountains." *She can't be behind this.*

"Mark's right," Aaron said, and John didn't dispute him.

"Come daylight, I'll ride with you to where the cattle were stolen," Evan said. "I've already thought about alerting Bob Culpepper and Uncle Parker."

John allowed the tragedy of the night to sink in. "Parker's here. And we've got about three hours until daylight."

The door squeaked open, and John realized Davis had wasted no time in getting Mama out of bed.

"Mark's been hurt?" Mama's voice cracked.

John and Evan carried him between them into the house.

"Looks like Ember's had a hand in this," Aaron said. "Our cattle are gone. John was shot. Now Mark's got a lump on his head. Men are dead. What did we do to her that she's caused all of this trouble?"

John should have defended her. He should have said Aaron didn't have proof. But John didn't know what the truth was anymore. And he feared they were right.

CHAPTER 54

As soon as the pink and purple hues of near dawn touched the horizon, John, Parker, Wirt, and Evan dug their heels into their mounts and rode across the 5T to where the cattle had been stolen near the summer pasture. At the site where sparse and worn grass and shrub existed together, all that remained were cattle prints and the telltale remains of a campfire.

John dismounted first to look for boot prints. Lack of sleep and feelings as torn as a battle-scarred flag, he weighed finding Ember's small footprints as proof of her guilt or not locating her tracks at all, which meant she could have been killed. In his near panic mind-set, he continued to tell himself she was alive. But visions of the recent dead men would not let him go.

How did a man deal with mixed feelings? He despised the thought of her betraying him, using his love against him. Had she lied to all of them about the abuse and the beatings? And what about using his family? Yet the prospect of finding her dead wrenched at his soul. God forgive him, but he didn't know which tragedy would be worse. He was a selfish man, not a godly one. The realities of life took priority over feelings. He knew it. He tried to accept it.

"Over here," Evan called.

John swung his attention to his brother who'd bent to examine tracks. Evan lifted his head and peered at him. "She was here." His voice barely registered above a whisper. "I'm sorry."

John stopped. He willed his feet to join his brother. "Are you sure?"

Evan pressed his lips together and nodded, his focus glued on John. "She's been wearing Mama's old shoes, the ones that had a worn heel on the left foot."

John forced himself to walk toward Evan. With a deep sigh, he knelt and saw for himself. The prints were Ember's. Every nerve ending in his body went numb. Then the sensation turned to grief. Every indication pointed to her guilt.

Bert counted three other men who rode with Clint and Lester. She recognized one as a man who'd ridden with Leon. Where could they drive this many cattle without the law catching up? Unless they planned to change the brands.

At daybreak, the men drove the cattle into a canyon on the far west side of the Wide O. Now that was stupid. Mr. Oberlander had ranch hands who'd discover them, and they had orders to shoot trespassers. She supposed a few more dead men meant nothing to her brothers.

With the gag in her mouth, she couldn't ask questions. Instead she allowed the why's and where's to roll around in her head. The filthy bandana tasted of dirt and smelled of sweat and tobacco. Much more of this and she'd be sick all over Clint's back.

John pulled his slicker from his saddle bag and shrugged into it. The rain had started in spits, then increased to a downpour. He, Evan, Bob, Wirt, and Parker followed the herd south. When the thieves had left miles behind them, they'd find a place to hide in one of several canyons. This was an organized plan, strategically set in place by a clever man. The manner in which the cattle had disappeared left John believing someone had spent time watching his every move. *Ember.* He'd trusted her ... believed her. If he weren't a grown man, he'd shed a few tears. But his concern about her was turning to betrayal.

"It's rained nearly every day for the past two weeks," Evan said. "Hard to follow a herd of cattle when the tracks disappear and the rain blinds you. But it can be done." He pulled his poncho up around his neck. "All we have to do is look harder."

Rumbling from the mountains behind him seized John's attention. He turned to see a steadily blackening sky over the mountains, moving their way. Rain soaked a man to the bone; lightning killed him. But John preferred taking his chances with the storm on an open range to losing his cattle.

Parker rode up next to John. "They're at least six hours ahead of us," he said. "Maybe more, depending on how fast they drove the herd last night. Let's get out of this weather and talk about what we can do."

John wanted to shout that Parker looked like a coward wanting to stop the search because of bad weather. But John knew he was the foolish one. He also knew trekking out alone invited a shooting—his own. Riding on for several feet, he searched for words and reasoning.

"Uncle Parker's right," Evan said. "The lightning's getting closer. There's no denying another storm's coming through."

"John, I understand how you feel with all of your livestock gone and Ember missing," Parker said. "But the cattle won't move fast in this storm."

Lightning flashed a jagged sword across an angry sky followed by thunder that shook the ground. Horses reared. John turned to Bob and saw the man slumped over his saddle. Alarm jolted him. "Bob, what's wrong?"

The marshal weaved and fell from his horse onto the mud splattered ground.

The men pulled their horses to a halt and dismounted. Parker got to Bob first. "My chest," Bob whispered. "Been hurting me for a while."

His heart. John remembered those times he'd seen Bob clutch his chest. "Can we get him on his horse and to shelter? The High Plains Ranch is the closest. Sparky and his wife will lend a hand."

"I'll hurry to town and get Doc Slader." Evan swung around his horse.

Parker peered up at Evan. "Be careful in this storm."

Evan didn't take the time to respond, but dug his heels into his horse's side and raced toward Rocky Falls in the blinding rain.

John helped Parker and Wirt hoist Bob onto his saddle. He glanced toward the mountains where stone canyons stood guard over a strip of land that stretched for hundreds of acres. That stretch belonged to the Wide O, right where those cattle thieves had driven his herd.

"Why don't you ride on to the High Plains? I'll be right behind you."

"Where are you headed?" Parker said.

John pointed to a ridge. "I want to see if I can spot anything from there."

"I'm not taking you back thrown over your saddle." Wirt had been quiet up to this point. "And I'm not allowing you to ride into a snake pit. You can't bring in cattle thieves and murderers singlehandedly."

"Right," John said, irritated that Wirt and Uncle Parker still viewed him as a kid instead of a grown man. "All I'm doing is taking a look. With these binoculars, I can see into some of the canyons.

"Not in this rain," Wirt continued.

"Take care of Bob. I'll be there in a while." John spurred his horse on toward the ridge and calculated how much time he had before the storm's fury was unleashed on all of them.

With the devil riding on his heels, John lost no time in climbing to a higher elevation where he could catch a glimpse of the terrain. Oberlander's hired guns wouldn't think twice about opening fire on him, but he'd risk it. Odd how losing everything had aroused fury and vengeance he didn't know he had. The storm above him moved closer. Perhaps he *was* a fool.

Raising his binoculars to his eyes, he frowned. Wirt had been right. His visibility in the rain was poor. From what he could see there wasn't a soul in sight. No men riding over the terrain or a large herd of cattle waiting out a storm. Holding his breath, he studied an area to the west that led to canyons large enough to hold his cattle and more. John hadn't explored those rocks in years, but what he remembered was plenty of hideaways with only one way in. *Wide O land.*

John's suspicions about Oberlander deepened. The owner of the Wide O was far too shrewd to allow his ranch hands to operate a cattle rustling outfit right under his nose.

The foolishness of venturing on by himself picked at John, but an invisible force urged him to continue. Anger, bitterness, and a desire for revenge had taken over. He should rein in those feelings that characterized him as a possible killer. He seemed blinded, yet he couldn't stop himself. If he found where the thieves were holed up, they wouldn't be going anywhere for a while. And was Ember riding with them, or was she a captive?

The sky, a deep navy blue, grew more menacing. A jagged sword of lightning flashed, followed by a thunderous roar that spooked his horse. John swung his attention back to where the others had ridden in the direction of the High Plains Ranch with Bob. *God, what next? Was Bob strong enough to survive a heart attack?* Evan had disappeared in his flight to Rocky Falls to fetch Doc Slader. John hoped and prayed Bob would recover. The man definitely needed shelter from the impending storm.

The wind whipped around him, as though daring him to see what lay on the other side of the strip of Wide O land. His mind drifted back to the canyons he'd explored as a boy. With a deep breath, he dug his heels into his horse and raced toward the foothills of the canyons where he believed the thieves were holed up. They'd been looking for the cattle for weeks, and the site of one particular canyon was well-hidden, more like a stone corral. The perfect location to hide cattle—secluded and on Wide O land.

What were a few more miles when he'd lost everything?

Without the cattle, Mama and Wirt had nothing to build a home and provide for his brothers. John would never agree to relinquish the 5T to a power-hungry man like Victor Oberlander. And he hoped Wirt wouldn't either.

And Ember ... he wanted to hate her. All the good he'd seen and the sweetness were a mask for the evil in her heart. John shivered with anger so intense that he realized its fervor matched the fury of nature around him. How could God allow this to happen? Or was this punishment for not seeing through Ember's lying ways? He'd fallen in love with a woman who'd set out to use him. John stiffened in the saddle. He didn't understand how God could allow him to be deceived. The need, the vengeance to go after the men—and the woman—who had stolen his cattle stalked him like a lone, hungry wolf. They were about to meet the end of his smoking gun.

CHAPTER 55

John followed the tracks of cattle and shod horses toward the canyon, its narrow entrance hidden by rock. The thieves would have a difficult time herding cattle through the narrow opening and down into the canyon, but once inside, the area opened wide.

He dismounted and led his horse through the canyon opening. Squeezing the rifle in his hand, he was ready to use it, itching to take revenge. Rain poured from the rim of his hat and off his slicker while thunder cracked with ear-piercing closeness. Standing behind a slab of rock that jutted out like an old man's knees, John bent to study the canyon where he remembered it widened to a copper and gray stone corral. He brought his binoculars to his eyes. This was the site where his pa had taken him years before. They'd climbed down the gradual descent amazed at the beauty of rock streaked with gray and copper color. But not today.

Today the canyon was filled with his cattle and those of his friends.

In the distance, he saw Racer. So had Ember chosen to ride his stallion like she'd ridden Oberlander's mare?

About two hundred feet from where he crouched, four men stood at strategic points ready to defend the canyon. He searched for anymore men. A small, slumped figure caught his attention and would not let him go. He held his breath. Ember huddled down in the rain with her back against the rock.

Her hands were tied.

Not what he expected from one who'd assisted cattle rustlers. He couldn't see her face ... Inching closer, he had to see if she was all right. How could he love her and want her behind bars at the same time?

"When's this storm gonna stop?" a man cursed. "All we need is a rush of water running through this canyon and causing a stampede."

"Stop your bellyachin'. It'll quit soon."

"Good. I'm hungry."

"Lester. You're an idiot. We ain't buildin' no fire here."

Lester. Ember's brother.

"Aw, we ain't had no good cookin' since Bert stole Simon's mare." He pointed toward the herd. "At least we got the stud horse."

"It's her fault we're holed up in this canyon. She told Timmons about Simon and got him arrested." The man turned toward Bert and delivered a kick to her thigh. She tumbled over, but she didn't cry out. "She'll get her due."

John winced. *Dear Lord, what have I done?* His heart thudded against his chest, and his face flushed hot. He'd been wrong; he'd accused, judged, and destroyed Ember Rose without knowing the truth. He'd taken off like a foolhardy kid who thought he had the answers to everything.

The rain beat down harder in time to the misery consuming his soul. Should he attempt to free her or head back for help? Another man emerged from the shadows. Five men against one, and they were all armed. A part of him wanted to believe God would help, but why should He when earlier John had questioned God's hand in all that had happened?

God, forgive me. I didn't know. He remembered when Ember said she'd rather die than see any of them hurt.

Ignorance of her sacrifice didn't make him feel any more righteous before God. He'd ignored God and hadn't tried to listen for His wisdom and guidance. He'd gotten on his unholy horse and rode away with vengeance on his mind. He'd yearned for blood.

All this time John had longed for someone to help him through the hard times pressing down with a yoke too heavy for any man to bear. God had been there all along, waiting for him to ask. But he'd been a bullheaded fool, insisting on living life his way and giving Him respect when times were good. What happened to the ideals of a godly man, the ones he'd tried to instill in his brothers? Oh, he'd made a few steps toward giving all of his problems to God. Then he'd snatch them back again. Did his brothers sense his stubborn pride? He hoped he hadn't lost their respect when he'd lost his hold on God.

God, I'm so ashamed. Forgive me for pretending to be You. Worse still, for judging Ember. Help me to get her free. I don't care about myself. Just her.

John could ride to the High Plains Ranch for help. It was less than thirty minutes away. Possibly Bob had taken a turn for the better, and Wirt or Parker could ride back with him. He'd been so full of hate that he hadn't tended to Bob like he should have. What if the man died before John could thank him for teaching him so much about law ... the nature of man ... and life. Next to Parker, Bob had been a man John had modeled his life after.

He studied the rustlers again. If the rain held, the men would be here for a while. His gaze returned to Ember. If there was a way to reassure her that he'd do his best to get her free—

A rifle poked him in the back. "Don't move, John. I'd hate to use this on a neighbor."

Victor Oberlander.

B ert heard the commotion above the thunder and the rain splattering around her. She turned her attention to the canyon's entrance. In the fog of the downpour, a familiar figure took form. *Not John.* The man she'd tried so hard to protect from her brothers walked her way. Then she saw who held a rifle on him. *Victor Oberlander.* How could this be? He and John were friends. He attended church. Mr. Oberlander even wanted to court Leah.

She blinked, thinking she must be daft. A Christian man didn't get involved with cattle rustlers and killers … Did he?

"Mr. Oberlander," Clint called. "Did you bring someone without an invite?"

"Sure did." Oberlander pushed John toward the men, the rifle firmly fixed against his back. "Guess he didn't take me serious about shooting trespassers."

"Maybe you should have told me your new ranch hands were hired guns." John's voice sounded strong and confident. But it would take more than a fearless stand to save him from these men.

"Bring him over by Bert," Clint said, "where we can keep an eye on both of 'em."

Her gaze flew to John's face, hoping he looked her way so she could silently tell him her many regrets. And her love.

Oberlander shoved him toward her, and one of the other men tied his hands behind him.

"The rain's let up a bit," Oberlander said. "I need you men to get the cattle branded."

"Yes sir. That means buildin' a fire, but if that's what you want, then we'll get it done. Can't get 'em all done before nightfall though." Clint sneered. "What about Timmons here?"

Oberlander lifted his chin. "Do I have to tell you everything?"

"No sir."

"And get rid of the girl too before leaving in the morning."

Lester stepped forward. "Despite the trouble she's been, she's still our sister."

Oberlander frowned. "And do you think she's going to keep quiet after turning Simon into the law?"

And I once thought he was a good man.

"There's a place in Denver," Lester continued. "I talked to a man there who'll pay a good price for her."

Oberlander hesitated. "I probably know the same man. She won't run from him. Those who do end up dead." He swung his glance back to Lester. "Go ahead and sell her to him. But if she takes off, I'll gun you down myself."

Lester nodded. Bert saw the possibility of getting Lester to help her and John. Her brother had taken up for her in the past, and he'd not been as influenced with money and broken promises as Clint.

Oberlander peered into Clint's face. "I'll contact a lawyer in Denver about Simon once these cattle are branded and driven back to my herd."

"How long will it take to get him out of jail?"

Now Bert more clearly understood what had been going on. Stealing John's cattle had given them some assurance of getting Simon free.

"Have no idea. Might take more money on your part."

"But you said you'd handle it all."

Oberlander laughed. "I said I knew a lawyer who had the means of freeing him. If he wants more money than what I've paid him, then you two will have to take care of it."

Bert's gaze flew to Clint. His face tightened, and he bit down on the corner of his mouth. For sure, her brother was making his own plans.

"You take care of things here, and I'll do my part," Oberlander said. "We don't need Bob Culpepper, Wirt Zimmerman, and Parker Timmons out looking for John. I'll set up a diversion in town to buy you some time."

"You won't get away with this," John said. "Folks already suspect your hand with this. Hired guns put you at the top of the list."

Oberlander shook his head and chuckled low. "You should have let me marry your mother, and none of this would be happening. Blame yourself, John Timmons. I would have treated her like she deserves, much better than that poor excuse of a US Marshal."

"Right. Then you could have added our ranch to yours without so many killings."

"You got into the middle of things when you stopped Leon from hanging this girl."

"Does that mean you gave the mare to Simon?"

"I'm not stupid. He stole it thinking it would cause me to keep my side of the bargain. Simon had no idea who he was dealing with when he took Queen Victoria."

"So all of this has been about adding acreage to the Wide O?"

"Land's about to double. The stone quarry has more business than it knows what to do with, and gold's been found. Breeding good horseflesh and adding to my herd of cattle means more money for me."

"You're getting rich at the cost of the men you've murdered?"

Oberlander shook his head. "I didn't kill those men."

"But you ordered it," John said. "Makes you just as guilty."

"Money buys whatever I want."

Bert studied Oberlander's hard features. *Not while John has breath in him.*

"You'll be stopped," John said. "If not by me, another man will make sure justice is served."

"Big talk for a dead man." Oberlander's words were laced with bitterness. He whirled around and pointed at Clint with his rifle. "See if you can follow orders."

Oberlander disappeared from the mouth of the canyon. Clint barked orders at the other men and stomped toward a wagon that held branding tools. Ember drew in a ragged breath and turned to John.

"I'm so sorry."

"I'm the one who's sorry for what I've been thinking about you."

She couldn't blame him, not when she hadn't given him a reason to trust her. "Clint threatened all of you if I didn't leave with him."

"I know that now."

She had to make sure he knew all of the truth. "I didn't help them steal a single cow. They made me ride with them so it would look like I lied to you."

His eyes moistened, and seeing his emotion moved her to shed one tear after another for all the trouble she'd caused. "I've been such a fool. Not trusting you. Doubting why you'd disappeared."

"If I'd given you a reason to trust me, then perhaps I could agree." She wanted to say so many things before their lives were forever changed. "Maybe I can convince Lester to let you go."

John's eyes narrowed. "We're in this together. Both of us will walk away from these men."

She shook her head. "You don't understand. I give up."

"Where's your spunk? Your faith?"

"Faith? I left it at the 5T."

"Then you'd better find it 'cause faith is the only thing that will save us now."

Anger swelled in her. "Do you think God's going to send an angel in here with some flaming sword?"

"Nope." His jaw tightened. "But he could send a posse."

She stopped her unfaithful thoughts. "You're right. I'm just scared. We have to pray for God to deliver us."

"Look at those two love birds." Clint stomped their way. "Shut up, before I blow a hole right through both of you."

Bert no longer cared. "I thought you wanted me home. Someone to tend to Pa. Now I hear you're selling me to a brothel."

"Pa's dead. A rattler got into the cabin and bit him while he slept."

She should have had a reaction—and she did. Sorrow for never having a pa who cared for her or saw her as anything but a nuisance. Grief for a family that had never been or would ever be. Faith? She had to believe in God because she had nothing else that truly mattered.

CHAPTER 56

Leah paced the barnyard. How long would John, Evan, Wirt, and Bob be gone? Shadows loomed around her. She should be cooking for the boys. Reading to Mark while he lay in bed. She should be on her knees. Yet all she could do was pace with Rowdy at her heels.

"Mama, I've cut slices of ham and bread," Davis called from the doorway. "And there are beans too."

Her precious baby. She choked back a sob. "Your brothers will appreciate supper. Thank you, son."

"Can I bring you a plate of food?"

"No, darlin'. I'm too upset to eat."

"Me too," his voice cracked. "I'm worried about John and Evan—and even Bert. She was nice to me, Mama. And now it looks like she played sweet to us so her brothers could steal and murder."

Leah hated that her youngest knew so much about life when he should be playing, fishing, anything but experiencing harsh reality. "God will make sure it works out."

"Do you really believe He will?"

"Of course." She walked toward him. All of her sons' needs took priority over hers.

"But where was God when Pa died? And when John got shot? What right does God have to pick and choose? Does He have favorites?"

Such heart-wrenching questions from one so young. She lifted her skirts and stepped onto the porch. The confusion on his young face yanked at her heart. She wrapped her arms around him. "We have to believe God knows best and to anchor our prayers in Him. I've been angry at God too. Remember when you read how David didn't understand why God allowed King Saul to try to kill him? All David could do was trust God to bring an end to the bloodshed."

"It's hard, Mama." Davis wiped the wetness from his cheeks.

"I know," she whispered. *Almost impossible.*

She heard horse hooves pounding against the ground and whirled around to see riders headed their way. She released Davis and grabbed her rifle, but then she saw a familiar painted horse. Drawing in a breath, she saw only three men. What had happened? She hurried back down the steps to await them. Wirt arrived first.

"Where's John?"

Lines etched into his face. "Leah, we thought he might be here."

"What do you mean? And where's Bob?"

Wirt dismounted. His face held the lines of worry—and trouble. "Bob had a heart attack. He's at the High Plains, and Doc Slader is with him."

She glanced about and attempted to gain her senses. Davis was watching, listening. "Will he live?"

"Doc thinks so. But he doesn't want him moved for a few days."

"But John ... Why don't you know where he is?"

"When Bob had the heart attack, Evan went back to town to get the doc. John rode on to the next ridge to see if he could spot the cattle. He didn't show up at the High Plains. We hoped he was here."

"Well, he's not!" She lifted her shoulders and slowly let them fall. "I'm sorry. I simply need to know if he's all right."

"We'll find him." Wirt pulled her into his arms, and she laid her head against his chest. "He probably took shelter from the storm."

"It didn't rain here. Just got black." Her own words mocked her. Was the devil himself trailing her son? "When can we leave to find him?"

Wirt breathed in deeply. "Parker and I have decided to round up a posse in the morning. Not sure where he went, but we'll pick up his trail."

Fear twisted through her. "But you have an idea where to begin. You saw where he rode."

When Wirt didn't answer, she drew back away from him. "You think he's dead, don't you?"

"Of course not, we—"

"Don't lie to me, Wirt Zimmerman. That's my son out there. Did he take out across Wide O land? You know Victor has armed his ranch hands with orders to shoot trespassers." She tensed not only her voice but her whole body.

"Leah, we all know the circumstances."

"So what are you going to do about it?"

"Soon as I leave here, we're riding to the Wide O to talk to Oberlander."

Leah could not believe her ears. "You mean you're going to ask permission to ride over his land? Aren't you a US Marshal?" She flashed her anger at Parker. "You two sound like a couple of schoolboys asking permission to use the outhouse."

"That's not it at all." Parker dismounted. "His men may have reported seeing John. And we can't find him in the dark. Tonight we'll round up some men to leave at first light."

"And what if the all-powerful Victor Oberlander refuses to let you ride over his land?"

"That would make him look guilty of harboring information," Wirt said. "He'd be a fool to try to stop us."

Angry tears rolled down her cheeks, and she quickly whisked them away. "In the meantime, my John could be lying out there—bleeding and hurting."

"Mama, getting upset won't fix things." Evan stood beside her. When had he dismounted? She wanted to acknowledge his words—the truth. But the panic had taken residence in her throat, and she couldn't speak.

"Leah," Parker said, his tone gentle. "He's my nephew and soon to be Wirt's stepson. We want to find him too. But it won't happen until daylight. Taking the road back to town is one thing, but trailing John in the dark is impossible."

How could she exist through the night not knowing if her dear son was alive?

Early morning Leah paced the porch with four of her sons seated around her. Parker and Wirt had ridden into Rocky Falls last night with a plan of leaving at first light in search of John.

Thoughts of John repeated in her mind. She remembered the joy of the infant she carried inside her. The proud day of his birth and Frank's tears when she presented him with his first son. John's first steps. His first words. The way he cared for his family. *Oh God, don't let his life be over.*

The anguish tearing her apart grew worse. She wasn't a coward, and she knew how to fight. Evan, Aaron, Mark, and Davis stared at her. They were men. Even Davis would soon show signs of being a young man instead of a child.

"You boys get your rifles. We're going after John. Mark, if you aren't steady, then I want you to stay here."

"I'm fine, and I'm going." Mark stood.

She turned to Davis. "I want you to ride into Rocky Falls. I'm hoping you can find Uncle Parker and Mr. Zimmerman on the way. Tell them that we're riding after what's ours. If they want to join us, that's fine. And if they don't, then they're cowards."

"Where do you think he is?" Aaron said. "I'm afraid he might have fallen for another one of Bert's lies."

Leah lifted her head, refusing to look at Evan. "Whatever we find, God is already there. We've all prayed for John. I'm holding on to those prayers."

"I agree," Evan said. "We're in this together."

Leah's confidence raised a notch. "Mr. Oberlander says he won't let anyone cross his land because he's protecting it, but I think he has something to hide. And I have an idea where John might be."

"Where?" Mark turned his head as though disbelieving her words. Oh, but he was so much like John.

"When your father and I first moved out here from Virginia, we used to explore the mountains and canyons along the strip of land currently belonging to the Wide O. Several canyons there could hold cattle."

"But there's no grass in a rocky canyon," Evan said. "They couldn't stay there long, except for the rustlers to change the brand."

"I'm thinking the same thing too," Leah said. "That's why we're leaving now."

"His ranch hands are armed," Aaron said with a firm grip on his rifle. "I'm ready for whatever it takes to help John."

"Let me go too." Davis stood and stretched to his full height.

Evan bent to Davis's level. "What you're doing is more important than anything right now. We need help, and those men can provide it." He placed a hand on the boy's shoulder. "We're counting on you to ride fast. Tell them about the canyon. I bet Uncle Parker knows where it's at too."

"Yes sir. I'll show you I know how to be a Timmons man."

Leah blinked back the tears. "All right. Let's get our horses, and make sure you have plenty of ammunition."

CHAPTER 57

The sun steadily rose across the canyon, and John realized if the good Lord had decided to call him and Ember home, then he needed to say a few things to the woman beside him. He hadn't given up on getting out of this mess, but he had no idea what the future held. He'd made so many mistakes with Ember that he would not make one more. The smell of burnt hide and the constant bawling of cattle while Oberlander's men branded stolen cattle with the Wide O brand gave him time to talk to Ember.

Victor Oberlander had tricked a town full of good people. To satisfy his greed, he'd stolen cattle and murdered to scare folks into selling out. He'd have prime property when businesses got word of railroad expansion into Rocky Falls.

He hoped Wirt or Parker pried into Oberlander's dealings and demanded a bill of sale for all the extra cattle running over the Wide O. That would nail Oberlander and his thieving and murdering ways. He turned his attention to the woman he loved.

"I wanted to ask you to marry me," he said. "I know I hinted at it, but I never asked you proper. Never made it serious."

She slowly turned to look at him, as though she'd heard wrong. "With all you know about me?" Her brown eyes moistened. "I have nothing to offer. No loving family. A brother who did unspeakable things to me." She glanced away then back to him. "Your brothers are good. Mine kill and steal."

"I don't care about Simon, Clint, or Lester. It's you I want in my life. It's you I want to spend the rest of my days with. It's you

I want to be the mother of my children." John realized something he'd never thought possible. "I ... I need you, Ember. My life is useless without you beside me."

"And I love you. I think I always have." She turned toward the sound of her brothers swearing at each other, and the men helping them brand the cattle roared within the canyon. "I want to believe that it's not too late to have a life with you."

"We're not giving up. God hears our prayers, and He'll deliver us."

"From what I've read, sometimes our prayers are answered in this life, and sometimes our prayers are answered in the next."

She was right, but he refused to cease hoping until he breathed his last. "We're not giving up, not until we breathe our last breath."

Clint walked their way. John had seen the grim look of determination before, and whatever he planned was not for Ember's or his benefit. He jerked Ember up from the rocky floor and untied her hands from behind her back.

"You wanna live, little sister? I have a job for you." Without waiting for her to answer, he slipped his revolver from his gun belt and shoved it into her hand. He forced her to face John. "Pull the trigger. That will prove your loyalty."

"I will not." She spoke her words quietly yet full of strength.

"Save yourself," John said.

"No. I'll not shoot him."

"Then I'll do it, and you can watch him bleed."

"No, Clint." Her face blanched, and her body trembled.

"Kill him." Hatred poured from Clint's words. "Do you want me to give you over to these men as a reward for finishing up a good job?"

"If you're anything like Simon, you would anyway."

His hand smacked hard against the side of her face, and she'd have fallen if not for Clint grabbing her.

Haven't you hurt her enough? John struggled against the ropes binding him. "Leave her alone."

Clint pushed her against the rock and aimed the revolver at John. But she scrambled between him and Clint. "Shoot me first, Clint. Because I won't watch you kill an innocent man."

"What's going on?" Lester called.

"Shut up. I'm taking care of business."

"Killin' Timmons and Bert?" Lester said. "I thought we agreed to sell her?"

"I changed my mind. I haven't forgotten what she did to Simon."

"Ember, move out of the way," John said. "Don't let it happen this way."

Clint snickered and raised his revolver.

"Do it," Ember said. "You're the one who'll have to live with all the murdering."

A rifle shot echoed through the canyon, and then another. Clint and the other men grabbed their weapons and raced toward the incline of the narrow rock entrance.

Leah and her sons had taken positions inside the mouth of the canyon so their rifle fire sounded like more than four people. But when she heard Wirt's voice behind her, she realized Davis had flown like the wind to find them.

"I'm here," Wirt repeated. "Parker's with Evan. And Davis is back with the horses."

Later she'd cry. Right now, she had a son in trouble and a battle to win.

"You're surrounded by US Marshals," Wirt called, his voice booming around them. "You men had better put down your guns and walk on out here with your hands up."

"We got John Timmons and Bert. Sounds like you'd better be the ones to back off, or we'll kill them both."

Ember?

"We're no fools," Wirt said. "You plan on killing them no matter what we do."

A coarse laugh from inside the canyon told Leah that Wirt was right.

"Let Ember go," John said, and Leah stifled a cry.

A man swore, letting them know what he thought of John's request. Leah saw a shadow above her as Mark and Aaron crawled up and over rock. *Oh, God, protect my sons.* She saw where the two could slip down undetected. Rifles in hand, they inched closer to the men inside. Where was Parker? *We have to free John. We have to.*

"Name who's behind this, and the law will go easier on you," Parker said. "No point in all of you hanging to protect one man."

"I don't believe you." A different man responded. Perhaps the two were Ember's brothers.

"It's the truth," Wirt said, creeping farther into the canyon and hiding behind rock. "We want who's started all the trouble. Is it Victor Oberlander?"

Leah wanted to aim her rifle at any of the men who might attempt to harm her sons. Frantic, her gaze darted back and forth. She couldn't protect them all. Only God could keep them safe.

"What makes you think Oberlander's behind this?" said the second man.

Wirt laughed. "You're on his land, and my guess is some of you are his ranch hands. Do you think he'd risk his neck for any of you?"

Leah understood Wirt and Parker were stalling for time, and yet her heart pounded for her sons who'd managed to get closer.

Rifle fire echoed around the canyon. Evan, Wirt, and Parker rushed inside. Leah followed, ready to end the life of anyone who attempted to harm her sons.

Bert bent next to John and feverishly untied the knots binding his hands. She hadn't seen the men hiding in the shadows to rescue them, but she'd recognized Mr. Zimmerman's and Mr. Timmons's voices. John's prayers had been answered, but they weren't rescued yet.

Her attention swung to Clint with the understanding he'd not be taken alive, and he'd take anyone he could with him. She glanced back at John, fearing for him.

"I warned you." Clint aimed his rifle at John. "Timmons is a dead man."

Bert screamed and rushed toward her brother. White hot fire knocked her backwards. And blackness overtook her senses.

CHAPTER 58

All John could see was blood. Ember's blood. He leaped to her body while another shot sent Clint sprawling to the canyon floor. He'd not move again.

"Ember." His words breathed out into a prayer. He knelt beside her and attempted to wipe away the blood pouring from her left shoulder. She didn't answer him. Neither did she look to be breathing. Quiet. Still. *No, God. Please.* He leaned his ear to her chest. A faint heartbeat, like a distant mantel clock, met his ears. Could one so frail survive this?

"John." Evan's voice shook him, and John realized his brother had been the one to shoot Clint. "Let me see if I can help."

Every nerve in his body stood at alert while emotion spilled through him. "Yes, please. Ember's hurt bad." He moved so Evan could tend to her.

Evan wrapped his arm around John's shoulder. "I'll do what I can until we get her to Doc Slader's."

All John could do was nod. Evan gently examined the wound, being careful not to touch her any more than was necessary. He lightly lifted pieces of cloth from the glaring hole. "The bullet's still in her shoulder, and it'll have to come out. But she shouldn't be moved."

"I'll ride for Doc Slader," Mark said, and took off at a run. "He's still at the High Plains taking care of Mr. Culpepper."

Evan removed his shirt and ripped it into bandages. Life continued on around John, but he failed to pay attention. All of his senses focused on Ember and watching her take short, shallow breaths.

"Hey, brother. What can I do?"

John tore his gaze away from Ember to see Aaron standing beside him. As if shaken in a dream, it occurred to him that Evan, Aaron, and Mark had helped Wirt and Parker. "Why ... why are you all here?"

"You know Mama and her feelins'." Aaron bent beside him. "She said you were in trouble and needed help. Told us to get our horses and rifles. Then sent Davis to town to find Uncle Parker and Wirt."

John looked about. Clint and Lester Farrar lay in a puddle of blood, no doubt dead. Three other men were staring at the end of Uncle Parker's and Wirt's rifles. Mama had a rifle on a fourth man.

"How did she know I was here?"

"She said her and Pa used to explore these canyons."

"Praise God," he whispered and studied Ember's pale face. "Victor Oberlander is behind the cattle rustling and murders. Simon and his brothers were working for him."

"Wirt will make sure Oberlander gets his due," Evan said, his focus on wrapping his torn shirt around Ember's wound.

"Good thing it's not up to me. He confessed to all of it." John picked up Ember's hand, so small. "Evan, tell me how she's doing."

"We'll get her fixed up," Evan said. "You know your Ember. She's a fighter."

"I want to believe so."

"Good. 'Cause I want to be there when you two get married."

John smiled while choking back the tears. "I'll need a best man."

"Deal. Like Mama, I think you two should get married at Thanksgiving too."

"Did you hear that, Ember?" John said with a light squeeze to her hand. "Evan's agreed to be best man at our wedding. Fight hard. Please."

Hours later, Ember laid on a bed at the High Plains Ranch. John held her hand and watched Doc Slader fight to save her life.

"I've got the bullet." Doc wiped beads of sweat from his forehead. "Keep praying, and I'll stitch her up."

"She's got to live," John said.

Doc wiped blood from his hands. "I think she has a fighting chance of pulling through this."

A finger moved in John's hand, and that's when he knew his Ember would live. They *would* have a life together.

CHAPTER 59

EIGHT MONTHS LATER

Ember burst into the marshal's office waving a letter. She tingled with excitement. "I have something for you."

John lifted a brow with a half smile that she recognized as meaning more than brief amusement. "Mrs. Timmons, what are you suggesting?"

"No, not that." She blushed red, knowing how he felt about their intimacy. "This is the letter you've been waiting for."

Laughing, John stood and gathered her up into his arms and kissed her soundly. "Now what could be more special than this?"

"I have to agree, but the letter's from Austin, Texas, for Marshal John Timmons."

She put the letter behind her back. "I think I'd like a kiss, please."

"I just gave you one."

"Delivery charges." She giggled.

He planted a kiss on her forehead, nose, and lips. "Thought you might like a few extra for your trouble."

She handed him the letter, hoping and praying it was good news. Parker had written the school on John's behalf to recommend him for their law program. Since then Bob Culpepper had retired, and John had been voted in as town marshal.

John opened the envelope and lifted the letter from inside.

"It's good news. I know it is." She stood on tiptoe to read it over his shoulder. But he hid it from her.

She watched his face while he read the contents. Not one trace of emotion revealed what the letter stated. For a moment she feared the worst. John folded the letter and placed it back into the envelope. He caught her eye. Still nothing readable.

"John, tell me what it said. I have to know." She'd help him work through bad news.

He nodded slowly. "I don't know how to say this."

Her heart sank, feeling his disappointment. "Oh, John. We can try another law school."

"Looks like we'll be moving."

Her breath caught in her throat. "Really? You're accepted."

"That's what the letter says."

"And you're going to be a lawyer?"

"I'm going to try." He drew her close to him. "It will be a lot of work on my part. A lot of studying. And the times I want to spend with you might mean reading a law book."

"But you can do it."

"With you, I know I can."

She laid her head against his chest and listened to his heartbeat. "I'll always be here for you, John."

"I need you, Ember. God knew what this man needed when He sent you into my life."

"By saving a scrawny kid from hanging?"

"By igniting my heart with what I needed to fulfill my dreams."

TRUTH

Truth is light
Unending
Everlasting
A choice for the day
A solace for the night
A comfort for tomorrow
Confronting evil with courage. Marching from the portals of heaven.
A javelin of light that pierces the soul. An anchor for the weak and oppressed
The choice of devout believers.
Truth is unconditional
Truth restores the broken
Truth beckons the lost
Truth is mercy
Truth is grace
Truth is Light.

By Ember Rose Timmons

AUTHOR'S NOTE

DEAR READER,

I hope you enjoyed *The Fire in Ember* as much as I enjoyed writing the book.

Ember's story has been a part of me for several years, waiting for the right moment to unfold. She was a complex young woman, and at times I didn't understand her fears and reservations about life. When she revealed her past to me, I began to understand her inability to trust. She had pain that only God could heal.

The humorous part of John learning that the boy he saved from a hanging was really a girl swung a wide pendulum as to why Ember was forced to run from those who'd abused her. The more I thought about Ember's plight, the more I realized the strength hidden behind her shame for a past she could not change. She set out to protect her brothers without the understanding that her behavior prevented truth and justice.

I hope secrets do not stalk your life. But if they do, I pray you have the courage to take the first step into light. God does not want any of us to experience abuse. Ember found the joy of a changed life that promised love and purpose. I hope you do too.

SINCERELY,
DIANN MILLS

DISCUSSION QUESTIONS

1. When John saved Ember (Bert) from a hanging, she deceived him by not telling him her gender. How did you feel about this aspect of her? Have you ever deceived someone to save yourself from the unknown?

2. John lived to take care of his mother and brothers. He also believed in upholding the law. What do you think drove John to carry the burden of responsibility alone?

3. Leah was a single parent. Have you been or are you now a single parent? Do you know someone who is a single parent? What challenges do you see there?

4. Ember was afraid to tell the truth about herself. Why do we often keep our real self secret?

5. John had a dream, but he couldn't reveal it. Why? What about you? What is stopping you from reaching out for your dreams?

6. Ember possessed the gift of music and song. How did that affect her relationship to the Timmons family? Do you think the story would have changed without this gift?

7. Evan believed he loved Ember too. A love triangle has the ability to show the best and the worst of those involved. How do you think Evan, John, and Ember were forever affected? Why or why not?

8. Did Leah have a favorite son? If so, which one? If not, why?

9. Wirt loved Leah and wanted her to marry him. What obstacles stood in their way?

10. Betrayal sears the heart. Do you think John overreacted to Ember leaving the ranch with her brothers? How would you have handled the situation?

11. Our best friends may not tell us the truth about ourselves. If you were Ember's best friend, how would you have advised her about Simon?

12. John thought he might lose Ember when she was shot. What do you think went through his mind while he waited to see if she would live?

ACKNOWLEDGMENTS

Julie Garmon, Louise Gouge, Mona Hodgson, Catherine Madera, Dane and Melissa Money, Melanie Stiles, and always my dear husband, Dean Mills, who puts up with me and my characters.

Ectotame vit eturia aliquatiae as enem inctore peleseq uassit faccus, quos aut aut que dolore que earchil ligenda qui ut optur aliqui voluptia vellect otatem quam, sitium inctotaspere vel eumquod utas dolest lauda cusdand aecaest aspitatas mintion rendam asped mi, conet, ventemo loritas quis di consequate quat plab iusa qui dolorero volor sim hitatinis velluptae volorit pernatest et mil ipicienit, occus.

Quis volupta eum re volupta duci doles dellit untemolupta volupta tiberis maione derovid elit fugit essus.

Aborepe ribusae. Ut millaborrum rest omnis essum, conecum quos molecation poreptatur, sinciatum audias doluptae voluptas quunt harunt, cum dolut di cullam, quiaerumqui rem sitassi muscimo luptat rem consed minctus tempora doluptatque quistec totaqui autae volupta menietus atur rent quiasi ra a pelenti ut labore, conse velecus anderit, optatur, omnihil et accus es mil est fugitat estiis simus aut modit la nulparum soloreium re erovidere possima iorrum quo quamus et eiume sumet et quo cusam qui simet, acidus minim id molorep eriaturitate imaginimusci quunto verae. Itat autemquodit, eum voles sequam que el essi dolorit offici di cor sit et verci aut ipsanditis et asperi te occus quuntur, est quis imaximp oreprov idebis consecum nihicipsam faccullation commoluptat etum aborro bearum quisita tiuntot atempor eperate omnia quatiunt optas dem dio od et pos quatet

A Woman Called Sage

A Novel

DiAnn Mills

They took away everything she loved … now, she's out for revenge.

Sage Morrow had it all: life on a beautiful Colorado ranch, a husband who adored her, and a baby on the way. Until five ruthless gunmen rode up to their ranch and changed her life forever.

Now Sage is a bounty hunter bent on retribution. Accompanied only by her majestic hawk, she travels throughout the Rocky Mountains in search of injustice, determined to stamp it out wherever it's found. The stakes are raised when two young boys are kidnapped and Sage is forced to work with Marshall Parker Timmons to rescue them. But Sage may ultimately get more than she bargained for.

In this exciting historical romance set in the late 1800s, murder, intrigue, kidnapping, and questions of faith will keep you in suspense until the final pages.

Available in stores and online!